MYTH IN MALMÖ

Torquil MacLeod

Published by McNidder & Grace
21 Bridge Street
Carmarthen SA31 3JS
Wales, United Kingdom
www.mcnidderandgrace.com

Original paperback first published 2025

A catalogue record for this work is available from the British Library.

ISBN: 9780857162823

Designed by JS Typesetting Ltd, Porthcawl
Printed and bound in the United Kingdom by Short Run Press, Exeter

To my late, beloved father Norman, whose own
Norse saga sadly never made it into print.
I hope this partly makes up for that.

GLOSSARY OF VIKING NAMES AND TERMS

Asgard – the dwelling place of the gods
Draugr – a ghost or reanimated corpse of the deceased
Eastern Sea – Baltic Sea
Freyr – the Norse god of peace, fertility, rain and sunshine
Hamingja – the female guardian spirit that decides a person's luck and happiness
Hel – the Norse underworld
Miklagård – Constantinople
Náströnd – the hall in Hel where murderers, adulterers and perjurers were tormented with the venom of serpents and the dragon Nidhogg sucked the blood from their bodies
Norns – the Norse goddesses of fate
Odin – the Norse god of war and death, often depicted as a protector of heroes
Svear – Sweden
Thor – a Norse god of enormous strength associated with thunder and storms
Valhalla – the great hall where the souls of brave warriors killed in battle were received
Vi – Visby on the island of Gotland
Wends – Slav inhabitants of what is now northeast Germany

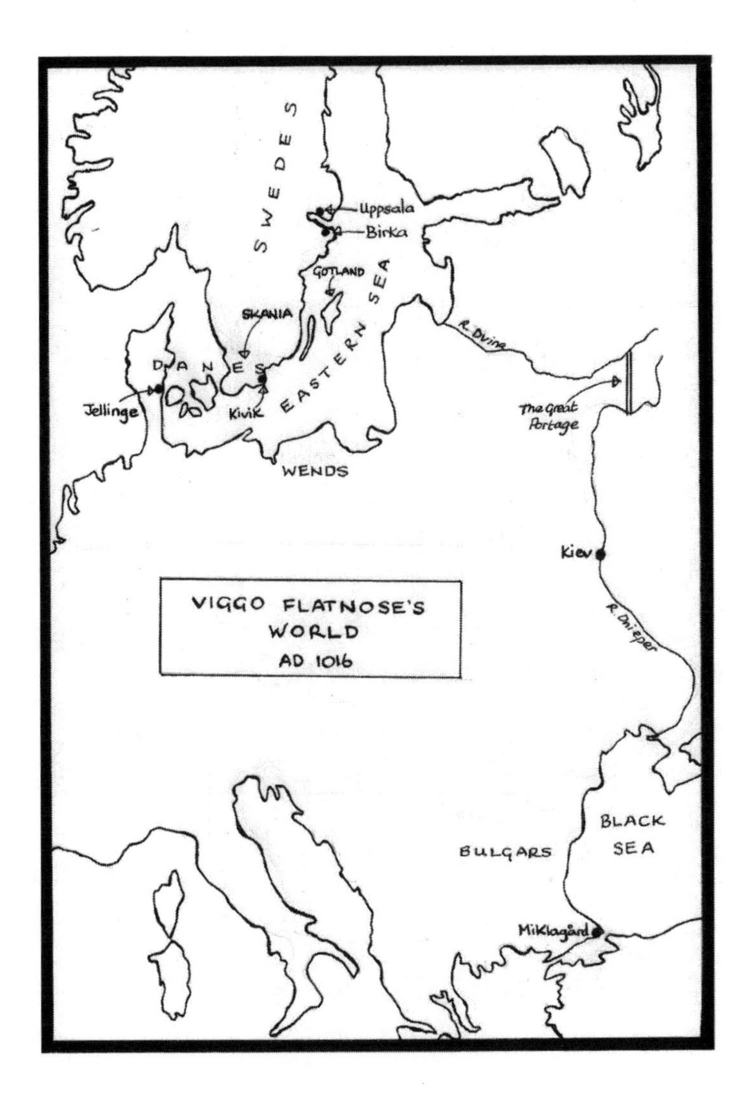
VIGGO FLATNOSE'S
WORLD
AD 1016
SWEDES
Uppsala
Birka
GOTLAND
SKANIA
DANES
EASTERN SEA
Jellinge
Kivik
WENDS
R. Dvina
The Great
Portage
Kiev
R. Dnieper
BLACK
SEA
BULGARS
Miklagård

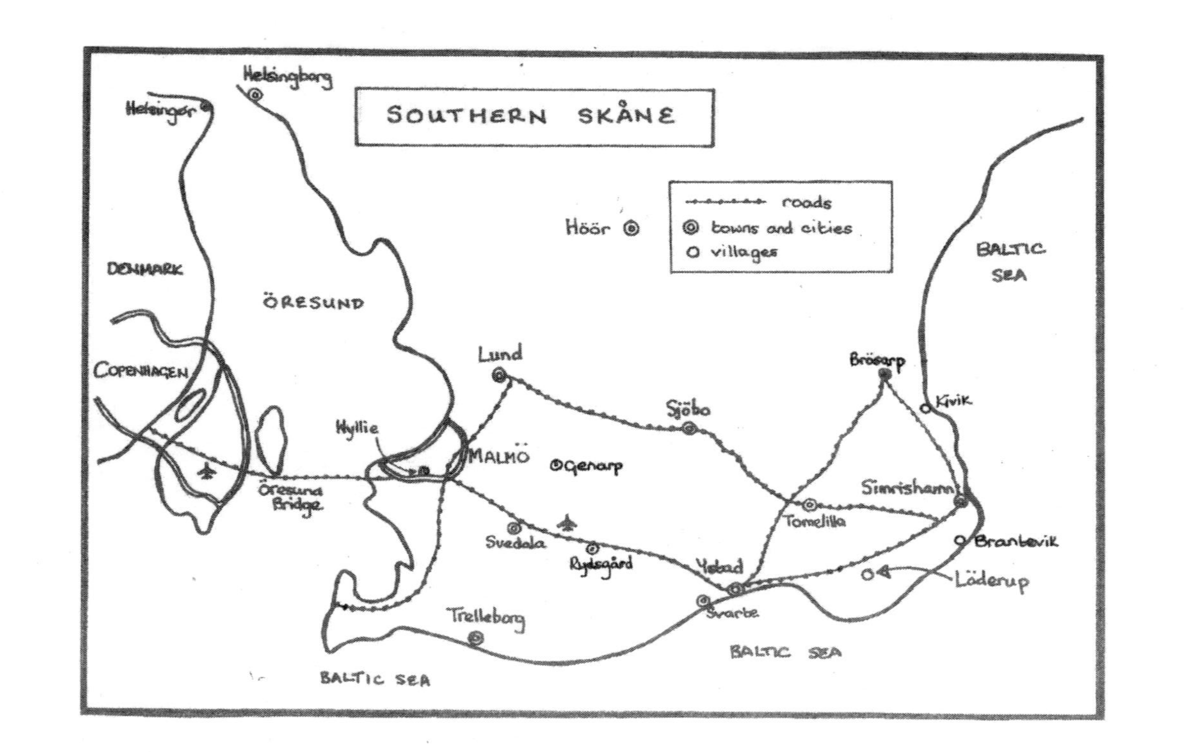
SOUTHERN SKÅNE
roads
towns and cities
villages
Helsingør
Helsingborg
DENMARK
ÖRESUND
COPENHAGEN
Öresund Bridge
Hyllie
MALMÖ
Lund
Höör
Genarp
Sjöbo
Svedala
Rydsgård
Trelleborg
Ystad
Svarte
Tomelilla
Brösarp
Kivik
Simrishamn
Brantevik
Löderup
BALTIC SEA
BALTIC SEA
BALTIC SEA

PROLOGUE

Kiev, early autumn, AD 1016

'Blinded?'

The young Norseman sounded incredulous. He had recently arrived from Novgorod and the north.

''Tis true.'

'But from the tale you tell, that is thousands of men!'

'The word was fifteen thousand or thereabouts.' For effect, Viggo Flatnose let his gaze wander over the rapt audience in the Kiev alehouse. 'Ninety-nine in every hundred. The hundredth only lost one eye,' he said, raising a solitary finger, 'so that he could lead his comrades back home to Samuel of Bulgaria. They say the shock of what we had done to his soldiers killed him,' he added with a grim laugh. Viggo made an imposing figure with his wild blond hair and feral beard. The broken nose that gave him his epithet did little to diminish his fine sculptured features, while giving the impression that he would think nothing of gouging out the eyes of his enemies.

'And who gave the order?' enquired the old Rus man with the facial scars that were testimony to an eventful life, though what he was now being told was clearly beyond his comprehension.

'The Emperor himself. Basil may look like a runt, but inside him burns a passionate hatred of the Bulgars and all those who revolt against him. He would kill his own mother if she proved disloyal. That is why he loves us so, the Varangian Guard.' He raised his beaker in salute. 'They may think of us as barbarians,

but we are the only ones he can depend on. The Greeks, on the other hand...' he sneered. 'Basil may have trusted them once, but with all their plotting and scheming, they are truly corrupt. They are but rats that skulk in the shadows and scuttle away at the first sign of trouble.'

Viggo took another deep draught of his drink and belched loudly.

'More!' he bellowed, and a lad rushed forward with a pitcher.

'And what is Miklagård like?' the young Norseman asked in awe. ''Tis said that it is the most beautiful place on this earth. Here in Kiev, they have wondrous buildings of the like I have never seen. I cannot imagine anywhere finer.'

A flash of pity crossed Viggo's rocky features.

'This is a fine place to be sure.' Viggo was not about to upset his engrossed listeners but he wanted to impress. 'Miklagård is indeed the world's greatest city with the world's greatest emperor. It stretches as far as the imagination can take you. It is full of splendid palaces, much grander than your late Khan's up the hill yonder. And the Church of the Holy Wisdom is such a wonder to behold, it takes the breath from your body. It has the most magnificent dome in Christendom, and inside its great doors, you could squeeze every man, woman and child that lives in Kiev and still have room for more. And there are dozens more churches, and many elegant houses – homes of rich merchants and men of power. For there is enormous wealth in Miklagård, as all the world's trade passes through its wharves and market places. Whatever a man needs or desires,' he said with a knowing wink, 'can be found within the city walls. Walls that have kept out the Rus many times in the past.'

'If Miklagård is such a city as you describe, why are you here in our humble little Kiev?' asked one of the crowd boldly. Viggo took an instant dislike to the man; he had the eyes of a weasel. He might have to teach him a lesson for his impudence.

'I am only passing through your humble little town,' he mimicked, 'on my way to my homestead in the land of my ancestors. I have been in these lands for nigh on ten years. During that time, I have served my Emperor well and now I am taking home the rewards for my loyalty.'

'And where might these "rewards" be now? I see no sign of "rewards", eh, lads?' Weasel-face wanted an audience of his own.

Viggo made an effort to keep his temper. 'They are in my ship down at yonder wharf and on the morrow will be stored ashore. With winter approaching, I may tarry awhile and enjoy what Kiev has to offer before I venture north. In the spring, the rivers will be easier to navigate and the Great Portage will be possible.'

To prove he had the means for munificence, Viggo bought ale for all those who had been spellbound by his tales. Later, much later, as dusk was falling, accompanied by cheers and back-slapping, he left the alehouse and headed up the hill towards his billet for the night. Nadira would be waiting there, and he was in the mood for a woman of her beauty and skill in the arts of love making. That was something else that the worldly ways of Miklagård had taught the raw adolescent from the north who had ventured south in search of fighting, fame and fortune. He had found fighting aplenty, and the fame and fortune had fallen into place as a result. Like all his race, he trusted to hamingja, the luck that was such an important element of a Norseman's life. Odin had been watching over him.

He liked Kiev. The High City of the Rus would serve him well during the coming months. He felt an affinity with the place, though it was a far cry from the unsophisticated Skanian homesteads awaiting him back in Denmark. Established by the Norsemen of old, carving out trade routes along the great rivers which wound their way through dense forests and vast steppes inhabited by barbarian tribes, Kiev would now be unrecognisable to those early pioneers. As Viggo climbed the hill towards his lodgings, below him on the Dnieper, where his ship was berthed, a multiplicity of sights, sounds and smells assaulted his senses. A nautical confusion of hulls, masts, ropes and sails filled the wharves, while on the waterfront, the hammering and sawing in the shipyards added to the cacophony created by the movement of merchandise, sailors with too much ale in them and traders haggling for better deals on their goods: furs, skins, walrus-tusk ivory, honey, beeswax and slaves heading south; silk, spices, glass, silver, gold and slaves heading north. Some of the larger ships were spewing out their cargoes onto the quay in readiness for transport to the merchants' quarter a little way further down the river.

Viggo smiled with satisfaction. He, too, was part of this commercial bustle. His slaves were safely manacled down there, and they would be an added source of riches when he sold them in the north, though he had lost three of them – and two of his own men – when their overnight camp on the river had been attacked by a party of nomadic Patzinaks, who roamed and pillaged the steppes between the great rivers of the Dnieper and the Don.

Drifting around him was the bluish haze of evening cooking fires, and a mouth-watering aroma wafted on the air. The log-paved streets were steep and narrow and hemmed in by wooden houses with turf roofs. Before he reached the hill's summit and the Khan's palace, Viggo turned into an alleyway, at the end of which was his lodging house. It belonged to a ship's captain whom he had befriended in Miklagård and who was wintering in Amastris. Awaiting him was Nadira.

His carnal thoughts were interrupted when he became aware that there was a man standing in his way – a man he vaguely recognised. Though it was dusk, it quickly dawned on his slightly inebriated brain that it was Weasel-face from the alehouse.

'I forgot to say, back there in the alehouse, "Welcome to Kiev!"'

Viggo sensed rather than saw the two large Rus standing behind him. He swung round. One was wielding a long knife, the other an axe. He glanced back at the man barring his way. Now he, too, was armed with a long knife.

'Out of my way, scum!'

'Not until we have relieved you of some of those "rewards" you were boasting about.'

'I spent them all in the ale house.'

'I doubt you spent all. Hand over what you have or I will cut out your bragging tongue,' said the man, raising his weapon.

Viggo only had a small knife on him. More fool him to go out unarmed! But he had to act quickly. He whipped it out and, in a stride, he was onto the Weasel before the other two ruffians could grab him from behind. The knife ripped into the man's stomach and he cried out in pain as he frantically tried to use his own weapon. But the long knife was too unwieldy and he missed his mark. Viggo twisted the man round just as the other assailants came at him. The axe came crashing down on Weasel-face and clove his skull while the sharp blade of the other ruffian's knife cut into Viggo's left shoulder. The two men were momentarily dazed by what they had done – just long enough for Viggo to pick up the Weasel's knife. As their leader slid to the ground, gushing with blood, the two Rus further hesitated. They were facing a mad, battle-hardened Norseman, and now a gang of Viggo's armed men, led by his cousin Harald, were rushing out of the captain's house on the other side of the street. The Rus cut their losses and fled, empty-handed.

A cock crew nearby. Viggo stirred himself and felt a jolt of pain in his shoulder. It could have been worse. His men had heard the noise outside and saved the day. They had got him inside their lodgings, and Nadira had gently patched up his wound with one of the Eastern salves that so intrigued and bemused him. He smiled at the memory of the soft wooing that had followed. Was she at last taming him? Or was it the other way round? He gazed down at her naked shoulder as she lay beside him. Her dark, flashing eyes and smooth olive skin had mesmerised him from the moment he saw her in Antioch. The look in those eyes! It could turn from hatred to love in an instant. For a short time, the hatred had overcome the love. Then, on the voyage to Miklagård, her attitude towards him had changed and the passion had won through, despite his not being able to speak her Eastern tongue, or the Greek and Latin spoken in Miklagård. It was his faithful Harald, with his mastery of the languages of the East, who had acted as his interpreter on their journey. Now, surrounded by Norsemen, Nadira was learning Viggo's tongue; she had a sharp and nimble brain.

While unable to resist the feelings that he had for this powerfully exciting and exotic woman, Viggo was well aware that such a match was fraught with potential dangers. He was not such a fool that he did not realise that she had used him to escape her suffocating, gilded cage, and that there may be consequences regarding her betrayal. There was also the reaction of his fellow Danes to consider. He was returning to his cold, wet, coarse homeland to assume his rightful position of jarl after the deaths of his father, and elder brother, Rune, who had been slain on an expedition to the land of the Angles. He would be in a revered position: a nobleman of importance. How could his people, who would assume Nadira was no more than a simple slave girl bought at a Miklagård market, accept her as his wife? No! He chastised himself for harbouring such doubts; he was forgetting what a formidable force the girl was! He had not known her long, but long enough to know that she had the charm to win over the men, and the strength of character to deal with the waspish tongues of the women of Vǫllrbý. He smiled at the thought of how she would put them in fear of her god.

Viggo leant over and kissed her shoulder. He would have to let her follow her strange Eastern faith. Like the Christians, the followers of Islam believe in a single god. But how can just one god control all the elements that make up the earth? When in Miklagård, he had had to pay lip service to the Christian Emperor's creed, and he remembered that, back in Skania, before he left, many Norsemen had converted to the worship of the Nailed God. But in his heart, he clung to the old beliefs; it was Thor and Odin who had protected him and kept the Valkyries from gathering him up from the battlefield and transporting him to Valhalla. Of course, he knew that one day, the Norns would cut his thread of life, and he would embrace the moment when they did. But if he did not die gloriously with sword in hand, he would make sure he had enough riches buried with him to see him comfortable in the afterlife. And the spoils of the blood he had spilt in the name of the Emperor would ensure that fate. And of those spoils, he thought, looking at the sleeping beauty at his side, Nadira was the greatest prize – or almost.

He gazed longingly upon her, wondering if the simpler life he was planning for himself would bring her the same happiness. The life he had plucked her from was a world away from overseeing a plentiful rye harvest or helping to bring in an abundant catch of herring. Viggo wanted to be a beneficent jarl and protect his people as he had done his Emperor. Yet he would be ready to fight if there was a call to arms from his King or the prospect of a profitable raid across the Eastern Sea to the land of the Wends on the opposite shore. If that were to happen, he would leave Nadira in charge.

He rose and pissed in the corner of the room and, still naked, opened the wooden door into the next room. Five of his men were sleeping. A couple of them had whores next to them. He was about to wake them from their slumbers, as he wanted all the cargo unloaded today, when he saw Harald standing by the outer door. His cousin had been but a boy when they set out from Vǫllrbý, and he had been by his side from that day on. He was now a strapping man whose axe had split many a head. Harald was the one man he trusted above all others. The concern on the young warrior's face alerted Viggo that something was amiss.

'You look as though you have seen a draugr.'

'It is not an undead troll that causes me fear,' whispered Harald. 'It is the living.'

'Have you upset some husband by stealing his wench?'

'I leave that task to you, Viggo. I have just been down to the ship to ready it for the moving of the cargo. I got talking to a merchant just disembarked from Berezan Island.' Viggo and his ship had passed through that trading post before heading into the Dnieper River from the Black Sea. 'He told me that two men were asking for you...'

'Maybe they are admirers and heard I was venturing north again.'

'...and Nadira!' This wiped the confident smile from Viggo's face. 'From the description, they were from the East. And they were too heavily armed to be traders.'

'Did one of them have a cut down his face across his left eye?'

'The merchant did not say.'

Viggo stroked his chin in deep thought.

'Did he think they would make it to Kiev before winter?'

Harald nodded.

'We must act. We must leave this very day.'

'But Viggo, the weather is turning. It may be too late for the Great Portage, and the rivers could freeze before we reach the Eastern Sea.'

'The further north we travel, the safer Nadira will be, even if we cannot reach Vǫllrbý until the spring. These men will be held back until the spring thaw and we will be safely out of their reach by then.'

Harald shot Viggo a sceptical look. 'Why not wait for them here and make sure they go no further... or return from whence they came?' he asked as his hand curled around his sword hilt.

'We are too close to Miklagård. More may follow in their footsteps.'

'Is she that precious?'

'Yes,' replied Viggo firmly. 'Now go and prepare the ship,' he ordered, turning back to the slumbering men. 'Get up, you lazy dogs! There is much to do today!'

As he strode through the room, kicking his men into wakefulness, he knew they would not be safe if they tarried longer in Kiev. Not even his faithful Harald guessed the real reason why armed men were on his tail. Was Odin about to forsake him?

CRIMINAL INVESTIGATION SQUAD

Anita Sundström, Chief Inspector
Klara Wallen, Inspector
Dan Olovsson, Inspector
Khalid Hakim Mirza, Inspector
Pontus Brodd, Inspector
Bea Erlandsson, Inspector
Liv Fogelström, Technical Assistant

CHAPTER 1

April.

Oskar picked his way over the rocky foreshore on his return from the beach. He wandered nonchalantly along the track through the trees which led to the main avenue of the *August Hagmanskoloniträdgård.*

It was a fine day, and the vegetation in the allotment plots was burgeoning in the unaccustomed warmth after the wet, cold winter. The gravel path was bordered by neatly clipped hedging or wire fencing; each section, bisected by a small gate, denoting different ownership. Every allotment had its own particular layout but all had well-tended gardens and a substantial wooden cabin. Every cabin was different. Though some were modest, others would not look out of place among the holiday homes along the Baltic shoreline. Many were painted bright colours, and some had extensions or outbuildings. Even with the smaller, simpler designs, there was a charming disparity between the basic exteriors and the more sophisticated interiors, which tended to be comfortably furnished with sofas, beds and kitchen sinks. For these cabins didn't merely serve as storage for gardening equipment: they were summer homes. This was when the local community could escape the confines of their apartments or houses and lead an outdoor lifestyle. From April to the end of September (the period when the water and electricity were turned on), these rustic homes could be inhabited full time if the occupant so wished. The only thing lacking was a toilet, but this could be found in the communal block.

Oskar meandered contentedly up the path, pausing at Elna Thysell's small plot on his left. Elna was now in her late seventies, but her cabin looked spanking new with its coat of blue paint, and the little lawn which ran up to the front door was always neatly trimmed. Nowadays, she was more interested in growing flowers than vegetables. The onions and the beans and the cabbages had been more her husband's thing. Since his death six years before, the patch had been transformed into a riot of colour, which perpetuated throughout the growing season. From daffodils to roses to hollyhocks, Elna lovingly tended and cherished them all.

Opposite Elna, on Oskar's right, were the Kristofferssons. Herr Kristoffersson's immaculate coniferous hedge bordered an equally immaculate garden. The wooden cabin, of larger proportions than most, was, of course, pristine, and the flag pole was the tallest on the allotments. Herr Kristoffersson was very keen on gadgets – one of his favourites being his leaf blower, which he was forever using even when there were no leaves to blow. Fru Kristoffersson meekly put up with her husband's bombastic attitude but sought solace in her friendship with the handsome Viktor Bjelk, two plots along. Conversations with the welcoming widower, when her husband was on one of his fishing trips with his former employees from his auto components company, gave her inordinate pleasure and helped relieve her loneliness.

Oskar continued up the path. Opposite Viktor Bjelk's was Sigrid Clausson's patch. She always offered Oskar a cheery 'hi' as she pottered over her vegetables or tended to her tomatoes in her greenhouse. Often on a summer evening, she and her friends from other plots would gather on her decking and enjoy a gossip over a few glasses of rosé. A relatively recent arrival, Sigrid was divorced and there was no current man in her life. In her sixties, she was still an attractive woman and she had several admirers, though few would have tried to take liberties with the ex-cop.

Next to Sigrid Clausson were Alma and Tord Cederholm. Both were on their second marriages and had numerous offspring between them. There wasn't any love lost between the two families, which put a strain on the relationship at times. When arguments ensued, it tended to be Tord who sought sanctuary on the allotments, where he'd bend Viktor Bjelk's ear. Today, Tord was sprucing up the Falun red on his little cabin.

Thora Tarland was the Cederholms' immediate neighbour; her domain was on the corner where the two main paths crossed. A neat metal gate opened into a little orchard of stunted apple trees, behind which her squat green cabin nestled cosily. The trees, old and gnarled, were, according to Thora, whose stories were prone to fabrication, one of the few remaining remnants of the original purpose of the land. In a more satisfyingly philanthropic age, the site of the allotments had belonged to August Hagman, the owner of a canning factory, one of the town's main employers. Hagman had donated the land for allotment use in order to afford his workers the chance to grow their own produce in their spare time. This had expanded into the hundred-and-thirty-odd plots today. Thora was fond of her apple trees. She had owned an orchard near Kivik, where her apples were sold to a well-known cider factory. But after a couple of disastrous growing seasons, her business had gone bust and she'd lamented her financial ill-fortune ever since. She blamed it on global warming, and had channelled her inner Greta Thunberg into embracing a greener way of life, one consequence of which was giving up her car. The bicycle which she used to come in from her home in Brantevik was propped up against the garden shed. Though forced into retirement, she liked to keep her horticultural hand in. Her old trees still produced a good yield and she always had some apples to spare for the people she liked. She often popped across the path with an offering to Viktor Bjelk, but only when that Kristoffersson woman wasn't sneaking round while her husband was away.

Where all the allotments on this row were neat and orderly, the one immediately behind Thora Tarland's was a notable exception. The cabin looked neglected and was in need of repair and a lick of paint. The flower beds were randomly filled with an assortment of scraggy plants which spent their days fighting with dandelions, buttercups and nettles. Many of the allotment holders felt that Gerda Brink's plot was letting the site down and had complained about her to the committee. To the newer inhabitants, it was a mystery that she hadn't been thrown off. The others, who had lived in the town a long time, knew perfectly well why: Gerda Brink had worked for the firm of a local lawyer and, over the years, she had become privy to secrets that could prove embarrassing to certain members of the community. She was untouchable and she knew it. Her most vociferous critic was her neighbour, Thora Tarland. They hardly exchanged a civil word. Their mutual boundary was a wire fence that ran behind their respective cabins. The narrow gaps between the fence and the buildings couldn't have looked more different: Thora Tarland's was gravelled and neat, Gerda Brink's was overgrown with yet more invasive weeds.

Yet there was some soil that had been disturbed on Brink's neglected strip. It was ideal for scratching. And for peeing on. Which was what Oskar, leg cocked, was doing now, when a voice shouted, 'Bugger off, you filthy mutt!'

Oskar scampered off through the fence as a stone whistled past his left ear. He darted through Thora Tarland's apple trees onto the pathway and then nonchalantly trotted off to find somewhere else interesting to sniff before heading home to the far end of the site, where his owner would be busy in her beloved greenhouse.

CHAPTER 2

June.

Kevin Ash carried his mug of tea back to his desk in the large office he shared with three other colleagues at the headquarters of the Cumbria Constabulary's Carleton Hall headquarters on the outskirts of Penrith. He plonked his mug down and stared at the mud-brown liquid. He marvelled that during his years in the North of England, he had gone from the soppy, weak tea of his youth to a consistency of brew you could almost stand a spoon in. He had affection for the North – after all, his two daughters were North-East born and bred – but he had never felt accepted either on Tyneside or in the North West. His Essex accent probably didn't help. The moment he opened his mouth, his roots were betrayed, and the Northerner's natural suspicion of anyone from south of the Humber kicked in. It also led to a lot of banter with his fellow officers: mostly good natured, occasionally not. When serving in Newcastle, he was known as 'Cockney Ash', though he was brought up over fifty miles from the sound of the Bow Bells. He had long accepted that he was always going to be regarded as an outsider.

He took a sip of his tea and turned his attention to the notes he needed for the following day. A fifty-year-old man was being tried for grievous bodily harm after a Friday-night fracas in the town, and Kevin was required to give evidence. The man may have been provoked, but he had a history of violence, and Kevin didn't expect there would be much sympathy floating around the magistrate's court.

'Hey, Kev!' a voice said loudly.

Kevin glanced up and saw the burly figure of bluff Yorkshireman, DS Si Braithwaite lumbering into the room, a piece of paper in his chunky hand.

'Just been up seeing the Super,' he said, brandishing the paper.

'Your lucky day.'

'No, Kev, yours!'

Kevin's heart sank. Another waste of his time beckoned.

'What now?' he asked resignedly.

'A missing person.'

'And why me?'

'I suggested you, as a matter of fact.'

'That's so kind of you. Why not send uniform?'

'Because the man who's lost his granddaughter is a friend of the Super's. I assume he's one of the funny-handshake brigade.' The Masons. That was another group Kevin was on the outside of, though this time from choice. 'He wants a detective to go and show we're serious.'

'So why not you, then?'

'Because you're the one with the Scandinavian bird.' Kevin might be a Southerner, but he did have some kudos at the station in the shape of his long-distance relationship with Swedish detective, Anita Sundström. Modifying the word 'woman' with 'Swedish' seemed to have a mystical effect on the British male. At headquarters, this led to envious wisecracks that now, in the days of #MeToo, were restricted to times when no female colleagues were within earshot.

'And what's that got to do with the price of fish?'

'The girl's missing in Scandinavia.'

There were no two ways about it. The dog was definitely dead. Stiff as a board.

'Where did you find it?'

'*Him*, not *it*,' said Judith Vesterlund vehemently, wiping a tear from her cheek. 'Down in the undergrowth above the beach.'

'It was deliberate,' Sigrid Clausson said firmly. 'It's not the first dog that's been attacked in recent weeks. But Oskar is the first to be actually killed.'

It was because Clausson was an ex-cop that Inspector Joel Grahn was here in the first place. It seemed daft that he had been called out. This wasn't what a detective should be wasting his time doing. But Clausson and his boss at Ystad went back a long way.

'What sort of dog is it... he... Oskar?'

'A cross of some kind,' said Vesterlund with obvious incredulity that the inspector didn't know a mongrel when he saw one.

The inspector bowed to Vesterlund's superior knowledge with a conciliatory grimace on his chubby face. He could see the woman was upset. And he didn't want to get on the wrong side of Clausson; any negativity might get filtered back to the station. He could see the cause of death – it left nothing to the imagination. The animal had been hit over the head with something heavy.

'Who found him?' The dog was laid out on the table inside Vesterlund's cabin.

'Viktor did. That's Victor Bjelk.' This was Clausson, who clearly thought that she should be the one to deal with the authorities. A clear-headed approach was needed and Vesterlund was too emotional. 'Oskar had been missing for twenty-four hours. He liked to wander off sometimes, but he always came back. When Judith hadn't seen him for a while, she went out to look for him. Kidnapping dogs is not unknown. There's quite a trade in them.'

'Was there anything special about Oskar?' asked Grahn,

who wouldn't have known the difference between a poodle and a Great Dane. What he really wanted to know was where his next cup of coffee was coming from. He hadn't had time for one before he left the station, as his boss had stressed the urgency of his mission with the words 'it looks good for community policing'.

'Well, no,' conceded Clausson. 'Hardly the point.' She was back with the upper hand. 'When Oskar had been missing for several hours, we sent out search parties. That's when Viktor found the poor thing under some bushes. He'd been killed then shoved out of sight.'

Grahn wasn't quite sure what he should be doing.

'You say there have been other attacks?'

'Yes. Even my little Maisie was kicked.'

'Pardon?'

'My cockapoo. Damaged her ribs. And there have been other incidences around the site.'

Grahn scratched his head.

'Have you any idea who might be behind this?'

'Gerda Brink,' Clausson and Vesterlund said in unison.

CHAPTER 3

Kevin Ash drove onto the M6 motorway and headed south. His destination was the home of James Vaux – somewhere near Sizergh, beyond Kendal. He thought it was ridiculous that he should have to go all that way. Why couldn't someone from the Kendal cop shop pop along and see the old buffer? Even a phone call would do. But no, Superintendent Kellet had insisted on a personal visit and that Kevin, with his knowledge of Scandinavia, was the man for the job.

The motorway was an incongruous slice of tarmac through the mountainous Cumbrian terrain: great for getting somewhere fast, not so good if you valued the rugged, wild aesthetics of the area. Today, with dark clouds gathering around the peaks, the fells looked particularly forbidding, and Kevin was glad to be eating up the miles.

He had first met Anita Sundström on a similar assignment, when he'd been appointed to liaise with the Swedish detective in search of a missing heir hunter. He'd been immediately smitten by the sexy, feisty, independent woman, and, in time, the relationship on both sides had blossomed into love. Over the years, they had come to an understanding. Both knew how impractical it would be to live together on a permanent basis, though Kevin was keener on giving it a try than Anita – he would like to have married her, but his proposal hadn't been accepted. So now, they had agreed on a long-distance arrangement, and Kevin had reluctantly accepted the status quo. Anita had persuaded him that it was for the best; she had known that neither of them could ever really settle in the other's homeland. Too many family ties. Anita's son Lasse and his partner Jazmin, and her granddaughter Leyla lived in Malmö; and Kevin's daughters Abigail and Hazel both lived in and around Newcastle, only a couple of hours' drive away. And Hazel was about to make him a grandfather!

So the time Kevin spent with Anita was precious. They usually managed an annual holiday and occasional long weekends at various locations. However, since Anita's elevation to chief inspector in the Skåne County Police, her new responsibilities meant they had seen less of each other, which Kevin found annoying and frustrating. Furthermore, Anita was finding the role difficult, and he spent much of their weekly FaceTime sessions trying to reassure her and calm her anxiety. He knew – and she knew deep down – that she was a very good detective, and a good manager, though he was aware that she loathed the administrative chores that took up much of her daily work. He also knew that her team respected her, though she had had some trouble with Klara Wallen, who felt that Anita's promotion should have been hers. But Anita had had the advantage of the backing of her commissioner, Theo Falk. If truth be known, Falk's unstinting support for Anita didn't always sit comfortably with Kevin. He'd heard that Falk and Anita had been friends at the Stockholm Police Academy and that the commissioner still held a candle for her. Kevin couldn't ignore the occasional twinge of jealousy, which he acknowledged was completely unreasonable, as Anita was clearly not remotely interested in Falk. All the same, it didn't stop him from fretting. After all, his own ex-wife had strayed into the bed of a senior officer, among others.

When Kevin came off the motorway at Junction 36 and headed towards the signs to Barrow, the weather, in typical Cumbrian fashion, changed, and the dappled verdancy of the landscape, enhanced by the June sunshine, lifted his spirits.

June was Kevin's favourite month. The countryside was still sparkling with youth: the trees were fresh and full, lambs gambolled in the fields, and the hedgerows were alive with chattering fledglings. It was a time to be treasured before the languor of late summer kicked in.

After the next roundabout, the dual carriageway began a steady incline. At the top of the bank, there was a sharp turn to the left onto a narrow lane. A couple of hundred yards further on, Kevin reached White Gables, a detached, 1930s villa set back in spacious gardens. He parked behind the SUV sitting in front of a garage which didn't look quite wide enough to take a large modern car. The front door was answered by a man that Kevin judged was in his early eighties. He was tall and slim with neatly cropped, pewter hair and matching moustache. Despite his advanced years, this was a man who was still in good shape.

'You must be DI Ash,' he said, holding out his hand. Kevin took it carefully, fully expecting some weird grip, but it didn't come. Maybe the Super had tipped him off. 'I'm James Vaux. Thank you for coming so promptly.'

'No problem.'

Kevin shut the front door behind him and followed Vaux through a well-appointed kitchen with an enormous Aga. Behind a small dining table was an open French window. On his way through, Kevin noticed a framed photo of a plump girl, about ten years old, with a freckled face tentatively grinning at the camera.

'Better out here,' Vaux said as they stepped onto a wide patio, beyond which was the garden. 'It's a nice day now. I'm afraid my wife is indisposed. She's taken all this very badly.' Vaux's delivery was clipped, which immediately made Kevin think of the military. 'Tea or coffee?'

'Tea, please.'

While Vaux went back into the kitchen, Kevin took a

brief stroll round the garden. Certainly, the layout indicated precision. Every border was ruler straight, the flowers lined up for inspection. The striped lawn was as immaculate as a cricket pitch. Even the fruit cages resembled fortifications. He came back to the patio and sat down on a metal mesh garden seat. The sun was now beating down, and Kevin shut his eyes and let the warmth caress his pallid skin. This was better than sitting in the station with his sweaty colleagues. He was given a jolt when he heard a voice say 'Shall I be mother?' Had he momentarily dropped off?

Kevin nodded. Vaux had brought out a tea tray laden with welcome refreshment. The older man, with just a hint of a tremor, poured the tea and handed it over. 'Help yourself to milk and sugar. And tuck into the biscuits.'

'Thank you,'

'Do I detect an Essex accent?'

'I'm afraid so.'

'No apologies needed. Spent a number of years in Colchester. Army, of course.' Kevin, in his early policing years with the Essex force, had, on occasion, been called upon to help sort out over-exuberant, drink-fuelled squaddies on nights out in the town.

Kevin added milk and two lumps to his tea and stirred it all together with a neat silver teaspoon.

'I'm afraid, Mr Vaux, I haven't really been given much background information on your granddaughter's disappearance. I gather her name is Linda and she's twenty-two years old.'

'Yes, Linda. She's gone AWOL, so to speak.'

'Do you know where she was last seen?'

'Well, the last we heard from her, she was in Copenhagen. Got a quick call. She was on her way to Sweden. That was a week ago.'

'Was she alone? Or with somebody?'

'On her tod.'

'And she hasn't been in contact with her parents or friends?'

'Her parents are both dead.'

'Oh, I'm sorry.'

'Linda's my son Harry's daughter. Harry followed me into the Army. Killed outside Basra after the invasion of Iraq. My daughter-in-law was distraught. Struggled to look after Linda, who was only two at the time. We believe that ultimately led to her cancer. Anyway, when Anna died, we took over nine-year-old Linda and brought her up. Clever girl. Loved history. Developed a passion for archaeology after I took her to Vindolanda up on Hadrian's Wall. She was fascinated watching the on-going dig they have there.' Vaux's eyes momentarily glinted at the memory. 'Wanted to turn it into a career. She studied archaeology at Newcastle University, and during her first summer holiday, she went on a dig in Orkney. The Brough of Deerness.'

'I've heard of that,' Kevin interjected. 'I've always wanted to go to Orkney. Maeshowe, Skara Brae and... sorry,' Kevin stopped himself before he got too carried away. 'History is one of my things.'

'You would get on well with Linda. Anyway, the Orkney dig was a huge success where she was concerned. Her other grandfather originated from the islands and filled her head with stories of Vikings and sagas and all that stuff. She found a Viking comb. Very proud of that. There's a picture of it up in her bedroom.' The words seemed to catch in his throat. 'Then last summer, she went to southern Sweden. Scor-ner.' His pronunciation was precise.

'Skåne. I know it.'

'It was a Viking settlement. She had a wonderful time. Full of it when she came back.'

'So, was it the same dig that took her back to Sweden?'

'Not exactly.' Kevin waited to be enlightened as Vaux

carefully picked up his tea and took a sip. All his movements were measured. 'The dig actually finished at the end of the summer last year. During it, she became good friends with a young British man called Tony Yealand.'

'Was this a romantic involvement?'

'I don't believe so,' Vaux said, wafting a hand in the air. 'Platonic sort of thing. Anyway, she's just finished her degree course and she decided to go and find him.'

'Find him?'

'Yes. He'd sort of dropped off the radar.'

'And this Tony was in Sweden?'

'Yes. He lives there. Older than Linda. He's been in Scandinavia for a number of years.'

'It must have been quite a strong relationship for her to make such an effort to find him after a year.'

'Yes, I thought it a trifle odd. But she told me he'd contacted her after she left the dig. She had to come back home before the end. He'd sent a text saying he thought he'd made a significant last-minute discovery. Sounded very excited. Then... nothing.'

Kevin was half way through munching a piece of shortbread. He swallowed it quickly.

'Didn't she follow it up at the time?'

'She sent him a few emails but he didn't reply, and she was busy with her final-year studies. And probably other distractions, no doubt.'

'Were these summer digs organised by the university?'

'The Orkney one was. She went to Sweden because a visiting professor encouraged her to join his team. She couldn't resist the lure of the Viking homeland.'

'And this professor was from Sweden?'

'I think so.'

'Did anybody else from Linda's course go on that Swedish dig with her?'

'Yes. A girl called Jane Caldbeck.'

'Have you contacted her, or any of her friends from the university?'

'Yes. Jane's in Crete at the moment but is due back on Sunday. She hadn't heard anything from Linda except a WhatsApp message on the same day that she phoned us. I have no idea who her other friends were. Jane was the only one we met. She's from near Carlisle.'

'How is Linda travelling? By air? Train?'

'No. She's got a second-hand Dormobile. Very second-hand. But she was happy enough with it. We paid for it as a present for getting her degree. She wanted to travel this summer before finding a permanent job, if there is such a thing these days,' he added cynically.

'I'll need a description of the vehicle. And she was in Copenhagen when she last contacted you?'

'It was the morning of June the sixth. She was on a campsite outside Copenhagen and she said she was crossing over that big bridge –'

'Öresund Bridge.'

'Yes. That day. Didn't expand on her plans. Told us about the journey from Amsterdam. She took the ferry over from Newcastle. It took her about four days to motor up through Germany and Denmark.'

'Is there anybody else you've been onto besides Jane Caldbeck?'

'Of course.' This came out as a bark, his anxiety coming to the fore. 'I've been onto the British embassies in both Denmark and Sweden. They say all the right things... she's bound to turn up... all that guff, but one wonders. It was in desperation that I got onto Jack Kellet.'

Kevin nodded. 'I'll need an up-to-date photo of Linda.'

'Of course.'

'What's she like? Out-going? Impulsive?'

'If you're implying that she would just rush off on a whim,

you're sorely mistaken. She's a thoughtful girl. Bright as a button. Works incredibly hard. Diligent.'

'A boyfriend? Girlfriend?'

'Not the latter,' Vaux snorted indignantly. 'There was someone briefly in her second year, I think. But nothing serious since.' Kevin wondered how well James Vaux really knew his granddaughter. How open would she be with her grandparents and how close were they in reality? There may be more to the relationship than meets the eye. Maybe Linda had gone off-grid deliberately.

'Presumably, she's got a mobile and computer with her?'

'Yes.'

'Well, I've a contact in the Skåne County Police. They might be able to trace her phone. But initially, they should be able to establish whether she did actually cross the Öresund Bridge into Sweden.'

CHAPTER 4

Gerda Brink's plot was a blot on the landscape. That was Joel Grahn's immediate impression. Not every plot was pristine – some needed a little TLC – but Gerda's was a veritable eyesore. Even the rickety greenhouse had some glass panes missing, allowing a rapacious vine to make a break for freedom. The whole area was a two-fingered gesture to Swedish order and neatness.

Brink herself wasn't much better. She was sitting outside on an old wooden chair, in a haze of cigarette smoke. Grahn put her in her late-sixties, though that may have exaggerated her age, as she had the sallow skin of a lifelong smoker. Her untidy, greasy grey hair looked as though it needed a good comb. But it was the eyes that struck Grahn most. The blue of the irises lacked lustre, and the stare was hard and suspicious.

'Gerda Brink?' he asked tentatively.

'Who's asking?' she rasped back.

'Inspector Joel Grahn.' He fumbled to produce his warrant card.

'Is that meant to impress me?' The snarled question was accompanied by a plume of smoke.

'I just need a word.'

'Go! That's a word.'

'I'm here about the dead dog found down near the beach. Have you heard about it?'

'Difficult not to,' she huffed. 'All that caterwauling over a dead dog. For God's sake, it's only an animal!'

'And one that was very close to the owner's heart. A companion.'

'If you say so. What of it?'

'I'm asking people if they heard anything or saw anything a couple of nights ago.'

Brink shook her head and flung her nearly smoked cigarette into the nearest weed bed. Grahn noticed a collection of butts.

'It has been brought to my attention that you don't like dogs. You've been known to kick one belonging to one of the plot holders.'

'That damned nosey cop! Don't listen to the likes of her – and the other soppy women round here. Cows, the lot of them. I can't abide these animals running loose, sniffing round my garden and pissing on my plants.' Grahn couldn't see any plants worth pissing on, but he supposed it was the principle.

'So, you know nothing about the incident?'

'No.'

'And this dog – Oskar – hasn't been on your plot? It's a mongrel. Brown and white.'

'Might have. They all look the same to me. If I'd seen it, I would have chased it off. That's not the same as killing.'

Anita Sundström took off her glasses and pinched the bridge of her nose. Kevin ringing her at work had been unexpected. Their regular calls were on FaceTime at the weekends. But this was about a case he'd been landed with, and he was asking for help. She was happy to oblige. He wanted to know if a missing British woman had come over to Sweden from Copenhagen and, if she had, could the Skåne County Police find her? When Kevin's name came up on her screen, she'd been worried that he was going to cancel their summer holiday. It had been a subject of much debate, and finding a compromise hadn't been easy. Anita wanted somewhere warm so she could laze around and unwind, but she knew Kevin wouldn't be too keen on that. He always wanted to *do* things: visit places of historical interest, go for long walks, trail round endless museums and art galleries. They finally agreed on Sicily, which seemed to offer them both what they were looking for. She could relax in the sun and he could wander off to yet another ruin. The only downside of allowing him to indulge his passion was that she would have to listen to a detailed break-down of his adventures at the end of each day. Maybe it was good for their relationship that Denmark and the North Sea lay between them.

She put her glasses back on and picked up the phone.

'Hi Hakim. Can you pop along?'

A couple of minutes later, Hakim Mirza entered her office. Jazmin's brother was not only part of the family, he was a dear friend. He was no longer the beanpole he'd been when he first started working with the team: marriage and fatherhood had seen him thicken out. He had found contentment in family life and was pleased that his wife Liv was back at work at the polishus. Liv had had more than her fair share of tragedy: shot in the line of duty and now in a wheelchair, she had found her *métier* as the team's IT expert. And Anita was equally delighted at the happy conclusion – Liv was a wizard with the technology that so often baffled and infuriated her.

'I've just had Kevin on the line.'

'How is he?'

'Good. But it was a professional call. A twenty-two-year-old British woman called Linda Vaux has gone missing. She was heading for Sweden, but she was last heard of on the sixth at a campsite in Copenhagen.'

'A week ago.'

'Firstly, we need to establish whether she made it across the Bridge. If not, we'll have to hand it over to the Danes. She was travelling in an old green-and-white Dormobile. Kevin's sending over the details of the vehicle. Can you get Liv onto the Bridge CCTV? He's also sending her mobile phone number, so can you ask if she can pinpoint the girl's movements? They're going to check out her social media activity over in Cumbria. There's an up-to-date photo coming through, too.'

'Was she coming here on holiday or for work?'

'Neither. She'd just finished an archaeology degree and she'd been on the Vollerby dig last summer.'

'I remember. The Viking hoard they found was on TV.'

'Yeah, that's right. She was coming back to find someone she was on the dig with. A fellow Brit. Seems they'd lost contact, so she decided to come over and look for him. We need to track him down.' Anita squinted at the notes she'd made during Kevin's phone call. 'Tony Yealand. That might be Anthony, officially.'

'She may have met up with him and be safely in his arms as we speak,' Hakim said with a grin.

'Apparently not. Well, according to Linda's grandfather. Purely platonic. Yealand's lived over here for some years, so he should be easy enough to locate.'

'OK. I'll get straight onto it.'

'The dig was carried out by Malmö University. If we find she did cross the Bridge, it might be an idea to contact the archaeology department. She may have got in touch with them first.'

Hakim left her office. Anita smiled to herself. Kevin had sounded fed up having to deal with this case. Apparently, it was as a favour for his boss. The only time he'd become animated during their conversation was when he was telling her about the Viking dig. Typical!

CHAPTER 5

On Monday morning, Joel Grahn got a call to go down to the front desk just as he was about to pour himself a coffee. Two 'elderly' women wanted to speak to him about an ongoing investigation. His heart sank. It was likely to be Judith Vesterlund and another of the allotment coven hassling him about that wretched dog. To his surprise, it wasn't Vesterlund. It was worse: the ex-cop, Sigrid Clausson. She was accompanied by a scowling, grey-haired, dowdy woman, whom Clausson introduced as Thora Tarland, Gerda Brink's immediate neighbour. Tarland's sad, rheumy eyes gave her a permanent air of disappointment. In contrast, Clausson exuded vivacity. Since meeting her the previous Thursday, when Oskar's body was found, Grahn had done some digging around the station. Clausson had been a detective, which meant she knew how the system worked. She'd been popular among her colleagues and, by all accounts, good at her job, though it was best not to get on the wrong side of her. More pertinently, she was a pal of his boss.

Grahn ground his teeth. After the exhilaration of working on the case of the sauna murders and the disappearing bank robber with the team from Malmö a couple of years before, life had got a bit dull in Ystad, but now he'd really reached the bottom of the pit.

'Well?' Clausson demanded.

'Well what?'

'The dog's murder. Any new leads?'

Grahn laughed then saw Clausson's stony face. 'Oh, that wasn't a joke.'

'Where are you with the case?'

'We all want to know,' Tarland added dolefully.

'Enquiries are ongoing.'

'For goodness sake! Have you spoken to Gerda Brink?'

'Yes.'

'And?'

'She denies knowing anything about it.'

'Of course she does.'

Before Clausson had time for another huff, he jumped in with 'But she did admit that she'd chased dogs off her patch.'

'She's had a go at my Maisie on more than one occasion.'

'You know I can't just arrest her. There's nothing to indicate that Oskar was anywhere near her garden.'

Clausson nodded at Tarland. 'Thora...' she prompted.

'Yes. I've seen Oskar in Gerda's so-called garden. It's almost wild,' she added in horror. 'I heard her shout at him.'

'There's a big difference between shouting at an animal and killing it.' Brink had pointed that out herself.

'Is there?' Clausson said caustically. There spoke a committed dog owner, thought Grahn.

'I need more evidence than that.'

'Then you'll have to find some.'

Grahn thought that was an unreasonable request in the circumstances.

'I'm surprised that Brink's so protective of her plot,' he observed. 'It's a bit of a –'

'Mess,' chimed in Tarland. 'It's a disgrace.'

'So, why doesn't she get voted off the site?'

Clausson and Tarland exchanged glances that Grahn couldn't interpret.

'Not that easy,' Clausson muttered. It was clear that she wasn't going to enlighten him.

'All I can say is that the investigation is in hand. If you come across any information that you think is relevant, please get in touch.'

Clausson and Tarland left without another word. Grahn shook his head wearily. He really needed that coffee now.

Anita was in the midst of her weekly Monday-morning meeting with Commissioner Theo Falk. As usual, the day's newspapers cluttered the commissioner's desk as he assiduously scoured the pages for any references to the Skåne County Police. Fear of bad publicity seemed to stalk the holders of the highest office in the force. Anita thought these meetings were a waste of time, but Falk insisted on them so he could catch up on her team's ongoing cases. From Anita's point of view, the only benefit was the quality of Falk's coffee. It was better than most of the local cafés could provide. She always had at least two cups.

'Anything else?' Falk asked with the beaming, unctuous smile that colleagues had noticed only seemed to be reserved for Anita. Things were less fraught for the commissioner now that the Eurovision Song Contest was over. With thousands of extra visitors, the participating artists' protection and anti-Gaza war protests to cope with, he'd had to call in help from Norwegian and Danish police forces, as Swedish resources had been stretched to the limit. All had breathed a sigh of relief when the last of the glittering bandwagon had departed the city.

'One thing... it maybe something or nothing. My friend Kevin Ash at the Cumbria Constabulary in the UK –'

'I know of him.' Falk mentally chastised himself for sounding irritable at the mention of the man in Anita's life.

'Anyway, there's a young woman from the area who's gone missing while on her way to Sweden. She was last heard of in Copenhagen on the day she intended to cross the Bridge. She's an archaeology student who was on the Vollerby dig down near Trelleborg last year, and she was coming back here to track down a fellow Briton who was on the same excavation. They'd lost touch.'

'So, he's still over here?'

'Yes, he's lived here for a number of years.'

'And has anything come up?'

'Yes. Liv Fogelström did find her on CCTV actually crossing the Öresund later that morning, so she did make it to Sweden. But not a sign of her since.'

'And the boyfriend?'

'Apparently, it wasn't that sort of relationship. Tony Yealand was living up in Stockholm, but we haven't been able to trace him so far. I've got Dan and Liv digging. For all we know, he may have left the country.'

'And this young woman?'

'Linda Vaux. She rang her grandfather – she was brought up by her grandparents – from a campsite outside Copenhagen on the morning of Thursday the sixth. That seems to have been the last time anyone heard from her. According to the grandfather, it's very unlike her not to keep in touch. We're checking her mobile phone, which may give us an idea where she is. And the Cumbria police are checking out her socials. Kevin told me yesterday that he's going to see a friend of hers from university who was on the same dig.'

'So she could be anywhere.'

'Hopefully, nothing untoward has happened. In theory, she'd be heading to Stockholm if that's where Tony Yealand lives. In the meantime, Hakim's going to the university archaeology department later to see if she's made contact with anyone from there.'

'Good. Keep me informed. But I don't want this taking up too much of your team's time if it's some silly girl who's got herself lost. Another coffee?'

'Oh, go on then.'

CHAPTER 6

Hakim and his colleague, Inspector Bea Erlandsson, were sitting in the Malmö University archaeology department. The secretary had explained that Professor Nordin shouldn't be long but his conference call with a Norwegian university had slightly overrun. And he had another lined up, so he couldn't give them much time. They were left alone among the quiet corridors and rooms, which were virtually deserted during the long summer vacation. They were lucky that the professor was still around, as he was usually away during the excavation season.

After about five minutes, Ari Nordin breezed in, with a laptop under his arm.

'Sorry for keeping you waiting. Once Norwegians get talking about Vikings, they can't stop.'

Nordin sat down beside the two detectives. He was in his early forties and had very short, fair hair, which disguised the fact that he was balding. He had a ready smile on what Erlandsson, if she had been interested, would have said was a handsome face: bright blue eyes, prominent cheekbones and a square jaw with the requisite amount of stubble. He had clearly been athletic in his youth. He wore slim blue jeans, expensive trainers and a baggy, collarless shirt, which hid any advancing middle-age spread. With a sigh, he placed the laptop on the seat next to him.

'How can I help?'

'We're trying to locate a British woman who was on your

archaeological dig last year at Vollerby,' Hakim began.

'Really?'

'Linda Vaux,' put in Erlandsson.

'Linda Vaux?' Nordin repeated as though the name wasn't immediately recognisable. 'Oh, yes, of course. Linda, that's right. I think she came over with a friend as well, though her name escapes me.'

'Jane Caldbeck,' Erlandsson reminded him.

Hakim continued, 'Linda Vaux was coming to Sweden to find someone.' Was that a hint of panic on the professor's face? 'Tony Yealand.' Was there now a look of relief? 'It's just she seems to have disappeared. She hasn't been in contact with anyone for over a week.'

'I still don't understand what you want with me.' An appropriately concerned smile accompanied the question.

'Apparently, she didn't know where Yealand lives. We thought she may have got in touch with you, or perhaps a member of your staff, to see if you could help.'

'Well, she's certainly not contacted me. But you can ask Moa. She's the department secretary. She'll have all the details of everyone on the dig.'

Erlandsson stood up. 'I'll do that now.'

'Are there any other people she might have tried to get Yealand's address from? Other students? Other archaeologists?'

'I couldn't say what students she was friends with. The other two main academics on the site were Alice Asplund and Jan Hansson. Alice is attached to Lund University. They've got an excellent department – we're relatively new, so we needed some of Lund's expertise. Jan Hansson is from Stockholm University. He was our osteoarchaeologist. Our bones man,' he added to clarify the role. 'We'd worked together on a dig at Birka six years ago. Again, Moa will have their details.'

'What about Tony Yealand?'

'Nice fellow. British.'

'We haven't been able to find him, either.'

'I believe he lives up in Stockholm... or certainly did. He was at Birka, too; that's where I first met him. He came down with Jan for the season. In fact, he was there when the Vollerby dig finished. Most of the others had gone by then, me included. Can't say I've heard from him, or about him, since. But that's not unusual. Then you run into these people again at conferences and things.'

'Do you know much about him?' Hakim said as he caught Nordin glancing at his watch.

'Sorry, next Zoom in five minutes. No, don't know much about him other than that he studied archaeology in the UK. Not sure what brought him over here, but when I met him, he was working as a guide, dressed as a Viking, on the daily tour boat to Birka. Tourists like that sort of thing, apparently. He was always interested in what was going on at the site and, eventually, the excavation director at the time let him join the team for the rest of the season.'

Nordin stood up and picked up his laptop. 'Look, I've got to go. Is there anything else?'

'Not at the moment.'

'If you need to know anything more, just give me a call. I'm around most of the summer because we've been analysing the results of last year's excavation and I'm doing some talks on the conclusions.'

Hakim raised himself to his full height. 'Thanks.'

Nordin began to move away then stopped abruptly. 'Why was Linda Vaux trying to contact Tony Yealand?'

'We're not entirely sure, but we know he'd contacted her at the end of the excavation to say he'd made a last-minute discovery... something really exciting. Then she never heard from him again.'

Nordin pulled a puzzled expression.

'Something last-minute? I doubt it. It was an astonishing

dig which produced an amazing hoard: one of the biggest found in southern Sweden. But when I left, the team were just tidying up and completing the recording of finds, etcetera. I'd have been the first to be told if anything significant had been found.'

'If you weren't there at the end, who oversaw the completion of the excavation?'

'Alice. Alice Asplund.'

Nordin nodded and swiftly disappeared down a corridor, and Hakim heard a door shut in the distance.

Erlandsson appeared from the opposite direction, brandishing a couple of sheets of paper.

'Got all the names and addresses.'

'Is Alice Asplund on there?'

Erlandsson scanned the list. 'Yes.'

'It might be worth having a word with her next.'

It didn't take Kevin Ash too long to reach the Carlisle area – it was straight up the M6 motorway. He came off at junction 42 and made his way across country to the south of the city and the large village of Dalston. Jane Caldbeck's parents' home was set back from the main road that ran into the village centre. He was expected, as he'd arranged with Jane's parents to call in after their daughter's return from Crete the previous evening.

The afternoon was bright enough for Mrs Caldbeck to show Kevin into the garden, where he found the young woman sitting at a slatted table reading a newspaper, a mug of tea and ubiquitous mobile phone next to her.

'Hello, I'm Kevin Ash,' he said, introducing himself.

Jane pushed her sunglasses onto her head as she stood up. Kevin was surprised at how tall she was. She was casually dressed in blue jeans, and a white cotton top which accentuated the tan she'd picked up on her Mediterranean holiday.

'Hello.' She sounded rather nervous. 'It's about Linda, isn't it?'

'Yes. May I take a seat?'

'Of course, of course.'

They both sat down.

'Sorry. Would you like a tea or a coffee?'

'You mum's getting me one, thanks.'

Beyond the patio, there was a swathe of neat lawn, edged by colourful, well-stocked borders. At the far end, the grass had been allowed to run wild, in contrast to the rest of the garden. Over the boundary fence was a field, and some of the neighbouring Herdwick sheep were attempting to poke their heads through the wire to get at the greener grass on the other side. Jane noticed Kevin's glance in that direction.

'That's my idea. I'd let the whole garden go back to nature if I had my way. Dad hates it,' she added with a smirk.

'I imagine a lot of your archaeological work is done on difficult terrain?'

'Yes, often we have to cut our way through undergrowth or trees to get to a site. The worst places are the rocky ones – they can be a nightmare.'

'What was Vollerby like?'

'That was in a field overlooking the sea. That was an easy one.'

At this point, their conversation was interrupted by Mrs Caldbeck, carefully carrying a tray sporting a small, flowery china tea pot, matching cup and saucer, tiny milk jug, and sugar bowl complete with cubes and tongs (Kevin felt he was in a time warp). There was also a plate with two slices of lemon drizzle cake and some chocolate biscuits. Having deposited her offering on the garden table, Mrs Caldbeck surreptitiously took away the mug her daughter had been using as though it was an unwanted ornament that visitors shouldn't see.

'Thank you,' Kevin said as Mrs Caldbeck headed for the house.

'How long has Linda been missing?' Jane asked as she

watched Kevin pour out some milk before adding the tea.

'I'm a milk-first man.' He stirred the concoction. 'Linda's been missing since the sixth: a week and a half ago.'

Jane's face creased with worry. 'I thought it was odd that she hadn't been in touch. We've got a uni WhatsApp group, and we were always sending each other daft messages. I know it's out of date, but she also did some Facebook. That was for the benefit of her grandparents so they could see what she was up to... or what she wanted them to think she was up to.'

Kevin shifted in his seat; he'd only recently stepped into the world of social media by reluctantly opening a Facebook account so that he could catch up with his daughters' activities. He had to be *au fait* with such things at work, of course, but he'd shied away from getting personally involved. He still wasn't completely happy with his decision: one downside was that he'd been spotted by some former schoolmates from whom he thought he'd escaped when he moved north.

'And were there things that she wouldn't want her grandparents to know?'

Jane grinned sheepishly. 'A few.'

'Anything to do with Sweden? Her relationship with Tony Yealand?'

'Tony?' she said in surprise. 'No, he was really sweet but not Linda's type, nor she his.'

'He's gay?'

'Yeah.'

So Linda wasn't going to Sweden to rekindle a summer romance.

'When was the last time you were in contact with her?'

Jane picked up her phone and fiddled with it at a frightening speed. She held up the screen for him to inspect. It showed a smiling Linda with her green-and-white Volkswagen Dormobile behind her and a caption: *'Donny got me to Denmark!'*

'I take it Donny's the vehicle?'

'Yeah,' Jane said, replacing the phone on the table. 'Linda liked to name everything. That was sent on the sixth. I've already told Linda's grandad this. I suppose you know he tracked me down on Crete via my parents?'

Kevin stared at Linda's pretty face, lit up by a delighted grin. The chestnut hair was scraped back into a ponytail, which helped to accentuate the features – deep-hazel eyes above a wide mouth, and a hint of youthful freckles. The puppy fat in the photo at the Vaux home had long gone. A pretty girl who was enjoying her freedom. She had appeared just as happy in a couple of selfies taken in Lübeck that Kevin had seen on her Facebook page. They had appeared two days before the Copenhagen WhatsApp photo.

'Since then, I've tried to call her several times, but I keep getting her voice message.'

'Her grandfather had no luck either.'

Linda's face disappeared off the screen.

'Do you know the reason why she was so keen to track down Tony Yealand?'

'I know he texted her after she came back to uni. Something about finding something right at the end of the season. Apparently, he'd sounded excited but didn't say what it was.'

'Why her and not you? The text that is.'

'They got on really well. I left half way through the dig.'

'Why did you do that?'

'I was pissed off,' she said casually, but Kevin got the impression that there was something more.

'Linda's grandfather thinks she tried to contact Tony after receiving his text.'

'Yeah. She said she did. But then he didn't get back to her, and we were both in our final year, so work rather took over. It was only when we were coming up to finals that she wondered what had happened with his discovery. She tried to contact him again but drew a blank. Then she got this idea into her head that she would go and find him. She really took to Sweden when she was there, so it was an excuse to go back. I thought she was bonkers. I tried to persuade her to come to Crete with me and Jason and some of the gang.'

'Jason?'

'My boyfriend. Linda's not too keen on him,' she shrugged. 'But she's still my bestie,' she quickly qualified.

'Linda's grandfather suggested that she went to Sweden last summer because of some visiting professor.'

Jane gave a guttural groan of disapproval. 'Ari Nordin. Professor Ari Nordin of Malmö University.'

'You don't sound a fan.'

'I'm not.'

'Why?'

'He's a creep.' She blushed.

'That describes a lot of men. Any particular reason why this one is?'

She appeared flustered at the question and glanced around to make sure her mother wasn't within earshot.

'Ari is very charming. Very persuasive.'

'Is that bad?'

'When dealing with young female students, yes. He came and gave a lecture at the uni. It was brilliant. *He* was brilliant, but he didn't half know it. He certainly cast his spell over me. There were drinks after the lecture to give the students and staff a chance to chat to him. Afterwards, he seemed up for seeing a bit of Newcastle's famed nightlife. Me and Linda and a couple of others ended up taking him down the quayside and then onto a club.' Kevin could imagine the scene only too well from his time on the force on Tyneside. 'By the end of the night, there was only him and me. We went back to his hotel, and the inevitable happened.' She gave a regretful shrug.

'And that was what persuaded you to head off to Sweden?'

'Oh, yes. It's embarrassing now, but a summer season with a handsome, charismatic excavation director in a country I had never been to sounded too good to be true.'

'So, it was you, not Linda, who was the instigator?' Kevin took advantage of Jane's thoughtful silence to have a mouthful of the lemon drizzle cake he'd been eying up.

Eventually, she spoke. 'Yeah. I persuaded her to come along. She'd planned to go back to Orkney, but I thought it would be great if she came with me. Besides Ari, I wouldn't know anyone else.'

'So, I take it the dashing director didn't meet expectations?'

'Oh, the first week, he was lovely. He was happy to take advantage of a naïve and daft British student, but he soon lost interest. Then he set his sights on Linda and dumped me. That was even before I discovered he had a wife! He had a reputation.'

'And did she...?'

'Yes. But she could handle it. I was too emotional.'

'And she was OK that he was married?'

'Didn't seem to worry her unduly when I pointed it out. Anyway, I couldn't take the situation any longer and left after about three weeks. I've no idea what happened after that. The thing with Linda might have lasted or he might have moved on to someone else.'

'Didn't you discuss it when you were back in Newcastle?' Kevin asked in some surprise.

'Taboo subject. I was too annoyed and embarrassed to bring it up. And she knew how I felt. But I do know she loved the dig – just threw herself into the whole Viking vibe. The Romans are more my sort of thing. There's more to unearth.'

'And what was Professor Nordin like around the site? Generally, I mean.'

'Arrogant. He was *so* full of himself.' She shook her head. 'I mean, he knew his stuff. He was good from that point of view.

Meticulous. Everything had to be done just so. But he could be unpleasant with people. Like Tony.'

'Tony Yealand?'

'Yes. I think they had history. They'd been on a previous dig together up at Birka.'

'The name rings a bell...'

'It's a site on an island not far from Stockholm. It was an important Viking settlement and trading centre. Anyway, something must have happened up there between the two of them. Ari was pretty nasty to Tony, and one or two of the others. He doesn't like to be thwarted.'

'Was he the only senior archaeologist there?'

'No, there were others. Doctor Jan Hansson was one. He was a pal of Tony's, I think. Anyhow, there was some link. And Doctor Alice Asplund. Nice but intense.'

'But Nordin ruled the roost?'

'Very much.'

Kevin pursed his lips thoughtfully.

'Linda was trying to find Tony, whom we believe lives in Stockholm. But we don't think she knew exactly whereabouts.'

'No, she didn't.'

'Presumably, Professor Nordin has access to address details of all those who were involved in the season's work. We know Linda crossed the Öresund Bridge, so, knowing her, do you think she would have contacted Nordin?'

Jane paused. 'Given what happened between them, probably yes.'

CHAPTER 7

Jesusparken is neatly squeezed between the corner of Nobelvägen and Ystadsgatan: a little haven in a world of concrete. The central grassed area was strewn with an assortment of semi-naked sun worshippers, desperate to catch the summer rays. Two of them rose from their recumbent positions to have a cigarette. Dog walkers picked their way through the corporeal obstacles, some passing mutual greetings, while others pulled their pugnacious pooches apart with an annoyed tug on their leads. One middle-aged woman sank to the ground to enjoy the warmth, oblivious to her two white poodles vocally objecting to this interruption to their exercise regime.

Around the edge of the park, most of the benches were occupied. At the far end, three noisy, heavily tattooed men smoked, and drank from cans that were evidence of an early visit to the *Systembolag*. Along from them, a vagrant of indeterminate age with a pork pie hat sat next to his ageing bicycle. He was already inebriated. From time to time, he would spring to his feet, call out, and cackle with laughter before returning to his seat. The unsteady routine was repeated, but, this time, it was concluded with a snatch of a long-forgotten song. This also greatly amused him. On the next bench sat a slim, middle-aged woman, who ignored the presence of her neighbours with well-practised ease.

From the entrance near the apartment block behind the park came a stout woman in a pair of ill-fitting Lycra shorts and a garish T-shirt. On her back was a knapsack and in her hand, a plastic bag full of breadcrumbs. On spying the woman, the scavenging pigeons which had already been pestering the park's patrons flocked to her feet in a scene reminiscent of *Mary Poppins*. The middle-aged woman, annoyed by the close proximity of the avian gang, moved to another bench. But she wasn't left in peace for long. The rubbish bin next to her new refuge had attracted the attention of the inevitable bin diver, a common sight in Malmö. These particular foragers ransack the city's waste for used metal cans and plastic bottles that can be inserted into reverse vending machines in exchange for much-needed cash.

'Right, let's give her another go,' said Hakim, standing up.

Erlandsson finished her water and then handed the bottle over to the bin diver, who was hovering close by in case it was thrown away.

They walked out of the park, reversing the route of the pigeon woman, and stopped at the entrance to the apartment block: the home of Doctor Alice Asplund. Though Asplund worked at Lund University, she lived in Malmö. They had buzzed her intercom earlier, but she hadn't been in. A neighbour coming out of the block had suggested they give her half an hour; she was probably at the gym. This time they were in luck.

Asplund opened her apartment door, with a towel wrapped round her neck. She'd obviously just got back – her black gym vest and matching leggings showed patches of sweat from her recent exertions. Her chocolate-brown hair was scraped back into a ponytail. Her body was toned and muscular, and with facial features that were strong and heavy set, she could not be described as beautiful. She was, however, striking, with dark, arching eyebrows that gave her eyes a brooding intensity.

'I was just about to shower,' she explained.

'Sorry to disturb you. This shouldn't take long,' Hakim reassured her.

Asplund slumped in an armchair while the two officers seated themselves on an uncomfortable, minimalist sofa. The room was crammed with books and files: every shelf and crevice stuffed to the gills. A desk in the corner, close to the window overlooking Jesusparken, seemed to be the epicentre of activity. There was no television or other evidence of more frivolous recreational pursuits.

'We believe that you were on the Vollerby excavation last summer,' Hakim started.

'Correct.'

'There was a British student on the dig called Linda Vaux.'

'Of course. I remember her. Very enthusiastic.'

'It appears that she has gone missing.'

Asplund looked blankly at them. 'I'm sorry to hear that. But she must be in England, so why –'

'No, she came over to Sweden the week before last. She seems to have disappeared over here.'

'Well, we can't find her,' clarified Erlandsson.

'That's odd.' Asplund absently took one end of her towel and dabbed her face. 'What was she doing in Sweden?'

'She came over to see Tony Yealand,' said Erlandsson. Hakim was happy for Bea to take the initiative.

'Tony? Oh, I suppose that makes sense. She phoned me a few weeks ago. Out of the blue. Said she was trying to contact Tony but couldn't get hold of him. She wondered if I knew where he was. I didn't. But she didn't say anything about coming over here.'

'We've been led to believe that he was in contact with her at the end of the dig, and then they lost touch. She was trying to reconnect.'

'Which presumably is why she contacted me. They did seem quite close.'

'It's just that we can't find him either.'

Asplund gave a little laugh. 'Me, neither.'

'What do you mean?'

'Tony and I were overseeing the tidying up of the site. Professor Nordin had had to leave a couple of days beforehand. I was managing the return of the equipment, taking down the finds tent... and sorting out all the other paraphernalia that goes with a dig. Tony's brief was the actual site. It was just a field when we started the excavation, and we had to leave it as we found it. A couple of weeks after we'd finished, I couldn't find some context sheets –'

'What are they?'

'They're used for recording everything: soil composition, timber, masonry, skeletal remains... whatever. Anyhow, I tried to contact Tony, as he might know where they'd gone. I emailed him first and when I didn't get a reply, I phoned him. Got one of those "unobtainable" messages.'

'Did you follow it up?'

'No. The sheets turned up. They'd been misfiled.'

'Did you wonder where he might be?'

'I assumed he must have gone home. I mean, back to the UK. I know he intended to stay in Sweden, but I wondered if he could have been sent back officially.'

'Sent back?'

'Well, quite a lot of British people have been sent back since Brexit. From what I've read, Sweden's sent more back to the UK than any other EU country. I know he was worried about it. He told me he'd applied for Swedish citizenship, but he certainly hadn't been granted it by last summer. I did tell Linda all this when she called.'

'The thing is,' said Hakim, 'Tony sent an SMS to Linda Vaux right at the end of the dig, after she'd returned to the UK, about something he'd found.'

'What do you mean?'

'He was excited about something he'd found on the site.'

'Really?' Asplund was now sitting up, her back ramrod

straight. 'What was he referring to? Linda didn't mention anything about that.'

'Yealand didn't tell her what it was. We hoped you might be able to enlighten us.'

'It was an exciting dig.' Asplund became quite animated. 'One of the best I've worked on. As you probably heard in the news, we found a hoard. Mainly silver dirhams – they're coins from the Middle East. Hundreds of them! And quantities of other pieces of silver: rings, arm rings, chains. Much prized. We also found a number of burials, which are offering intriguing insights into Viking times in what was then Denmark. And quite a number of artefacts. It was all around what we believe was a substantial Viking longhouse.'

'Could any of those finds be news to Linda?'

'From what I remember, she left before the very end of the dig, and I'm sure nothing of significance emerged after that. We were working to a time limit and were starting to wind things up.'

'As far as we understand it, Linda lost contact with Tony Yealand after that SMS. So, you were both there at the end of the dig?'

'That's right. I was there on the last official day. So was Tony and a couple of the others. When I left, there was only Tony.' She thought for a moment. 'Well, I'm pretty sure. I did go back the following afternoon to double check that everything had been done. The team had done such a good job that it was hard to believe any activity had taken place over the previous six weeks. There was no one around.'

'Tony was gone?'

'Well, yes. I assumed he'd headed back to Stockholm. The Vollerby site was deserted.'

'And no contact with him after that?'

''Fraid not. Certainly not from me. Some of the others might have kept in touch. I'm sure Jan would. That's Doctor

Jan Hansson. He and Tony were... close.' Her meaning was clear. 'Though there was a...'

'What?'

'Nothing, nothing.'

It didn't appear that Asplund was going to elaborate.

'Right,' said Hakim, rising from the sofa. 'Thank you for your time.'

Asplund showed them to the door.

'Please let me know when you locate Linda. She's such a nice girl.'

'We will.'

Out on the street, they were hit by the strong sunshine. Hakim squinted in the light.

'What do we do now?' asked Erlandsson, popping on her sunglasses.

'It would help if we knew what Tony actually wrote in his SMS.'

CHAPTER 8

It was a call of nature that caused Sigrid Clausson to rise early and visit the communal toilet block. By the time she returned to her cabin, she was too awake to go back to bed, despite it only being just after five. Maisie was also up and pacing around. She was ready for a walk.

They strolled down towards the beach. Maisie loved to run around on the sand, while Clausson was content to gaze out across the sea. The morning was bright and clear. The sun was rising quickly: a great gelatinous orb on the horizon. In the far distance, she could see a large cargo ship ploughing through the calm waters of the Baltic. The sound of the rippling water along the shoreline was tranquillising, almost mesmeric. While Maisie was happily scrabbling around in the dunes, Clausson allowed herself some reflection. Certain things had been difficult over the years. Police life had taken its toll in a number of ways – the most serious being the breakdown of her marriage. The unsocial hours, the absorption with her cases and the resulting tiredness and irritability had fostered a disinterest in her home life that had pushed her civil-servant husband into the arms of someone who had more time to give him. She was no longer bitter. Between them, they had produced two great kids, and now the void that had opened up in her life when she retired was filled with the thrill and enjoyment of being a grandmother. She had her family, and she had her allotment. Pottering about amongst her flowers and plants and vegetables, she was at her happiest. And the social scene that she'd become part of since returning to Simrishamn and taking over her plot had enriched her life even further.

Basking in this pool of contentment, she felt particularly irritated by this dog business: it was an itch she couldn't scratch; it upset the status quo. Gerda Brink was at the bottom of it, of course. She was a disruptor, always had been. When Clausson had been a young cop briefly based in Simrishamn, before moving up through the ranks to Malmö, she'd come across Brink working in the office of one of the town's law firms. Even then, she'd thought the woman unpleasant. Sneaky and sly. In her privileged position, Brink had had access to many of the clients' deepest secrets – divorce resulting from indiscretions, criminal proceedings, contentious wills, land disputes and discreet out-of-court settlements – and she was not averse to using her knowledge to her advantage. The woman was poison, and no one who was unfortunate enough to come under her scrutiny was safe.

Clausson made an effort to push these uncomfortable thoughts away and turn her mind to more pleasant things. Time to return home for a well-earned cup of coffee. She whistled to Maisie, who obediently dashed across the beach and happily trotted ahead along the short track which led to the allotments. The warm weather had accelerated the growth around the trees either side of the track. Lost in her own reflections, Clausson abruptly became aware of Maisie snuffling in the long grass. She called to her to stop, but the dog was too engaged to listen. Tutting, she strode over to where Maisie was rootling. Suddenly, the ex-detective was brought up sharp. All her senses on the alert, she fixed her gaze on what had attracted her dog. A foot protruded from the undergrowth – a woman's foot, judging by the size and design of the sandal. Clausson ushered Maisie out of the way and carefully pushed back the foliage to reveal two blotchy legs, stiff from rigor mortis. At the top of the legs was a pair of faded red shorts. Clausson thought the shorts looked familiar. As she investigated further, her professional training kicked in and she was careful not to disturb the scene any more than she had already. But she didn't have to touch the body to know whose it was. The woman's head was turned slightly to the side; the pale blue eyes were sightless and the lank, grey hair was matted with blood. It was Gerda Brink.

It was at eleven o'clock that Kevin came on screen in the polishus meeting room. Anita, Hakim, Erlandsson and Liv Fogelström were already seated round the table. After a few 'hi's were exchanged, they got down to business. Hakim led the discussion in English for Kevin's benefit.

'There are two strands to this investigation. Obviously, we're trying to locate Linda Vaux. At the same time, we're also trying to find Tony Yealand. He, apparently, was her reason for coming to Sweden. We believe that she was coming as a result of an SMS – that's a text to you, Kevin – from Yealand sent last August, saying he had found something exciting: a significant, last-minute discovery. Unfortunately, no one that we've talked to saw the SMS.'

Kevin interrupted, 'We can't trace the phone; it must have been switched off. But I can ask our tech lads to contact the server – see if there's any way of finding out what the text actually said. Possibly the wording might give us some kind of a clue.'

'That's great. Thanks, Kevin.' Hakim took a drink of water and continued. 'Neither of the two leading archaeologists on the Vollerby dig – Professor Ari Nordin of the University of Malmö and Doctor Alice Asplund from Lund University – have any idea what Yealand allegedly found.'

'OK. So, where are we with Linda?' Anita asked.

'Firstly, we now know that she phoned Alice Asplund some weeks ago asking if she knew where Tony Yealand might be. She didn't. And Asplund was unaware that Linda was actually planning to come over to Sweden. We know Linda's movements up to the sixth. She travelled by ferry from Newcastle to Amsterdam and drove up through Germany and over to Denmark via Lübeck.' Hakim pointed at the board, where photos of Linda, taken from her Instagram account, were smiling at him. 'Then we know she was camped outside Copenhagen and was about to cross the Öresund Bridge. She phoned her grandfather from there.'

'And sent a WhatsApp message that Jane Caldbeck saw on the same day,' added Kevin.

'Yes, *Donny got me to Denmark!*' Hakim pointed at the pertinent photo. 'Irrefutable proof. And we *do* know that she drove across the Bridge.'

'The green-and-white Dormobile went through the toll at 11:23,' Liv confirmed.

'Then she disappears. Contacts no one... well, no one that we're aware of. Given that it's been eleven days since we know she was last in touch with people close to her, we've reason to be seriously concerned. As Kevin said, her phone's off. She had a laptop with her, but there's been no internet activity since leaving Denmark. When she crossed the Bridge, did she head straight for Stockholm? Or did she try and find out where Yealand lived from someone down here in the Malmö/Lund area? Both Ari Nordin and Alice Asplund deny having heard from her.'

'We're trawling through CCTV in Malmö, especially round the university,' said Liv. 'But it's a needle-in-a-haystack job. She could have driven anywhere – perhaps nowhere near the city.'

'You'd have thought a Dormobile with UK plates would be easy enough to spot,' opined Anita.

'You would!' answered Liv, smacking her wheelchair in frustration. 'We've also been on to Stockholm to keep an eye open.'

'OK. Let's keep looking,' said Anita. 'And what about Tony Yealand?'

Hakim took over again. 'The last known sighting that we've been able to establish was last August, on the twelfth – it was a Saturday. Two nights before, there'd been an end-of-dig party. It was held then because that was the last day Professor Nordin was going to be around. Virtually everybody left the dig on the Friday afternoon, when it officially finished. Linda had gone back to the UK the Monday of that final week. On that Saturday, Alice Asplund saw Yealand, who was tasked with making sure the site was left in the condition they found it in. That may well have been the day that he sent Linda the SMS. Asplund went back the following day, the Sunday, for a final check. Yealand wasn't around, and the site was back to normal. So, nothing untoward. However, she did try and contact him a couple of weeks later but couldn't get hold of him. No reply to an email. Mobile number was unobtainable.'

'Did she leave it at that?' Anita asked.

'Yes. She was asking about context sheets she couldn't find, but they turned up, so she didn't bother any further. Interestingly, she did think that Yealand may have returned to the UK, either under his own volition or been sent back as a result of Brexit. Apparently, it was something that was worrying him at the time of the excavation. He'd applied for Swedish citizenship so he could stay. Liv's looked into it.'

'Yes,' said Liv. 'We've sent back over a thousand British citizens; that's about half the number that have been expelled from the whole of the EU put together.'

Anita quickly jumped in before Kevin could start chuntering on about the UK's withdrawal from the EU.

'And was Yealand one of those?'

'No. I can't find any evidence that Tony, or Anthony, Yealand was sent back, though there is a record of his application for citizenship. There seems to have been no reason why he wouldn't have been granted it, as he'd been in Sweden for at least five years, which is the new rule.'

'Nor can we find him in Sweden,' put in Erlandsson. 'The address we got from our list from the university was an apartment in Stockholm. It turns out it was only rented up until the end of July last year. The rental company told me he'd paid up and didn't leave any of his possessions behind, so he must have stored them somewhere while he came down here to Vollerby.'

'Sounds as though he was planning to move somewhere new after the dig,' Anita said. 'Another apartment in Stockholm?'

'Possibly. Maybe because of the uncertainty about his future here, he decided just to head back to Britain anyway.'

'I'll check that out at this end,' said Kevin. 'Though if he did, you'd think he might have contacted Linda over the last year. Or at least told her where he was.'

'Someone who might know is a Doctor Jan Hansson,' Hakim said. 'He's an academic from Stockholm University and was the bones specialist on the dig. According to Asplund, he and Yealand were close. The way she said it, I took it to mean that they were maybe more than just friends.'

'Yeah, that makes sense,' Kevin cut in. 'I went to see Jane Caldbeck, the Newcastle University student who went over to Vollerby with Linda, and she told me he was gay.'

'And Professor Nordin said Yealand came down to the dig with Doctor Hansson,' interrupted Erlandsson. 'I've tried to reach him, but he's been on an exchange to South America this last year. The National University of San Marcos in Lima, Peru. The university thought he was due back this week.'

'Right, follow that up Bea,' Anita instructed.

Hakim interjected, 'There was one thing that struck me when we were talking to Professor Nordin... I don't know if you noticed it, Bea, but when we said that Linda Vaux was coming over to Sweden to find someone, I thought he looked slightly worried. Then relieved when we said it was Yealand.'

'I did notice that.'

'I'm not surprised.' They all turned to Kevin on the screen. 'Going back to my chat with Jane Caldbeck: it was very illuminating. According to her, she ended up in the professor's hotel bed when he was over in Newcastle for a lecture. In fact, it was Jane who persuaded Linda to go to Sweden. However, during the dig, Nordin dumped her and took up with Linda. It was at that stage that Jane discovered Nordin was married and she decided to leave. She doesn't know how it panned out between Linda and Nordin throughout the rest of the dig, and they didn't discuss it when they were back in Newcastle; it was a taboo subject.'

'Hmm... that explains his panic,' Hakim huffed.

'What's more, Jane confirmed that Linda didn't know where Yealand lived. She thought it likely that Nordin would be Linda's first port of call in her quest to find him. I got the impression that Linda would have been quite happy to rekindle whatever happened in Vollerby last summer.'

Anita twiddled her empty coffee mug. 'That puts a slightly different complexion on things. Could she have gone to see Nordin when she arrived in Sweden?'

'Or she might just have contacted him before she left home and asked for Yealand's address,' Liv pointed out.

'True. The university wouldn't officially be allowed to give out any personal information, but Nordin probably could,' Hakim said, backing up Liv's suggestion.

'Nordin didn't say anything when we saw him,' remarked Erlandsson. 'And remember, Yealand went off the radar in August last year.'

'Maybe Linda thought Nordin might know where he was proposing to live,' said Hakim. 'They seem to have got on. He described Yealand as a "nice fellow".'

Kevin tutted. 'Again, this is not what I got from Jane.

According to her, Nordin treated Yealand badly. Well, she used the word "unpleasant" when speaking about his attitude to some of the archaeologists, Yealand in particular. And she described the professor as "arrogant", though her opinion may have been coloured by his treatment of her.'

'Was there a reason why he was unpleasant to Yealand?' Anita asked.

'Jane thought they had history. It was something to do with another dig some years ago at Birka, the site near Stockholm. That's when they first came across each other.'

Anita suddenly noticed the commissioner hovering through the glass in the door. When he caught her attention, he waved for her to come out.

'OK, let's keeping digging. By the way, that's not meant to be a pun, Kevin. I'll ring you later.' She made a phone gesture as she stood up. 'The longer Linda's missing, the more worried I'm becoming.'

Anita led Commissioner Falk to her office. She hoped this was actually important and not one of his surprise social visits. Fortunately, he didn't beat about the bush.

'There's been a suspicious death over in Simrishamn.'

'And?'

'A bit like a couple of years ago with the sauna murders, they think we should be involved. They haven't the manpower these days. And, naturally, I thought of you. It's your part of the world.'

'Any details?'

'The woman was found near the August Hagman allotments.'

'I know them. My *morfar* had one of the plots.'

'Good. So you'll know your way around. The woman appears to have been battered to death.'

'That'll have come as a shock to the community. Do you

know the name?'

'Gerda Brink.'

Anita pondered for a second. 'Rings a distant bell.'

'You'll be dealing with Detective Grahn at the Ystad end.'

Anita smiled. 'Joel. I like him.'

'Oh, and I'd better warn you. The crime was called in by an ex-detective who's one of the plot holders. She worked out of here at one time.'

'What's her name?'

'Clausson. Sigrid Clausson.'

'Don't know her personally, but I've heard of her.'

'I know what old cops are like – they can't help interfering. Make sure she doesn't get in your way.' Then he added with a grin. 'Be diplomatic.'

Falk reached for the door. 'By the way, any developments on the missing British girl?'

'No sign of her. Or of the man she was hoping to link up with. We've got some inconsistencies cropping up.'

Falk didn't like the sound of that. 'Don't let it be a distraction.' His hand stayed on the door handle. 'Unless it's likely to cause an international incident. It won't, will it? Is it getting press coverage in Britain?' His face flooded with concern.

'I have no idea. I'm talking to Kevin Ash later. I'll ask him.'

'Whatever.' He opened the door. 'For the time being, I want your team focussing on the Simrishamn murder.'

CHAPTER 9

Anita entered the tent that had been erected over the body of Gerda Brink. With her, Klara Wallen, Dan Olovsson, Pontus Brodd and Joel Grahn were all squeezed in, together with three members of the forensics team. Unlike the sauna murders, Anita was grateful that they had been brought in while the body was still in situ. She didn't recognise the forensics technician – a large man, sweating in his protective white suit, called Degermark. Unsurprisingly, he was irritated by such a large audience while he was examining the body.

'Do you all have to be in here?' he grumbled moodily.

Anita nodded to the others, and the officers left her with Grahn.

'So, how did she die?' Anita ventured.

'Straightforward. Blunt force trauma. It appears that she was hit with some venom,' he said with distaste.

'Any idea of the murder weapon?'

'Judging by the evidence of the unfortunate woman's skull, nothing as simple as a heavy instrument. My guess – and don't quote me yet until I've got her out of here – is some sort of stone or rock. Dirt... jagged edges...'

'Could have been picked up anywhere round here,' observed Grahn. 'Do you think that makes it unlikely that this was pre-mediated?'

'Bit early for speculation.' Degermark raised himself to his feet with a grunt. 'I doubt she saw the attack coming. It looks like the wounds were all inflicted from behind.'

Now that Degermark was standing, Anita was able to take a closer look at the body. The back of the head was a mess of dried blood and splintered bone.

'Would it have taken someone with a certain degree of strength to do this?'

'If you're trying to get me to say whether it was a man or a woman, then I'll have to disappoint you. Most people could have done this, as the victim was unaware of the attack. No defence wounds. Age is also a factor. She must be late sixties... seventy. And I suspect her health wasn't great.'

'How can you tell?'

'See how stained her fingers are on her right hand? Points to a life-long smoker. Having said all that, it took several blows to kill her. She might not have fallen after the first one. Oh, and it appears that the attacker is right-handed.'

'Time?'

'Between eleven and one last night. Probably nearer midnight.'

'OK, we'll leave you to it.'

Degermark seemed relieved that the interrogation was over.

Anita and Grahn stepped out into the sunshine, where the other detectives were gathered. Olovsson already had a comforting cigarette in his mouth, though it would remain unlit at the crime scene.

'OK, Joel. You mentioned there was some background to this?'

Grahn nodded. 'Yes. A dog called Oskar.'

'So, what do we make of our Professor Nordin?' Hakim asked. He and Erlandsson were sharing a coffee break round Liv's desk.

'Mmm, now that we've heard Kevin's version of the dig?' Erlandsson said before biting off a bit of *knäckebröd*. It made a sharp, snapping sound. She and her Brazilian partner, Maria, had become fiercely vegan in the last year and, with no butter or cheese, to Hakim, the *knäckebröd* looked dry and unappetising. 'If this Jane Caldbeck is right, Linda may well have tried to contact Nordin. They were lovers, after all.'

'The Dormobile certainly wasn't anywhere near the university that day or the next,' said Liv. 'I've checked all the CCTV we can get hold of in that vicinity.' She pointed to the large screen on her desk. The frozen image showed a street choked with traffic. Next to the screen was a photo of little Linus, Liv and Hakim's son, sitting on a garden rug, dark hair tousled, and a wide, toothy grin on his chubby face.

'Let's put ourselves in her position,' said Hakim. 'By all accounts, she didn't know where Tony Yealand was before she set off, other than that he lived in Sweden. You'd have thought she'd try and find his address before she left the UK. It's a long way to come for nothing.'

'But she couldn't go through the university, as they wouldn't give out personal information,' Erlandsson pointed out. 'She obviously approached Alice Asplund but had no luck there. Doctor Hansson? He was the closest to Yealand. Were they an item?'

'Hansson's been away this past year, so Linda might have found it difficult to contact him,' countered Hakim.

Liv's lightening fingers went straight to her keyboard. 'She could have gone onto the Stockholm University website. He's on here. Email address. Wouldn't matter where he was in the world, he's still reachable.'

'Maybe she did and he didn't know where Yealand was. Remember, Hakim, when Asplund told us they were close, she was about to say something else and clammed up?'

'That's right.' Hakim took a drink. 'I still can't get my head around Yealand disappearing – or leaving Sweden without anybody knowing. Maybe Kevin will find him. But that doesn't bring us any closer to locating Linda.'

'Which brings us back to Nordin,' said Erlandsson with some force. 'He's all surface charm. But the picture Jane Caldbeck painted was very different. He's a plausible liar. He lied to us about liking Yealand. And presumably, his wife doesn't know about his various extracurricular activities. It's all right having his bits on the side when they're at arm's length. But what if Yealand was only an excuse for Linda coming back to Sweden and the real reason was to take up with Nordin again? And then her sudden reappearance causes him to panic. What if she turned up at his home? By the way, where does he live?'

'Near Genarp,' replied Liv.

'If Linda *did* contact him,' said Hakim, 'it would be highly unlikely he'd want to meet her at the university or at his home. It would be somewhere more discreet.'

'Then there are the other students on the dig,' suggested Erlandsson. 'Perhaps she got in touch with one of them.'

'We need to check them out. See if any of them had contact with Linda recently – or Tony Yealand. Or if they knew of Yealand's plans after the dig.'

'We'll go through the list from the university,' said Erlandsson.

'And I'll try and source CCTV round Genarp,' said Liv, 'though there aren't likely to be many cameras out there.'

'Thanks.' Hakim gave his wife an indulgent smile. 'Maybe another word with Nordin might be in order, Bea. It would be interesting to find out why he was so down on Yealand.'

Klara Wallen snorted. Pontus Brodd appeared bemused. Dan Olovsson just fiddled with his unlit cigarette.

'This was a vicious attack,' said Anita after Joel Grahn had filled them in on the background to Oskar the dog's demise. 'I just can't believe someone could do that to another individual because of an animal.'

'Beloved pet,' Grahn corrected. 'A member of the family.'

'I get that entirely; dog owners can be very passionate about their pets. But I still think it's a stretch that the dog was the motive for what happened here last night. Gerda Brink sounds to have been a deeply unpopular woman, so there might be other things at play here. Thinking back, I seem to remember my mother knowing her – and she didn't like her. Then again, my mother didn't like many people. But I suppose the dog's a starting point. Who was Oskar's owner?'

'Judith Vesterlund,' Grahn said. 'She's up there and round to the right. Brown cabin with white trim.'

'Right. Klara can you go and have a word with her?'

'Fine.' This was said with resignation and accompanied by a hard stare. Anita stared back, hoping Wallen wasn't going to give her a difficult time. Her one-time friend had grown distant and resentful since Anita's return to the force and elevation in rank.

'Dan, can you and Pontus start talking to the owners nearest to the place the body was found? Did they see anything? More importantly, at that time of night, *hear* anything? Then work your way up the row. We need to establish a timeline. The victim was killed between eleven and one in the morning, though we're probably talking around midnight.'

'Sure,' said Olovsson, who immediately strode away and whipped out his lighter.

'Actually, Pontus, before you start, can you first disperse this lot?' Anita said with a wave at the small inquisitive crowd that had gathered beyond the police tape. 'And don't say anything to any media people.' She knew better than to let Brodd anywhere near a half-intelligent journalist.

'Joel, I think we'll start with the victim's allotment.'

They set off back towards the allotments while Brodd ushered the onlookers away from the cordoned-off crime scene.

'Excuse me!' a voice called. Anita turned round and saw someone breaking ranks from the crowd. The determined, bottle-blonde woman had already brushed aside Brodd's feeble attempts to stop her.

'Yes?' Anita asked as she heard Grahn mutter under his breath, 'Head of the coven.'

'Sigrid Clausson,' she introduced herself. 'Former Detective Sigrid Clausson.'

'Ah. I believe you found the body.'

'Technically, it was Maisie.'

'Pardon?'

'My cockapoo. She sniffed out the body.'

'We'll need a statement.'

'Of course,' Clausson snapped as though Anita was stating the obvious. 'But I can give you a lot more than that.'

'We'd be grateful for any relevant information you can supply us with.'

'I'm ready now.'

'I'm just... OK. Pontus!' Brodd lolloped over. 'Could you take fru Clausson's statement, please? That's ex-Detective Sigrid Clausson,' Anita added with a wry grin.

'I do think we need to talk.' Clausson was persistent.

'I'll speak to you soon.'

Clausson was not to be fobbed off. 'And you are?'

'Chief Inspector Anita Sundström.'

A light of recognition came into her eyes. 'I know the name. You've come a long way. Weren't you the one who shot the wrong man on the top of the Torso some years ago?'

'It's nice to be remembered.'

Anita turned on her heel and marched up the path, with Grahn in her wake.

CHAPTER 10

The door wasn't locked. The outside of Gerda Brink's allotment may have been unruly with its tangle of plants and weeds, but the inside of her summer residence was as tidy as the outside was chaotic. It did smell heavily of a habitual smoker, though the large ashtray was clean. The furniture wasn't new but the television was. So were the appliances in the basic kitchen. It was an odd mix. Was the external eyesore a deliberate ploy to wind up the other plot holders?

Anita scrutinised the L-shaped room.

The body of the L housed the bed and the kitchen area; the leg contained two armchairs and a television. The divan bed had seen better days, as had the small bedside table, on which sat two half-burned candles and a holiday brochure. The faded-green kitchen cupboards ran along one wall under the window. The microwave, toasting grill and kettle were all top-brand products. Brink had cleared up after her evening meal, as everything was in its place. There was no indication that anyone else had been in. From what Grahn had gleaned, Brink wasn't likely to have had any visitors.

Anita picked up the brochure. 'Was Gerda Brink planning a holiday?' she mused. 'This isn't your cheap resort or bus tour: it's high-end stuff. Luxury hotels in Italy and the south of France.'

'I'm surprised she could afford something like that,' huffed Grahn. 'Perhaps it was just an unfulfilled dream. I can't see her wandering through Monaco dressed like a tramp – she didn't exactly dress to impress.'

'It'll be interesting to see what her home is like. Do we know where it is?'

'She lives in Brantevik.'

'You can check it out after we've finished here.'

'OK,' said Grahn as he leant down and started opening the kitchen drawers one by one. In the bottom one he found a newspaper clipping with the headline: *A BELOVED BOY REMEMBERED*.

'What's that?' Anita asked.

Grahn scanned it quickly.

'It's about a five-year-old boy who was killed in a hit-and-run incident... five years ago.'

'Don't remember it.'

'He was called Anton Lagerberg. Died on the road near Kivik. Family on holiday from Stockholm. He'd wandered off one evening from their camper van. They've paid for this bench overlooking the sea with a plaque on it commemorating the child.'

Grahn's eyes continued down the text.

'Quotes from the bereaved parents about how much Anton loved the sea and coming on holiday here.' He paused as he read on. 'The driver was never found. Blah, blah, blah. They were trying to locate a dark-blue Volvo seen in the area about the time of the incident. Nothing turned up. No one found. All a bit of a tragedy.'

He passed the clipping over to Anita. She looked at it. The article was accompanied by a photo of the bench with the parents and two siblings standing behind it. There were a couple of council officials and a bank of bystanders behind the family. Anita couldn't see any immediate relevance.

'Bag it.'

She gave the cutting back to Grahn.

'Oh, look! My uncle's got a namecheck. He took the shot.

Back in the day, he was a press photographer up in Stockholm. Then he moved down here a few years ago and still does the odd job for the local papers.' As Grahn was about to put the cutting in a bag, he noticed a word written on the back in blue biro. 'What's this? *Garage*.'

'We can look at it later.' Anita glanced round the cabin. 'Doesn't look as though the killer was after anything in here.' With that, she went outside onto the peeling decking. She stood for a few minutes, surveying the plots. Memories of her grandfather working his small patch came wafting back. She remembered sometimes sneaking off after school and sitting on the bench outside his cabin to have an illicit smoke. She always picked a time when her grandfather wasn't there, of course. Like her mother, he wouldn't have approved even though he was a smoker himself. She'd also had her first heavy petting session in that cabin – her grandfather never kept it locked. Ironically, the boy was called Björn, just like her ex-husband. She wondered what the first Björn was doing now. Any further reminiscences were cut short by Grahn joining her. He was clutching a shoebox.

'You're not going to believe this, Chief Inspector!'

He opened the lid with a flourish. The box was packed with krona notes.

Kevin wiped a trickle of sweat from his forehead as he put down the phone. Yet another wait until someone got back to him with the information he needed. He scribbled a note on the pad on his desk. All the way through the last conversation, he'd been dreaming of a cool pint. As soon as he got off work, he'd go and sit in the beer garden of his local pub and take advantage of the unusually warm weather; Cumbria wasn't normally noted for heat. And then there was that large pork pie in the fridge, which would be the centrepiece of a salad he'd cobble together when he got home. The perfect evening.

'Ah, Ash!' The images of the pint and the pie immediately dissipated as Superintendent Jack Kellet breezed into the office. 'I've just had James Vaux on the blower. Says he hasn't heard anything. I was under the impression that *you* would keep him abreast of any developments so he wouldn't have to bother *me*.'

'That's because I haven't got any positive news to give him.'

Kellet seated himself next to Kevin's desk. A thick-set man, he loomed over his subordinate.

'So, where are you at?'

'I've been liaising with the Swedish police. All they've been able to establish is that Linda Vaux entered Sweden on the sixth and there's been no sign of her since. No sightings, no contact with those close to her. CCTV and hospitals have all been checked. Her social media activity stopped at the same time. I'm waiting to hear back from her phone provider. That might give us some clues. Have to say, it doesn't look good.'

Kellet rubbed his chin thoughtfully.

'So what are you doing at this end?'

'I've been building up a picture of what she did in Sweden last year and why she was going back. And there we've run into another mystery. The Englishman she was trying to locate has also disappeared. Well, he's not in Sweden anyway. I'm trying to find out if he came back to Britain.'

'What have you got on him?'

'Well,' Kevin said, revisiting the scribbled notes on his pad, 'Anthony Yealand is thirty-one. Born and brought up in Evesham in Worcestershire, then university in Bournemouth to do archaeology. He seems to have gone to Scandinavia within a year of graduation and ended up staying there doing various jobs, including summer seasons.' Kellet frowned. 'Summer seasons as in excavations. Not the end-of-the-pier type,' Kevin clarified.

'Relatives?'

'From what I can gather, his parents split when he was very young and he didn't have any contact with his father after he walked out on the family. Mother died during his first year at university. No siblings. I got that from a cousin who hasn't seen Tony for years, though they have exchanged Christmas cards. Strangely, the cousin didn't get one last year. Maybe that's why he settled in Sweden – he had nothing to come back to in the UK. Anyway, as no one in Sweden seems to have seen him since the end of last year's dig, I've been trying to establish if he did in fact return here in the August or September. I've been going though passenger lists, border force, etcetera.'

Kellet slowly raised himself to his feet with the hint of a groan.

'Keep me informed, and get onto James Vaux and give him an update.' Kevin nodded. 'But go gentle.'

Easier said than done, Kevin reflected. The familiar twist in his gut wasn't anything to do with the thought of the impending pork pie; it was that horrible feeling he got when a missing person's prolonged silence only meant one thing – they were dead.

CHAPTER 11

It was the end of a long day. Anita, Wallen, Olovsson, Brodd and Grahn had gathered at the Simrishamn police station. The entire red-brick building opposite the town's railway station had once been fully occupied by the police. The force was now reduced to a skeleton staff on the bottom floor, and there was still plenty of space left for an incident room. On the table in front of them was the cash-filled shoebox Grahn had found at Gerda Brink's allotment. Next to it were two plastic carrier bags full of yet more money that Grahn had discovered in Brink's Brantevik house.

'Robbery wasn't the motive,' Olovsson observed wryly when the discussion began.

'There was no sign that anybody had been in her house,' Grahn confirmed. 'By the way, forensics will be giving it the once-over tomorrow morning. Not that we're expecting to find anything.'

'Stealing her money might not have been the motive, but it might have played a part.' Anita stared at the bags. 'What on earth was she doing with so much? Why wasn't it in a bank? And where did she get it from?'

'It's not as though anyone carries much cash these days,' added Wallen blankly. She still didn't appear happy.

'OK. Klara, how did you get on with the dog's owner?'

'Judith Vesterlund. Didn't get much out of her other than that she was the wife of a Church of Sweden minister. They came south about ten years ago to retire, though he must have been much older, as she would only be about fifty then. He died two years ago. Heart attack. She's a leading light in the church here in town. She was obviously upset and bitter about Oskar's death, and she seemed to think that Brink killed the dog. Not that she has a shred of evidence to back up that accusation. I think she was persuaded by the community, which had made up its collective mind that Brink was responsible. She just went along with it. Whether that's because Brink clearly had no time for animals or the fact that she was universally disliked, I can't tell.'

'We got that impression, too,' agreed Olovsson as he looked towards Brodd for confirmation.

'Could Vesterlund have bashed Brink on the head?' Anita asked.

'She might have wanted to, but she didn't strike me as the type. Her late husband was a priest. She's quite a spare woman, so whether she would have had the strength...' Wallen shrugged. 'Claims she was asleep by half ten.'

'Dan?'

'Pontus and I have spoken to the plot holders nearest to the crime scene. Most of them say they heard nothing. The closest one is an elderly lady called Elna Thysell. She says her hearing isn't too good these days but she thought she heard voices in the trees. She thought she must have dreamt it, but then again...'

'Time?'

'She wasn't sure, but it was definitely around midnight.'

'OK. Now, Pontus, what else have you got?'

'Tore and Alma Cederholm, who live second from the end of that row, remember seeing Brink sitting outside her cabin on their return from a meal on Storgatan. That was around ten. Alma said "Good evening". Brink ignored her. That's the last confirmed sighting we have of her. The owner of the neighbouring plot is away on holiday and the one behind her,

Thora Tarland, says she didn't *see* Brink, but she did smell cigarette smoke wafting over at about the time the Cederholms saw her. Brink's smoking seems to be one of many sources of irritation for Tarland.'

Olovsson interjected, 'The head of the Allotment Association Committee, Henning Kristoffersson, has the plot opposite Elna Thysell's – so that's the other cabin nearest the trees. He said that Brink was a creature of habit. She often went for late-night walks down to the beach when no one else would be around. He sometimes saw her if he'd stayed up to watch some television after his wife had gone to bed.'

'And the night of the murder?'

'He says he was watching something on Viaplay. Didn't see anyone going past, but he admits he was probably too engrossed to notice.'

'Presumably, he wouldn't have heard anything either because of the television.'

'Exactly.'

'So the murderer could have known Brink's usual movements and was waiting for her.'

'That might fit in with this,' said Olovsson, holding up a plastic evidence bag with an unfinished cigarette in it. 'This was found near the body. As you can see, it's half smoked, so she might have been attacked before she could finish it.' He also had another, larger bag with more butts in it. 'All these are from the same brand – Level, the cheap ones. They match the butts that we found strewn around her plot.'

'Isn't that what you smoke?' laughed Brodd.

'I don't get paid enough to buy fancier ones.'

'So, having a smoke may have been part of her midnight-wanderings routine?'

'Could be. All these others were found when we combed the area. We'll get them tested – make sure they *were* all smoked by Brink. The walks and the smoking... could be a pattern which a number of people were familiar with.'

'Maybe Thora Tarland got so fed up with her smoking, she did her in,' Brodd joked.

Anita then turned her attention to the kronor. 'OK, the money. We need to find out about Brink's financial situation. Why on earth would she have all this cash lying around?'

'Doesn't trust banks,' Olovsson smirked.

'None of us do, but it's difficult to function without them. Let's look into her finances. Another thing we found in her cabin was a brochure for luxury hotels in the Mediterranean. Was she planning a holiday? Had she been on expensive holidays before?'

'Her house was quite revealing,' said Grahn. 'The word is that she was normally quite shabbily dressed, but her wardrobe tells a different story. I'm no expert, and maybe Klara can help on this front, but some of her clothes looked expensive. And there was some fancy leisure wear and evening wear. Sort of stuff you might wear during a cruise or in a posh hotel in a climate warmer than Sweden's.'

'Interesting. We need a thorough check on her background. Her finances are the first port of call. Did she even *have* a bank account? And we need to check out the travel agent on that brochure you found. But, above all, let's find out why she was so disliked.'

'I'm sure Sigrid Clausson can fill us in on that,' Grahn said with a raised eyebrow.

'Oh, shit! I haven't spoken to her. I'll see her in the morning. Right, Klara, I want you to head up this investigation. It might help that you have some local knowledge.'

Her announcement didn't get the positive reaction Anita was hoping for. Wallen was always bleating about not having enough responsibility. Now, she was being handed a murder case and yet she looked as happy as a funeral director consoling a bereaved client.

'That OK?' Anita prompted.

'Yeah, 'course,' was the low-key response. Even Brodd, the main sounding board of Wallen's bitching, was surprised by her lack of enthusiasm.

Anita sighed; Wallen was beginning to get on her nerves. Ignoring her, she addressed some practicalities: 'This will be the base for the investigation. I know it's a pain to keep coming out here, but needs must. We'll meet up tomorrow at nine.'

CHAPTER 12

It was Wednesday morning. Kevin Ash brought his car to a standstill. He'd come off the motorway at Shap and taken the country road towards Orton. He was parked on the rough grass on this quiet moorland road. Far below him, the motorway, the River Lune and the main train line between Glasgow and London criss-crossed each other, fighting for space as they snaked through the neck of the narrow Tebay Gorge before winding their way through the Howgills, a remote arm of the Pennines, on one side and the Lakeland Fells on the other. The bleak grandeur of this panorama always impressed Kevin. Up on the slopes of this unrelenting landscape were several farms, their sheep strewn across the barren terrain like confetti. He was always amazed that farmers could make a living in such uncompromising surroundings. But, like their animals, they were a tough breed. Sheep were their livelihood, as they were for so many farming communities in Cumbria. Kevin breathed in the clean, dry air. The only sounds were the bleating of the sheep, and a skylark high in the heavens; even the hum of the motorway was inaudible at this distance. Way down from his vantage point, he could see the large clump of trees which surrounded the Shap Wells Hotel. Despite its remoteness, this watering hole had become a popular Victorian spa and later, in the Second World War, it had been requisitioned as a prisoner-of-war camp for captured German navy and Luftwaffe officers. With little chance of escape from an inaccessible place like this, their war had come to an end in threadbare luxury.

Kevin had taken Anita there for coffee once. She'd switched off when he started relating its history.

He took out a bar of chocolate and broke off a row. It had been a testing morning. After being ticked off by Superintendent Kellet yesterday, he thought he'd better go and see James Vaux in person. He'd tried to be as positive as possible while also laying the ground for the prospect that Linda might already be dead. It was a delicate balancing act that the gruff Vaux had seen through. As an experienced soldier who'd lost men in Northern Ireland and the Falklands, he'd been used to hearing – and relaying – bad news. His main concern was protecting his fragile wife from such a devastating possibility. She'd already lost a son and daughter-in-law.

Vaux hadn't been able to give Kevin any more useful information on Tony Yealand. This was increasingly concerning, as an early-morning conversation with Hakim had confirmed that Yealand's Swedish bank account hadn't been touched since August last year. He had also heard back from the UK Border Force that there was no record of Yealand entering Britain in August or September. Furthermore, having done a trawl of university archaeology departments, including his alma mater in Bournemouth, there had been no sign of Yealand in any of them.

Kevin snapped off another row of chocolate and bit into it reflectively. He had inadvertently stumbled into a double mystery. Yealand's message to Linda Vaux appeared to be the last known communication he'd had with anyone. And having heard back from Linda's phone provider, he now knew exactly what the text had said. Frustratingly, all that did was confirm what her grandfather and Jane Caldbeck had told him: *Made an amazing find. This'll show him. Will tell all later. Tony x.* It had been sent last year at 16:12 Swedish time on Saturday, August 12th. So Tony Yealand *had* discovered something, but they were working with that knowledge anyway.

The other bit of information gleaned from the phone provider corroborated Alice Asplund's statement that Linda had called her on May 5th. The conversation had lasted twenty-three minutes.

There was little more Kevin could do here. He would talk to Kellet and see if he could swing it to go to Sweden and join in the search there – but he would have to get that okayed by Chief Inspector Anita Sundström as well.

Anita was trying to keep a professional open mind with regard to Sigrid Clausson, but she had to confess she hadn't warmed to the ex-detective. Clausson still had connections in the force, and Anita knew she had to tread carefully. It was that fine line between respecting an old police officer and not letting her interfere with the investigation. According to a couple of colleagues in the polishus who had known Clausson, she'd been a decent, no-nonsense cop, if somewhat opinionated – a characteristic which had occasionally rubbed a few people up the wrong way.

Anita sat at the little table inside Clausson's neatly appointed cabin. The ex-detective's dog, Maisie, had initially sniffed around Anita's ankles, but had slunk off to lie on her bed in the corner when the visitor failed to show the requisite amount of interest. It was raining hard, and the sound on the corrugated-tin roof drowned out the bubbling of a fresh pot of coffee. Streams of water spilled down the window panes, blurring the vibrant colours of the roses, geraniums and Oriental poppies into an Impressionist aquarelle. Next to the flowers, young brassicas and salad plants in the raised vegetable beds were enjoying the drink. Anita could appreciate the appeal of this pretty, productive plot. Though she loved her own apartment, she missed having some outside space. Maybe sometime in the future, she'd move back into the country.

Her first mouthful of coffee jolted her back into the

present. She was used to strong coffee, but Clausson's was already stripping the lining off her stomach after the first gulp. It produced an involuntary cough.

Clausson eyed her beadily. 'How's the case progressing?'

Anita recovered enough to produce the stock answer: 'Early days.' It elicited a suppressed huff. 'I need to know more about the victim. Of course, we're already looking into her background, but you have seen and, presumably, dealt with her in recent weeks. Your impressions would be useful.'

'First and foremost, Gerda Brink was a very disagreeable woman. I've only been on the allotments a year. I retired three years ago. I'm not from Simrishamn, though I served here for a couple of years when I first joined the police. I come from Kristianstad originally. My ex-husband was from up the road at Hammenhög, so we often came over this way during our marriage to see his family, and I loved the idea of retiring here.'

'Is your ex still around?'

'No. He's somewhere in Thailand shacked up with God-knows-who. He always liked oriental girls.'

Anita wasn't going to venture into that potential minefield. 'Gerda Brink?'

'I'm getting to that,' Clausson said brusquely. 'She was messy and untidy – you've seen her plot. And she was rude. An acid tongue. I don't think she had any friends. Certainly not among the plot holders.'

'The state of the plot puzzles me. I assumed that having an allotment, you have to keep it tidy as part of the deal. At least be seen to be making an effort. Why was she allowed to get away with things?'

'Ah, that surprised me, too, until I made a few enquiries of my own. Once a detective...' she shrugged. 'She used to work for a local solicitor called Knut Fredriksson.'

'I remember the name from when I lived here as a teenager.'

'Well, Gerda worked as his secretary-cum-office-manager.

From what I gather, Fredriksson had quite a dubious reputation: took cases other solicitors wouldn't handle. Seems he was unscrupulous in his methods. A lot of things never reached court. Rumours of backhanders, fraud, bribery... even blackmail. All sorts of unsavoury dealings. None of it provable, of course. Fredriksson was always careful. And clever. And rich as a result. And right in the middle of his spider's web was Gerda Brink. Everything passed through her hands. I can't quote you specific examples or who she might have had dirt on, but I can tell you this: she was feared.'

'Is Fredriksson still alive?'

'No. Died a few years ago.'

Anita took a careful sip of her coffee.

'If what you say is true, then there may be a long list of suspects. People with secrets to hide.'

Clausson nodded. 'Oh, yes. She was the kind of person who would enjoy that power over people. And probably hint that it would only take one slip of her tongue to destroy a reputation.'

Anita's mind went back to all the cash they'd found. Had Brink gone further than mere hints? Was it blackmail money?

'Do you know if anybody ever threatened Brink directly?'

'No. I know people were upset when Oskar was killed, and some people said things...'

'Including you?'

Clausson grimaced. 'I did, actually. I was so upset. How could anyone kill a defenceless animal?'

'Why did everybody – including you – think it was her?'

'She made it plain she didn't like dogs. Or cats, for that matter. I told Inspector Grahn that Brink was seen trying to kick my Maisie. And Thora – that's Thora Tarland, who backs onto Brink's plot – saw her chasing Oskar off at least a couple of times.'

'Maybe Oskar shouldn't have been there,' Anita observed.

'He wouldn't have been doing any harm,' Clausson said dismissively.

Anita pushed her coffee away, only half-drunk.

'It might be significant that the dog and Brink were killed in the same way. Maybe the killer is one and the same.'

Clausson was about to object. Then, after a pause, the urge subsided and she picked up her mug.

CHAPTER 13

Professor Nordin lived a couple of kilometres outside Genarp, east of Malmö, close to Häckebergasjön, a beautiful, small, wooded lake with many islets and promontories, much admired by tourists. On one of these promontories stood Häckeberga *slott*, a castle in the French Renaissance style, which had in recent years become an exclusive, boutique hotel. Nordin's house stood back from the road and was surrounded by trees. To a certain extent, it resembled its much more imposing neighbour: cream, stuccoed walls; tall, rectangular windows set within semi-circular arches; and a high double entrance door. Above the door was a substantial balcony. Hakim and Bea Erlandsson stopped their car a little short of the property and agreed that, impressive as the house was, it was still a poor imitation of the grand *slott*, and out of keeping with its rural surroundings. On the gravel drive, two cars were parked – a family-sized Volvo and a green Mini Cooper. A sensible combination for town and country, thought Hakim. He wasn't quite sure what he'd been expecting, but knowing what he now knew about Nordin's colourful private life, he'd envisaged flashier wheels.

The heavy rain that had swept through Skåne that morning had ceased, and the sun was fighting to break through the shifting clouds. Erlandsson rang the doorbell. It was answered by Nordin's wife. Her initial worried reaction changed when Erlandsson reassured her that they were only 'making routine enquiries'. When she disappeared inside to fetch her husband,

Hakim whispered that he was surprised that Nordin wanted to fool around with other women when he had such a nice-looking wife at home. 'It's never enough for some men,' Erlandsson mouthed back.

Nordin wasn't pleased to see them.

'Was it really necessary to come to my home? Couldn't we have met up in Malmö?'

'We did contact the university,' explained Hakim, 'and they said you were working from home today.'

'Is it *that* urgent?'

'Don't you think a young woman disappearing is urgent?'

Nordin muttered what may have been an apology under his breath. However, it was clear that he wasn't going to invite them in. 'How can I help?'

'New information has come to light about Linda Vaux,' Hakim said.

'What new information?'

'About your relationship with her. It was more than just digging up artefacts together, wasn't it?'

Nordin was startled and his immediate reaction was a furtive glance over his shoulder.

'Let's take a walk,' he said hurriedly, and quickly closed the door behind him.

Nordin led them across the gravel where the cars were parked, and onto the lawn that ran down to the road. The grass was still damp from the rain. They were now out of earshot of fru Nordin, though Erlandsson noticed that she was peering out of a window.

'It sounds as though your relationship with Linda Vaux started on your visit to Newcastle,' said Hakim.

'I met her there. That's true. There was no actual relationship other than I liked her.'

'Not then. It was Jane Caldbeck you actually slept with in Newcastle.'

That stopped him in his tracks. He wore the expression of a man caught in a theatrical farce with his pants down. This audience didn't laugh.

'Ah, so you've been speaking to Jane.'

'A British colleague has. It was Jane who persuaded Linda to go on your dig in Vollerby. Then, according to Jane, you turned your attentions to Linda and gave her the heave-ho.'

'That's a bit simplistic.'

'Well, give us the complicated version.'

'There was more to it than that. Jane was clingy. Linda was... was more easy-going.'

'She would be less likely to make waves,' said Erlandsson sarcastically. 'Less likely that your wife would find out.'

They were standing close to an overhanging beech tree. Drops of rain still clung to the fresh leaves.

'I'm not proud of what I did.'

'You took advantage of vulnerable girls.' Erlandsson was warming to her castigation.

'Hardly. They were young women. They knew exactly what they were getting into.'

'Sounds as though Jane didn't. You used your position to –'

'Let's cut out the moral judgements,' Hakim butted in, giving Erlandsson a warning look. 'We've got a missing woman and we need to find her. We know that you had a relationship with her. What we need to know is whether she's been in touch with you since last year.'

'No.'

'Are you saying that at the end of the dig you merely parted? End of?'

'Yes. It was a summer fling. She knew it. I knew it. Her head was screwed on. She's a bright young woman.'

'No emails? No SMSs? Phone calls?'

'Nothing. I've already told you,' he added with some irritation.

'That's before we knew that Linda was your lover. We know that before leaving the UK, she did speak to Alice Asplund. *She* didn't know anything about Yealand's movements either. And Linda didn't mention anything about coming over to Sweden, so she obviously hadn't decided to come at that stage.'

'So, you haven't found Yealand yet?'

'No. He, too, seems to have totally disappeared. There seems to have been no trace of him since the dig.'

'Beats me where he's gone.'

'That's another thing you weren't truthful about. According to Jane Caldbeck, you treated Yealand badly.'

'That's just Jane being bitter,' he said dismissively.

'Are you sure? She thought there'd been some history between you.'

'Oh, that,' he said with a wave of his hand. 'Just a misunderstanding.'

'Misunderstanding?'

'Heavens, it goes years back! On another dig. Nothing really. Archaeological disagreement, that's all. Petty feuding. You know what academics can be like,' he said with a false laugh.

Hakim processed what Nordin was saying. Was it relevant? Possibly not at the moment.

'OK, Professor. One last question. Where were you on Thursday, the sixth of June? That's the day Linda entered the country.' Nordin stared back thoughtfully as though he was trying to recall. 'It was only thirteen days ago,' Hakim prompted impatiently.

'Ah, I know. I was working from home that day.'

Hakim nodded back towards the house. 'And your wife can confirm that?'

Nordin pursed his lips. 'No, actually. She and Eddi – that's our son – were in Roskilde staying with my in-laws. Bente's Danish,' he added unnecessarily.

'So, you were alone.'

Hakim left the implication hanging in the air as he and Erlandsson turned their backs on the professor, leaving him stranded in the middle of his lawn.

'She didn't come here,' he called plaintively after the retreating detectives.

Anita was making her way back to the police station in Simrishamn. She walked past the church (though not religious herself, it was still one of her favourite buildings in the town) and across the square before heading down Järnvägsgatan. Suddenly, she heard a voice call out 'Hey, Sundström! Anita Sundström!' She turned, expecting to see someone from the old days. It took a few moments before she realised who it was. The large man was unshaven, with long, greying hair sprouting out beneath his baseball cap. His clothes were scruffy as though he'd just walked off a building site after a day's labour. His demeanour wasn't friendly.

'Hello Rolf,' she said without enthusiasm. It was Klara Wallen's ex-partner: belligerent, controlling, a nasty piece of work. Anita hadn't seen him since before the break-up.

'You're a conniving cow!' he spat out.

'I beg your pardon.'

'It was your fault. You encouraged her.'

'Klara left because you treated her like a slave.'

He took a step towards her and she thought for a moment that he was going to take a swing at her. She could smell the alcohol on his breath.

'There was nothing wrong with the way I treated her. She was happy with me.'

'That's the last thing she was.'

'It was *you*! You got into her mind,' he said, repeatedly jabbing a finger into his head. 'You poisoned her against me.'

'I didn't have to. You made that woman's life a misery. It

took her some time, but she saw sense in the end. Leaving you was the best thing she ever did.'

He raised a warning finger and waggled it in front of Anita's face. 'You bitch! You've ruined everything. I'm going to make you pay!'

'I hope you're not threatening a police officer.'

'Being in the police won't protect you.' He spat at her but misdirected the spittle, which landed on her shoes. Then he stormed off, cursing. Presumably, he was heading for the *Systembolag* to buy more booze.

Anita took a deep breath. She felt winded by the confrontation. The blazing hatred in Rolf's eyes had really shocked her. This was a man who would never take ownership of his coercive behaviour. It had to be someone else's fault, never his.

Slowly, she took out a tissue and wiped the spittle off her shoes. Did this explain why Klara was acting so strangely?

CHAPTER 14

Klara Wallen was on her mobile phone when Anita entered the meeting room. She'd already caught Olovsson having a sly cigarette out in the car park. He hurried in after her.

'Any luck?' he asked Anita breathlessly.

'Yes. Some useful background on Brink.'

'Thanks,' Wallen said into her phone and placed it back on the desk. 'That was confirmation that the cigarettes found near Brink's body had been smoked by her. By the way, I've also got initial findings from Degermark. He's sure the murder weapon is some kind of stone or rock. He mentioned the dirt when he first looked at the body, but now, they've also found traces of moss and lichen in the wounds. I've sent Grahn off to organise a search.'

Anita nodded. 'Good.'

She hung up her jacket and bag and sat down before imparting her news.

'Well, Sigrid Clausson has proved quite helpful filling me in on Brink's background. Though she's only been on the allotments for a year, she's been nosey enough to discover a few juicy morsels about Brink's past life. She worked at the law firm of Advokat Knut Fredriksson, and her privileged position gave her access to client information, much of it of a sensitive nature. Clausson believes she'd been using this information over certain people for her own benefit. "Fear" was a word she used.'

'Extortion?' pondered Olovsson aloud. 'All that cash?'

'That occurred to me. They're not exactly going to pay hush money by direct debit, are they? Though Clausson didn't know any specific details, we can be pretty sure that a number of Brink's targets are allotment holders. That, in turn, means they're likely to know her nocturnal movements.'

'Does the firm still exist?' Wallen asked.

'Fredriksson died some time ago.'

'It's not listed,' confirmed Olovsson, who had quickly consulted his phone.

'Can you find out if it was taken over? Files might still exist. If so, that's a good starting place.'

'Might have a problem with client confidentiality,' warned Olovsson.

'We'll have to overcome that if it's an issue. Have we got a full list of all the plot holders?'

'Yes,' said Wallen, brandishing the information.

'Let's check whether any of them have criminal records.'

'The whole bloody lot?' groaned Wallen. 'There's a hundred and thirty-two plots. We could be talking about two hundred people!'

'Got to be done,' Anita said firmly, brooking no argument. 'Right, Brink's finances, obviously not including the cash we found.'

'Comfortable, I would say,' said Wallen, looking at papers on the desk she'd commandeered. 'Seven hundred thousand kronor or thereabouts. House paid for, so no mortgage. Allotment also paid for; just the usual fees to fork out. She made two cash deposits in the last year. Not particularly big sums. Usual sort of outgoings: property tax, utilities, supermarket, a number at the local pharmacy, occasional Skånetrafiken fares, petrol for her car, etcetera.'

'What about the expensive clothes in her house?'

'Bought abroad mainly, judging by the labels. French and Italian. Last June, she took out ten thousand kronor in euros.'

'One of her holidays?'

'Pontus is in Malmö checking travel agents.'

'But there's no sign of her paying for a holiday with a bank card?'

'Not that we can find.'

'Right. We've got lots of potential suspects – we just haven't a clue who any of them are. By the way, have we found any relatives?'

'Gerda wasn't married,' said Wallen. 'Had an elder sister who she was estranged from.'

'Not surprising,' Olovsson commented dryly.

'The sister lives outside Örebro. She's got terminal cancer and isn't able to travel, even if she was inclined to.'

'We'll have to get Clausson to do the formal identification. OK... local law firms. Dan.'

Olovsson took the hint and scurried off.

'Klara, can I have a word?'

'Yeah, sure.'

'Correct me if I'm wrong, but I get the feeling something's worrying you. You seem distracted.'

'There's nothing. I'm fine.' Her protestations didn't sound convincing.

'Is it because we're in Simrishamn?'

'What do you mean?'

'Rolf.' Wallen fixed her eyes on her desk. 'Does he live here now?'

'He moved back in with his mother after I left Ystad,' she mumbled.

'I met him on the way here.' Wallen's head jerked up. 'He wasn't best pleased to see me.'

'Did he say anything... about me, I mean?'

'He's under the impression that I was the cause of your break-up. Apparently, I poisoned your mind.'

'He's such a shit.'

'That's as may be. But why is he blaming me?'

'That might be my fault,' Wallen said with an apologetic grimace. 'When I finally stood up to him and said I was leaving, he was really furious. I was so angry, but I was frightened, too. I... I said my friends had noticed how controlling he was and how he was destroying my life. When he demanded to know who these friends were, I sort of came out with your name. Sorry.'

'I do understand. But he's looking for someone to blame, and I wasn't expecting to be verbally threatened in the middle of Simrishamn. However, I can see why you did it. He's a potentially violent man, and I don't want him coming after you and doing something silly. If this is going to be a problem, I can move you onto the Linda Vaux case. Get you out of here.'

Wallen bit her lip.

'Thank you. But I'm going to stay. I haven't seen him since I left. He turned up at my apartment in Malmö once. Drunk. Fortunately, I was out. If I run now, I'll always be frightened of him.'

'Only if you're sure.'

'I'm sure,' she said. 'We've got a case to solve.'

Hakim and Erlandsson were making their way back into Malmö.

Erlandsson had made the mistake of asking how Hakim's son, Linus, was doing. It opened the floodgates of parental pride, and if he hadn't been driving, he would have shown her all the latest photos on his phone. As they reached the outskirts of the city, Hakim realised that he was dominating the conversation somewhat. He quickly changed tack.

'How's Maria?'

'She's good, thanks. We're just about to move into a new apartment. Same block. Just a bigger place. We'll have a party to celebrate. You and Liv are invited, of course.'

'Of course! he smiled. 'Does she miss Brazil?'

'Sometimes. But she loves it here.'

'I always think we must seem rather boring compared to such an exotic place.'

'It's certainly livelier than here,' Erlandsson laughed. 'But I think she actually rather likes our sensibleness. If there is such a word.'

Hakim laughed. 'We're definitely more restrained. My parents still can't get their heads around Swedes not saying what they think.'

'Ditto Maria. And it also drives her mad when I won't get into an argument. "You Swedes just don't like confrontation! What's wrong with a good shouting match?"' she mimicked. 'But she's getting used to it, and learning to be a bit more diplomatic, especially on her nursing course – doesn't do to upset the patients too much. And now she's applied for citizenship, she'll have to practise being even more Swedish.'

'Has she really been here that long?'

'Yeah, over five years. Of course, she'll have dual nationality. But, hopefully, being a citizen will stop her being regarded as an immigrant.'

'Sorry, Bea, but, sadly, it doesn't work like that. I was born here, but a lot of people don't think of me as Swedish. Even some of our colleagues. I hope Linus won't have to live with that label.'

'Linus will be accepted. Things change.' She was interrupted by her mobile bleeping into life.

'Bea Erlandsson. Oh, hi Liv.' She listened to the voice at the other end. Hakim glanced across as he drove, in case it was something important. Erlandsson grew more excited. She finished with an enthusiastic 'Thank you.'

'Good news?'

'Traffic's been on to Liv. Linda Vaux's Dormobile has been spotted on CCTV!'

'Where? When?' gabbled Hakim excitedly.

'On the day she drove over the Bridge. The vehicle was on the E65 approaching Svedala.'

They came to a halt at traffic lights.

'Svedala?' Hakim mused.

'12:06. Now we know she didn't head into Malmö.'

'Nor was she heading north towards Stockholm.' The lights changed and they moved off. 'From Svedala, she might have headed south to Vollerby, to the site of the excavation.'

'Or towards Genarp. And to Professor Nordin's place – with his wife conveniently out of the way.'

'Exactly.'

CHAPTER 15

Saint Nicholai's church was quiet that morning. A couple of tourists had wandered in and taken the obligatory photographs before leaving her in peace. She sat in the back pew in the side aisle so that she had an uninterrupted view of the large cross on the wall at the opposite end. In her eyeline on the right was one of the magnificent model three-masted sailing ships that hung from the ceiling – a reminder of Simrishamn's rich maritime heritage – and on the left, an ornate golden crown hovered above the baptismal font. To the right of the cross, through the archway, she could just make out the altar. Within the stark white walls of this uncomplicated church, she could find solace in her complicated world. To her, this was a place of harmony, tranquillity and spiritual replenishment. She had much need of the latter.

For Judith Vesterlund it was also a place where she sought sanctuary. Life had tossed her around so much in recent years. Yet despite all the battering, her faith had kept her afloat. She had clung on desperately to her belief, and now her frequent prayers of supplication had been answered, though maybe not in the way she had envisaged. God certainly works in a mysterious way.

Oh, Sture, Sture! Her husband was never out of her thoughts. How she missed him! Her love for Sture had been pure and Godly, though it had often been sorely tested. Despite his devotion to Christ, the Devil had whispered in his ear more than once, turning their world upside down, and the religious conviction that had protected and comforted her all her life had been ripped asunder. She thought of Sture's own personal demon as the Great Evil, and their escape to this place of refuge was part of the Purge. Little did she know that the Devil would follow them. He had taken on human form, of that she was sure, and she was equally certain that he had had a part to play in Sture's passing and the death of her faithful Oskar. But now, through God's will, he had been ousted. She raised her eyes to the cross and thanked Him again for her deliverance. Her only sorrow was that Sture wasn't there to witness their salvation. He had gone to his grave a tormented soul, but now she could be certain of his place in Heaven, relieved of his burden.

She was about to leave when she saw Thora Tarland emerge from behind one of the pillars. Tarland went to the spherical votive stand next to the font. Vesterlund saw her take a prayer candle and place it in one of the holders. How strange, she thought; she had never seen Thora in the church before. She watched as Tarland lit her candle. Maybe she was seeking comfort; many of the allotment holders had been knocked off balance by Gerda Brink's death.

Vesterlund didn't know Tarland well, though she had always been friendly, and she had been very supportive when Oskar was killed. Tarland contemplated the flame of the candle she had lit. Vesterlund watched and waited; it wasn't for her to intrude on the woman's private thoughts.

Vesterlund shuffled in her seat and Tarland started, turning to face the source of the noise.

'Sorry. I didn't mean to surprise you.'

'I didn't realise you were there. I thought I was alone.'

'I think we're all a bit jumpy after recent events.'

'Yes.' Tarland looked drawn, as though she hadn't had much sleep. 'I think everything that's happened has taken its toll. Particularly for you, losing Oskar like that.'

A wave of sadness hit Vesterlund at the mention of her

pet's name. 'I miss him so much.'

Tarland glanced back at the candle, the little flame flickering defiantly.

'I think we all feel unsettled. I may not have liked Gerda... but I keep thinking about how she died. And where. It just doesn't bear thinking about.'

Vesterlund reached out a comforting hand and tapped Tarland's arm reassuringly.

'I know. But she's gone now. There's nothing we can do about it.'

'But has she really gone? It feels like her death has cast a dark shadow over all of us.'

Vesterlund knew exactly what she meant.

Pontus Brodd came out of the travel agent's. It was the fifth one he had visited that day. He'd started at the one whose name had been stamped on the brochure found in Gerda Brink's cabin. The friendly girl behind the counter was unable to supply the information he wanted: Brink hadn't used the firm for a couple of years. Nor did he have any luck in the next three places. After all his stomping around central Malmö, he decided to treat himself to a *fika*.

Five minutes later, he was stretching his long legs under a table which bore a cup of steaming black coffee and a large slice of chocolate cake. All his colleagues were either over in Simrishamn or rushing around Skåne interviewing academics, so he felt like he was skiving off school. It was a good feeling, especially as he had something positive to report: it was at the last travel agent's that he'd struck gold. Alongside his coffee were a couple of holiday brochures he'd picked up on the way out. Asking questions about sunshine locations abroad made him think it was time he headed somewhere warmer than Sweden this summer. He hadn't treated himself for a few years. The last holiday he'd planned had had to be cancelled after he'd been stabbed in a park in Svedala. The brochures he had in front of him were for Lanzarote and Turkey. Certainly, they would be cheaper than the holidays Gerda Brink had taken.

Her trip abroad last June had been to Nice, in the south of France. She'd stayed at the Hotel Boscolo on the Boulevard Victor Hugo in a room described as *Chambre Supérieure*. She had eaten at the in-house Anglo-Italian restaurant. He knew this, as she'd paid for it all in advance. When he'd seen the hotel on the website in the travel agent's, he'd been amazed at how grand it all looked. And the year before, she'd been to an equally upmarket hotel on the Amalfi coast in southern Italy.

It was a real conundrum. A double life? What he'd gathered from the allotment residents he'd spoken to was that Brink was a mean and mean-spirited woman who spent no money on her plot and even less on her appearance. As far as they were concerned, her only conspicuous spending was on her cigarettes. They had reported that she disappeared for about a fortnight most summers but she would never reveal where she'd been. Not that folk were particularly interested – they were just pleased that her malign presence was gone for a short while.

But what was most intriguing – and this would be of real interest to the team – was the fact that she always put down cash as payment. At first, this had surprised the girl who had booked the last trip, until a colleague informed her that Brink had used them before and had always paid in cash. Was this a tax-dodge? Brodd wondered. It was definitely odd; Sweden was fast becoming a cashless society, and Brodd, like countless others, never carried the stuff with him. Whatever. He'd report back soon, but first he was going to plan a holiday of his own. Besides, he was convinced that the girl in the agency had been flirting with him; he'd make sure he got her again when he booked.

*

At the end of the day, Anita had time to catch up with the missing person's case – or was it missing persons', plural? At least they now had a sighting of Linda Vaux in Sweden. That had raised various possibilities. Hakim and Erlandsson were keen to point the finger at Professor Nordin. He was obviously terrified that his wife might find out about his affair with Linda, and if she *had* turned up at his place (a strong possibility – she *was* driving along the E65), surely that would be a solid enough motive for kidnapping – or even murder! Unless, as Anita pointed out, Nordin had simply squirreled her away in some love nest somewhere. Of course, that didn't explain why there was no trace of Tony Yealand: the man she was allegedly looking for. Perhaps that was just a story she'd spun to cover up the fact that she was going back to see her married lover. Whatever the truth of the matter, Yealand had simply disappeared. They really needed to know what had happened last summer down in Vollerby.

Doctor Jan Hansson, who was a friend of Yealand's, had just returned from South America, and Hakim was due to have a Zoom call with him the next day. And Erlandsson had tracked down one of the students who'd been on the dig, and was going to her apartment in the morning. Between them, they hoped to get a more in-depth picture of both Yealand and Vaux – and Nordin. Meanwhile, Linda's photo and description of her Dormobile had been more widely circulated, and there was an appeal for help on the local news scheduled for tonight, and an item in the newspapers tomorrow.

Brodd had reported back about Gerda Brink's holidays. That fitted in with the cash they'd found around her properties. Anita was now even more convinced that Brink may well have gained it through extortion. Given the randomness of the notes, it was also likely that they came from more than one source. And the more sources, the more potential suspects they might unearth. So some progress. But Anita's optimism was dampened to some extent by her decision to leave Klara Wallen in charge of the case. She could understand Wallen not wanting her professionalism to be compromised by the Rolf business, but if her competence or judgement were affected in any way – perhaps simply by being in the vicinity of a man she fears and may easily bump into in the course of her duty – then it could have negative consequences not only for Wallen herself but for the whole team. On her return from Simrishamn, Anita had consulted the police database and found that Rolf Häggel had a record: two counts of violent conduct. Both had involved too much alcohol. Had he ever laid hands on Wallen? She'd never mentioned it. But the possibility made Anita even more uneasy. She had given Wallen an out, which she hadn't accepted. So, what was the alternative? Put her on a different case? That would probably stoke up further resentment and increase the animosity Anita now knew Wallen felt towards her. It would also make Wallen look weak in the eyes of her colleagues. She would just have to pray that Rolf and Wallen's paths didn't cross. To be honest, *she* didn't like the thought of running into him again, either. He was unpredictable.

Further thoughts were pushed to the back of her mind as her phone burst into life. It was Kevin.

'Are you using Linda Vaux as an excuse to keep ringing me?'

'Of course. I've arranged the whole thing.'

'I wouldn't put it past you.'

'Ha ha! Seriously though, I've made no headway with Tony Yealand over here. There's no indication that he's been in Britain over the last twelve months. We do know he was here in April last year – he attended a conference in Brighton. Apparently, he met up with some of his lecturers from his days at Bournemouth Uni. – and a guy who was a student at the same time as Tony and is now on the staff. Anyway, I managed to get hold of this John Finlay. He said that Tony was looking forward to the Vollerby dig and seemed to be enjoying life in Stockholm. He also mentioned that Tony had been on a WhatsApp group of former students and had posted some photos from Vollerby. But he hasn't posted anything or made any comments on other posts since' – Kevin consulted his notes – 'August last year.'

Anita sighed. 'Not good.'

'No. Presumably, nothing at your end?'

'No. But we have had a sighting of Linda's Dormobile. She appears to have bypassed Malmö, which is a bit of a surprise. Still looking.' Kevin didn't respond. 'Are you still there?'

'Yeah, yeah, that's good. Look, I was wondering if it would help if I came over and joined the investigation. I've drawn a blank here, and there's nothing more I can do. And we've got two British citizens missing in Sweden.'

Anita smirked at Kevin's sudden earnestness. 'Can you sell it to your boss?'

'Already have. He's keen to have this solved. He's taking a particular interest in the case. I think he and James Vaux must be Masons. They're like the bloody Illuminati: they like to help each other out. But Kellet said it would all depend on the Swedish end.'

'So I'm the "Swedish end"?'

'You've got a very nice Swedish end, but I was thinking more about your permission.'

Anita sniggered.

'Actually, you might even be quite useful.'

'Glad to hear it.'

'I've also got a murder on my hands.'

'Didn't know that.'

'Couple of days ago. I've had to split the team, so an extra body would help. You'd be working with Hakim.'

'Excellent.'

'I'll get it rubber-stamped by Theo Falk.'

'I'm sure your boyfriend won't say no to you.'

'You've been talking to Hakim.'

'Might have. Have I got competition?'

'Piss off, Detective Inspector.'

'I'll try and get a flight on Friday.'

'And I suppose you'll want to stay at Roskildevägen?'

'Be rude not to visit my girlfriend while I'm over. I'll do the cooking,' he added hastily.

'There's only one thing I'm slightly worried about.' Anita sounded serious. Kevin could sense a 'but'.

'What?' he asked tentatively.

'The last foreign law-enforcement officer I worked with tried to kill me.'

CHAPTER 16

Bea Erlandsson made her way to Östra Sorgenfri and parked in between two blocks of apartments off Kiviksgatan. Though Nour Haddad had an Arab background like himself, Hakim had decided it would best to send a woman to talk to her, as it may be less potentially intimidating. Like many of Malmö's ethnic residents, the Haddad family might be wary of the police.

It was Nour who met Erlandsson at the apartment door. She wore jeans, a white, casual top and a light-blue cotton hijab. A nervous smile crossed her pretty face.

'Come in. I've sent my mother out to do some shopping so she won't be fussing around.'

They went into the living room. The third-floor balcony beyond looked out onto the next block. The apartment was immaculate. The furniture was typically Swedish, but the room was embellished with some ornaments and pictures reflecting the family's Algerian roots. There was a large woven rug of many colours on the floor, and bright, patterned cushions bestrewed the sofa and armchairs.

'Tea? Coffee?'

'No thanks, Nour. Had a coffee just before I came out. Is it OK to call you Nour?'

'That's my name,' she said pleasantly.

Erlandsson sat down and took out a notebook.

'Right, Nour, I gave you a brief outline of why I wanted to see you.'

'Yes, the dig at Vollerby. I must admit when I got a call from the police, my parents got into a panic. They're scared that if we've done anything wrong, we'll all be sent back to Algeria.'

'Oh, don't worry. This is just routine. We need some background on some of the people involved in the archaeological excavation.'

'Poor Linda! I saw it on the news last night.'

'Yes. We're trying to put together a picture of what went on. It may have a bearing on her disappearance.'

'Really?'

'Yes. The reason she was coming over to Sweden was to try and find Tony Yealand.'

'I haven't heard from either of them, I'm afraid. Not since the dig finished.'

'What was their relationship?'

'They were both nice people. Friendly. I really liked them. And they got on well together. I suppose it helped that they were both English. Shared the same sense of humour. They often had a joke which went over the heads of the rest of us.'

'We know that they had differing relationships with the dig director.'

'Professor Nordin?'

'We know that Linda had an affair with the professor.'

'Yes, we all knew that, but everybody sort of turned a blind eye to it. It was awkward because the professor had also had something going on with Linda's English friend. But *she* left half way through the dig.'

'And we've heard that Professor Nordin's relationship with Tony Yealand was strained.'

Nour pulled a face. 'I don't know much about that. It's true they hardly spoke. Don't really know why. They had obviously come across each other before. Archaeologists can be a bit funny about things. Protective. I study under the professor, so

I don't really want to say too much. I've another year to go.'

'Nour, I totally understand. Rest assured, anything you say to me is in confidence. I'm not going to put it into a report or anything. It's all background.'

Haddad looked relieved.

'Was it only Tony that the professor didn't get on with?'

'Well, he can be acerbic at times. Sort of making fun of people.'

'Such as?'

'I don't think he was being nasty as such, but he sometimes had a go at Alice. That's Doctor Alice Asplund.'

'About anything in particular?'

'It's just an archaeological thing. I'm sure he didn't really want to cause her offence. Though she got a bit fed up of the jibes, I think.'

'What was it?'

'Long story. She has this thing about a crown that she believes belonged to the Emperor Basil the Second.'

'Sorry. Who was he?'

'Basil the Second was a famous Byzantine emperor. He lived in Constantinople. At that time – that's the early eleventh century – his imperial guard consisted of Vikings. They were brave and loyal and well rewarded. Alice thinks that some of those Swedish or Danish Vikings might have had something to do with the crown's disappearance. I don't know why she's got this into her head; most historians don't believe the crown ever existed, that it's just a myth. But Alice has been looking for it on digs all over the place... Turkey, Ukraine, Bulgaria, here. She's found nothing, of course. Anyway, Professor Nordin was very sceptical about the whole thing, often deriding her about it. You know, making jokes at her expense... that sort of thing. As I say, archaeologists are a weird breed.'

'So, why are you joining that "weird breed"?'

Haddad gave a bashful grin. 'Good question. It's because

I want to go back to Algeria and work on the sites there. Some of them are really amazing: everything from prehistoric cave paintings to Roman cities, and way beyond. It's my history, really. I know I was born here. It's just... I don't know... sometimes, I don't feel as though I fit in.'

'It's not easy in the current climate,' Erlandsson said with some sympathy. She remembered the hard time she had had coming out about her sexuality in the testosterone-fuelled police force. She, too, had had to cope with the jibes of a superior: the snide remarks of Chief Inspector Alice Zetterberg still left a bitter taste. Certainly, Nour Haddad's observations were exacerbating her dislike of Professor Nordin. 'But coming back to Tony. Obviously, he and Linda didn't have a sexual relationship.'

'Tony was gay.'

'Precisely. But we've heard he was close to Doctor Jan Hansson. Was there more to it than mere friendship?'

Haddad appeared uncomfortable; she didn't find it easy discussing such a topic. 'I couldn't say for definite. I think it was assumed by the group that they were... together. But they didn't do anything outwardly. Very professional on site.'

'My colleague is talking to Doctor Hansson later today. Maybe he'll give us an idea of their relationship. Maybe he actually knows where Tony has been this last year.'

Haddad appeared doubtful.

'Is there something I should know?'

'I don't know if I should be saying this... A couple of days before we finished, they had a falling out.'

'Who? Jan and Tony?'

'Yes. It sounded quite serious. I was in the finds tent cleaning some of the artefacts, and I heard them outside. I couldn't hear what they said exactly, but Jan sounded really angry. I think Tony was trying to calm him down. Jan must have stormed off. Then Tony came into the tent rather shamefaced and was seriously embarrassed when he realised someone might have overheard them. I didn't say anything and neither did he.'

'You didn't catch anything?'

'Not really. Well, other than Tony saying it had been "a mistake". I don't know what the mistake was.'

Klara Wallen was examining the board. There wasn't much on it. An enlarged photo of Gerda Brink taken from her passport, another one of her lying dead in the undergrowth, and several crime-scene shots. There was a diagram of the section of allotments nearest the scene, with the names of the plot holders. As yet, none of those names came into the category of 'suspect'. There was also, courtesy of Joel Grahn, a photograph of the deceased Oskar. Was there a link? Wallen doubted it. However, as progress was limited, she had to keep an open mind.

Olovsson and Brodd were also in the room. Olovsson had taken on the task of trawling the police database to see if any of the plot holders were on it. Brodd was going through the bits of CCTV they were able to access. Despite there being only a few cameras around the town, Brodd was painfully slow. Wallen wished she could get Liv involved.

Olovsson was drumming his fingers on his desk, which usually indicated he wanted a cigarette. The noise was an annoying distraction – Wallen couldn't concentrate on the board. As she stared at the images, seeking inspiration, her mind wandered. She couldn't get Rolf out of her head; he was lurking somewhere in the town.

'Well, well, well,' she heard Olovsson behind her.

'Found something?' she asked hopefully.

'Possibly. Our very own allotments commissar. The upright herr Henning Kristoffersson.'

'He has a criminal record?' Wallen gasped in amazement.

'Not exactly.' Wallen was immediately deflated.

'But his name came up in a criminal investigation.'

'When?'

'2009. At that time, he was the manager of a motor dealership outside Tomelilla.'

'Dodgy cars?' ventured Brodd, who had torn himself away from watching endless CCTV footage.

'A Saab dealership. The cars weren't dodgy – far from it – but Kristoffersson probably was. It was at that time when a lot of Swedish vehicles were getting nicked and ending up in Poland and Eastern Europe.'

'*Go to Poland. Your car is already there!*' Brodd quoted the old joke with a laugh.

'Yeah, exactly. Seems like a number of high-end Saabs from Kristoffersson's dealership were among them. One of his customers was suspicious, as he'd only had his car for four days before it disappeared off his drive. He went to the police and reported his suspicions. Kristoffersson was investigated. The police couldn't prove anything, but he left under a cloud. As we know, Saab eventually went bankrupt, and the dealership closed. Meanwhile, Kristoffersson bought into a small auto-parts distribution company here in Simrishamn and became a respected local businessman. The investigation petered out as far as he was concerned.'

'So the police thought he was tipping off the Polish gangs,' said Wallen. 'Presumably for a price.'

'It was probably what paid for the small business he took over. Basically, the investigators believed he was involved but didn't have any concrete evidence.'

'It certainly means he had something to hide. Is there a connection to Brink?'

Olovsson chuckled. 'Kristoffersson was worried enough to hire a lawyer to help him cover his tracks. And guess which one?'

'Knut Fredriksson!' Wallen and Brodd said together.

CHAPTER 17

The coffee was just as good, though Theo Falk wasn't his usual amiable self. He had grudgingly agreed to Kevin Ash joining the team in the search for Linda Vaux and Tony Yealand. But it had come with the proviso that Ash could only observe when they were interviewing suspects – nor did he have any authority to arrest anyone or do any investigating on his own.

'He'll be fine,' Anita said with a bright smile. 'I'll keep him on a tight lead.' She immediately regretted the choice of phrase, as she wondered what unwanted image that would conjure up in the commissioner's mind.

'As for potential suspects, Hakim and Bea have their sights set on Professor Ari Nordin, the dig director at Vollerby. We know Linda skipped Malmö and was on the Svedala road, so she could have ended up at his country residence. He was working from home that day – the family was away. And they had been lovers the previous summer.'

'Mmm...' Falk muttered. Was he even listening?

'Nordin has quite a reputation with the opposite sex. We certainly need to find out more about the randy professor.'

'Yes.' Falk seemed to be back with her. 'It's the name. Nordin. Professor Nordin. I thought it sounded vaguely familiar.'

'You know him? You might have come across him at one of your fancy functions.'

'No, no, nothing like that. Back in Stockholm.'

'I'm not sure he ever worked up there.'

'It was a dig.'

'Ah. Was it Birka? I believe he and Tony Yealand were on an excavation there a few years back.'

'I don't know about Yealand. I wasn't on the case as such, but a friend was.'

'There was a case?' Anita said in some surprise.

'A girl. A student from Stockholm Univeristy. She drowned off the island that summer. She was working on the dig. It was investigated and the verdict was accidental death. She'd gone swimming one night. Got out of her depth and died.'

'How sad. So why did Nordin's name come up? Was he the dig director?'

'No. It was a Stockholm-University-led project. Nordin was just one of the senior archaeologists. They did look into the possibility of foul play. Nordin came into it because there were rumours he was having a fling with the dead student.'

'He certainly has form.'

'It turned out it was just one of those unfortunate things.'

'The English student that Kevin... Detective Inspector Ash talked to believed that there was history between Nordin and Yealand. It could have been that dig.'

'Could be. I suggest you get hold of the case notes from Stockholm. They might shed some light on your current investigation.'

'Yes, I will. Thanks for the tip.'

'No problem.' The benevolent smile was back.

Anita drained the last of her coffee and stood up.

'Oh, Kevin will be flying in tomorrow. Do you want me to introduce you to him?'

'That won't be necessary,' Falk said stiffly.

Doctor Jan Hansson had the slightly mottled, worn-out look of someone who was jet-lagged. He stared out blearily from the screen. The police knew he was a man of forty-seven, though the unshaven, thin face and the severely curtailed hairline made him appear older. They had also checked out his history. He was a native of Skåne and had been brought up in Simrishamn. In fact, he'd gone to the same school as Anita, but they weren't contemporaries. Once he'd left for higher education in Uppsala, he never returned. His academic career had been stellar, taking him to universities in Germany, England, South America and now Stockholm. The only person Hansson could see on his screen was Hakim. Watching, out of Hansson's eyeline, were Anita and Bea Erlandsson.

'Thank you for linking up with me,' Hakim began in a friendly tone. At this stage, he was unsure how the interview would pan out. 'I appreciate that you must be tired after your flight.'

'That's fine. I'm not quite sure what this is about.' Hansson said, stifling a yawn. The doctor may have been well travelled, but he still betrayed traces of his Scanian accent.

'It's about the Vollerby dig you were on last summer. One of the women on that dig – an English student called Linda Vaux – has gone missing in southern Sweden.'

'Gone missing? What do you mean?'

'Do you remember her?'

'Vaguely,' Hansson said, shaking his head slowly as though he was trying to conjure up Linda's image.

'She became very friendly with the dig director, Professor Nordin.'

Realisation dawned on Hansson almost immediately. 'Now I remember. Is that why she came back to Sweden? To see Ari?'

Was that a telling comment?

'That wasn't her intention. The person she wanted to reconnect with was Tony Yealand.'

Hansson flinched at the mention of Yealand's name and immediately had a coughing fit. It was an obvious ploy to cover up his reaction. When he eventually removed his hand from his mouth, he didn't speak.

'You know Tony Yealand? You're friends, I believe.'

'I suppose.'

'Very good friends, actually, according to some of the people we've been speaking to.'

'We *were*,' Hansson said in little more than a whisper.

'You mean you're friends no longer?'

'I haven't heard from him for a long time.' There was a hint of sorrow in his voice.

'Really? And why would that be?'

'I've been away for a year.'

'Distance doesn't normally stop friends from communicating with each other. Not in this day and age. Zoom... Skype... Facebook...'

'What has my former relationship with Tony got to do with Linda? If she was over here looking for him, why don't you just ask him?'

'He's gone missing, too.'

Hansson's demeanour suddenly changed to one of concern.

'What do you mean, "missing"?'

'Just that. We can't find him. In fact, we have found no trace of him since the end of the dig.'

'Oh, Christ!' Hansson buried his head in his hands. 'That must be why his things are still here!'

'I think you had better fill me in on what happened in Vollerby. We have it on good authority that you and Tony had an argument.'

'Who told you that?' Hansson said, taking his hands away from his face. He was ashen.

'Part of it was overheard.'

Absent-mindedly, Hansson began to chew the end of his little finger. 'As you said, we were close. Very. After the dig, Tony was going to move into my apartment while I was away in Peru, and he'd moved his things in before he went down to Vollerby. Let's say I didn't expect him to move out when I returned.'

Hakim made a note. It explained why Yealand had wound up his rental agreement.

'Everything started to go wrong at Vollerby. Tony wasn't comfortable being there.'

'Why?'

'Because of Ari. They'd fallen out on a previous dig.'

'Birka? Six years ago?'

'Why, yes.'

'What did they fall out over?'

'I'm not entirely sure. A student died. Drowned. It cast a shadow over the whole dig. I know Tony was very upset, though he wouldn't talk about it. He'd got on well with the girl. He didn't want to go to Vollerby because he knew Ari would be there. It was me who persuaded him. It meant we could spend the summer together doing what we loved. Precious time, as I would be disappearing for the whole of the next academic year.' Hansson stopped and gulped. He was becoming emotional.

'So, what went wrong?'

'It was Ari Nordin. He was being nasty to Tony. At one stage, Tony wanted to leave. Again, I talked him into staying. Near the end of the dig, I told him to go to Malmö for a couple of days to give himself a break. It was there he met some guy in a bar. Just a one-night stand. But this guy was young. I was always conscious of our age difference. It made me hypersensitive – worried that someone younger would come along. He said it was a mistake and he was sorry. But instead of treating it as a one-off fling, I had a meltdown. I buggered everything up.' Tears were forming in the corners of his eyes and he used his shirt sleeve to wipe them away.

'So, when was the last time you saw him?'

'Two days before the end of the dig. The day after... the day after I stormed off. I missed the end-of-dig party, as I had to go back to Stockholm to make arrangements with the university before I flew out to South America. I didn't say goodbye to him.'

Hakim thought he was going to break down.

'And that was it?'

'No.' He pulled himself together. 'No. When I got back here, I realised how stupid I'd been. He'd admitted his fling had been a mistake. Anyway, I knew he was overseeing the tidying up of the site, so I went back down to Vollerby to see him. He wasn't there. The next week, I left Sweden. I did try to contact him. I wrote at least a dozen emails saying how sorry I was and could we patch things up. I even offered to pay for him to come out to Lima.'

'But you didn't hear anything?'

'No. I just thought he didn't want to make up and that he didn't want anything more to do with me.'

'I'm afraid no one seems to have been able to contact him.'

'What could have happened to him?' Hansson sounded desperate.

'We have no idea.'

'It must be something awful...' His voice broke.

Hakim and his colleagues were coming to the same conclusion but weren't articulating it just yet.

CHAPTER 18

'Why do you think Gerda Brink was allowed to stay on the allotments?' asked Wallen.

For the first time, Henning Kristoffersson appeared uncomfortable.

'Her cabin was in a state and her plot was a mess. I thought you had rules about that sort of thing.'

Wallen and Olovsson had interrupted Kristoffersson's hedge trimming. He was wearing a khaki shirt and shorts. And goggles – an unnecessary affectation for such a low hedge. He'd seemed delighted to be talking to the police again, as he was the self-appointed expert on all things to do with the allotments, and he'd greeted Olovsson like an old friend. (During their initial enquiries, Olovsson had asked him about the night of the murder, and he felt he'd made a valuable contribution to their investigation by pointing out Brink's nocturnal routine. They clearly regarded him as the font of all knowledge.)

He'd immediately ordered his wife to prepare coffee for these 'fine officers of the law'. He also stipulated that they partake of the biscuits she had baked that morning. Anna-Marie was unhappy about his demand – the biscuits had been allocated as an excuse to call in on Viktor Bjelk that evening when her husband was at the cinema in Ystad. When they had all squeezed into the living room, coffee and biscuits to hand, he banished his wife. Any contribution she might make would be valueless, as she'd spent that night at home to give her a break from Henning's snoring. Even in his sleep, he commanded attention.

Initially, all had gone well. He repeated his experience of the night in question for the benefit of the lady police officer. They had also been interested in his general observations on life on the allotments and, in particular, people's attitudes to the murder victim while she was alive. Then Inspector Wallen ambushed him with a broadside that he hadn't expected and didn't want to answer.

'It's not that easy,' he found himself mumbling.

'Aren't you Chair of the committee? Surely, there are minimum standards of maintenance?'

'Well, y... yes,' he stammered. 'The council insists on it.' This sounded half-hearted.

'Surely Brink fell short of them?'

Kristoffersson felt a trickle of sweat run down his back.

'We did speak to her.' He didn't sound convincing.

'She clearly ignored you. Could it be that she had some kind of hold over people?'

'What on earth do you mean?'

'Let's say that certain allotment members wouldn't want to cross her because she was privy to matters they might not want to be generally known.'

'I have no idea what you're talking about,' he said defensively.

'OK,' said Olovsson. 'Tell us about Knut Fredriksson.'

'Who?'

'The lawyer.'

'Y...yes, I have heard that name mentioned. I believe he practised round here.' Kristoffersson's voice was becoming hoarse.

'I think you knew him quite well. In a professional capacity.' Olovsson had been so nice before. He wasn't being nice now.

'What makes you think that?'

'Because he dealt with the police on your behalf. Back in 2009.'

'No... well, I can't really remember,' Kristoffersson blustered. 'It can't have been important.'

'The police didn't agree. Nor did the owners of the car dealership outside Tomelilla you managed.'

The colour drained from Kristoffersson's face.

'I was innocent.'

'Just because the police couldn't prove it, it doesn't mean you were innocent.'

'I didn't do anything wrong.'

'So, why didn't you stay on at the dealership?'

'I was insulted by their lack of support and totally unfounded lack of trust.' He'd regained some of his poise.

'We hear differently. Fredriksson managed to hush things up. He also acted for you when you set up your business here in Simrishamn.'

Kristoffersson suddenly stood up. 'I don't have to listen to this!'

'Yes, you do,' said Olovsson calmly, 'when you're our chief suspect in the murder of Gerda Brink.'

That took the wind out of Kristoffersson's sails.

'That's ridiculous! Why would I kill Gerda Brink?'

'Because she knew all Fredriksson's clients – and their secrets, including yours.' Olovsson said this so positively that the fact that this was only conjecture was convincingly disguised.

Kristoffersson sank back onto his chair. Olovsson had hit his target.

'You wouldn't have wanted the folk round here to know you were associated with Polish car thieves,' weighed in Wallen. 'Guilty or not, mud sticks. Brink had the power to destroy your reputation at any time.'

'And we know you were awake when the murder took place,' added Olovsson. 'You told me so yourself.'

'Can your wife vouch for you that night?' Wallen asked.

Kristoffersson shook his head. 'Erm... actually, no. She was back in our apartment.'

'So no alibi.'

'This is preposterous! I didn't touch the woman. I didn't have to.' These last words were blurted out.

'Was that because you were paying her to keep her mouth shut?'

'Of course not!' he expostulated. 'I didn't pay her anything. You've got it all wrong. I didn't kill that bloody woman!'

'Do you think it's him, Dan?'

Wallen and Olovsson were walking out of the allotments.

'We certainly rattled him. He has a motive...'

'Which we have no evidence for.'

'True. And he certainly had opportunity.'

'What we might be able to prove is the hush money. Check out his bank and see if he made any significant cash withdrawals.'

CHAPTER 19

The plane was on time and touched down on a cloudy day at Kastrup Airport. As Kevin Ash descended the passenger stairs, the sun was trying its best to br eak through. He took this as a good sign. He was excited to see Anita again – he always was after months apart – but he knew that this wasn't a normal visit. They were both working on a case; he must be professional.

He got through passport control reasonably quickly, though he was annoyed that he had to get his passport stamped (a post-Brexit requirement), and as he only had a cabin bag and a small backpack, he didn't have to wait at the baggage reclaim area. The train arrived within ten minutes and he found himself being whisked across the Öresund Bridge. He always enjoyed the moment when he first caught sight of the Turning Torso. He knew he was back. Malmö was a city he had fallen for almost from the first time he'd visited. The fact that Anita lived there obviously helped. June was a great time to be in the city: the parks, the squares, the canal area and Gamla Stan – the old town – were all abuzz with happy Swedes making the most of their short summer.

He got off the train at Triangeln and made his way past the Opera House and along the edge of Pildammsparken. It was in the middle of the afternoon, so Anita was unlikely to be in her Roskildevägen apartment. It was Lasse who opened the door when he pressed the buzzer. They gave each other an affectionate hug. Lasse had accepted him very early on in his relationship with Anita. Football had been the first bonding topic; now they had developed more in common.

Leyla was in the living room. How she had grown! At first, she was a little shy and wouldn't say hello. But when Kevin produced a fluffy feline stuffed toy, the eight-year-old melted and grabbed it with delight.

'Say thank you,' Lasse said to her in Swedish.

'*Tack*.'

When he visited his sister's grandchildren, Kevin normally brought chocolate, but with Leyla he couldn't. Her T-shirt didn't cover the Libre, which monitored her blood sugar, attached to her arm. She had Type 1 diabetes, and it was a constant reminder of her condition.

'Another stuffed toy!' Lasse sighed. 'She's got hundreds. But she loves them. Cats are a good choice.'

'Your mum tipped me off. I got it at the airport. I'm afraid I didn't have time for any proper shopping. It was all very last minute.'

'So I gather. Mamma will be pleased to have an extra person involved now she's got this murder over in Simrishamn. So it won't be a holiday,' he warned as an afterthought.

'Don't worry. I won't treat it like one.'

'Having said that, we're all going to Rosegarden for lunch on Sunday.'

'Sounds like a plan.' Kevin liked Rosegarden – eat as much Oriental food as you like and not be stuffed with a huge bill. He thought he'd treat them as a thank you to Anita for putting him up. He could put it on expenses, as he was saving the Cumbria Constabulary the cost of his accommodation. Happily, the exchange rate was also in his favour.

Kevin cast his eye round the unusually clean and tidy living room. 'Blimey! Your mum's done a job on this place. And at such short notice!'

'You are kidding, aren't you? This was down to me. I cleaned up before you arrived.' Kevin couldn't help smiling.

He was usually the one who kept the apartment tidy whenever he visited.

'Coffee?' Lasse asked.

'Only if it's not as strong as your mum's.'

'Don't be a wimp.'

Kevin followed Lasse into the kitchen, leaving Leyla to play with her new friend, who was already being sucked into an imaginary game.

Lasse ladled an inordinate amount of coffee grains into the percolator.

'How's things?'

Lasse shrugged. 'Same old. Still doing shifts at the café, but I try and work them round Leyla.'

'Your mum still on your case?'

'You mean getting a career?' he laughed. 'I get it worse from Papa. He can't understand his son not doing something academic. Can't get it into his head that I'm quite happy as I am.'

'That's what counts. And Jazmin?'

'Loving her new job. I don't know if Mamma told you, but she's got a job with the Green Party. Just part time at the moment, but she was really lucky to get something so soon after her course ended.'

'Yeah, your mum did say something. The Greens are quite big over here, aren't they?'

'They were in the last coalition government with the Social Democrats until the right-wingers took over a couple of years ago.'

The percolator began to bubble and hiss.

'So be prepared! You can expect a few lectures from Jazmin. She gives Mamma a hard time every time she flies off to see you.'

'Ah, the famous Swedish flight shaming.'

'*Flygskam*.'

'Mmm. It's not so easy for us Brits being stuck on an island, especially now all the ferries to Scandinavia have stopped. But I'll try and avoid the subject.'

'Wise move.'

'Pull him in for questioning.' Anita's message to Wallen couldn't be clearer. 'Make him sweat.'

They were referring to Henning Kristoffersson. Already an early candidate for the murder of Gerda Brink, Olovsson had gone into his banking affairs. His balance had been healthy after he'd sold his auto-components company. However, over the last four years, it had been regularly depleted – every six months, twenty thousand kronor in cash had been withdrawn. Significantly, one of the withdrawals was the week before Brink paid for her expensive holiday in the south of France. The team were sure that this pointed to him paying her off. Now they had to prove it.

Kristoffersson had been particularly indignant that he had had to go to the police station on a holiday weekend – 'It's Midsummer for God's sake! Haven't you got better things to do?' Wallen and Brodd hadn't, but Olovsson had, which made him particularly crotchety.

'I take the money out for my fishing trips. I go twice a year,' was Kristoffersson's defence when confronted.

'Why cash?' asked Olovsson

'Easier to buy drinks for the boys. Some of these fishing places are in the back of beyond. You know what they're like.'

'I don't, actually. And as far as I can see, the dates of the withdrawals don't coincide with your trips.'

'Best to be prepared.' Kristoffersson had regained the bumptious calm that he'd lost during his initial outburst.

Grudgingly, they had to let him go. As long as he kept denying it, they couldn't link the cash payments to Brink, let alone find any evidence that Kristoffersson had killed her. He probably had a motive, definitely had the opportunity, and certainly had the means – rock and stones proliferated at the murder site. They had retrieved various geological lumps from the area, but none yielded any evidence. They had also tested the notes found in Brink's homes for fingerprints. Another dead end – no matches on the database. The trouble was that Brink's victims were unlikely to have criminal pasts. And they couldn't force Kristoffersson to provide his fingerprints without charging him.

It all added up to a potentially frustrating holiday weekend for the team.

CHAPTER 20

Both Anita and Kevin were champing at the bit to get stuck into their investigations, but, as Anita explained, 'The whole of Sweden comes to a standstill at the beginning of Midsummer, and half Sweden can't stand up by the end of it.' While many people like to keep the old festive traditions alive – dancing round maypoles while imitating frogs, wearing garlands of flowers in their hair, singing, drinking, and eating herring, strawberries and *smörgåstårta* – Anita and family hardly indulged in the celebrations. A meal at Rosegarden and a barbecue at Hakim and Liv's had been enough to pay lip service to the holiday mood. Both outings had been enjoyable, if somewhat abstemious, as Hakim and his parents were non-drinkers, and Anita had volunteered to be the designated driver. As a result, Kevin and Liv, who would normally have partaken of a glass or three of schnapps, both felt obliged to keep themselves in check.

Anita and Kevin had tried to avoid the topic of work but, inevitably, it seeped into the conversation. In both the ongoing cases, there were a number of suspects, some of them vague and insubstantial. Henning Kristoffersson did not come into this category. The arguments against him were building up nicely, but, as yet, the team hadn't enough evidence to act. The Linda Vaux disappearance was more problematic; they weren't sure exactly what they were dealing with. The longer she was missing, the more likely it was that some harm had come to her. They believed that Professor Nordin knew more about her whereabouts than he was letting on. And as he had strong connections with the missing Tony Yealand, he was very much a person of interest.

On the Monday morning, Anita had the whole team come into the polishus for a meeting. There were no casualties from the weekend's celebrations other than Olovsson looking tired and Brodd hung over. Kevin was invited to observe.

They dealt with the Gerda Brink murder first.

'We really think that Henning Kristoffersson could be our murderer,' Wallen stated. 'We have a motive. We think – though we can't prove it – that he was paying Brink off to keep quiet about his involvement with the Polish car thieving gangs. The dates of his cash withdrawals don't match his supposed fishing trips, but one withdrawal coincides with Brink paying for one of her expensive holidays in cash. He had opportunity – in fact, it was he who told Dan about Brink's regular nocturnal walks – and he admitted that he was awake around the time of the murder and that his wife was not on the allotments that night. So he has no alibi.'

'You need to find more evidence,' said Anita, 'and I don't want you to concentrate solely on Kristoffersson. Brink had a lot more cash than Kristoffersson's hush money, if that's what it was. Others may have been paying her off, too. We need to cast the net wider.'

'I'm afraid we've had a bit of a setback there,' said Olovsson as he stifled a yawn. 'Sorry,' he apologised. 'A weekend with boisterous grandchildren is knackering. Knut Fredriksson, the lawyer. He retired in 2013 and his clients were taken over by L. Wennås Group AB. They're now in possession of all the files and documents. The trouble is they won't allow us access because of client confidentiality. So we have no idea what dirt Brink may have dug up.'

'We could always get a warrant,' said Anita.

'Actually,' a bright-eyed Grahn, who had sensibly done

his drinking at the beginning of Midsummer, chipped in, 'I've been thinking about the files. If Brink was blackmailing folk, wouldn't she need to have them to hand? They're not much use to her if they're secreted away in another law firm's office. Any one of her victims could have just turned round and refused to pay if she hadn't got the evidence in her possession. Otherwise, it was just hearsay – nothing more than malicious gossip which might, or might not, be believed, especially when it came from someone as poisonous as Gerda Brink.'

'That might still be enough to damage a person's reputation,' pointed out Wallen. 'It can still be toxic.'

'Possibly. But enough to keep paying out blackmail money? I'm not sure.'

'You've got a point, Joel,' Anita said. 'It makes sense that when the Fredriksson office closed down, Brink salted away the files she needed. So, working on that hypothesis, if she did do that, where would she keep them?'

'Nothing has turned up on the plot or in her house,' confirmed Wallen. 'Both were searched thoroughly.'

'Both places would be a bit obvious,' continued Grahn. 'And risky. Her victims would be desperate – surely she would be crafty enough to guard against one of them trying to break in. I think she would probably keep such precious information somewhere really safe: somewhere known to no one but her.'

'Some sort of lock-up?' Olovsson ventured. 'A garage we don't know about?'

'Could they be stored with her lawyer?' asked Wallen. 'But then access would be a pain.'

The following silence was broken by Brodd. 'A safe deposit box?'

Everybody stared at him. Brodd's single contribution to the meeting was a surprisingly good one.

*

After Wallen and her team had left, the discussion turned to the disappearance of the two Britons. A fresh round of coffee was accompanied by Kevin's favourite cinnamon buns that he'd bought on the way in.

'No further sightings of the Dormobile,' reported Liv. 'No reported accidents and nothing from the hospitals.'

'I must admit, I fear the worst,' sighed Anita.

'Whatever has happened, I'm sure Professor Nordin is involved,' said Erlandsson emphatically.

'What about Tony Yealand?'

'Zilch,' said Hakim. 'Not a trace.'

'When he was down here on the dig, he must have had stuff with him,' said Kevin. 'A computer... mobile... toothbrush... clothes. Everything that he'd need for six weeks.'

'He was staying at the university student accommodation at Celsiusgården,' explained Hakim. 'No sign of anything there. He was due to leave on the Sunday and he was gone and the room cleared by the Monday morning, when the cleaners went in. We've doubled checked. No one saw him leave, but there was hardly anybody around that weekend. The others on the dig had gone by then, and the place was virtually empty.'

'I'm sure you have,' Kevin said quickly, not wanting to sound as though he was being critical. 'It's just that we can safely assume he never made it to Stockholm. Otherwise, he would have gone to Jan Hansson's apartment to collect his other belongings.'

'Unless he just didn't want to bump into Hansson,' Erlandsson suggested. 'He might have been too embarrassed after their falling out.'

'Yeah, but Hansson was off to Peru. Yealand could have picked up his things after he left.'

'He could,' mused Hakim. 'Unless he thought he'd just let the dust settle and come back later when Hansson returned – perhaps he hoped they could make up and start again. When she couldn't get hold of him, Alice Asplund thought Yealand may have returned to the UK. Perhaps he had the idea of giving Hansson some space. Except he never came back.'

'I can see the reasoning, Hakim. The thing is he never made it to Britain. At least, we haven't been able to trace him.'

'There is another scenario,' said Liv. 'Say Yealand's find really was amazing – and therefore potentially very lucrative if he sold it on to some private collector. Maybe he just did a bunk and is on some tropical beach living off the proceeds.'

'Unlikely,' cautioned Anita. 'Why send Linda the SMS? He's already alerted someone. And he wrote *'This'll show him'*, which I think we all agree refers to Ari Nordin. Skipping the country wouldn't afford him that satisfaction.'

'True,' conceded Liv.

'But I suppose we can't rule out the possibility. So, what do you reckon we should do next?' Anita asked Kevin.

'Well... where was the very last place we know he was seen?'

'Vollerby,' said Erlandsson.

'We should start there. Visit the site. After all, it links our two missing people.'

'It's just a field now,' Hakim pointed out.

'Mmm... We need to go with someone who was on the dig. Someone who could point everything out to us.'

'Professor Nordin?'

'Maybe not. Keep him on ice,' said Anita.

'Maybe Jan Hansson then,' Hakim suggested. 'No one knew Yealand better, and I know he's starting in Malmö today doing further work on the skeletons found at the site.'

'That's a good idea,' said Anita by way of rounding off the meeting. 'The case notes about the student who drowned on the Birka dig are being sent down from Stockholm. Between them and any information which Hansson may have, we might be able to shed further light on why Yealand and Nordin fell out.'

CHAPTER 21

Klara Wallen felt uneasy. She picked up her sandwich and gave it a withering look. She wasn't hungry any more. When she'd popped out from the Simrishamn police station for her lunch break, she'd spotted Rolf down the street, sitting outside a café. He looked rough. She noticed that people were giving him a wide berth. Of course, she was bound to see him at some point – after all, Simrishamn isn't a large town – but it was still a jolt.

Her coffee was going cold. Maybe she'd been foolish to carry on leading this investigation. But she couldn't turn down such a golden opportunity – and it would have made all her bitching about Anita seem nothing more than sour grapes. Yet the situation with Rolf was a big issue. He'd had such a tight grip on her life. Little by little, he'd driven away her friends and family, and she had floundered in the wake, becoming totally reliant on him. Which was just what he wanted. The only people whom he couldn't stop her seeing were her work colleagues, and it had been they – mainly Anita – who had given her the courage to make the break: to pack her bags and move back to Malmö. What worried Wallen now was not the invective – Rolf had plastered her Facebook page with so many lies and slurs on her character that she had taken it down – but the threat of violence. He'd hit her on three occasions and had threatened to do so a number of other times. It had usually happened when he was drunk, and he always appeared mortified afterwards, begging her forgiveness. But she knew the attacks were calculated; he'd always been careful not to harm her where the bruises would show. Her colleagues had known she was having problems, but she was too ashamed to be completely honest about what was going on; it would make her look weak. She was a police officer for God's sake! It would have undermined her credibility in the force had she come clean. But there was also the moral dilemma that as a police officer, she should make a stand on behalf of all the other women in her situation. She knew better than anyone that if she reported him, the years of coercive behaviour and violence might lead to a hefty prison sentence and may deter other potential abusers. But how would that look to her superiors? So she'd moved out and let it go. But Rolf hadn't gone away. The malevolent effects of his influence on her life still dogged her. And since being assigned to the Gerda Brink case, all the fears and doubts and dread had resurfaced.

She pushed away her uneaten sandwich and forced herself to think about the case in hand.

Henning Kristoffersson was their leading suspect. Wallen was experienced enough to realise that she couldn't get hung up on the ex-car dealer to the exclusion of other potential suspects. Grudgingly, she knew Anita was right and they must cast their net wider. Nothing had emerged from the numerous interviews they'd had with the allotment holders. She had to think about the possibility that Brink's murderer had no connection with the allotments at all. Perhaps someone else she'd been blackmailing. They, of course, wouldn't necessarily know her late-night routine but they could have found it out from somebody who did.

And was there a connection with the dead dog? Or was that a totally separate incident? There was so much to think about. For a fleeting moment, she felt a small wave of sympathy for Anita having to balance two investigations. It soon passed.

She picked up the sandwich and dropped it into the bin beside her desk. What a waste. She chided herself, just as her mother used to do: 'Think of all those poor children starving in Africa!'

Her phone buzzed. It was Joel Grahn.

'Hi, Joel. Anything for me?'

'Oh, yes!' He couldn't disguise the excitement in his voice. 'I'm in Handelsbanken in Ystad. Gerda Brink has a safe deposit box here!'

Anita had been glued to her computer screen for the last fifteen minutes. The file on the drowning of Hilma Moll off the island of Björkö, where the Birka site is situated, in 2018 had been sent through from Stockholm. It made interesting reading. The student's naked body had been found on the beach on August 8th, and the pathologist's report concluded that it was a straightforward drowning. She had consumed a large amount of alcohol, which may have contributed to her getting into difficulties in the water. There was no evidence of sexual assault and no foul play was suspected. The inquest concluded that Moll's death was accidental.

But the circumstances surrounding the death were not so banal. That evening, there had been an impromptu drinking session instigated by one Axel Råberg from Stockholm University, the leading archaeologist on the site. Some of the recollections of the participants were blurry, but at some stage, Hilma Moll just wasn't there anymore. No one had noticed her absence and no one had seen her leave. Among the revellers were the familiar names of Professor Ari Nordin, Doctor Jan Hansson and Tony Yealand. At just after midnight, Hilma's body had been found by Nordin on the shore. The police had asked Nordin what he was doing wandering around at such an hour; he said he'd been looking for Moll. Further enquiries had revealed that he was having a sexual liaison with the young woman. Anita read the transcripts of the interviews. At first, Nordin had been reluctant to admit to the affair but when, eventually, he did confess to the relationship, it transpired that he'd expected Hilma to visit him that night, and when she hadn't turned up, he'd gone searching for her.

The police had believed him. They concluded that, in a drunken state, Hilma had decided to go for a swim, had taken off her clothes (found further along the beach) and gone skinny-dipping. She'd got into trouble and drowned. Case closed.

Anita picked up a bar of Marabou chocolate and snapped off a piece. This was likely to be her lunch today. She didn't have time to go out and buy something. Normally, she would have taken the report at face value. Now, she viewed it differently.

Ari Nordin had been a central figure in the Birka incident. Now, he was central to the investigation into the missing Linda Vaux. He had been involved with both women. He also had an antagonistic relationship with the missing Tony Yealand, supposedly stemming from that dig. She still hadn't got to the bottom of why they had fallen out.

Jan Hansson put down the lid of his computer. He stood in pensive inaction for several moments. The lab assistant asked him if he was all right. He wasn't sure. His work on the bodies from the Vollerby skeletons had been interrupted by a Zoom call from Inspector Mirza. Should he be troubled? It had raised so many questions: ones he had been asking himself. The answers still eluded him.

'Is Professor Nordin around today?' he asked the assistant.

'I saw him in the corridor a couple of hours ago.'

Without further word, Hansson left the lab.

He found Nordin busy at his desk, typing a document on his computer.

'Sorry to bother you, Ari.'

'No, come in. I'm just putting some finishing touches to my first talk on the Hoard of Vollerby.'

Hansson took a seat.

'It's Vollerby I wanted to talk to you about. I've just had a call from Inspector Mirza.'

Nordin pulled a pained expression.

'I've had a couple of conversations with said inspector myself... making all sorts of insinuations. He even had the bloody nerve to come to the house! I'd be quite happy never to see the man again. What did he want with you?'

'He wants me to accompany him to the Vollerby site on Monday.'

'What? What on earth for?'

'I don't really know. Apparently, they want someone there who's familiar with the site. I'm not sure what they expect to find.'

Nordin lapsed into silence.

'It can't be anything to do with the disappearance of Linda Vaux,' ventured Hansson.

'No,' Nordin said at last. 'That wouldn't make sense. Might be to do with Tony Yealand, though.'

'I was afraid of that.'

'You really don't know where he is, do you?'

Hansson shook his head mournfully. 'That was the last place I saw him.'

'No contact since? Are you sure?'

'I tried to get in touch, but nothing.' Hansson shifted uneasily in his chair. 'The police seem to think he found something. Something that excited him.'

'Let's be honest, Jan. I know he was your... your friend, but it wouldn't have taken much for him to get turned on. He wasn't exactly the best archaeologist we've worked with.'

'He was keen,' Hansson said limply in Yealand's defence.

'He was a liability.'

Hansson was about to speak, then appeared reluctant. Nordin noticed.

'What is it?'

Hansson scratched his chin.

'There was something else. When I was first talking to the police, Birka came up.'

Nordin was startled.

'Christ! Why?'

'I had to explain why Tony wasn't happy at Vollerby. They'd heard rumours about you and he not getting on.'

'Was there anything else?' There was panic in Nordin's voice.

'Well, they already seemed to know about the Birka incident. I had to say it cast a gloom over the dig.'

Nordin got up from his desk and turned to the window. 'Hell. I can't afford to have all that dragged up again.' He turned back to face Hansson. There was sweat on his forehead and damp patches under his arms.

'I'd better get on,' said Hansson, rising from his seat. 'Just thought you should know.'

'Thanks, Jan. And for God's sake, don't let the idiots mess around with the site.'

CHAPTER 22

Uppsala, summer AD 1017

The sacrifices had been made and the gods rewarded. The Temple of Uppsala, on its prominent site, dominated the bustling settlement. Built of wood and decked in gold, it was the seat of worship to the three most important deities of Asgard: Thor, Freyr and Odin. In the sacred grove close by, hanging from the trees, human and animal corpses were putrefying in the summer heat.

Viggo Flatnose felt uplifted. The gods had protected him on the perilous journey he and his men had made after their hasty flight from Kiev. They had faced much hardship, even more than on the journey to Miklagård ten years earlier. The great rapids on the River Dnieper had lived up to their names – 'The Ever Fierce', 'The Yeller' and 'The Drinker' – as their waters had been swollen by torrential rain. Such hazards tested the strength and willpower of all the men, and supplications to the gods were many. Then on leaving the Dnieper, there was the Great Portage. The ship was emptied and hoisted onto wooden runners prepared from fallen trees before being dragged by the male slaves and hired oxen. For days, they toiled up and down hills, through forests and over moss and grassland, the weather deteriorating all the while. Many were the times that Viggo and his fellow Norsemen had to bend their backs to help. When they reached the next river, the Dvina, their reward was rowing with the current, aiding them in their journey towards the sea.

Then the Dvina froze over. They were forced to winter in a small trading settlement before setting off in the early spring. They reached the Eastern Sea without further mishap and set sail for Gotland. But somehow, again, they had fallen out of favour with the gods. Rough seas battered their ship and they limped into Vi, the principal settlement on Gotland. Then their fortune turned again. During the three weeks they spent on the island while the ship was being repaired, Viggo was able to trade many of his goods: the rich Gotland merchants bought his silks, spices and jewellery. With much silver in their chests and the smell of home in the air, they sailed with light hearts and a fair wind to the Skanian coast. At Kivik, Viggo sold the ship and the slaves, except two of the women whom he kept for Nadira. And thence to Vǫllrbý to claim his inheritance. He was welcomed by karls and thralls alike, and his return was celebrated with days of feasting. Nadira, as he had anticipated, was greeted with suspicion, but he let it be known that any animosity towards her would be considered an affront to himself. He only ventured to Uppsala when he felt his people had grudgingly accepted this 'woman with strange beliefs and potions'. Some even thought her a witch, but that suited Viggo, as it meant they feared her and would do as she instructed.

Harald and a few retainers accompanied him on his journey north. Ostensibly, he went to thank the gods for his safe return and to ask them to give him the strength to combat the scourge of Christianity that was already widespread in the southern lands and was now creeping into his own community. But another reason was more secular: the trading contacts would help cement his wealth.

It was such a contact that would warn him of a grave danger.

Viggo and Harald were quenching their thirst in the sunshine of the market place while they reminisced about their years in distant lands and how good it was to be back among their own people. The rhomphaia that Viggo had laid on the table was the object that had sparked off the memories. In their early days in Miklagård, Viggo had taken the long, curved Byzantine sword from a Greek soldier after a violent altercation in a brothel in a dispute over one of the girls. The Greek had not taken kindly to being thrown out of the room by an uncouth barbarian when he was about to satisfy his lust. Viggo, in his youthful enthusiasm, had underestimated the man, and the fight had resulted in a broken nose. The story had so amused his fellow Varangian Guards that they had awarded him the soubriquet of 'Flatnose'. The name had stuck. To Viggo, it was a proud battle scar. From that day on, the rhomphaia and his trusty axe had never left his side.

The retelling of this tale led Harald to ask about Nadira.

'You will never need to look further now that you possess the most beautiful woman in the East... and the West.' Harald's admiration was clear.

'You never possess a woman like Nadira,' Viggo said with a deep laugh. 'She possesses me!'

Viggo's mind went back to the day he first saw her in Yusuf's home in Antioch. Yusuf was said to be the richest man in a rich city, and he was keen to catch the eye of the Emperor. He also had a vast property in Miklagård, where he fashioned himself as 'Joseph' in order to smooth his path in a Christian imperial capital. He had his sights set on the governorship of the eastern province, which he could exploit for further wealth and power. Viggo had been sent to protect a precious cargo on its way back to Miklagård and the Emperor. He had not met Yusuf personally; he had been greeted by his most trusted wife, Nadira. Small and slender, she was dressed in an elaborately embroidered, three-quarter length robe, underneath which Viggo espied a pair of delicate sky-blue, silk trousers. Her head was covered by a scarf, held in place by a bejewelled clasp. Surprisingly for her evident status, her face was unveiled, and her perfectly symmetrical features – straight nose, wide mouth and dark, intelligent eyes – captivated Viggo from the instant he saw her. His obvious attraction to this unusual emissary did not go down well with the tall, ugly brute who was standing behind her. His malevolent scowl was accentuated by a deep scar which clove the left side of his face from above his eye down to his cheek. It was difficult to tell whether the eye functioned or not. Viggo learned that this was Bilal, the man who ensured his master's transactions were completed when worldly incentives had failed. The threat of a quick entry to the next world usually sealed the bargain. Those who did not comply soon met their chosen god.

Nadira, though cordial, had remained distant. She had looked at Viggo's unwashed state, wrinkled her nose and suggested, through her interpreter, that he and the four Varangian Guards accompanying him should, before discussing her husband's business with the Emperor, visit the city's great baths. Viggo soon realised that it was not so much a suggestion as a polite order.

It was on the voyage back to Miklagård that a bond formed between Viggo and the olive-skinned beauty, particularly when he impressed her by navigating their ship through a fierce storm in the Aegean; Nadira and many of the crew thought their final moment on this earth had arrived. As waves crashed over the prow of their ship, she had found herself desperately clinging to the Norseman for fear of being swept overboard. All he had done was laugh. It was then that she began to see this rugged, filthy and commanding heathen as a way of freeing herself from a stultifying marriage that had been arranged as little more than a trading agreement between Yusuf and her father. She had been saddled with an aging, pot-bellied tyrant who lost interest in her sexually when she failed to produce the children expected of her. However, Yusuf had realised that she could offer more than sexual favours. She was resourceful and astute: clever enough to win his trust and reliance. He found that her looks and charm were an asset in his business dealings, and he began to use her as a go-between in his ventures. And so it was that Nadira was assigned the important task that would, he hoped, endear him to the Emperor.

After their eventual arrival in Miklagård, Nadira worked her wiles on an already-infatuated Viggo. When word reached her that Yusuf was on his way to Miklagård, she persuaded her Norse lover that it was time for them to head north, which he was keen to do. Word had reached him that he was now head of his family and he wanted to return to his ancestral home. And as the Emperor was away campaigning, there was nothing to keep him in the great city any more.

'Will Nadira be content among our rough folk?' Harald asked.

'If she can teach them to wash, then my hopes are high!' Viggo was in a buoyant frame of mind. 'I think more ale is needed. Let us drink to the woman who has brought us good fortune.' Harald was unsure of what Viggo meant, but he was happy to secure the ale.

It was at this moment that Viggo heard a man call his name. He recognised him immediately. It was Gorm, with whom he had done good business on Gotland earlier in the year.

'What brings you to these parts, Gorm?' he asked.

'I have come to resell the silks and spices I bought from you – at twice the price!' They all roared with laughter, though Viggo knew that there might be some truth in the jest. But he did not care. He was basking in the good fortune his hamingja was affording him.

'Harald, buy our friend a drink,' Viggo ordered. When Harald hesitated, Viggo shook his head in merriment. 'Gorm, my cousin is miserly with his Byzantine bounty. That bag that hangs upon his belt is full of gold Arab coins. They never leave his side, as he trusts no-one.' Harald was embarrassed by the

teasing, though he went for the ale, albeit grudgingly.

'And how is life on Gotland?' Harald asked on his return. He had met a buxom wench there and had fond memories of their short time on the island.

'Rich.' Gorm beamed. Then his face turned serious. 'However, I may have ill news for you, Viggo.'

'How so?'

'Just before I left, I came across two swarthy men from the East who, at first, I took to be traders. But their business was not trade. Their business was you!'

'Did they speak to you?'

'They did. They learned that I had had dealings with you. They wanted to know where you had gone. I pleaded ignorance, though they offered many dirhams – and gold besides – for an answer.'

'That was good of you, my friend.'

'I wish that had been the end of it. But I heard shortly before I set sail for Svear that they had gained knowledge of your destination.'

'Did one of the men have a deep scar upon his face?' asked Viggo as he ran a finger from his own forehead to his cheek.

'Why, yes! The main one was scarred exactly how you describe.'

'Bilal!'

'Who is he?' enquired Gorm.

'He is a man who plagues my dreams. These are Yusuf's men. By Thor, this news disturbs me greatly.'

'Nadira?' Harald gasped in concern. 'They may be headed for Vǫllrbý even as we sit here idly drinking.'

'You are right, Harald. We must make haste, for it will take us many days to reach home. We must beg your leave, Gorm. But I thank you for your warning.'

With that, Viggo grabbed his sword and hastened from the alehouse.

Kivik, Skania, summer AD 1017

Two ships were gently swaying against the quay. A strong sun was shining on the calm Eastern Sea. Seagulls screeched above a small boat that two fishermen were unloading. Erik walked away from the shore and followed the smoke that rose from the smithy. He knew that the smith would be the font of all local knowledge. The heat from the forge hit him as he ducked under the eaves of the thatch. He waited for the smith to finish his hammering, for his concentration was intense. Erik spied a couple of ploughshares propped against the wooden wall. On a bench, there were harness buckles, iron nails, axeheads, knives... all manner of metal paraphernalia in various stages of completion. One corner of the shed was devoted to a large pile of scraps and fragments waiting to be transformed by the craftsman.

The smith glanced up, and ran a hand across his sweaty brow.

'How can I help you, stranger? I can make anything you desire, except for Mjölnir.'

Erik smiled at the smith's jest about Thor's hammer, which he assumed was a standard greeting.

'It is not your skill I need, but your knowledge. And your keen eye.'

The smith eyed him suspiciously.

'I will reward you handsomely,' Erik added quickly.

'You must have come from Gotland. Be you with the two dark men outside?'

'I am their guide and interpreter.'

'I do not like the look of them, especially the one with that battle scar on his face.'

'Have no fear. They do not mean the folk round here any harm. They have travelled all the way from beyond Miklagård to bring good news to a Norseman lately come from the East.'

The smith spat in the fire and it hissed.

'What news?'

'That I cannot divulge, as they have not told me. I am merely here to help them find their way. I am familiar with their tongue, as I have often taken the route to the East in the company of Gotland merchants.'

Erik pulled out a small bag and let a few dirhams drop into his palm. The silver coins twinkled in the light from the forge. This brought an appreciative nod from the smith.

'Who is it that these men seek?'

'A noble Norseman who is late of the Emperor's Varangian Guard. He is called Viggo. Known as Viggo Flatnose.'

The name was clearly known to the smith.

'He and his companions passed this way in the late spring. They bought horses from Thorkell up yonder.' He smiled at the recollection. 'I well remember a beautiful woman that accompanied them.'

'That is good news. Do you know where they were going?'

'I might.'

Erik took the hint and let another two dirhams drop into his hand.

'A place they call Vǫllrbý. It is two or three days' ride from here. On the coast.'

Without a word, Erik tossed the coins onto the bench. 'Where will I find Thorkell?'

Erik stepped out into the sunshine and blinked. He saw Bilal and Zohan near the shore and waved. They would be pleased. Now he would seek out three horses and they would be on their way. He glanced back at the smith, who had returned to his hammering with increased enthusiasm. He shook his head. The man had been easily bribed. Would he have been so forthcoming if he had known the real reason why these strangers had come all this way? Viggo Flatnose had stolen something from their master. And Erik had been promised rich rewards if he helped them retrieve it. And if the Norseman be despatched to Hel!

CHAPTER 23

As Hakim had said, it was just a field.

The grass was lush after the recent mix of sun and rain, and a dozen cows were munching their way from one end to the other, totally unconcerned by the four visitors who had invaded their space. There was no evidence that any archaeological activity had taken place here a year before. The trenches had gone, the postholes hidden, and the tents that had housed the extraordinary finds and the bones of long-forgotten Vikings had been dismantled.

The Vollerby site overlooked the sea. A fresh breeze was rippling the water, which twinkled in the sunlight. Its proximity to the shore had made the spot a perfect location for a Viking community, and it had the added benefit of excellent grazing and fertile soil. The nearest modern buildings were a farmhouse and large cowshed: a common sight in Skåne, they were in the middle of a ploughed field further inland. A ribbon of small homesteads, a comfortable distance from the site, was sparsely stretched along the coast on either side.

Doctor Jan Hansson was proving to be a difficult guide. Returning to where he'd fallen out with his lover was clearly having a negative effect on him, and he was tense and agitated. He kept glancing at a particular spot, which turned out to be where the finds tent had been pitched – the scene of his bust-up with Tony Yealand. Kevin decided the best way to calm him was to get him to describe the lay-out of the site.

Hansson took them to near the centre of the field.

'This was the main focus of the dig. The longhouse was here,' he said, waving his hand over the ground. 'It was much larger than we expected.'

'So, who did it belong to? Somebody important?'

'High status. Possibly the residence of some jarl or chieftain. We found that it was the centrepiece of a small community. There were smaller dwellings and what we think were farm buildings. The people would have had animals, though their primary diet was fish, judging by what we found in the midden over there.' Hansson indicated another patch of grass further away. The information was imparted as though he was reading from some lecture notes. He still didn't seem happy.

Kevin swiftly moved on to what the dig had uncovered. 'I understand the excavation was a remarkable success. One of the biggest hoards ever found in southern Sweden.'

'Very much so. A huge amount of silver of all kinds including a large number of dirhams. They're Arabic coins. Hundreds.'

'So this place had an Eastern connection?'

'Certainly, the hoard indicates there must have been some trade links.' Hansson was warming to his theme. 'The Danes in Skåne and the Swedish Vikings had strong connections with the East. They ventured to Constantinople, which they called Miklagård, and beyond, to places like Baghdad and the Caspian Sea. There was huge wealth to be gained. Furs and slaves went south from Scandinavia and silks, spices, silver and gold headed north along the rivers of what is modern-day Ukraine and Russia. Dangerous waterways that the Vikings and Eastern merchants were willing to risk. There were dramatic rapids, marauding nomads along the trade routes and, of course, the Great Portage.'

'The Great Portage?' Hakim asked.

'The Vikings had to carry their ships overland between the rivers. That took some ingenuity.'

'And the hoard? Why bury all that silver?' Kevin was intrigued.

'Possibly offerings to Odin in preparation for the afterlife, or maybe just something to pass down to their descendants. Except in some cases, the hoards were left untouched. Perhaps the children died or had to flee – who knows? Or perhaps they didn't even know about the wealth that was under their feet. Of course, the Viking we found may not have had any direct connection to the artefacts at all.'

Kevin could see that Hakim and Erlandsson were impatient to ask questions concerning the case. He judged that Hansson wasn't ready to open up yet.

'Tell me about the bones you found.'

Hansson's jitteriness seemed to vanish and a glint came into his eyes. 'Yes. We found two bodies. Well, two and a half. In the main grave, we found a man buried with a horse. Probably the chieftain. Certainly a warrior. There were some impressive grave goods – a Viking sword and two axes – but what really caught our attention was the *rhomphaia*.'

'Sorry?'

'A curved sword.'

'Arab?'

'Well, certainly common in the Byzantine Empire. Its discovery led to all sorts of speculation. Had it been traded? Or had this man been to the East? And an even more exciting thought: could he even have been in the Varangian Guard?' Faced with blank expressions, 'Sorry. The Byzantine emperors' personal guard, mainly comprised of Swedish Norsemen.'

Kevin was fascinated. 'I had no idea the Vikings got so far. Any idea who your Viking was?'

'Not really. The Norse name for this site was V□llrbý. Ari Nordin found an Anglo-Saxon source which mentioned it in reference to the Viking invasion of England under King Cnut. A warrior from here was believed to be one of the dead at the

Battle of Sherston in 1015. Rune was his name. Though our Viking dates from a similar time, I doubt that it's him. It's unlikely that his body was brought all the way back here. He'll be lying somewhere in English soil. But we do know that our man met a violent end.'

'What about the other bodies?'

'Well, there was a human head in the midden over there.'

'How bizarre.'

'We thought that. Who would be so unimportant that he was thrown in with all the rubbish? And where was the rest of his body? He could have been a slave, though why he would have been beheaded is a conundrum. Whoever it was, he must have committed a heinous crime to have been punished in such a way. Actually, one of the reasons I'm down in Malmö is to continue with the osteoarchaeological analysis of all the remains, so, hopefully, we'll find out more.'

Kevin could see that Erlandsson was finding it all rather boring. Notwithstanding, he ploughed on, 'And the third body?'

'Actually, it was that one I found the most intriguing,' Hansson continued. 'Female, laid close to the chieftain. And many of her grave goods were from the East. She had a wonderfully worked gold filigree bracelet and other beautiful objects that would have been incredibly valuable in Viking times. We also found traces of silk: also much prized by the Norse. But she is an enigma. She wasn't a Viking woman who had this wealth bestowed on her by her husband. I measured the strontium and oxygen isotopes ratio on the skeletal remains to determine where she grew up. Basically, using the teeth. It turned out that she had been brought up in what is modern-day Syria: either on the edge of the Byzantine Empire or the Abbasid Caliphate.'

'What on earth was she doing here?' asked Hakim, aware that his parents had made a similar journey from the Middle East.

'It would appear that she was a woman of substance. I have to admit we had a few lively discussions over this. Ari Nordin argued that no woman with that kind of background would end up in the backwaters of Skåne with an uncultured Norseman. He believed she was probably a slave girl picked up in a Constantinople market, who became a favourite of our dead Viking. He lavished gifts on her that he'd acquired out East, which would also explain the *rhomphaia*. Alice Asplund was of the opinion that she was a slave girl that he'd purchased over here – somewhere like Gotland – and that the Eastern artefacts were the result of trade. Of course, Alice is interested in the economic side of history, but she did agree with Ari that the woman was probably a favourite slave who replaced the chieftain's own native women in his affections.'

'And you?' asked Kevin.

'I'm a romantic,' Hansson said with a rueful smile. 'When you work with bones, you can't help wondering and imagining what these people were like in life. What they looked like, what they did, what they ate, who they mixed with. It makes their deaths less of a mystery. And we can often determine these things. We'll be recreating a digital portrait of our exotic lady this summer, so we'll find out what she looked like.'

'That sounds fantastic!' said Kevin, caught up in the wonder of it all.

'Whoever she was, it would have been one hell of a shock to the poor woman's system living round here,' said Erlandsson with some feeling as the wind began to whip up around them. By now, the sea was becoming choppy and the grey swell was turning unfriendly.

'This is all very interesting, Doctor,' said Hakim decisively, 'but we need to know more about the dig itself, not the history.'

Hansson's melancholy glance rested on the young inspector as he was brought back to reality.

'And what do you want to know?' His chirpiness was gone.

'We're trying to trace the whereabouts of your friend and colleague, Tony Yealand. As you know, he seems to have vanished. We're here in this field because this is the last place he was seen. Alice Asplund saw him on Saturday, the twelfth of August. When she returned the next day, he'd gone.'

'You think some harm's come to him.' It was said with pragmatism.

'We can't discount it. Where were you on that day?'

'You can't possibly think...' Hansson started to protest. He shook his head sadly. 'As I explained, I came back to Malmö to make up with Tony. I caught an early train from Stockholm. He wasn't where he'd been staying, at the student residence, so I thought I'd leave it until the Sunday. When he didn't appear, I came down to the site here on the Sunday morning... on the off-chance... you know. He wasn't here, and I couldn't hang around, as I had to get back to Stockholm to get my flight to South America on the Tuesday.'

'You didn't think to come to the site on the Saturday?' Erlandsson asked.

'I didn't want to in case there were still other people around. It might have been' – he hesitated – 'awkward.'

They began to wander back across the field in the direction of the farm.

'Linda Vaux. Was she close to Tony?'

Hansson stopped for a moment and looked at Hakim.

'They were friends. They bonded because they were both British. Shared the same culture... laughed at the same things... you know.'

'Linda seems to be the last person Tony was in contact with,' said Hakim. 'He left her that cryptic message, which we think was sent on that Saturday. What could he have found that he was so excited about?'

'I've been thinking about that. Honestly, I can't think of anything. All the trenches had been dug and filled in. Perhaps something in the spoil turned up, though I doubt it. Ari made sure everybody was very thorough. If he had found something, I'm sure he would have told someone senior on the dig.'

'Would he?' Hakim queried.

'Well, maybe not, given the circumstances. And I suppose not Ari,' he conceded.

'Alice Asplund?'

'He had no problem with Alice. But I can't think of anything that could have been more exciting than what we'd already found. It was an amazing thrill for everyone on the project. It certainly papered over any tensions on site.'

'The tensions. That's what we need to know about. Obviously, between you and Tony,' Hakim said pointedly. 'What about Ari Nordin?'

'He did rub certain people up the wrong way. Usually the ones he didn't respect. And some people didn't approve of his carrying on with the English girls.'

'When we spoke to you on Zoom, you said that Linda Vaux might have gone to see Professor Nordin,' said Erlandsson.

'It's just that she was quite smitten with Ari. Of course, he was always careful to keep his flings separate from his domestic life.'

'So Linda turning up out of the blue would be potentially damaging for his marriage. A huge embarrassment at the very least.'

'I suppose.'

'Let's get back to Tony,' Hakim said, though he was coming to the same conclusion as Bea Erlandsson that the professor had something to do with Linda Vaux's disappearance. 'There was bad feeling between him and Nordin.'

'Yes. I blame myself for encouraging Tony to join the dig.'

'How did the bad feeling manifest itself?'

'Just little things really. Ari wasn't open to Tony's suggestions. Mind you, that applied to a lot of us. Even though the hoard wasn't found in his trench, I could see that Ari would claim all the credit. Indeed, his reputation in the archaeological field has rocketed since last summer and will soar even higher when all the data is revealed later this year.' Absent-mindedly, Hansson kicked at a tuft of grass. 'Ari annoyed Tony by not putting in a trench over there.' He pointed in the direction of the far end of the field, which sloped down towards the sea and was not visible from where they were standing. A clump of trees also shielded that section of the site from the beach below. 'Before we started the dig, we had geophys go over the area... that's a geophysical survey. It creates a sort of map of the properties under the earth, highlighting possible archaeological features. Physical structures, minerals, metals, disturbances in the earth –'

'Bones?'

'No. Unless they're in some kind of casket or container. Basically, the survey gives us an idea of where to dig. Naturally, Ari chose the area with the most activity, and he turned out to be totally correct. As I say, Tony was interested in an anomaly over there, but Ari refused to put a trench in, as he said we hadn't the time or the resources or the budget to work on other parts of the site. Tony took it as a personal slight. And Ari also criticised his opinions of some of the finds. To be honest, I don't think he regarded Tony as a proper archaeologist.'

'But what was the root of this antagonism? Birka?'

Hansson nodded wearily. 'It seemed to be. Tony never really told me what sparked it all off. He just wouldn't talk about it. I assumed Ari was annoyed because Professor Råberg brought Tony onto the dig half way through.'

'Do you think it may have had something to do with the student's death on the island?'

'Tony wouldn't talk about it but, yes, I think that may have had something to do with it. He was very cut up by the incident. As I say, Tony and this girl had hit it off. Maybe Ari didn't like that – jealousy perhaps. But, of course, Tony had no interest in her romantically.'

'We believe the Stockholm police interviewed the professor at the time.'

'Yes. He was the one who found the body. Tragic accident.'

They reached the farm gate.

'Thank you for coming down, Doctor Hansson. Bea will give you a lift back to Malmö.'

'You must find Tony. And the girl, of course,' he added as an afterthought.

'We're trying our best.'

'It's been fascinating talking about the Vikings,' Kevin added.

'Pity you weren't around here a thousand years ago.'

'Why?' he laughed.

'You could have investigated a serious crime. Our Viking had his head split open from behind. I think he was murdered.'

CHAPTER 24

It had taken twenty-four hours to unravel the red tape which was officially tying Gerda Brink's safe deposit box. Once allowed access, Joel Grahn and Dan Olovsson had pored over the contents at the Simrishamn police station.

The box contained nothing of monetary value. However, the contents had clearly been used to generate an income for Brink. There were six files, stolen from Knut Fredriksson's law firm, each neatly labelled, and a notebook containing a record of payments with dates of receipt, and initials matching the names on the files. HK was particularly interesting – Henning Kristoffersson. The dates of the biannual payments next to Kristoffersson's initials exactly corresponded with the amounts he had withdrawn from his bank. Attached to his file, they also found handwritten notes – some in Brink's small, neat, cursive longhand and others in a more flamboyant style, which they assumed to be Fredriksson's. Olovsson felt smug – he had been right! All the details of Kristoffersson's involvement with a gang of Polish car thieves, and the high financial price he had paid for Fredriksson's services to ward off the police were there. It also seemed the lawyer had charged an exorbitant legal fee for Kristoffersson's purchase of the auto-parts company. If Knut Fredriksson had done as well out of his other clients, he would have retired a very rich man.

'We've got him!' Grahn announced triumphantly. 'At least we should be able to bring him in.'

'Klara will be pleased,' agreed Olovsson. 'But before we do

anything, we need to look through the rest of the files.'

They divided the task. After twenty minutes correlating the information, Olovsson drew an inference: 'Brink doesn't seem to have gone for any big, one-off payments... look, they seem to be small and steady, like a regular income. Intriguingly, this one stopped four years ago – and another one stopped on July the ninth last year.'

'Maybe they'd paid up an agreed amount.'

'I don't think blackmailers work like that,' said Olovsson thoughtfully. 'They could have died, I suppose.'

'Oh, that's a thought. The first one might have gone during Covid.'

'Mmm... yes, that's a possibility. We need to check them both out. It's interesting that the amounts vary. Kristoffersson appears to have been extorted the most.'

Grahn stood up, groaned and stretched before rubbing his eyes. 'Maybe it's based on the severity of their misdemeanours,' he suggested.

'Do you think someone like Brink would make those moral distinctions? I suspect it was purely pragmatic. How much could the victims afford to be squeezed? Here's one for example. Judith Vesterlund.'

'Really?' Grahn gasped incredulously. 'The meek churchy lady? Oskar's owner?'

'Yeah, and the wife of a minister of the Church of Sweden, to boot. He had a parish outside Växjö.'

'Not exactly blackmail material.'

'You wouldn't have thought so, would you?' Olovsson scanned the notes. 'Turns out he was hassled out of his parish and forced into early retirement. Seems his pastoral care for a recently bereaved widow went above and beyond offering spiritual comfort' – he paused as he continued reading – 'and she wasn't the only one.'

Grahn sniggered. 'So all his unfrocking led to his

defrocking! But how did Brink get hold of that information?'

Olovsson scrutinised the papers in front of him. 'The Vesterlunds had to move from Växjö, so they decided to buy a house in Simrishamn. But they had to sell fru Vesterlund's family summer home on Öland to do so. Some cousin objected and they turned to our friend Knut to sort out the legalities. He dealt with the cousin's lawyer up in Växjö. It's all here in Brink's notes. Looks like she had a conversation with someone at the Växjö law office about the Öland sale and picked up the tittle-tattle about the molesting minister.'

'I thought lawyers were supposed to keep client confidentiality.'

'Well, somebody let it slip.'

'I mean, I understand Brink blackmailing the minister, but he's dead.'

'So then Brink turned her attentions to his wife. And she was kind enough to let her off with a smaller payment,' Olovsson said sarcastically. 'I suppose as a pillar of the local church community, Judith's reputation is still on the line.'

Grahn sat down again. 'So that gives her a motive, too. I must admit, she didn't kick up as much fuss about her dog being killed as Sigrid Clausson and some of the others. It wasn't Judith who came to the station with Clausson: it was Thora Tarland.'

He jumped back up. 'What if Brink did kill the dog? Her way of making sure Judith Vesterlund kept on paying? Perhaps Oskar's death was a warning.'

Olovsson consulted the notebook and flipped over a couple of pages.

'When was Oskar killed?'

'The sixth, if I remember rightly.'

'Well, Vesterlund paid up on the tenth – the following Monday. That's four days after the incident. All her previous payments were twice-yearly, at the end of November and the end of May, regular as clockwork. Maybe Judith had missed one and needed a reminder.'

Kevin let the sun kiss his shaven head. It wasn't hot enough to be annoying, just gentle enough to be soothing. The water in the canal did little more than hint at a ripple. He knew enough about Malmö to know that the wind off the Sound rarely dropped, so this was an unexpected and welcome hiatus. He turned to Hakim, who had accompanied him on his jaunt out of the polishus. Ostensibly, they were on a mission to bring back snack lunches for Liv and Bea Erlandsson, but the truth was they needed a break, and the weather was too good not to take advantage of. The change of scene, albeit brief, was doing them good. They had reached an impasse in the investigation. The trip down to Vollerby that morning had been interesting from an archaeological point of view, and useful in terms of understanding a little more about the involvement in the dig of the two missing people, but it hadn't actually got them any closer to finding out what had happened to them.

The team had metaphorically gone all round the houses, grasping at any threads of information which might lead them to a more concrete course of action, but all to no avail. And everyone had purposefully avoided the elephant in the room. But now they were freed from the confines of the polishus, Hakim and Kevin voiced what they were all thinking.

'Do you think...?' Hakim asked tentatively.

'That they're dead?' Kevin blinked up at the sky. He hated wearing sun glasses; he reckoned they made him look like a cheap gangster. 'Probably.'

'Murdered?'

'That's the question, isn't it? It's got to be a possibility. Seems odd that they should both disappear.'

They started walking along the embankment in silence.

'I think Linda's been killed,' said Kevin. 'It's been too long since she went missing. If she'd been in an accident, she would have been found by now. A Dormobile is a hard thing to miss. What I can't work out is why someone would want to harm her. What are we not seeing?'

'And Tony Yealand?'

'The same premise applies.'

'Or perhaps he just doesn't want to be found,' Hakim suggested half-heartedly.

'Mmm, I'm not so sure about that. That last text... sorry, SMS he sent to Linda Vaux doesn't suggest that he was a man who wanted to vanish. He thought he'd made a big discovery. Big enough to *show him*, presumably Nordin. Sounds like he was on the verge of something exciting. And then to disappear... doesn't make sense.'

'Granted. Unless what he found would put him in danger. Unlikely though.'

'Let's just think about it for a minute,' suggested Kevin. 'What if the two disappearances *are* linked? The only person who seems to connect them is our Professor Nordin.'

'Little more than circumstantial. He wasn't even around when Tony Yealand was last heard of.'

'He certainly wasn't on the site, at least as far as we know. The last time we think he was there was the end-of-dig party. And that was held early because he was going off somewhere else. Where?'

'Don't know. We've only really been looking at him as a person of interest in connection with Linda.'

'What if' – Kevin clicked his fingers as an idea sprang into his head – 'what if Tony Yealand was so pleased with what he'd found that he took it straight to Nordin? To show him his trophy, and show him up at the same time. And Nordin couldn't take it – jealousy, embarrassment, professional humiliation... whatever. Perhaps the professor snapped and killed him.'

'Not sure about that.' Hakim said doubtfully. 'If that was

the case every time someone made a big find, there'd be a lot of murdered academics.'

Kevin smiled. 'You might be right there. I suppose I'm clutching at straws. But it would do no harm to ask him about Yealand.'

CHAPTER 25

Speaking in English seemed to have a calming effect on Ari Nordin, who had initially shown some agitation when the two detectives turned up at his office. A neutral language seemed to create a barrier between him and his interrogators, making the questions seem less intrusive. Nordin seemed impressed with the British policeman, awarding him more integrity than his Swedish counterparts. He reminded him of Inspector Morse (a great favourite among Nordin's limited television viewing), and, as a result, he elevated Inspector Ash's intellectual level to nearer his own. There was no actual evidence of this other than that Kevin appeared genuinely interested in his work on the Vollerby dig and had enthused about the finding of the hoard. Kevin would have been both bemused and amused if he had known Professor Nordin's assessment of him.

Kevin and Hakim had found Nordin in his university department. He seemed happier in his academic surroundings than he'd been at home, where the presence of his wife spying on him from the window had made him edgy and defensive. After that particular encounter, she'd put him through an even more rigorous inquisition than the police had. With some slick lies and fancy side-stepping, he'd managed to fob her off with a watered-down version of the truth: the police were making general enquiries about two missing British people who had been on the Vollerby dig. He had to tell her who they were, and when he mentioned Linda Vaux, he pretended not to know much about her, as she wasn't one of his Malmö students.

Did his wife suspect? It was possible; the interview had been animated and accusatory. But he'd always managed to cover his trails of deceit before. Or so he assumed. Did she know more than she was letting on? He pushed this disquieting thought to the back of his mind.

'Can we go back to Birka?' asked Hakim. He'd already explained that they'd continued to draw a blank as far as Tony Yealand was concerned.

'Really? I can't see the relevance.' It was clear that Nordin was trying to brush this line of enquiry aside. 'Only in that I met Yealand there for the first time... we've been through this already.'

'We've now read the Stockholm police report into the drowning of Hilma Moll.' At the mention of the student's name, the professor's gaze immediately shifted to the open window in his office.

'As I've already said, it was a tragic accident.'

'And the police agree.'

'Well, there you are.'

'You were interviewed on a couple of occasions.'

Nordin distractedly swept a hand over his head as though his hair might have become unruly. It was too short for that.

'Routine. That's what they said. *Routine*,' he emphasised.

'Specifically, they asked you about your connection with the girl.'

'It was all very difficult. I was the one who found her. Can you imagine the shock? Such a young life.'

'Doubly shocking, as you were in a relationship with her.'

After a pause, 'I admitted that at the time.'

'Which is why you were a subject of their investigations – in case there'd been foul play.'

'I take issue with that!' Nordin's voice was raised. 'The whole thing was ludicrous and went nowhere.' He raised a warning finger. 'I hope you're not going to make the mistake of trying to reinterpret the situation.'

Hakim smiled. 'Of course not. But the fact remains that you had a fling... or whatever you want to call it... at Birka with a young student. And you did the same at Vollerby with *two* students. In the great scheme of things, such behaviour is your own business, though it does lay you open to the accusation that you were abusing your position. I wonder if your employers have an ethical conduct policy,' Hakim added in an effort to puncture Nordin's composure – he didn't like the man. 'What interests us is that we have two digs: on one, a young student dies, while on the other, a girl goes missing. And you're intimately connected with both.'

Hakim's little lecture had got Nordin flustered. He wiped a trickle of sweat from his neck.

'You're insane if you're implying I had anything to do with either event. And technically, Linda didn't go missing on the dig,' he rallied.

'Which brings us back to the other missing person. Tony Yealand. When did you last see *him*?'

'I don't know,' Nordin said airily. 'Probably at the end-of-dig party. That's the last time I saw everybody.'

'Where were you over the weekend that the dig was wound up?'

'I wasn't at Vollerby. That's why our end-of-dig party was early.'

'Please answer the question.'

Nordin took a deep breath. 'I left for Denmark on the Friday because it was my in-laws' fiftieth wedding anniversary. In Roskilde.'

'And the Saturday?'

'It was a weekend do.'

'OK.' Hakim turned to Kevin. 'Have you anything you'd like to ask, Inspector Ash?'

'Yes, if you don't mind.' He flashed Nordin a warm smile,

which was greeted with relief by the academic. 'As I said earlier, we visited the Vollerby site. Jan Hansson gave us a good insight into the whole excavation. There was just one thing I wanted to ask you. I understand that Tony Yealand was intrigued by the geophys... I think that's the term used. Well, that's what they called it on the British archaeological programme, *Time Team*. Sorry, I digress. Yealand seemed especially interested in a section of the field that showed up certain anomalies. Again, I think that's how they are referred to. He was keen to put a trench in that particular spot, but you didn't allow it. Was there a reason for that?'

'Look, we can't dig everywhere. There were time and budget constraints. I have to make some tough decisions. Besides, we'd already made such amazing discoveries that it seemed rather pointless wasting more time and resources expanding the dig. We were unlikely to find anything half as good.'

'Yes, I see. Obviously, the conundrum we have is that that weekend, Linda received a message from Yealand saying he'd found something really important.'

'I know. I can't for the life of me think what it could have been. But to be brutally honest, it wouldn't have taken much to get Tony going. He wasn't a very good archaeologist.'

Kevin leant forward in his seat. 'Nothing has surfaced in the last year that might be construed as unusual? I don't know... something of the Viking period that could have "got Tony going"?'

'What are you getting at?'

'Well, correct me if I'm wrong, but if he *had* found something – and he obviously thought it was important enough to send an excited SMS to Linda Vaux about it – surely it would come to light in some way... in academic circles... in a museum... even on the open market. After all, there's hardly any point finding some archaeological treasure and then doing nothing with it. You see, Professor Nordin, I'm trying to establish the veracity of Yealand's claim. It might help us find him.'

'I suppose so,' Nordin conceded.

'I mean, for example, someone on your dig talked about Doctor Asplund's theory about some imperial crown. Is that the sort of thing that would get Yealand going?'

Nordin burst out laughing. 'Oh my God! That is just pure myth! Alice has got it into her head that the Emperor Basil's crown actually existed. Do you know about this?' Kevin shook his head. 'There's an obscure reference by Theodore of Ephesus which mentions a crown that disappeared while in the care of a barbarian at a time when the Byzantine Emperor, Basil the Second was away on campaign. The Byzantines sometimes referred to the Vikings in the Varangian Guard as "barbarians". Mind, it has to be said that Theodore has proved a rather unreliable chronicler. Anyway, the crown was supposedly made in the Middle East somewhere.'

'A golden crown?'

'Not in the conventional Western European design. If it existed at all, it would have been more like the famous Monomachus Crown.'

'Sorry, I'm none the wiser.'

'That was made for the Byzantine Emperor, Constantine the Ninth – he's a bit later than Basil. It has seven gold plates decorated in cloisonné enamel and depicts some of the royal family, two dancers and a couple of allegorical figures. It was found by a Hungarian farmer in 1860 and is now in the National Museum in Budapest. It's quite beautiful. Even if Basil had been presented with such a crown, it would have been wasted on him; he was a philistine. Anyway, going back to your original question... it's extremely unlikely that Tony Yealand found anything of value or import. And definitely not a mythical Byzantine crown!' he added with a knowing smirk.

'Oh well, it was worth a shot.'

Nordin pursed his lips in a thoughtful manner. 'There was something –'

'Yes?'

'Well, last month I was approached by an antiques dealer. She had a couple of gold dinars. Early Arabic coins. She said a customer had brought them in and she was wondering if they were authentic and maybe I could put a value on them. I could see they were from one of the Caliphates, so I passed them on to Alice Asplund. More her field.'

'And would they date from Viking times?'

'The coins were probably earlier, but could have been brought back from the East by Vikings, or used by Arab or Byzantine traders who'd ventured north.'

'Could they have come from Vollerby?'

'No way. The coins we found in our hoard were all silver dirhams. Five hundred and eleven to be exact,' Nordin added proudly.

'Did the dealer say where they came from?'

'Family heirloom, or some such tale.'

Klara Wallen hadn't wasted any time dragging Henning Kristoffersson into the Simrishamn police station. She'd barely listened to the protestations of Olovsson and Grahn as they attempted to outline the credentials of three other contenders for the murder of Gerda Brink. Wallen was so convinced that Kristoffersson was their man that she blithely brushed off any arguments to the contrary. A quick result would impress the commissioner, as long as Anita didn't try and hog the credit. And despite her best efforts, Wallen had failed to suppress another advantage of a swift conclusion to the case creeping into her mind: she could get out of Simrishamn and distance herself from Rolf.

With the evidence in black and white in Gerda Brink's notebook, even Kristoffersson could no longer deny that he had been paying his tormentor to keep her mouth shut about his former unlawful activities. He admitted the blackmail, but he wasn't going to readily admit to his dealings with the Polish car-thief gangs, as he was fearful that he might be retrospectively prosecuted. And despite Wallen and Brodd's aggressive promptings and threats, he was adamant that he hadn't killed Brink.

'But she was bleeding you dry,' persisted Wallen. 'I can't think of a better motive for getting her out of your life altogether.'

'I've already admitted that I paid the bitch. But there is no way I killed her.'

'Come on, Henning. Surely you don't expect us to believe that. You'd had enough. That last payment just tipped you over the edge. You had the motive and the opportunity, and the means was easy enough to find – there are plenty of rocks down by the shoreline.'

'I didn't bloody touch her, I tell you!'

Wallen swapped a sideways glance with Brodd. Kristoffersson wasn't budging. Then she decided on a change of tack. It was a suggestion Dan Olovsson had thrown into the mix during the last meeting.

'Your wife...'

'What about her?' For the first time, Kristoffersson appeared unsettled.

'Did *she* know about the payments to Brink?'

'No...' he said cautiously.

'Are you sure?'

'I deal with all our personal finances. She doesn't know what goes in or out.'

'Bit sexist,' said Brodd. Kristoffersson gave him a withering look.

'Did she know why you lost your job with Saab?' Wallen asked, wondering if they had stumbled across another possibility.

'I told her that I had had a disagreement with the owner and had resigned.'

'And she believed you?'

'Why wouldn't she?'

'What if she'd known more than she was letting on? What if she'd found out what Brink was doing to you?'

'What the hell are you implying?'

'You say that your wife was at your apartment that night,' said Brodd, taking up the thread of Wallen's probing.

'Yes, she was,' he said emphatically.

'How can you be sure?'

'Why wouldn't she be?'

'It's not far away. She must have known Brink's routine as well as anybody else round here. She could have killed her to stop her exploiting you.'

'You must be mad! I've never heard anything so ridiculous!'

'And why not?' asked Wallen.

'Anna-Marie is incapable of doing anything like that,' Kristoffersson said furiously.

'We'll have to ask her.'

'You just leave her out of this!'

'Can't do that, I'm afraid. Unless you confess, of course.'

CHAPTER 26

The traffic shuffled slowly along Norra Skolgatan. Bea Erlandsson felt lethargic, too, after spending the last half hour in the suffocating environment of Thilde Meerwald's antiques shop. Tightly packed from floor to ceiling, it had everything from quality antique furniture to tatty bric-a-brac. The eclectic mix would certainly appeal to anyone who enjoyed rummaging for a bargain. Even Erlandsson was drawn in – she liked retro, and ended up buying a lava lamp for Maria. It would give her a laugh and would fit in with the decor they were planning for their new apartment. Despite being Brazilian, Maria had bought into all the Scandinavian minimalistic chic – with a touch of British psychedelia thrown in, hence the lava lamp. Bea bowed to her partner's better taste. Though three years her junior, Maria had a boldness and self-possession Bea envied. Lacking in confidence when they first met, it was thanks to Maria that she now had the assertiveness, self-belief and self-esteem which were vital elements in a good police officer. Anita had recognised the change in Erlandsson – how she now took the initiative, trusted more in her intuition and contributed more to the team – and had allowed her to flourish after the crushing carping of former Chief Inspector Alice Zetterberg.

Thilde Meerwald was delightfully odd. An old hippie with uncontrollable hair, big hooped earrings, bright-red lipstick and a colourful skirt that was big enough to double as a Bedouin tent, she had been perfectly cooperative. It turned out that Meerwald had been intrigued by the gold coins that

Hakim had asked Erlandsson to enquire about.

Who had come in to have them appraised?

A grey-haired lady. Probably in her sixties. 'My sort of age, my dear.'

Anything else about her?

Not that she could remember. 'Unremarkable.'

Did she say where the coins had come from?

The woman had been vague. She'd mumbled something about them being in her family for ages, though Meerwald had been unconvinced. But the grey-haired woman didn't seem the sort to have stolen them! This observation had heralded a cackle of laughter that only a serious smoker could produce.

Meerwald explained that she'd taken the coins to Professor Nordin at the university. Nordin had then passed them on to an academic colleague. Her opinion was that they were authentic, though putting a commercial value on them was not in her range of expertise. The professor suggested to Meerwald that they should really be in a museum.

Erlandsson asked Meerwald if she'd contacted the woman to say she'd got the coins authenticated.

No. She hadn't left a phone number or an address. Or even given her name. She just turned up a couple of weeks later and asked if Meerwald was interested in buying them. Meerwald had said that she would have to have them properly valued by a numismatist. The woman had just pocketed the coins and left. Apparently, she hadn't been very keen on the idea of getting them authenticated in the first place; she'd just wanted to cash them in.

Erlandsson reached the corner of Norra Skolgatan and Föreningsgatan. Why had the grey-haired woman not gone straight to a specialist in the first place? And why hadn't she taken up Thilde Meerwald's offer to do so? The most obvious conclusion was that she didn't want to reveal where the coins had come from. So, where *did* they come from?

*

Kevin had taken his place at one of the wooden bench tables outside The Pickwick twenty minutes before he got the call from Anita to say she was on her way. That had given him time for a pint and to mull over a phone conversation he'd had with Alice Asplund an hour before. Following up Bea Erlandsson's report on her visit to Thilde Meerwald, Kevin had wanted to meet up with Asplund, but the doctor was out of town at her recently purchased country home. Hakim had made the call and asked if he could pass the phone over to his British colleague and she had replied in immaculate English. She explained to Kevin that she was at her new house for a few days, decorating and doing other jobs, and that she'd also be paying a flying visit to Stockholm.

When asked about the coins, Asplund confirmed that Nordin had passed them over for her to identify and authenticate. They had been genuine. The gold dinars were issued during the reign of al-Radi bi'llah, the twentieth Caliph of the Abbasid Caliphate. His seven years in power had ended in AD 940. She helpfully explained that at its height, the Abbasid Caliphate had covered an enormous area: what is now Egypt, Saudi Arabia and the Middle East, all the way across to modern-day Pakistan and Afghanistan. Dinars were circulated far and wide through trade. She was of the opinion that it was quite possible that some had reached Scandinavia in the Viking era.

'The woman who brought in the coins was very vague about how she'd got hold of them. In your opinion,' Kevin had asked, 'could they have come from Vollerby?'

'No.' Asplund had sounded emphatic. 'The hoard we found was exclusively silver – and that included the coins we unearthed. The owner must have been wealthy by Viking standards. If the gold coins had also been in his possession, they would have been with the rest of the hoard.' As an afterthought, she added, 'It was frustrating that we couldn't pinpoint their origin.'

'Yes, it must have been. Anyway, thank you for your time, Doctor Asplund.' Kevin finished with a jolly 'And have fun doing up your country cottage.'

'I will,' Asplund said in some surprise. 'Oh, is there any word on Linda Vaux?'

'I'm afraid not. We're still looking.'

Kevin had another beer, and there was a gin and tonic on the table by the time Anita turned the corner and flopped down opposite him. He gazed at her in concern; she was looking permanently stressed these days.

'How did it go?' He knew she'd been dragged into some budget meeting – the sort of thing she loathed, and one of the reasons he was happy not to advance any further up the greasy pole.

'Waste of bloody time,' she said between gulps of her G&T. Then she sat back. 'I needed that. Thanks.'

'Anything for my chief inspector.'

'OK, that's enough crawling. Except in the direction of the bar in a minute to get me another.'

By the time Kevin had bought the next round, Anita was unwinding.

'How's the Simrishamn case going?' he asked, now feeling it was safe to return to the topic of work.

'I had a chat on the phone with Klara. She's got Henning Kristoffersson locked up for the night. He's called his lawyer, but when he appears in the morning, he'll get him straight out. Klara's hoping a night in the cells might make Kristoffersson confess. It seems a long shot to me, but she's convinced she's got the right man. He admits paying money to Gerda Brink, but nothing more.'

They lapsed into silence.

'Oh, and Bea filled me in on the Arab coins. They don't strike me as relevant really, but everything has to be checked out.'

Kevin just grunted.

'OK, do *you* think they're relevant? You don't keep quiet for long unless you've got something on your mind.'

This raised half a smile. 'I'm not sure you'll think this is a good idea.'

'Try me.'

Kevin paused to take a sip of his beer as though this would give him the courage to speak.

'I think we should be doing some digging at Vollerby.'

'What? Are you serious?'

'It's partly the business of the gold coins.' He quickly raised his hands. 'I'm sure they have nothing to do with Vollerby. But it brought home something I've been thinking about since speaking to Jan Hansson and Ari Nordin. If you remember, Tony Yealand was keen to investigate an anomaly on the geophysics mapping of the site. Nordin wouldn't sanction it for obvious reasons – time and money – and besides, he'd found the archaeological motherlode with his hoard. Why would he bother?'

'Understandable.'

'But what if...' Kevin cleared his throat. 'What if, when he was winding up the site, Tony did a little dig of his own – at the spot where the anomaly was? And there he found something else. Something that got him excited – so excited that he wanted to tell his friend Linda Vaux about it.'

'Such as gold coins?'

'I was hoping so, but not likely, according to the experts. Possibly a weapon, or an artefact of some sort.'

'OK. Say Yealand did do some digging on his own initiative. What would be the point of us doing more if he'd already found whatever was there to be found? I know you'd just love it, but we're not on your beloved *Time Team.*'

Kevin smiled at Anita remembering the programme. 'We wouldn't be digging for treasure. The thing is I got the impression that Jan Hansson was... what should I say?... uncomfortable when we were down at Vollerby. It was a site he knew well, so why?'

'It's where he last saw his lover. Brought back bad memories.'

The tables were now filling up around them.

'You're right, I know. It was the last place Hansson saw Tony Yealand. It seems to be the last place anyone saw Tony Yealand.'

'And?'

'And I was wondering if he's still there.'

CHAPTER 27

It was one of those stultifying nights that happen only occasionally in Skåne. The clouds had rolled in and seemed to trap the heat of the day. Sigrid Clausson found it difficult to sleep. She brushed the sweat off her face before it dripped onto the pillow. The summer duvet had been kicked off nearly an hour before. Was it the heat that was keeping her awake? Or was it what she had found out earlier that day? She tossed and turned for the umpteenth time before sitting up and noticing the time: 02:09. The last time she'd looked, it had been 02:04. She picked up the bottle of water by her bed and drank thirstily. It had the annoying effect of making her want to pee. She needed a trip to the toilet block.

It was some time before she got up. Should she have tried to contact the police? She knew that Inspector Wallen was nominally in charge of the Brink investigation. Chief Inspector Sundström had indicated that if she had any useful information, Wallen was the person to approach. She'd decided it could wait until the morning. Yet again, she went over the events of the day. She'd received a visit from a distraught Anna-Marie Kristoffersson, telling her that the police had taken her husband in for questioning and were keeping him over night. Had they got it wrong? True, Henning Kristoffersson was a self-important pain in the arse who got everybody's backs up, strutting around the allotments as though he owned them. The only person he seemed to defer to – or certainly not cross – was Gerda Brink. Brink was a nasty piece of work and had a poisonous tongue, but surely that wouldn't be a reason for Kristoffersson to kill her? What motive did the police think he had? It was while comforting the weeping Anna-Marie that the woman had let slip a piece of information that might prove very useful to the police.

Clausson got up and Maisie stirred in her basket.

'Stay put.' Clausson shushed the dog and donned her pyjama bottoms, which she hadn't worn in bed due to the heat. She slipped on her flip-flops and quietly stepped out into the warm night. Her torch guided her to the toilet.

As she approached Gerda Brink's plot on her return journey, she thought she heard a rustling sound. She stopped in her tracks and chided herself; just another plot holder on the move for the same reason she was. She took a few more steps. No, this time she was sure. Someone was in Brink's garden. She flashed the torch, but the beam revealed nothing. Then her old instincts kicked in – the tightening of the stomach, the sharpening of the mind. She just knew something wasn't right, but she didn't want to call out in case she woke the neighbours. Slowly, she opened Brink's gate. It creaked. Clausson cursed Brink for not oiling it. She carefully crept up the weed-strewn path towards the cabin. She was sure that someone was behind it – perhaps breaking in? She tried a tentative 'Who's there?'

Silence.

Now she was at the corner of the building. Beyond the fence, Thora Tarland's cabin loomed eerily in the half light. Once again, she spoke, 'I know you're there.' She swore she could hear someone breathing. Screwing up her courage, she lurched round the corner. Suddenly, the torch was smashed out of her hand and it flew to the ground. She half staggered and was aware of a dark figure beside her. As she tried to steady herself against the wall of the building, a searing pain shot through her skull and everything went black.

*

'And this wouldn't happen to be Detective Inspector Ash's idea by any chance?' Commissioner Falk's captious tone wasn't unexpected.

'Sort of. But I have to say I agree with him.'

In fact, Anita hadn't agreed with Kevin's suggestion at first – far from it. She had taken some persuading right up to the moment they went to bed, but by morning, she had come round to his way of thinking. 'It was the last place anybody saw Tony Yealand. The least we can do is have a look at Yealand's anomaly – find out if that particular spot was disturbed a year ago. If there *is* any evidence of digging, it would most probably have been Yealand after the official dig had finished. And if he did find something, that would explain his excited message to Linda Vaux.'

'You're not expecting to find anything else there, are you?' Falk said with a frown.

'Who knows?'

'It could be an official nightmare.'

'All we need is the farmer's permission. It's nothing to do with the university now, as they were only granted access for the six weeks of the excavation. We'll need the geophysical survey from them though. There's no reason for them not to hand that over.'

'I suppose so,' Falk said reluctantly.

Just then Anita's phone buzzed. Klara Wallen's name came up.

'Sorry, I'd better take this.'

'Go ahead.'

'Hi, Klara.' There was an animated voice at the other end, but Falk couldn't decipher what was being said despite his best efforts to listen in.

'OK, I'll be straight over.'

She clicked off the phone.

'That ex-cop on the allotments, Sigrid Clausson. She was

attacked last night. She's in intensive care.'

'Is she going to be all right?'

'They're not sure she'll make it.'

CHAPTER 28

Klara Wallen was waiting in the car park outside Ystad hospital, where Sigrid Clausson had been rushed to. Anita drove up just over an hour after she'd received the call. She wound down her window.

'She's still in a coma. It's touch and go.'

'When did it happen?'

'Sometime last night. No one heard anything until Alma Cederholm became aware of Clausson's dog, Maisie, barking. That was unusual, as Clausson had it well trained. Alma went to investigate and realised that Clausson wasn't in, so she went looking for her. Eventually, she spotted a pair of feet poking out round the corner of Brink's cabin, and there she was.'

'You said on the phone that it was head trauma.'

'Yes. Similar to how Brink was murdered. And the dog.'

'Presumably, there's nothing we can do here.'

'No. Joel's inside,' Wallen said, jerking her head in the direction of the hospital. 'He'll let us know the outcome. If she makes it, there'll be a uniform on the door in case there's a second attempt.'

'Right. Let's go to Simrishamn.'

Gerda Brink's allotment was surrounded by police tape fluttering in the sea breeze. The curious plot holders who'd gathered to see what was going on had left some time ago to tend their patches and discuss the latest disturbing developments on what, until recently, had been a peaceful site. Where

Brink's murder had shocked, (but not been accompanied by a groundswell of sympathy), the attack on Sigrid Clausson had shaken the community to its very core. And the thought that the perpetrator might possibly be among their number was both unnerving and distressing.

There were still a couple of white-suited forensic technicians at work under Degermark's doleful eye when Anita and Wallen arrived at the crime scene.

'This is as many murders in a fortnight as I've had to deal with in ten years,' he muttered.

'Sigrid Clausson isn't dead yet,' Wallen pointed out.

'Technically,' he mumbled.

'Anything you can tell us?' Anita asked.

Degermark stepped round the back of the cabin, and Anita and Wallen followed.

'This is where she was found.' It was the bleak strip of weed-infested earth between the back of the building and Thora Tarland's fence. 'Her head was there.' The dried blood mixed in with the dirt was a good marker. 'The perpetrator was probably hiding or waiting here when fru Clausson came upon him – or her. Unfortunately, I didn't get to see the victim in situ, as she was whisked off to hospital before I arrived.' Degermark bent down and picked up an old, heavy spade wrapped in a polythene bag. He turned it over in his hand – the underside was smeared with blood. 'At least we have a weapon this time. And before you ask, no prints. The attacker must have been wearing gloves. He probably got the spade from the shed round the corner. It was unlocked, and there are a number of ancient garden implements in there. Judging from the state of the plot, this is the only use the spade has had in years.' Degermark seemed to have the same dark sense of humour as Eva Thulin. Maybe it was a prerequisite of the job.

'So, unlikely to be a premeditated attack,' Wallen commented.

'I see there are some scuffed footprints over there,' Anita pointed out. 'Any use?'

'You've got to be kidding,' Degermark huffed. 'There's the woman who found the body, of course, not to mention the herd of elephants who came to nose. Throw in the clodhopping ambulance crew, and you've no chance. I'm not a miracle worker.'

Oh, Eva, where are you when I need you? Anita thought. She glanced up at the window at the back of the cabin. 'Any evidence that the perpetrator was trying to get in there?'

'No. Nor on the door at the front. My guess is that Clausson disturbed the attacker before they had time to break in, if that's what they were about.'

'And then the break-in was abandoned. OK. Thanks.'

Wallen followed Anita back round to the front. They stood on the peeling decking, which creaked under their feet.

'What was Clausson doing here?'

'Disturbed during the night?' Wallen suggested.

'She's the other side of the Cederholms' property. I doubt if she'd hear someone padding about from there.'

'And Thora Tarland, directly behind, is away at the moment. Visiting a sister in Falkenberg.'

Anita's stomach gave an inadvertent rumble. 'Excuse me. Didn't have time for breakfast this morning.' She surveyed the plot as she tried to imagine the sequence of events. 'Maybe she was going to the toilet block. Heard something on her way there, or on her way back?'

'Possibly.' Wallen took out her tin of snus and popped a sachet in her mouth. Anita knew it was a sure sign that she was feeling stressed. She was tempted to ask for some herself. This case needed to be cleared up quickly. Clausson was an upstanding member of the community, not to mention an ex-cop. She would be under pressure from the commissioner as well as the people of Simrishamn.

'As I said at the hospital, kind of the same MO as Brink,' said Wallen with some regret.

'Looks like it.'

'If it's the same perp, it can't be Henning Kristoffersson. I had him locked up last night.' This was a keen blow to Klara Wallen's pride. And to be shown up in front of Anita was even harder to take.

'Unless we're looking at two different people,' Anita considered. 'Both attacks appear opportunistic. No weapon was brought to either scene. We need to look at other suspects,' she said matter-of-factly. 'And one of the first things we need to find out is why the perpetrator was here.'

'If someone was intending to break in, they must have been after something of Brink's.'

'The blackmail files?'

'That would be my guess.'

The meeting in Simrishamn police station didn't get underway until food and coffee had been brought in. They tucked into their overblown *fika*, then had to wait for Dan Olovsson, who was finishing his cigarette outside in the car park. He came back reeking of tobacco.

Joel Grahn had also joined them after returning from the hospital with no positive news: Sigrid Clausson was still in a coma.

On the board were four names:

Henning Kristoffersson
Judith Vesterlund
Viktor Bjelk
Einar Wallter

Anita let Klara Wallen take charge of the meeting.

'With regard to the attack on Sigrid Clausson, we'll discount Kristoffersson for the time being. He can't have been involved last night. He wasn't released till first thing this morning.'

'Will he try and sue for wrongful arrest?' Brodd asked with half a cinnamon bun stuffed in his mouth.

'Hardly. He knows we know what he was up to. He won't want that coming out. Dan, let's go through the others in the files.'

Olovsson cleared his throat with a grating cough.

'Right. Brink's notebook contained the initials of her victims and a record of their payments. We've linked the initials to the files she'd taken with her on Fredriksson's retirement, and we found six names. Since she started her nefarious activities, two of her victims have died and, obviously, their payments ceased. Of the remaining ones, we'll start with Judith Vesterlund, pillar of the church here in Simrishamn, whose husband was a Church of Sweden minister up in Växjö. This clergyman managed to get himself defrocked for giving a bereaved widow more than grief counselling. Apparently, there were others, too, who received his special ministrations. The couple seem to have come to Simrishamn to escape the shame, but Brink found out about them when Knut Fredriksson was acting for them with regard to a legal problem with the sale of Judith's family summer home. Some dispute with a cousin. Judith Vesterlund has been paying ever since.'

'But her husband is dead,' stated Wallen.

'The payments were reduced when he died, but they continued. Brink was clever. Never asked too much. She eschewed the big one-off payment approach and went for the slow trickle, twice a year. A bit like a direct debit, only cash.'

'Then there's Vesterlund's dog, Oskar,' said Grahn. 'Everyone believed he was killed by Brink: a motive for murder in itself.'

'I understand that,' said Brodd. 'It would explain her killing Brink... but the attack last night?'

'We think,' said Wallen, turning to Anita for confirmation, 'that whoever attacked Clausson was trying to break into

Brink's cabin. They may have thought that the incriminating files were stored there.' Brodd nodded. 'Right, what about Viktor Bjelk?'

'He seems to be the local heart-throb around the allotments,' Grahn said with a wry grin. 'He always seems to have a number of female visitors. He's a widower. He worked in the planning department of *Ystads kommun* before he retired. Lost his wife to cancer shortly before he finished his job, which was unfortunate timing. When he did retire, he took a year off travelling and ended up buying a place in Thailand, which he visits every winter for a couple of months.'

'So, he has money,' said Wallen.

'Yes, despite Brink sucking away at his bank account.'

'And on a council salary?' asked Anita sceptically. 'They aren't the most generous of employers.'

'Ah, therein lies his susceptibility to blackmail,' said Grahn with a trace of relish. 'Viktor ended up as Head of Planning. There was a farmer on the edge of Ystad who was having serious financial difficulties. This farmer was made an offer on some land at below-market value, which he could hardly refuse in his straitened circumstances. The man who made the offer was none other than Knut Fredriksson, acting on behalf of an anonymous client. Within a year, that land was sold on at a huge profit to a housing developer who... surprise, surprise... had no difficulty getting planning permission for over three hundred dwellings. And guess who Fredriksson's anonymous client was...'

'Viktor Bjelk!' shouted Brodd, which showed that he was keeping up.

'It was no coincidence that Bjelk bought the land, as he was already in cahoots with the developer long before Fredriksson made the purchase on his behalf.'

'Was Bjelk on the allotments when Brink was killed?' Anita asked.

'Yes. I interviewed him,' said Olovsson. 'And we'll find out if he was around last night.'

'OK,' said Wallen. 'What about this Einar Wallter? I can't remember seeing his name on the list of plot holders.'

'That's because he isn't one,' said Olovsson. 'He's the only person in Brink's files without a connection to the allotments.'

'So, what did she have on *him*?'

'It's all to do with a Will,' Olovsson announced. 'Or rather a disappearing Will. Wallter is of German extraction. He's fifty-eight. His father ran a successful import-export business in Trelleborg, which had been in the family since before the First World War. Einar was an only child, and his mother died when he was quite young. After he left university, he became involved in the business, but he wasn't suited for the cut-throat world of commerce, and he retreated into teaching in Malmö. So with no successor to take over his company, the father sold up. He did all right out of the sale and bought a big place along the coast here, and he still had plenty left in the bank. The trouble was that during his father's retirement, along came what Einar regarded as a gold digger – a far younger woman. A Romanian national called Elena Jenei. At this juncture, maybe because of Elena, Einar became estranged from his father, and Wallter senior changed his Will. Then, ten years ago, the old man died of a heart attack on a sunshine holiday in some upmarket Turkish resort. There were rumours that he was at it at the time of his seizure and that hotel staff had to lift him off the stranded gold digger. And this is where Knut Fredriksson came in. Not literally, of course!

'By the time Elena Jenei got back to Sweden with her dead sugar daddy, the new Will had mysteriously disappeared. Fredriksson claimed that it had never existed and that the original Will still stood. The gold digger was gutted, but there was nothing she could do, and Einar got the lot. The new Will should have been destroyed, of course, but Fredriksson kept a copy as a contingency measure. This very personal legal service presumably came at a price – and continued to do so once Brink got hold of the incriminating document (we found it among her papers). Anyhow, Wallter chucked in his teaching job and moved into the big house not long after probate was completed.'

'Good work, you two,' said Anita once they'd all had time to digest the information. 'OK, before we think about bringing this lot in to be interviewed, I want you to get their bank details to make sure they tally with Brink's notebook. That way we're in a better position to confront them. And we need to find out where each one was last night, and in Einar Wallter's case, where he was on the night Brink was killed.'

Brodd grabbed the last remaining bun. 'We could have this wrapped up pretty quickly.' This was said by a man who wanted to get back to Malmö as soon as possible.

'We can't assume that both attacks were carried out by the same person,' Anita warned. 'In which case, Henning Kristoffersson could still be in the frame for Brink's murder.'

Whether Anita believed that or not, it had the effect of cheering up Klara Wallen.

CHAPTER 29

Anita didn't get back to Roskildevägen until late on the Friday night. When she opened the door to the apartment, she could hear the dulcet tones of Sarah Klang. The Swedish singer was Kevin's latest obsession. One of his annoying habits was to latch onto certain songs and then play them continuously – fine for him but boring for the other people having to listen to them. And when he wasn't playing the tune, he was humming it in a dirgeful monotone. Whenever Anita pointed this out, he would immediately apologise, yet within five minutes, he'd be humming the same damn tune again. In this case, it was Jazmin's fault for introducing him to Sarah Klang on his last visit.

She was weary. So often these days, she came home to a lonely apartment to spend her time worrying about work problems and having no outlet for her fears and frustrations. At least Kevin was someone to whom she could unburden herself – albeit long distance. So to have him on the spot was heartening and reassuring, his cheery welcome appreciated even if she wanted a change of music. He had a bottle of her favourite Shiraz open on the kitchen table and a paella on the hob.

'How've you got on?' he asked as he poured her a glass of wine.

'Complicated. We've got more suspects to look at. But there's not much that can be done until Klara and the boys get more information.' She raised her glass. 'The slightly better news is that Sigrid Clausson, the ex-cop I told you about, has got no worse. All we can hope for is that she'll come out of her coma and be able to tell us what happened.'

Kevin proffered a bowl of crisps with a Ranch dip he'd made from a packet from the supermarket. Anita picked up a crisp and dunked it. Kevin could sense she was distracted.

'Good news on the Vollerby front.'

'Oh, yeah?'

'Hakim has got permission from the farmer and we can go down to the site on Monday morning.'

'God, I hope something shows up!' She bit into her crisp. 'Theo will give me hell if we come up with nothing. He thinks I only requested it to keep you happy.'

'Ah. I get the impression he's not a member of my fan club.'

'Not exactly,' she said with a grin. 'Which is odd, considering he's never met you.'

'I think we'd better keep it that way.'

He joined her in a drink and raised his own glass.

'Has Hakim got anyone from the university to help pinpoint the exact area you're going to dig up?'

'Yeah. Some student that Bea talked to. Hakim wasn't keen on Nordin or Hansson being there, as they're what he regards as "people of interest" in Tony Yealand's disappearance. He'd wanted Alice Asplund from Lund University, but she's not around until Wednesday.'

After their paella, Kevin did the washing up (for some reason Anita couldn't fathom, he didn't trust dishwashers), then they curled up on the living-room sofa in front of the television. There was an American movie on with Swedish subtitles. Kevin noticed that Anita wasn't paying much attention.

'Do you want to watch something else? Or just switch it off?'

'No, no. You watch it.'

Kevin picked up the remote and turned off the television.

'OK, what's up? Is it about the cases?'

She didn't say anything. He was about to ask again when she spoke.

'This may sound daft.'

'I'm happy with daft.'

'I'm probably imagining things. I was down at the allotments after our meeting, and I wandered onto the beach for a little think. It took me back. I spent a lot of time there as a teenager. Escaping Mamma, going for an illicit smoke or meeting a boy. Sorry, that's not relevant. Anyhow, I headed back through the town to the police station to pick up my car. There are a lot of people out and about at that time of the evening. Schools on holiday. Lots of tourists.' She seemed uncertain about carrying on.

'And?' Kevin prompted.

'I thought I was being followed.'

'Followed?'

'It seems stupid now I say it out loud. I didn't see anybody. It was just a feeling. Look, forget it. I shouldn't have mentioned it.'

The conditions on Monday were dry, so they wouldn't be wallowing in muddy soil. The digger gently sank its claws into the grass and scraped away the surface of the field, with all the care and precision of an art restorer revealing an old master under a modern daub. The face of Nour Haddad was alight with anticipation, while Kevin looked stressed and nervous. He had a lot riding on the outcome of this impromptu excavation – as had Anita, who had put her neck on the line for what he was now thinking might be a crazy idea. He wanted to rush over and stop the whole process, but he knew he had to grit his teeth and see it through. He hated to think of the consequences if nothing was found – or there was no sign of any recent digging. The commissioner would be furious. 'A waste of police time' would be putting it mildly. Kevin would be ridiculed, branded as incompetent and hounded out of Sweden. He could take all that, but he didn't want Anita to suffer as a result.

Haddad could hardly contain her excitement as she fixed her gaze on the machine at work. Kevin could appreciate the thrill that archaeologists must feel at the start of every dig. To anyone with a passion for history, bringing the long-dead back to life, recreating lost worlds and furthering the understanding of the development of our own civilisation through the discovery of even the smallest fragment of pottery, glass, cloth or bone must be an intense and exhilarating experience. The young student had been delighted to be asked to help interpret the geophysics map that had been digitally drawn up the year before. She had wondered if, from an ethical point of view, she should ask Professor Nordin's permission to use the results. Erlandsson had hurriedly assured her that this was purely a police matter and she didn't have to bother the professor. They didn't want to alert Nordin as to what they were up to.

After consulting the map, Haddad had pronounced where the area with the anomaly was to be found and the digger had been brought in. Hakim and Erlandsson were giving instructions to the driver. The burly farmer stood on the other side of the machine, closely watching its progress. He'd moved his Swedish Red-and-White dairy cattle into the adjoining field the night before, and a number of the cows now hung their heads nosily over the dividing fence.

Kevin confined his chit-chat with Nour Haddad to historical matters. He knew better than to ask her about her impressions of Linda Vaux and Tony Yealand, though he would love to have done so.

'Is everything tied up from last year?'

'Oh, no,' she said, her eyes never leaving the activity in front of them. 'A lot has been left for this summer. People have had their normal academic work to do over the last year. I know Doctor Hansson is down from Stockholm to do further work on the skeletal remains; Doctor Asplund is looking into the hoard items and dealing with the Viking Museum in Stockholm, where they will go on display this winter; and Professor Nordin's preparing for a lecture tour on the success of the excavation.'

They lapsed into silence.

'Professor Nordin didn't show you any Arabic gold dinars by any chance?'

'No. But I know the ones you mean. I'd have loved to have seen them. Abbasid Caliphate. He said he'd passed them on to Alice Asplund.'

'We wondered... well, *I* wondered if they could have come from here.'

'I very much doubt it. You mean the thing that Tony may have found?'

'I suppose so.'

'No. There was only silver coinage on the site. It wouldn't make sense to bury gold away from the main grave or the jarl's hall.'

'That's what the professor thought.'

'As you can see, where they're digging is quite a distance from the main longhouse and where the Viking skeleton was found,' she said with a sweep of her hand.

'If Tony *had* found something over there, what do you think it might have been?'

'Weapons, possibly. An axe?'

'It sounded as though it was more significant.'

'A Norse helmet would be nice. Or an arm ring, a torque, a brooch...'

Nour Haddad suddenly broke off. There was activity over by the digger, which, by this time, had tentatively scraped off a second layer of earth to form a shallow depression. Hakim, Bea Erlandsson and the farmer were all gaping at the ground.

Even the digger driver had swung out of his cab.

Hakim looked up. 'Kevin! Over here! We've found something!'

Kevin, with Haddad in his wake, ran the short distance to where the others were standing. He stared in horror at the newly dug earth.

'Oh, shit!'

CHAPTER 30

The countryside was familiar. Anita had been along this route endlessly since her teenage years. The breadbasket of Sweden in all its ripe abundancy. There was nowhere, in Anita's opinion, more beautiful in the height of summer than Österlen: the vibrant yellow of the corn, the intense greenery of the woodland, the cerulean sky and the sapphire sea – no wonder this magical pocket of Sweden is so beloved by artists. Anita would have loved to indulge herself and enjoy the scenery as she drove along the Scanian coast between Malmö and Simrishamn. But as she had Klara Wallen in the car with her this bright morning, she was unable to forget about the more pressing issue of the Gerda Brink case.

On their arrival at the police station, they had a brief meeting with the team. They had been looking into the finances of their suspects, and the record that had produced immediate results was that of Einar Wallter. Olovsson had managed to correlate the figure in Brink's notebook with withdrawals from Wallter's bank. While the others continued digging, Anita decided that she and Wallen would pay Wallter a surprise visit. She felt, particularly after the attack on Clausson, that she needed to be more hands on. The fact that an ex-detective from her own force was lying in a coma had upped the stakes, and the pressure was on to find the culprit. And there was a good chance that that same culprit was also Brink's murderer.

Back in the car, now on the road to Kivik, she and Wallen once again sat in virtual silence. There had been a time when

Klara had been Anita's best friend on the force. They had shared a lot over the years, and in the past, they would have chatted happily about work, holidays, men and a dozen other inconsequential things. Now there seemed to be a void between them. But today, Anita was happy to stew in the silence – she had far too many other things going round in her head. The biggest immediate worry was Kevin's Vollerby venture; that could end up making them both look stupid. Why on earth had she let him persuade her? Because they were getting desperate? Of course they were. There was still no sign of Linda Vaux. Liv was being her usual thorough self, scrupulously coordinating the search around Skåne: liaising with all the other stations and pulling CCTV footage from myriad sources. How could a young woman disappear into thin air unless she had been abducted? That was the obvious deduction, and the resultant natural conclusion was that she was probably dead. Sometimes Anita hated her job.

Wallter's house was a large modern building on a height overlooking the sea near the village of Vik. The villa was a flat-roofed confection of wood, glass and concrete, as far removed in style as it was possible to get from a traditional Scanian house. There were no curves to soften the angles and no decorative architectural details to please the eye. It was a soulless structure: stark and unwelcoming. Its one redeeming feature was the amazing view over the Baltic. A red Maserati GranTurismo sat outside on the gravelled forecourt.

'Jesus! That's worth more than my whole apartment block!' muttered Wallen as they got out of the car. Einar Wallter opened the front door. He was a tall man, stick thin with a wispy beard and spiky hair (a fashion statement which seemed incongruous in someone his age). They knew he was fifty-eight, though he was clearly making the effort to look younger. He wore a white polo top with tight blue slacks and had nothing on his feet. Designer sunglasses were perched on the spikes on the top of his head.

'Look, I haven't got the time. And I don't bloody believe in Armageddon and all that rubbish.'

'I'm not here about the end of the world,' said Anita, pulling out her warrant card.

'Oh, I thought you were Jehovah's Witnesses. I've had them round before.'

'I'm Chief Inspector Anita Sundström and this is Inspector Klara Wallen' – Wallen flashed her warrant card – 'and we'd like a few words.'

Wallter didn't move. 'OK,' he said guardedly.

'I think it might be better if you let us in.'

'If you think it's necessary.'

'It's very necessary.'

He took them down a neutral corridor into a massive living room with huge picture windows, outside which was enough decking to impress the captain of an ocean-going liner. At one end of the room was a suite of dark-leather chairs and sofa, while at the other were two loungers upholstered in white linen. The loungers were angled to face a long wall-mounted fireplace with decorative pebbles, above which was an enormous television screen. The other walls were bare save for one large splash of modern art. More chairs were positioned to take in the dramatic view of the sea, which today calmly glinted in the sunlight.

Wallter waved an airy hand in the direction of the sofa. He picked up a mug from a transparent cube of a coffee table and took a drink. He wasn't going to offer to make them one.

'So, what do you want?'

Anita nodded to Wallen.

'We're investigating the murder of Gerda Brink.'

'Who?'

'The woman who died at the allotments in Simrishamn two weeks ago.'

'Ah. Yes. I did read something about it.' He sat down and glanced out of the window.

'Are you saying you didn't know the lady?'

He shook his head. 'No, no. Why should I?'

'Well, you see, that's odd because you've been paying her money twice a year for five years.'

His face creased in surprise. 'I have no idea what you're talking about.'

Wallen took out Brink's notebook. She carefully opened it at a marked page and showed it to Wallter. 'You see the initials there – EW? That's you.'

'That could be anyone,' he blustered.

'It could be, but it's not. We also have a file with your name on it. Gerda Brink knew a lot about you. And we know she was blackmailing you. See the amount and the date written down next to your initials? You took the exact same amount out of your bank in cash two days before.' Wallen flicked the page over. 'Same again.' She flipped over another page. 'Same again.'

Wallter's face almost blended into the background as he turned the same pale shade as his walls.

'And why would I do that?'

Wallen glanced round the room. 'For this.'

'What do you mean, *for this*?'

'Your father built this when he sold his business. It was for him and his young woman friend, Elena Jenei, to live in. He even changed his Will so that she would be left the house and a chunk of his money. Except that Will never surfaced when he died, and the original Will, leaving everything to you, his only son, was produced for probate by your father's solicitor, Knut Fredriksson.'

'I can't believe you've had the audacity to look into my personal finances without my permission! I'll be taking this matter up with my lawyer!'

Wallen ignored the outburst. 'We don't know how much you paid Knut Fredriksson, but it was clearly worth it. But what you didn't factor into your calculations was Gerda Brink. We found the new Will in her possession, by the way. When did she approach you?'

Wallter laid down his mug and sat in deflated silence. When he saw Wallen was about to repeat the question, the manufactured indignation in his voice was gone. 'Not until Fredriksson died.' He slumped in his chair, broken. 'I went to his funeral. I thought I should pay my respects after what he'd done for me. Brink came up to me outside the church in Simrishamn. When I was offering my condolences, she came straight out with the threat to expose me. She said she had evidence of the second Will, and that it would only take a phone call to my father's Romanian whore and I'd be stripped of the house and a large slice of the inheritance.'

'She could have been bluffing,' said Anita.

'That's what I thought. I saw with my own eyes Fredriksson shredding the second Will in his office. That was part of the deal when I paid him off. So I told Brink to piss off.'

'Obviously she didn't,' said Wallen.

'Two days later, I got a package through the post. Inside was a photograph of the original new Will. That old bastard Fredriksson must have shredded a copy. When I met up with Brink a couple of days later, she said it would be far cheaper for me to pay her a meagre sum than lose all this. She said she knew I could afford it.'

'So her death was very convenient.'

'No, wait. What are you saying? You think I killed her?' He was flustered and the words spilled out in a torrent. 'You must be mad! Why would I do that? I could afford to pay her...' He tailed off.

'For now perhaps. But Brink could have bled you for the next ten, fifteen years. That's a lot of money in the long run.

It might have put all this in jeopardy.' Wallen waved her hand at the room then looked across to Anita. 'To us, that is one helluva motive.'

'You've got to believe me.' Now Wallter was visibly shaking.

'Well, let's go into where you were when the attacks took place.'

It took a moment for it to dawn on him what she had said. 'Attacks? Plural? Who else are you talking about?'

'Just tell us where you were on the night of the seventeenth.'

'I... I can't remember,' he stuttered.

'It was only thirteen days ago. It can't be that hard to recollect.'

He picked up his mobile phone, which was balanced on the arm of his chair. He nervously flicked through it. 'I was in Malmö that day,' he said hopefully.

'And that evening?'

'Well, I was here. All night,' he added as categorically as he could muster.

'And can anyone vouch for you?'

He shook his head dolefully.

'What about last Friday night?'

Wallter shot a quizzical look at Wallen. 'Why Friday?'

'Just answer the question, please.'

'I was at a party.' Now he perked up.

'Where?'

'Ystad.'

'Until when?'

'Late.'

'You need to be more specific.'

'I don't know. I can't remember.' He fixed them with a despairing look.

'Try.'

He groaned. 'As I say, late. I drove back after midnight, I suppose.'

'Through Simrishamn?'

After a pause, 'Yes.'

'I hope you hadn't been drinking,' Wallen said with a humourless smile. Wallter didn't answer.

Anita stood up. Wallen followed suit.

'That's all for the moment. Can you give Inspector Wallen the contact details of the person who was holding the party in Ystad? And don't rush off anywhere. We'll need to talk to you again.'

Anita stood on the forecourt and waited for Wallen to emerge.

'What do you think?'

Wallen pulled a face. 'Not sure. I don't buy that he hadn't heard about Clausson. It's been on the local news and it's the talk of the area. And there's a good chance that he was passing through Simrishamn at the time of the attack. A few drinks might have given him the urge to break into Brink's and find the Will.' She cast an envious eye over the Maserati. 'What will happen about the Will?'

'It'll be up to the prosecutor.' Nodding in the direction of Wallter's gleaming red phallic symbol, 'That'll go for starters. But we'll sit on it for the time being while he's still a potential suspect.'

They walked towards Anita's modest Skoda.

'I'm not sure that he would know about Brink's nocturnal walks,' said Wallen. 'If he did, he'd have to have watched her movements.'

'Good point. Circulate his picture among the plot holders – see if he's been seen hanging around.'

Anita was about to step into the car when her phone sprang into life.

'It's Hakim.' Her first thought was that they had drawn a blank at Vollerby.

'Hi, Hakim. Anything to report?'

'You can say that again!' Hakim sounded excited.

'Well?'

'We've found what could be the remains of Tony Yealand!'

'Oh my God!' Momentarily, she was speechless. Then, 'So Kevin's hunch was right! And we've got another murder case on our hands!'

'I'm afraid it's not that simple, Anita.'

'Why? Are the remains not enough to identify him?'

'No, it's not that. We've discovered two bodies!'

CHAPTER 31

By the time Anita had reached Vollerby, a tent had been erected in the corner of the field, and the presence of the white-suited technicians indicated that Hakim had managed to get hold of Eva Thulin and her forensic team. Anita was greeted by Kevin.

'You were right,' she said.

'Doesn't make me feel any better.'

'But two bodies? What the hell's going on?'

'Eva's the best person to talk to.'

'You've met her now.'

'Oh, yes. Quite a girl!'

As they reached the tent, Eva Thulin pushed back a flap and on seeing Anita, her face creased into a wide grin. She nodded in the direction of Kevin.

'Just met your fancy man.'

'I think you're referring to our British guest, Detective Inspector Kevin Ash of the Cumbria Constabulary.'

'God, do you call him that at home? Not very romantic.'

'Oh, shut up. What have we got?'

Thulin pushed back the hood of her protective suit and wiped her forehead.

'Well, you've given me some corkers in your time, Anita. But two bodies in the same grave... talk about buy one, get one free!'

Anita was used to Thulin's humour.

'Is one of them our missing man?'

'Could be. Two males lying on top of one another. The

uppermost one has significant head trauma: skull badly fractured. Big slice in it. As for the one underneath, he looks as though he's been there a long, long time, and there's no obvious cause of death. According to the archaeology student, this was a Norse site, but the grave itself isn't what you'd expect for a formal Viking burial. The bottom guy is face downwards.'

'How recent is the top man's burial?'

'Couple of clues. He still has fragments of clothing, which are definitely more Dressman than Dark Ages.'

It sounded like one disappearance had been solved. Thulin opened the tent flap so Anita could inspect the crime scene.

'And the other clue?'

'My history's not too good, but I'm almost certain the Vikings didn't have laptops.'

Anita had dropped Wallen in Simrishamn before speeding off to the Vollerby site. Wallen wasn't sure what to make of their interview with Einar Wallter. On the way back, Anita had reiterated that they mustn't assume that Brink's murderer and Clausson's attacker were one and the same person. In one way, that hypothesis was encouraging; it meant that Henning Kristoffersson could still be in the frame for the Brink killing. Wallen's gut told her that he was their man. However, the attacks were so similar that it made perfect sense that they were the work of a single perpetrator. And on the surface, Wallter had a clear motive and didn't seem to have much of an alibi for either occasion. She already had Joel Grahn checking out the party in Ystad to discover what time he left.

The next morning, Viktor Bjelk's banking details had come through, which was all Wallen needed to send Olovsson and Brodd off to the allotments to have a word with the ex-planning officer.

Viktor Bjelk may have been in his mid sixties, but it was

easy to see why he caught the attention of many of the female plot holders. He was undeniably handsome, with luxuriant grey hair, tanned features and amazingly white teeth. He had a lean-yet-toned physique, which his red singlet and khaki shorts showed off to perfection. He was sitting on the decking in front of his cabin. He had a twinkle in his eye and a pleasing smile, which he switched on as soon as he saw Dan Olovsson approach. He'd met Olovsson soon after Gerda Brink's death, and he greeted him like a friend.

'I hope you've come with some positive news. The community is getting increasingly nervous.'

Before Olovsson could answer, there was a rustle of movement at the door of the cabin, and out came out a slightly flustered Anna-Marie Kristoffersson.

'I was just dropping off some potatoes for Viktor.'

Olovsson's glance over to Bjelk's own potatoes in his vegetable patch only increased fru Kristoffersson's agitation. Bjelk came to the rescue.

'Anna-Marie has kindly brought me some earlies. As you can see, mine aren't ready yet.'

'Yes, exactly,' Anna-Marie twittered, her face turning an interesting shade of crimson. 'I must be getting back.'

'Thank you, Anna-Marie,' Bjelk said cheerfully as she beat a hasty retreat.

'We'd like a chat,' said Olovsson.

'Of course.' Bjelk was unperturbed. 'Please take a seat,' he said, indicating two vacant garden chairs.

'I think it might be better if we went inside.'

'Oh, really? It's such a pleasant day.'

'You might not want your neighbours to hear what we have to say.'

Bjelk's eyes lost their twinkle. 'Very well,' he said, 'you'd better come in.'

Inside, Olovsson and Brodd were invited to sit on the only

two chairs in the room, while Bjelk perched on a rather ruffled duvet on the bed.

'This sounds ominous.'

'It is,' said Brodd.

Olovsson interrupted before Brodd could elaborate. 'As you know,' he began slowly, 'we are looking into both the murder of Gerda Brink, and the attack on Sigrid Clausson sometime in the early hours of Friday morning. With the latter in mind, did you hear anything that night?'

'No. Sound asleep. I've already told this to the uniformed officer who came round on Saturday.'

Olovsson ignored the hint of annoyance which had crept into Bjelk's voice. 'For Sigrid Clausson to get from her plot, which, as you know, is directly opposite this one, to Gerda Brink's, she'd have had to pass your bedroom window.'

'True. But I still didn't hear her leave. I was dead to the world. A clean conscience makes a soft pillow. Isn't that an African proverb or something?'

'I've no idea, but it's one that I'm surprised applies to you.'

'Why so?' Bjelk picked up a tin of snus from a small rattan table next to his bed and loosened the top. He took out a sachet and popped it into his mouth. His smile had gone but he remained unflappable.

'One of the first things we always look into in a murder case is motive. Why was Gerda Brink killed?'

'She was thoroughly disliked,' Bjelk said with the bored air of having to state the obvious.

'We soon found that out. And when we dug a little deeper, we discovered that she had in her possession certain secrets.'

'She was secretary to that old rogue Knut Fredriksson. She would know lots of things.'

'She did indeed. Which brings us to your time as Planning Officer for *Ystads kommun*.'

'Happy days.'

'Perhaps for you, but not necessarily for other people. It was while you were working for the council that you teamed up with a certain developer to buy some land on the edge of Ystad.' Olovsson paused and waited for a denial. None came.

'So?' Bjelk said calmly.

'You bought the land from a farmer who'd hit hard times.'

'He needed the money; it dug him out of a hole.'

'But then, miraculously, planning permission for a large housing estate on the land was granted, and the value of the plot tripled overnight.' Bjelk shrugged casually. 'And it was Knut Fredriksson who handled the sale while you remained the anonymous buyer. A clear conflict of interest.'

'Sure Knut handled the sale. So what?'

'It was hardly ethical, or legal for that matter.'

'It's all in the past.'

'But it didn't remain there. After Fredriksson's death, it turned out that Brink had kept files and notes on a number of old clients.'

'Unfortunately, that's true.' Bjelk was still unabashed.

'She was blackmailing you.'

Bjelk smiled again. His teeth were on prominent display.

'Blackmail is a rather brutal word.'

'Nonetheless, that's exactly what she was doing. Twice a year. We've checked the payments with your bank.'

'It was a bit annoying,' he conceded as though he was merely swatting away a fly.

'Annoying!' Brodd burst out. 'It must have been more than that. She was screwing you!'

'*Mea culpa*. She caught me out. There are certain people I didn't want thinking badly of me around here – still don't – and I knew she could make a stink. So I admit that I paid the woman. Her demands weren't ridiculous – she was clever like that – but I kept her happy.'

Olovsson leant forward in his chair.

'Ah, but her death meant no more payments. No more potential scandal that would blacken your reputation in your happy little world. That's quite a motive.'

Bjelk thought about it for a moment. 'Put like that, yes, you're right. Except for one thing. I didn't kill her.'

'What about the attack on Sigrid Clausson?' blurted out Brodd. Bjelk's equanimity was really winding him up.

'Am I supposed to have done that, too? I *have* been a busy boy! Why would I possibly want to bang Sigrid Clausson over the head at two o'clock in the morning?'

'How do you know what time she was attacked?' Brodd demanded.

As though talking to a child, Bjelk patiently explained. 'The uniformed officer who spoke to me on Saturday told me. He asked if I had heard anything around two o'clock in the morning.'

'Just checking.'

Olovsson wished he hadn't been landed with Brodd. He got to his feet.

'OK. Thank you for your time, herr Bjelk.'

Olovsson couldn't help but admire how cool Viktor Bjelk had been throughout the interview, despite Brodd's aggressive interventions. That might be down to the fact that he was innocent or, conversely, that he was a cold-blooded killer.

CHAPTER 32

'I was hoping for a quiet week!' exclaimed Theo Falk. 'Now, we've got two bodies!'

A cup of the commissioner's excellent coffee would have been welcome compensation for Anita, being the bearer of bad news, but Falk had been too agitated to offer her one. She could have done with the injection of caffeine; it had been bedlam at the polishus since the discovery in the field at Vollerby. Now, it was officially a murder case. The bodies were still undergoing forensic examination, but there was little doubt that the top one was that of Tony Yealand; lying next to the computer, they'd found a mud-encrusted wallet containing bank cards with his name on.

'We're having the computer cleaned up, but the technicians aren't too hopeful that they'll get anything out of it – it's in quite a state after being underground for nearly a year. And there was no sign of the mobile phone Yealand must have used to send the SMS to Linda Vaux. We didn't find any keys either. The murderer must have taken them and cleared away Yealand's things from the student accommodation he was staying in.'

'And what about the second body?' There was panic in Falk's voice.

'Oh, that's much, much older, according to Eva Thulin. We're talking centuries here.'

'Thank goodness for that!'

'Could be another Viking, so we'd have to get the archaeologists involved.'

Falk fiddled with the newspapers on his desk, distractedly shuffling them into some sort of order. Anita had noticed that the longer he was in the job, the more fretful he was becoming. The relaxed, friendly manner of his early days in office had melted away as the pressures of his position wore him down. Even his delight at seeing Anita was showing signs of dissipating. She didn't mind that – she knew his feelings for her were stronger than mere regard and she didn't want any favouritism – but she did mind that the friend from her Police Academy days was now looking strained and haggard from the pressures of the job. She found being a chief inspector difficult enough without the added stresses of being the person behind the desk where the buck stops. And, of course, Falk was also the face of the force in a world where an often unforgiving media, a critical public and politicians of all persuasions were quite happy to use him as a football to be booted about to suit their own agendas.

'So, how do you think things played out?' Falk asked, now that he was satisfied that his pile of newspapers was neat enough.

'It's difficult to tell. We can speculate that Yealand decided to dig up the area that Professor Nordin ignored. He found something that excited him enough to bang off an SMS to Linda Vaux. That was at sixteen minutes past four on the Saturday. So we know he was alive then.'

'The other body?'

'Possibly. I'm not sure how much the discovery of yet another Viking burial registers on an archaeologist's scale of excitement. There are probably a number of graves around there, unless he thought this body was particularly significant. Besides, the bones themselves wouldn't have created the anomaly on the geophys. But metallic grave goods might. You would expect to find grave goods, and there weren't any.'

'Taken by the murderer?'

'Could be. Anyhow, it might not even *be* a Viking. We need to get it dated.'

'The point is there must have been someone else there with Yealand.'

'Or someone he contacted after his discovery. It looks like whoever it was smashed him over the head and killed him – again, we need confirmation – then buried his body along with his laptop, though the phone Yealand used to contact Linda Vaux is missing. Eva Thulin believes that a spade was used to strike the victim, so it certainly doesn't appear to be a premeditated murder. The killer must have taken that, too.'

Falk stood up and came round from behind his desk. He poured himself a coffee, still without offering one to Anita.

'It doesn't look good when we have a foreign citizen killed on my... our patch.'

'He may not be the only one.'

'Christ, don't say that! So, what news of the girl?'

'Nothing yet. We've put everything we've got into finding her.'

'Maybe it's a good thing we've got a British cop over here. Shows we're cooperating. Sorry, what's his name again?'

'Kevin Ash.' She knew Falk was being disingenuous.

'Yes, of course. Maybe, in light of developments, he should be given a bit more...'

'Leeway?'

'Yes, leeway. But within limits. I don't want him charging around Skåne causing chaos.'

'I don't think charging around is his thing.'

He took a sip of his coffee and, as he did so, realised that he hadn't offered Anita one.

'Do you want a coffee?'

Too late. She just wanted to get out of there and get on with the two separate murder cases she now had on her plate.

'No thanks.'

'Is it possible that whoever put Yealand into that grave is also responsible for the disappearance of Linda Vaux?'

'We can't rule that out.'

'But that would exclude your prime suspect for Vaux's disappearance.'

'Yeah. Professor Nordin has an alibi for when we think Yealand was killed. But we're still checking that out.'

'So, what do we do next?'

Bea Erlandsson was eager for an answer. It was a question Anita was asking herself.

'First, we need confirmation that it was Tony Yealand in that grave.'

'Surely –' Erlandsson began to protest.

'We have to be a hundred percent certain before we can start having serious conversations with people he was involved with – people who might have had a motive.'

'Ari Nordin would be top of the list if he didn't have an alibi for that weekend,' noted Hakim gloomily.

The smell of coffee pervaded the meeting room. The tension within the team was almost palpable. They now had a murder on their hands – they expected the body in the grave to be confirmed from dental records as that of Tony Yealand – and Linda Vaux was still missing. Anita glanced at the crime investigation board. There were still too many gaps. In the middle, there were various photos of Vaux and Yealand, and a copy of the last SMS he'd sent. But other than pictures of Professor Ari Nordin and Dr Jan Hansson, taken from their university websites, there was no one else of significance up there. They simply didn't know enough.

'What we need to do is establish a timeline, not just for the period around Yealand's disappearance, but for the whole dig. Who came and who left. Particularly Yealand. He arrived in Malmö... had his one-night stand... that sort of thing.'

'I'll sort it,' said Hakim.

'Another question we need to answer is what did he find in that grave? If, in fact, it was a grave. The archaeology student, Nour Haddad, expressed surprise that the other body was facing downwards... we need to know more. But whatever Yealand found has disappeared, presumably taken from the site by the murderer.'

'That raises another question,' said Kevin, who had bucked the trend by having a Lipton Breakfast teabag in his mug. 'Was Tony murdered for whatever he found or for some other reason?'

'And how is Linda Vaux's disappearance connected, if at all?' Anita ploughed on. 'Did her reappearance in Sweden and her search for Yealand spook the murderer? She would be asking questions about Yealand's whereabouts, and the perp wouldn't want that even if they thought the body would never be found. And if that's the case, they may have got to her, which means the chances of her still being alive are remote.'

The room went silent as everyone present digested this grim possibility. Then the tension was broken as the door opened and Liv wheeled herself in.

'I've just had technical on. Yealand's computer's too far gone. We can't get anything from it.'

'That's a pity,' groaned Anita. She turned to the board for help. The bearded face of Tony Yealand seemed to be pleading with her to find his killer. But without his computer, what chance did they have?

CHAPTER 33

The grey skies that Wednesday morning reflected Klara Wallen's mood. She had arrived in Simrishamn very early and as none of the other members of her team were about, she had taken herself off to the harbour. Not many people were around at that time of day; the throngs would come later, undeterred by the weather. Its pretty painted cottages, cobbled streets, picturesque port and inviting cafés made Simrishamn a magnet for tourists, and second-home owners, who had bought great swathes of Österlen property.

Wallen took a seat and watched a couple of big ocean-going yachts swaying in the water. She imagined herself jumping on board one of them and heading out into the Baltic to escape the frustrations of her life. Work was one of the problems; she was finding that being responsible for the Gerda Brink case was far more challenging than she'd anticipated. They had plenty of suspects: that was part of the trouble. All had motives. All seemed to have had opportunity. But there was no hard evidence against any of them. She felt herself breaking out in a sweat. What if she failed to get a result? Would it hamper her chances of promotion? Did she even want to become a chief inspector? An analysis of the rationale behind this obsession with her career was bringing her to an uncomfortable conclusion: perhaps it was merely to camouflage the fact that her personal life was going nowhere. She hadn't had a relationship with anyone since Rolf, not even a date. And she found it so hard living alone – no one to come back to, no one to discuss the day with. She had nothing to look forward to. She was fifty-four and had nothing to show for it. She stared at the twinkling water and felt overwhelmed by self-pity. She didn't even have any friends she could confide in. She'd been close to Anita once, and then, like a fool, she'd turned her back on her. Why? She knew why: pride and resentment... and, yes, she had to admit, jealousy. Anita had been promoted, Anita had a loving family, Anita had a long-term boyfriend. All the things that Klara wanted. She was only a year younger than her boss, yet Anita seemed to have it all.

With an effort, she forced herself out of her despondency. Positive action was the only way forward. Easier said than done... one step at a time.

She had spoken to Anita last night. Now the team had another murder on their hands, she assumed she would have even less help, but Anita had reassured her that that wouldn't be the case and that she was coming over this afternoon. By that time, she would have spoken to Judith Vesterlund.

Wallen decided to talk to the ex-minister's wife at her allotment. Dragging her into the police station would probably be counterproductive; the intimidating atmosphere could well make her clam up. She took Joel Grahn with her, as he had that boyish charm which seemed to appeal to older women.

Judith Vesterlund fussed round nervously as she made them coffee and laid out biscuits. Her cabin was quite basic, without much in the way of ornamentation. Wallen noticed a framed photo of Sture Vesterlund – not in clerical garb but in relaxed mode in jeans and a check shirt. The picture looked as though it had been taken in front of their holiday home on Öland. There was also a crucifix above the bed and a bible upon the bedside table. No other books were in evidence.

Vesterlund put down the tray and, under instruction, Grahn poured out the coffee. During this procedure, Wallen was trying to weigh up whether Vesterlund would have had the physical strength to commit Brink's murder and the attack on Clausson. Though she was a slim woman, she was no weakling, and she was certainly tall enough to inflict the injury which had killed Brink. But could she have done it? Was she the kind of woman to murder someone if she'd been desperate enough? Possibly.

'We need to talk about your relationship with Gerda Brink,' Wallen started.

Vesterlund blinked anxiously. 'I didn't really have one.'

'But you thought she killed your dog... Oskar, wasn't it?'

'I did. I do.'

'Why?'

'As I said to Officer Grahn here at the time, she'd been seen chasing Oskar away. She threw things at him.' Wallen thought she was going to burst into tears. There was a catch in her throat. 'Gerda hated animals. I'm afraid I didn't control Oskar as I should have. He often disappeared and ran around the allotments.' She paused and touched the corner of her eye. 'Oskar had been such a comfort since my husband's... A companion, you know.'

'It's terrible losing a pet,' said Wallen, sounding sympathetic.

'Yes... yes, it is.'

'It's really your husband we need to talk about.'

'Sture?' she said uncomprehendingly. 'He died two years ago.'

'We've had to look into his background.' Wallen almost felt as though she had to apologise.

'Oh, I see.' Vesterlund clenched her bony fingers tightly.

'We know why he left his parish. And that you had to sell your old family summer home on Öland to pay for the move down here.'

Vesterlund stared in wide-eyed mortification at her husband's past being discussed in such a way.

'Sture was a good man,' she whispered. 'But he allowed

the Devil to tempt him.'

'But you see, fru Vesterlund, the trouble is Gerda Brink found out about his... indiscretions, too. Did she threaten to expose him?'

'He never told me.' Again, her voiced was hushed. 'But...' She fell silent.

'But?' Wallen encouraged.

'She... Gerda did threaten him.' Her hands strayed to the hem of her skirt, not as an act of modesty, but one of apprehension. She took a deep breath. 'He didn't tell me, but I sensed something was wrong. We'd never had much money. We could only afford to move down here with what we got for the house on Öland. It had been in my family since the 1940s. Sture had always handled our finances and had always been careful. He wasn't mean but he used to get cross when he thought I'd overspent or bought something that wasn't essential. Then, one day, when I was dusting his desk, I found a bank statement. I wasn't prying, you understand; he just hadn't put it away. I looked at it. After all, the money was mine as much as his. Anyway, I saw on it a fairly large cash withdrawal. I thought it strange. I couldn't think what he would use the money for. Then I... I started to really worry. Was the Devil at work again? Was Sture going back to his old ways?' Her voice faltered.

'Another woman?'

She nodded in crestfallen agreement.

'But it wasn't that, was it?'

'No, it wasn't. I confronted him, ready to forgive him as I had done before. Then he admitted what the payment was for. He told me how Gerda had approached him and demanded a price for her silence. Twice a year.'

'So, you paid her.'

'Yes. We did think of getting out – moving again – but we were getting too old, and Gerda wouldn't have let us out of her clutches that easily.'

'Sture died two years ago. What about after his death?'

'I thought it would come to an end. But Gerda wouldn't let go. She said that if I didn't continue the payments – at a reduced rate – she would blacken Sture's name in the community. She relied on the fact that I play an important role in the church here. I couldn't bear it if the whole sordid business was dragged through the mud again. So I continued to pay.'

'We have a notebook of Gerda Brink's which highlighted all the payments made to her, including yours,' said Grahn.

'There were other people?' Vesterlund was shocked.

'Indeed there were. We noticed that the last payment you made was later than the previous year. In fact, it was four days after Oskar was killed. Was killing your dog a way of getting you to pay up?'

'I was having difficulty raising the last payment. I asked for more time. She wouldn't have it. I suspected that Oskar's death was a warning.'

This time, Vesterlund broke down, crying into her handkerchief.

Wallen gave her a few moments to recover. 'You can see why we're here,' she said.

'No... Why?'

'You loved your dog and you believed Gerda Brink killed him. She was bleeding you of money you found difficult to raise and there was the constant threat that she might expose your husband's misdemeanours.'

Judith Vesterlund suddenly looked older as the inference dawned on her. 'Oh, no! I c...couldn't! It would go against everything I believe in or what our Lord taught us. I even tried to forgive her, though I found I couldn't, and for that I feel guilt and shame. But causing her death... that would be the greatest sin of all and I could never live with myself. Despite the wrong she did me, I couldn't possibly have killed her.'

*

The investigation board was filling up. Photos from the Vollerby site were now displayed alongside a timeline that Hakim had produced:

VOLLERBY ARCHAEOLOGICAL EXCAVATION 2023 – TIMELINE

Monday July 3rd	*Dig begins*
Weekend July 22nd/23rd	*Jane Caldbeck leaves*
Monday August 7th	*Linda Vaux returns to UK – Tony Yealand goes for break in Malmö*
Wednesday August 9th	*Yealand returns to site and has argument with Jan Hansson*
Thursday August 10th	*Hansson goes to Stockholm*
	End-of-dig party as Ari Nordin leaving for weekend in Denmark
Friday August 11th	*Clearing site begins under Alice Asplund and Yealand*
Saturday August 12th	*Asplund sees Yealand at site – last person there (and last reported sighting)*
	Yealand sends SMS to Linda Vaux
	Hansson returns to Malmö
	Yealand's possessions cleared out of student room over the weekend (presumably by murderer)
Sunday August 13th	*AM – Hansson visits site to see if Yealand's there*
	PM – Asplund visits site to check all is clear

Anita, Kevin and Hakim studied the list.

'Hansson could have lied about when he visited the site,' Kevin said, scratching his chin thoughtfully. 'No one seems to be able to corroborate him being there.'

'If he did kill Tony Yealand, he couldn't have had anything to do with Linda Vaux's disappearance, as he was still in Peru,' said Hakim.

'We can't assume they're connected,' said Anita. 'And what would Hansson's motive be for killing Tony?'

'Jealousy? Revenge?' said Kevin. 'Remember the age difference. Hansson trying to cling on to a much younger man. There's nearly twenty years between them. Yealand has his fling and Hansson can't take it.'

'If it is him, then that still puts Ari Nordin in the frame for Linda's abduction. Unless, of course, he's got her stowed away in some love nest.'

Hakim demurred. 'She wouldn't have gone off the radar altogether – surely she'd have got in touch with her grandparents to let them know she was OK.'

'You're right, of course. The person we really need to be talking to is Alice Asplund,' said Anita. 'She appears to be the last person to have seen Yealand alive. We need to know exactly when she went down to Vollerby on that Saturday. Did she see anything odd – like Tony digging up a far corner of the field? And did she inspect the whole field on the Sunday or just the section they'd been working on?'

'We should also talk to the farmer,' Hakim suggested. 'Did he see anybody digging in the field on that Saturday? Did he notice either Asplund or Hansson or anybody else that weekend, particularly after four that afternoon?'

'OK. Hakim, I'll let you organise who talks to whom. Remember, at this stage, until it's officially confirmed, the commissioner has agreed to keep the finding of Yealand's body out of the press. The same goes for when you're talking to Alice Asplund and the farmer. Right, I'm off to Simrishamn to coordinate things with Klara.'

Anita made for the door.

'Will you be back tonight?' Kevin asked.

'Yeah. At some stage.'

'Do you want me to sort some supper for you?'

'No. Don't worry. Just feed yourself. I'll pick something up on the way home.'

As she opened the door, Erlandsson burst into the meeting room and nearly knocked Anita out of the way. She could hardly contain her excitement.

'Ari Nordin!'

'What about him?' Anita asked.

'His alibi has gone out the window!'

CHAPTER 34

On the drive over to Simrishamn, Anita found it difficult to concentrate on Klara Wallen's case, as Bea Erlandsson's news had thrown open the investigation into Tony Yealand's murder. As he had originally stated, Ari Nordin *had* gone to his in-laws' fiftieth wedding anniversary weekend in Roskilde. He *was* in Denmark that weekend, but he left on the Saturday to return to Malmö – 'Some university business', his mother-in-law had informed Erlandsson. Then he was back in Roskilde by the evening for the next part of the celebrations. She couldn't give exact timings, as there were a lot of friends and family around at the time. So Nordin was in the vicinity on the Saturday – the day that Tony Yealand had most likely been killed. That put him in the picture for both Yealand's murder and Linda Vaux's disappearance. Anita had left Bea with the task of finding out what the professor's 'university business' was on a Saturday during the summer vacation.

Anita drove into the police car park. At the station opposite, a train was standing at the platform ready for its return trip to Malmö, via Ystad. As a teenager, she'd often done the same trip with her friend Sandra for a day out in the big city. Malmö was exciting to a young girl; it had a vibrancy that Simrishamn couldn't offer. She and Sandra would go to the cinema or wander round the shops and then end up in a coffee bar. Then, she'd longed to escape the stuffiness and narrow-mindedness of a small town, where everybody knew your business. Now, she was getting to an age when all the things she had desperately wanted to leave behind were becoming more appealing. She was beginning to yearn for a less stressful environment, and Simrishamn had taken on the rosy hue of nostalgia. It was back in her affections, and she felt personally responsible for its well-being, which included catching Gerda Brink's killer.

Klara Wallen had assembled the team. Anita was greeted with the smell of half-eaten pizzas. Each one of the detectives took their turn to describe the three suspects they had interviewed – Einar Wallter, Viktor Bjelk and Judith Vesterlund. Anita had found the differing reactions of the three interesting. Wallter, as she already knew, had denied knowing Brink, until he was faced with the facts. Then he had disintegrated, pleading his innocence. Viktor Bjelk had admitted that he'd been paying blackmail money to Brink, yet had seemed relatively unfazed by the whole experience, though he wasn't keen for his misdemeanour to be made public. Judith Vesterlund hadn't even known her husband was being blackmailed. It was only when she saw an unexplained withdrawal on his bank statement that she got the truth out of him. And then after his death, Brink had threatened Judith with blackening his name and had continued the squeeze.

'As you can see,' Wallen said in conclusion, 'all three have a strong motive. All three had opportunity. And the means was easy – anyone could have picked up a rock or stone to hit Brink with. Same thing goes for the spade which was used to clobber Sigrid Clausson.'

'What are your thoughts on Henning Kristoffersson now?' Anita asked.

'It depends if we think the two attacks were carried out by two different people or were the work of one perpetrator.'

Anita reflected that both the cases she was overseeing had similar elements.

'I don't think we can discount Kristoffersson. After hearing about Brink's death, any one of the blackmail victims could have gone to her allotment to try and find the evidence she had on them.'

Olovsson's fingers were starting their irritating drumming again. It meant either he was unhappy about something or was desperate for a cigarette.

'Dan? Something on your mind?'

'Perhaps we should be looking at the two crimes as separate incidents, in which case there's the possibility that Sigrid Clausson was deliberately targeted.'

Anita noticed Wallen's face crease with anxiety at this suggestion. The thought of a whole new line of enquiry was daunting.

'I suppose we can't discount it,' Anita conceded. 'Though I'm not sure how the attacker would know that Clausson would be there at that time of night.'

'Unless it was a planned meeting,' Olovsson countered, 'though I have no idea why it would take place on Brink's plot. But I have heard that ex-Inspector Clausson was nosing around unofficially.'

'God save us from retired cops!' Anita exclaimed. She hoped that it wasn't amateur sleuthing that had led to Clausson nearly getting herself killed. 'I presume there's no news from the hospital?'

'No,' said Wallen. 'She's still in a coma, so she's not going to be talking to us any time soon.'

Alice Asplund was about to leave her apartment when Bea Erlandsson and Kevin Ash stepped out of the lift on her floor. She explained that she was just back from a flying visit to Stockholm, where she'd had a meeting at the Viking Museum about exhibiting the finds from the Vollerby hoard. She was now off to her holiday home; she was expecting a visit from her builders and she didn't want to miss them. It wasn't a very subtle hint that this chat wouldn't take long.

The conversation was in English. It always amazed Kevin how fluent most Swedes were in his native tongue. It made him feel quite inadequate and ashamed of the British attitude to learning foreign languages. A lot of it was down to lack of necessity, of course. The only good thing to come out of historical colonisation, he thought ruefully, was that so many people in the world spoke English. Kevin and Erlandsson seated themselves on the small, uncomfortable sofa while Asplund hovered impatiently on the arm of her chair.

'Have you found Linda yet? You can't miss the media coverage, even in Stockholm.' Asplund's concern was clear.

'I'm afraid we've got no positive news on that front,' said Erlandsson.

'I can't believe someone could just disappear in this day and age.'

'You'd be surprised how often it happens. But we're not here for that, Alice. Can I call you Alice?'

'Sure,' Asplund said.

'We're still looking into Tony Yealand's disappearance.'

'That's extraordinary, too.'

'There's been no sign of him since the end of the dig. You seem to be the last person who saw him.' Erlandsson just managed to stop herself adding 'alive'.

Asplund shifted on her perch.

'Well, as I told you before, I went down to Vollerby on that last Saturday. Two of the team helped me load up the last of the equipment and then left. I had a quick word with Tony, who was still patching up the ground, and he said he would be finished by the end of the day.'

'What sort of time are we talking about? I mean when you left.'

'I was probably away by ten.'

'And the Sunday?'

'I came down in the afternoon after I'd had lunch out with friends. As I say, the site was deserted.'

'Did you look over the whole field?'

Asplund looked baffled.

'What do you mean?'

'Everywhere in the field.'

'Well, no. I assume you've seen the size of it. It's massive. I checked where we'd been working. I don't understand. Why would I look elsewhere? After the initial geophysics, we decided as a group that we were only going to work on a certain area. And, as you know, it was the right decision; we struck gold. I don't mean literally, of course.'

'We heard that Tony Yealand was keen to put in a trench somewhere else. Some anomaly at the far end of the field.'

'I did hear from Jan... Jan Hansson that Tony had mentioned something about that to Ari. But that was never practical in the time we had left. Tony's lovely, but he does let his enthusiasm get the better of him sometimes.'

'In what way?' Kevin asked.

'I think he found it difficult being part of a team. He wanted to make an impression... make a great find. That gives you kudos in our field. I suppose we're all guilty of that. But successful digs are usually a team effort.'

'Even if some people hog the limelight afterwards?'

For the first time, Asplund's face cracked into a grin. 'It has been known.'

'Certainly, Professor Nordin's reputation has soared.'

'Well, it was *his* dig.'

'But he didn't actually find the hoard?'

She gave a little cough. 'It was actually unearthed in one of my trenches.'

'Ah,' said Kevin. 'Hence his digs about the Byzantine crown – excuse the pun.'

'What do you mean?'

'We heard he liked to tease you about a crown? Something to do with Basil the Second?'

Asplund shook her head ruefully. 'Yes, you're right. I do believe the crown exists, and if it's ever found, that would be remarkable. But the reason Ari teases me about it is that I know *he* believes in its existence, too, and he would kill to get his hands on it – any archaeologist would. Finding the Basil Crown would be like discovering the Holy Grail. Reputation made for life. Sadly, it's been lost for a thousand years, and I'm sure it won't emerge in my lifetime.'

'I did look it up on Google. Most people seem to think it's just a story.'

'Most academics would agree with that. And Theodore of Ephesus wasn't always right. But we go into archaeology as dreamers. The crown is the dream that keeps me going.'

Bea Erlandsson got to her feet. 'Thank you, Alice. When will you be back in Malmö, in case we want to speak to you again?'

'I'm at my summer place for the next week or so.'

Kevin stood up.

'Nice to have somewhere to escape the city at this time of year.'

'Yes, I'm lucky. Couldn't afford it on my salary, but my uncle left me a legacy.'

Erlandsson and Kevin made for the door.

'Anyway, you can contact me there. It's near Rydsgård. Just give me a call.'

'I hope you find your crown one day.'

'I live in hope,' she said with a sparkle in her eyes.

They burst out laughing. It was fun catching up with her oldest friend. Anita felt she needed the company of someone who had no connection to work. She'd phoned Kevin to say she'd be back late, as she'd made a last-minute arrangement to meet up with Sandra. She hadn't seen her for months, and her frequent trips over to Simrishamn seemed the ideal opportunity. Since taking over her role as chief inspector, Anita hadn't had much time for a social life other than with immediate family and Kevin. And as she didn't really have that many friends, her relationship with the girl who had taken the 'incomer' under her wing on her first day at school in Simrishamn was one to be treasured. Sandra had never married and had remained in the town virtually her whole life. Despite the fact that they were chalk and cheese in many ways – Anita had always had itchy feet and had wanted to marry and have a family as well as having a fulfilling career – they still always got on really well. Maybe it was the difference in their characters that bound them together.

After spending the afternoon with Klara Wallen and the team – and paying yet another visit to the allotments – Anita had given her friend a ring on the off-chance that she was free for a coffee or a bite to eat. Luckily, Sandra's hospital shift had finished and they were able to meet up in a little restaurant near the harbour. The day had turned blustery, and the churning waves looked grey and forbidding under the threatening clouds.

They had gone past catching up on what they'd been doing since they last hooked up and had reached the stage of dusting down familiar reminiscences that never seemed to lose their lustre despite frequent retellings.

'Do you remember that British doctor you fixed me up with years ago? Can't remember his name.'

'Colin something.'

'That was it! Colin Culshaw! CC! You really landed me in it there. Took ages to shake him off.'

'I thought you'd make the perfect match,' Sandra giggled, just as she'd done as a teenager.

'I swore I'd never date another Englishman again. Now

look at me.'

'How is he?'

'The same. He's over here at the moment, helping with a case. It's rather nice to have him around. Sometimes, the apartment's a bit too quiet when I'm there alone.'

'You're describing my life.'

'You've got your dogs.'

'True. And they need plenty of attention. I couldn't cope with a man, too!'

Anita watched her friend finish her glass of wine. She was sticking to mineral water. Next time they got together, she would make sure she didn't have to drive.

'You don't feel you've missed out?' Anita asked gently.

A broad smile broke out behind Sandra's spectacles. 'Not really. I value my independence too much. I really like my job at the hospital. And I have good friends close by... or not far away. I can go sailing when I want. I don't have to discuss with anyone where I want to go on holiday or how to spend my days off. I don't have to go through life having to compromise. And I've got my girls to take for long walks in the most beautiful area in Sweden. What could be better?'

Anita supped the last of her drink. In a way, she envied her friend and the simplicity of her life. Though she wouldn't swap Kevin, however annoying he could be, for a couple of canines. It must be love.

They left the restaurant and walked slowly up Storgatan. The hostelries and eateries were busy, and the pedestrianised street was still attracting a lot of strollers despite the heavy black clouds which now threatened a downpour. When they reached the square, they said goodbye with tender hugs, and promises to meet up soon for a proper evening together. Sandra carried on up Storgatan and Anita headed down Järnvägsgatan towards the police station to pick up her car.

The car park was deserted and Anita couldn't see any lights

on that side of the building. The team must have gone home, and she knew that there was only one officer on duty overnight these days. How things had changed! She peered at her car through the gloom. Something wasn't quite right. Oh, hell! One of her tyres was down. In fact both the back tyres were flat. How could that have happened? She bent down to inspect the damage. Did that look like a slash mark? She stood up. At that moment, she got a strong whiff of alcohol, and a second later, a fist smashed into the side of her head and she collapsed against the side of her car. Then she was roughly dragged back onto her feet, a hairy forearm was wrapped violently round her throat from behind and her glasses fell to the ground. Her arms were pinioned against the body of the car and she was gasping for breath.

'You fucking bitch! I said you'd pay!'

Groggily, she struggled to break away. She got one hand free and tried to kick out, but her foot missed its target. Her lungs were bursting and she was becoming increasingly dizzy. She called out, though she heard no sound. Swirls of colour exploded in her brain and she felt her body go limp. Then, suddenly, she was released and she slid to the ground, gasping for air. As she hit the concrete, she had a blurred image of her attacker. Rolf was standing stiffly with what looked like the muzzle of a pistol jammed against his head.

The hand on the grip was Klara Wallen's.

CHAPTER 35

The next morning, Anita stood in the police station car park watching the garage mechanic replace her two back tyres. Her mind was still seething with the events of the previous evening. She fingered the bump on the side of her head where Rolf had punched her. Other than that, she was physically fine, though the mental scars might take a while longer to heal. Oddly enough, the thing she focussed on most was the fact that in the fracas her glasses had got bent. What a stupid thing to think about! Perhaps some psychological reaction to the whole traumatic episode: concentrating on something trivial. Klara Wallen had probably saved her life, as Rolf had been so drunk, he obviously didn't know what he was doing. They'd slung him in a cell to let him sober up before deciding what to do with him. Anita had then phoned Kevin to say she was staying the night in Simrishamn, purposefully avoiding telling him what had happened. She knew he would be furious and full of thoughts of retributive justice – and that was the last thing she needed. She'd tell him when the time was right. Wallen had insisted on spending the night at the station to keep an eye on their prisoner and Anita, gratefully, left her to it and went off to find a bed at Sandra's house. Her friend had checked her over before handing her a large glass of Absolut.

Waking up in his cell, Rolf, though badly hung over, was full of remorse. Gone was the macho belligerence and sadistic swagger. He appeared genuinely frightened by his situation – and his gun-toting ex-partner. Wallen had risen to the occasion, her professionalism and loyalty to her colleague and one-time friend winning through. The worm had turned – at least that was the impression Anita got during the long conversation they had together over two mugs of coffee. Though Anita had been the victim of Rolf's hostility and violence, she let Wallen decide his ultimate fate. The time and energy involved in the prosecution process was a commitment she could do without. In the end, after much deliberation, Wallen had asked her, as a favour, to let Rolf go. This she agreed to do, but with the proviso that even the slightest misdemeanour in the future would lead to an immediate arrest. Wallen had then taken the miscreant in hand, laying down a set of conditions, one of which was to attend the nearest drug and alcohol rehabilitation centre. Rolf had been pathetically grateful. As far as Anita was concerned, it was more than he deserved.

The lab that Doctor Jan Hansson was working in looked impressive. Kevin and Hakim had seen bodies in morgues, of course. Depressing places, where the recently deceased, often dying through violent or tragic circumstances or both, were subjected to the most rigorous autopsical procedures in order to discover the cause of death. It was the part of the job that Kevin hated the most. The gruesome details which, written up in a report, would eventually land on his desk, he could deal with. What he found most difficult and emotionally draining was coping with the grieving friends or relatives, especially those whose unenviable task was to identify the body of their loved one. But in the world that Jan Hansson inhabited, each body was a voyage of discovery. There was no dead flesh to dissect, no next of kin to deal with, and no superior officers wanting quick answers. And Hansson was surrounded by a plethora of modern technology to help him. Scanners, printers, camera equipment, digitisers, computers and incubators all had roles to play – and must be fun to play with, Kevin reckoned. Yet all this paraphernalia was a mere sideshow to the star attractions. On two tables, bones had been painfully, precisely and respectfully laid out, each skeleton with a story waiting to be told: a story offering a tantalising glimpse into a frustratingly elusive and obscure past world which we can only ever visit in our imaginations. Jan Hansson's osteoarchaeological work brought him close up and personal to the people who inhabited that world, and Kevin, who loved his history, felt a pang of envy.

Hansson didn't seem to be particularly pleased to see them and was tetchy from the moment his lab assistant announced their arrival. This might have been because he didn't want his work interrupted. He watched as Kevin bent over the first table to take a closer look at the skeleton.

'This the Viking?' Kevin asked in English.

'No. It's a female,' Hansson said stiffly.

'Ah. Difficult to tell without clothes on.' Hansson didn't smile. 'So, this is your slave girl?'

'That's still up for discussion. If she was a slave, she was an important one, favoured by the jarl.'

'And you say she was from the Middle East?'

'Yes.'

'A long way from home. She must have an interesting tale to tell.'

'Very much so,' said Hansson, who had been somewhat mollified by Kevin's interest. 'She was in her forties, which would have been quite old at the time. She must have achieved some prominence, as she was given a special burial. I think I told you we found traces of silk among the grave goods. Much prized by the Vikings. High-status jewellery, too. No ordinary slave would have had such fine objects.'

Kevin wandered round to the next table.

'This must be your Viking chief?'

'Indeed.'

'Now you indicated to me that you think he was murdered.'

'Yes. Let me show you.'

Hansson went to the top of the table and picked up the skull. There was a deep crack down the back.

'He was only about thirty. It's clear he was struck from behind.'

'Couldn't it have been a battle wound?'

'I would have thought that unlikely. He would probably have worn a helmet in battle, and the blow wouldn't have been as deep. And it's likely that he would have had more wounds if he'd died in a battle or skirmish. There's evidence that he'd received a wound of some sort on the left shoulder, but that would have been some time before he died, as it had healed. He also had a broken nose – again, inflicted well prior to death. As for the blow that killed him, I suspect he didn't see it coming.'

'A sword?'

'No, we think it was an axe. I've talked to an expert in ancient weapons. He believes it was from the type of Norse axe that was common at the time.'

'The time being?'

'Late tenth, early eleventh century.'

'So, later Viking era.'

'Yes,' Hansson concurred in some surprise as he carefully put the skull back in its place at the top of the skeleton. 'Would you like to see what he looked like?'

'Absolutely!' Kevin was fascinated.

Hansson went over to a computer and hit some keys, and the reconstructed face of their Viking appeared on the screen. The man that stared out at them was ruggedly handsome, despite the crooked nose. His hair was a dirty blond and they'd given him a bushy beard. Kevin had seen many of these reconstructions on the history programmes he enjoyed watching on the television. When the technology was relatively new, he thought the reconstructions all looked fairly similar

– be it monk or thane, goodwife or queen. But techniques had improved, and this man's physiognomy had a character all of its own. It was a strong face, a courageous one. It was just a pity that he couldn't be identified.

'And this,' Hansson continued, pointing at a skull on a workbench along from the computer, 'is the one we found in the midden. It appears his head was severed from his body with one neat blow.'

'You thought he might be a slave?'

'I still do. It would explain why his head was tossed away among the rubbish. The interesting thing about him is what we've learned from the isotope analysis on his teeth. Turns out he was from the same part of the world as the woman.'

'The Middle East?'

'Yes. So he probably came as part of a package with the woman. Whether they were slaves brought back from the Byzantine Empire or sold through a slave market here in Scandinavia, we have no idea. But they both ended up in Vollerby. One had a dignified end, the other a gruesome one. I'm sure Ari will spin a good story out of that.'

Kevin nodded appreciatively before turning to Hakim. He'd softened Hansson up ready for Hakim to go in for the kill.

'We may have another body for you to examine,' said Hakim.

'What do you mean?'

'Possibly another Viking.'

'I haven't heard anything.'

'We dug him up at Vollerby.'

Hansson appeared taken aback.

'Why on earth were you digging there? And without the university's involvement. Someone senior from the department should have been there.'

Kevin noticed Hansson didn't ask where on the site they

had been digging.

'We were investigating the area where the anomaly that had intrigued Tony Yealand was.'

'This is totally out of order. It's an archaeological site of great importance. You shouldn't be trampling all over it.'

'We weren't looking for the Viking.'

'But you...' Whatever protest was coming next slipped away.

'We were trying to find Tony Yealand.'

Hansson was stricken. His mouth gaped and he grabbed the edge of the table. For a moment, Kevin thought the doctor might collapse.

'And I'm afraid we did find him.'

Confirmation, through dental records, that the body in the Viking grave had been Tony Yealand's had come through first thing that morning, and Anita had given Hakim permission to use the information when confronting Jan Hansson.

'I don't... I don't believe you,' Hansson stammered.

'There were two bodies in the same grave. Forensics thinks one may be a Viking, or certainly very old, so I'm sure you'll be given the chance to examine his remains in due course.' Hakim paused. 'The other is that of your friend.'

By now, it was clear that Hansson was no longer taking in what Hakim was telling him.

'It has been confirmed by our forensic technicians. We also found Tony's laptop and wallet in the grave. It's definitely him.'

'I don't understand.' It was barely above a whisper. 'What was he doing there?'

'We thought *you* might be able to tell *us*.'

Hansson's brow knitted in confusion. 'You can't possibly think...'

'We know you were down in Malmö on the day he disappeared.'

Hakim was fishing. The farmer who owned the Vollerby

field had been away on a booze run to northern Germany that weekend with his wife, and his teenage son, left in charge, hadn't noticed anyone on the site on the Saturday, other than when the equipment had been taken away in the morning, though he did notice the woman archaeologist there on the Sunday afternoon. The farmer had explained that there was no need to check the field; he was going to let it settle after the excavation and he wouldn't be using it for grazing until the following spring.

'I didn't go down to Vollerby until the Sunday morning.'

'We've only got your word for that.'

'It's true.'

'And you didn't notice any recent disturbance in the ground at the far end of the field?'

'I didn't go to the far end. Why would I? I could see no one was around.'

Hakim glanced around the lab. 'Thank you for the tour, Doctor. I take it you won't be leaving Malmö for a while?'

'No, no. I'm here until August.'

'We'll be in touch.'

Down the corridor from the lab, Hakim turned to Kevin.

'Strange he didn't ask how Tony Yealand died.'

'My thought exactly.'

CHAPTER 36

Hakim had already reported back to Anita when Kevin came to her office, wondering if she wanted to pop out for lunch. He hadn't seen her since yesterday morning.

'Sorry. Got a meeting with the prosecutor. Give her an update on the two cases.'

'Don't worry. Fancy a pint at the Pickwick after work? Maybe a carry-out after? Can't be arsed to cook tonight.'

'Sounds great.'

'How did it go in Simrishamn?'

'I'll tell you about it tonight.'

Kevin took the hint that she was busy. He was about to leave.

'Hang on. You're wearing different glasses.'

'Had a slight accident with the others. Popped back home to collect these.'

He looked at her suspiciously. 'That looks like a bruise.' He pointed accusingly at her temple. Anita instinctively raised her hand to cover it but was too late.

'What the hell's happened?'

'It was nothing.'

'That's not bloody nothing! What aren't you telling me?' he demanded.

'Honestly, it's nothing.'

'Something happened in Simrishamn. What the hell was it?'

'There was an incident. All sorted now.'

'Anita, tell me what happened.' The tone emitted both anger and concern.

'Something to do with my team.'

'One of the team hit you?' he exclaimed in disbelief.

'Of course not. But it concerned one of them.'

'Who?' he said sharply.

Anita was reluctant to go any further.

'Who?'

'Klara,' she admitted wearily.

'She did this to you?'

'No. Klara didn't touch me. The point is that it's sorted. It's an internal matter. End of story.' She was becoming defensively cross. 'Now I must get on,' she added brusquely.

Kevin held his hands up. 'OK. I get the message.'

He stormed out of the door.

Joel Grahn found the incident room empty. He put down the folder he was carrying and walked up to the board. Photos of the main suspects in the Gerda Brink murder case – Henning Kristoffersson, Viktor Bjelk, Judith Vesterlund and Einar Wallter – stared out at him. It was interesting – he also had images of three of them in the folder.

Klara Wallen came into the room. She appeared pre-occupied. Grahn was unaware of the events that had taken place the previous night. On seeing him, she flashed him a cheery smile. He was taken aback but responded in kind. Up to this point, he'd thought of Wallen as rather grumpy and uptight: someone who'd bitten off more than she could chew and was buckling under the pressure of an investigation that had hit a roadblock. Had something happened that he didn't know about? If it had, she wasn't going to enlighten him.

'Got something there?' she asked, noticing his file.

'Sort of. I don't know if it's much help, but I was struck by what you said about Einar Wallter being approached by Gerda

Brink at Knut Fredriksson's funeral. It so happens that it was one of the first jobs my uncle did when he came down from Stockholm.'

'Jobs?'

'Sorry. Tomas is a newspaper photographer. It was one of his first freelance assignments. I got him to run off all the shots he had of the mourners and outside the church afterwards.'

'Anything unusual?'

'Not really. But I was interested in who was there.'

Grahn laid out half a dozen photos on the table.

'There's Wallter,' he said, pointing at a group of people entering the church. 'And behind him, Henning and Anna-Marie Kristoffersson.'

He pointed to the next picture. 'There's Brink. She seems to be saying something to Viktor Bjelk. He's not smiling.'

'It's a funeral.'

'His funeral perhaps?' Grahn quipped. 'So that's three of our suspects all gathered together. Probably keen to make sure he really was dead so their secrets would remain safe. So, we know Wallter was approached there by Brink; I wonder if the others were too? No sign of the Vesterlunds. But I suppose they were unaware that their secret was out at that stage.'

'Any more of Brink?'

'Only this one.' Brink was talking to a woman, suitably dressed in black, who could be in her early thirties.

'Who's she?'

'That's Knut Fredriksson's niece. She gave the eulogy.'

'Yeah. Makes sense that Brink would know her.'

One or more of their suspects were in the other three shots.

'There's Tord Cederholm,' said Wallen, stabbing her finger at the photograph.

'No sign of his wife.'

'I wonder if he was one of Fredriksson's clients. Have we anything on him?'

'His initials aren't in Brink's infamous notebook. And we haven't come across his name in any of the documents she salted away.'

Wallen scrutinised the photos as though she was trying to tease out some clue they had overlooked. 'Better check him out all the same. Anyway, stick these up on the wall.'

Prosecutor Sonja Blom didn't seem to age, which Anita found annoying; *she* was getting increasingly bad feedback every time she looked in a mirror. Blom could still get away with a figure-hugging black suit, which perfectly complemented her immaculately trimmed hair and beautifully buffed nails. The wonder in the polishus was that such a clever and ruthless woman had remained so long in the backwaters of Malmö when she could have slipped seamlessly into Stockholm's more sophisticated environment. Her sharp tongue and no-nonsense approach not only put the fear of God into the villains she prosecuted, but also into those upholding the law. Anita could see why Eric Moberg had had so many run-ins with her. Bizarrely, she'd had a good relationship with Anita's immediate predecessor and nemesis, Alice Zetterberg, a fact which could well explain the edge the prosecutor invariably brought to her meetings with Anita. Blom always set the tone by refusing to offer her coffee or any sort of beverage – a courtesy extended to other colleagues.

'You seem to be stuck,' Blom said. She straightened up behind her desk and pushed away the papers she had been reading. 'It doesn't look good.'

Anita wasn't quite sure which case Blom was referring to, as she was 'stuck' on both.

'It seems you have several suspects.' She perused the papers again. 'Henning Kristoffersson, Einar Wallter, Viktor Bjelk and Judith Vesterlund. All appear to have been blackmailed by Gerda Brink, so all of them have motives. And all, according to you, had opportunity. Surely you can produce some sort of proof I can work with?'

Anita shook her head. 'We've drawn a blank. We can't prove any of them were at the murder scene. And as you can see, we believe the weapon that killed Brink was a stone or rock. Impossible to find in a naturally rocky area – and it could easily have been thrown into the sea. And even if we did by some miracle find it, we'd hardly be able to lift any prints.'

Blom gave an over-the-top, exasperated groan.

'And what about the attack on Sigrid Clausson? Now *there* was a fine officer.' The implication was that Anita wasn't. 'You don't appear to have got anywhere with that either.'

Anita managed to keep her temper.

'We do have the weapon that was used in that attack. But there are no fingerprints. And the scene was so scuffed by well-meaning plot holders that there was nothing for forensics to work with.'

This only produced a disapproving click of the tongue.

'It appears to me that these two events must be connected.'

'I'm glad you can see that, but I prefer to keep an open mind.'

The withering look said exactly what Blom thought of that.

'And then there's the missing British woman. You don't appear to be getting anywhere with finding her.'

'We *have* dug up her friend,' Anita countered.

'Yes. The commissioner is still keen to keep that under wraps. One dead Brit is bad enough. And the chances of another turning up must be a distinct possibility.'

'There I have to agree with you. The search is ongoing.'

'And have you given me anything to work with over the murder of Tony Yealand?'

Anita shifted in her seat. 'No. It's early days.'

'He died nearly a year ago.'

'Exactly! Difficult to pick up the trail after so long. But at least we found him! He could have lain there forever. That's down to good detective work.' That wasn't quite true – a Kevin hunch had done the trick, but she wasn't going to tell that to Blom. 'As you can see, we already have two possible suspects.'

Again, Blom made a play of checking her notes.

'Professor Ari Nordin and a Doctor Jan Hansson.'

'The former clearly disliked Tony Yealand, though, as yet, we haven't been able to establish the reason. The latter was Yealand's lover and they had a falling out only days before he was killed. Professor Nordin's alibi doesn't stack up and we're checking where he was at the time of the murder. We know he came to Malmö that day. Hansson was also in the area.'

'Any indication of what Yealand was so excited about?' Blom asked, holding up a copy of the SMS sent to Linda Vaux.

'Not yet. The academics involved in the Vollerby dig have no idea either. Of course, whoever killed him presumably took whatever he'd found.'

'Again, we are... or should I say... *you* are short of answers. I suggest you come back with some evidence that I can use to prosecute, before the public loses all faith in our department.' The cold stare only heightened Anita's discomfort and annoyance. 'And I suggest you do so very soon.'

Sweat seeped down her face from her brow as she crashed along the footpath through the trees. She wiped it away without breaking her stride. Alice Asplund had already done five kilometres and was pleased with her time. It was on course for being the fastest she'd managed on this route since she'd bought the cottage in January. Then, it had been too cold to do much running, or work on the building. That's why she had allocated a few weeks over the summer vacation to do the place up. There were some big decisions to be made.

The music through her airpods was helping her keep a

rhythm. She was only five minutes from reaching home and she was determined to set a personal best. Then she'd have a new target to beat. It was a competitive streak that had propelled her life and career. She didn't like to be beaten. It was an attitude that often didn't sit well with some of her more laid-back colleagues, yet it was exactly that outlook that had made her popular with the directors of the archaeological digs. She never gave up, and pushed others to work harder, whatever the weather or conditions.

The music was suddenly interrupted by her phone. She cursed as she realised that she'd have to speak to Ari Nordin and that she wouldn't be able to achieve her record-breaking time.

'Hi, Alice.'

Asplund had stopped and was breathing quite heavily.

'Are you all right?'

'Yes. Just out for a run.'

'OK. Sorry to interrupt.'

She could read Nordin's thoughts through the ether, imagining her in tight singlet and Lycra running shorts. She knew how his mind worked. But he had never tried anything on – she was far too old for him.

'No problem.' She disguised her annoyance.

'I've just been talking to the Viking Museum. They're very pleased and think the exhibition will be a great success. Well done there, Alice.'

'Is that all you're calling about?'

She heard him clearing his throat at the other end.

'All this police stuff. They've been talking to you?'

'Of course. They've been talking to us all, I should imagine. A couple came round to my apartment on Wednesday. One of them was a British detective.'

'The cops actually came to my house.' She could hear the horror in his voice. 'That was very embarrassing.'

'Was Bente there?'

'Yes.'

'Then I can imagine it being very embarrassing.' Fortunately, he couldn't see her grin.

'They keep asking me about Linda. She didn't get in touch with you, did she?'

'Yes,' Asplund said as she wiped away the last drops of sweat from her face. 'I told them that she'd rung asking about Tony Yealand... sometime in May. I couldn't help her. I hadn't realised that she'd actually come over to look for him.'

'So she didn't come and see you?'

'Why would she? Surely *you*'d be the first person she'd contact.'

'Shit. You didn't say that to the police?'

'No, don't worry.' She paused. 'You haven't done anything stupid, have you Ari?'

'No, no,' he blustered. 'I haven't seen her. It's just the police have this thing about bloody Yealand disappearing, too. I couldn't care less about what's happened to him.'

'They asked me about my movements on the Saturday at the end of the dig. They're saying that I was the last person to have reportedly seen him. They wanted to know my timings down at Vollerby that day.'

'When did you leave the site?'

'I told them around ten.'

The connection went quiet. For a moment, Asplund thought they'd lost contact.

'That's good. Look, I need to ask you a big favour.'

CHAPTER 37

The digital clock by Anita's bed moved to 04:32. She must have had some sleep at some stage during the night but she couldn't recall. Kevin was gently snoring beside her, but it wasn't that that had kept her awake. In fact, she'd dropped off shortly after they'd made love. The wine beforehand had briefly anaesthetised her worries and smoothed the path to the reconciliation process with Kevin, who hadn't taken her crankiness at the office as personally as she'd expected. She knew his concern for her had been genuine, and she was feeling guilty that she'd been so snappy with him. She hadn't gone into the details about what had happened in Simrishamn, and she could tell he was still anxious about her. It was the situation with Rolf that was one of the many things churning in her brain during the wee small hours.

Now, it was light outside. Anita got up and went to the bathroom and took an IBS tablet. She hadn't suffered from the problem before taking on this new job; now, it was a regular inconvenient visitor. Then she headed for the kitchen and put the kettle on. Maybe a herbal tea would settle her. She shut the door as the kettle boiled so the noise wouldn't wake Kevin. It sounded so loud at that time in the morning, when most of Malmö was still asleep. She sat at the table and dipped the camomile tea bag up and down on its string. That seemed to sum up her professional life at the moment – constantly finding herself in hot water. She still felt resentment at Prosecutor Blom ticking her off like a naughty schoolgirl who hadn't done her homework. But she had to admit Blom was right – they had numerous suspects in their sights yet not a shred of physical evidence in either case. Then there was her concern over the missing Linda Vaux. Talking to Kevin, she had built up a picture of the young woman in her mind. She was no longer a statistic on a list of missing persons: she was flesh and blood. What if she was faced with the same situation as Linda's grandparents and Leyla had disappeared without trace? That thought made the search more personal.

Then there was Rolf. Had she done the right thing? Should she have gone ahead and thrown the book at him as payback for all the dreadful things he had put Klara Wallen through? Had she given in too easily out of gratitude to Wallen for saving her from a vicious attack? After all, it was Wallen who had landed her in that situation in the first place. And thinking of Klara, Anita was beginning to regret giving her the responsibility of the Simrishamn case.

She took a sip of tea in an attempt to stop the griping pains in her stomach. If only they could make some sort of breakthrough, she might be able to cut down on the tablets.

The day was warming up and Anita had to open the office window. It relieved the stuffiness in the room, though it let in the traffic noise from the street below. She had spoken to Hakim and Liv – and then to Wallen – and nothing new had emerged. She hadn't seen Kevin since they'd both arrived at the polishus at half past seven that morning. She'd dragged him out of bed because she wanted to make an early start. She'd decided to go through all the information gathered from both investigations in case she'd missed something. It had turned out to be a frustrating morning. As far as she could see, she hadn't missed a thing.

There was a knock on the door, and Kevin popped his head round.

'Busy?' he asked, not wanting a repeat of yesterday's contretemps.

'Come in. I'm not getting anywhere.'

Kevin sat down at the other side of the desk. He was clutching some papers.

'I may have made a breakthrough,' he announced. 'Well, sort of,' he added as a qualifier.

'Anything would be helpful.'

'Blimey, this seems strange! Me reporting to you. Like you're my boss.'

'Aren't I anyway? Just get to the point.'

'The point. Yes. Remember I told you that Tony Yealand had met up with some of his ex-lecturers from Bournemouth University at a conference early last year in Brighton? And I'd managed to speak to one of the lecturers who'd been a student at the same time as him? A guy called John Finlay. Well, Finlay got back in touch yesterday. After I'd told him Tony had gone missing, he contacted a mutual friend who was also Tony's best mate from uni – a fella called Baz Stokes. They'd shared a house at one stage. Tony was best man at Baz's wedding and also godfather to one of his kids. Anyhow, John Finlay tracked this Baz down. He's now living in Toronto in Canada. I've just talked to him – it's the morning over there. He last heard from Tony two days before we think he was killed.'

'How?'

'It was an email. He's sent it over. In fact, he's sent two, both from the time of the Vollerby dig. The first one is very significant.' He held out one of the pieces of paper. 'This one is dated the twenty-ninth of July – just before the hoard was unearthed.'

Anita read through the email:

Hi Baz,

So, so sorry I haven't written for ages. I know you

wrote months ago. I'm hopeless at keeping in touch. Forgive an old mate? I hope you and Helen and the kids are doing well. Busy on a dig in the south of Sweden near Malmö. Viking stuff – I know, yawn, yawn. But it's what I like doing. And I love it here in Sweden, so much so, I'm applying to become a citizen. It'll make life so much easier after the Brexit fiasco.

This dig is looking really good so far. We've already found a substantial longhouse and a couple of important burials. One probably a chieftain, the other a woman. Can't wait to find out more about them. And we found a severed head! Ghoulish! More your sort of thing! It reminded me of that Hallowe'en at uni when you hired that headless costume and went poncing through the streets with that dummy head tucked under your arm. There are a few old dears in Bournemouth who I suspect never recovered!

The only fly in the ointment is the dig director. He's a total wanker – never agrees with any of my suggestions and takes every opportunity to belittle me as though I'm not a proper archaeologist. I only agreed to come down here because I wanted to be with Jan before he buggers off to South America for a year. I would love to have followed him out there, but I'm trying to get this citizenship thing sorted out. If I leave before it's granted, they might not let me back in. There's a decent doctor from Lund who sticks up for me, but the whole situation's really getting to me. I'm even thinking of quitting. One girl (a fellow Brit) has already left because of Nordin (the director). Of course, I should have known better. It all goes back to that bloody trouble

> *in Birka – remember I mentioned that? It was all so awful.*
> *Sorry, this isn't meant to be a big moan. What about you? How's Toronto treating you? Are the kids losing their British accents and becoming little Canadians? Your summer cabin sounds brilliant. Bet Helen loves swimming in the lake. She was always jumping into the sea back at uni. Mad as a hatter. Send her my love. And the kids of course. Tell Charlotte that her useless godfather won't forget her birthday this year!*
> *You take care, mate. I promise to be a better correspondent. And I promise I'll come over next year.*
> *Cheers, Tony*

'That backs up what we've already learned,' said Anita thoughtfully. 'Tony really did have a problem with Nordin. He's clearly referring to Jane Caldbeck leaving.'

'Interesting that Alice Asplund fought his corner,' Kevin remarked. 'He doesn't mention if Jan Hansson did.'

'You're right. But it all seems to go back to Birka. And the other email?'

Kevin handed over the second piece of paper.

'This was sent on Thursday, the tenth of August: two days before he was last seen. It's more rambling and lots of typos. Reckon he was drunk after the end-of-dig party. Revealing, nonetheless.'

Anita started to read:

> *I know I shouldnt be sending you this Baz mate. Bit pissed. we've just had a wrap party. Winding up thinGS but Ive really fucked things up with Jan.. Had a bit of r&r in Malmo as things with Nordin*

getting too much Went a bit daft. pppretty young Swedish lad. One nighter So so so fucking stupid I had to tell Jan. he lost his rag. said he could kill me. Not like him. He was so upset Look totally my bloody fault hES GONE back to Stockholm and then hes away. I don't know what to do my buddy Telll me

'Wow!' exclaimed Anita, shaking her head. 'All over the place, but the message is clear. He was feeling really bad about what he'd done. Did Baz reply to this?'

'Yeah. He tried to be sympathetic. Said he was sure Jan would forgive him eventually, but that maybe some time apart would help. Do them both good to reassess their relationship. Of course, Baz never heard back. At first, he thought Tony was being his usual unreliable self. But when no present arrived for his daughter's birthday, and then no Christmas card last year, he tried to contact him, but had no joy. He thought maybe Tony had taken umbrage for some reason –perhaps the advice he'd given him hadn't worked or something. Now we know the real reason, of course. Poor Baz was devastated when I told him.'

'Can't have been an easy call.'

'Not really. I tell you what, though: that reference to Jan Hansson losing his rag caught my eye.'

'Mine too. *Said he could kill me*. Just a figure of speech? Or maybe there was more to it.'

'We know Jan Hansson was back in Malmö on the Saturday. What if he went down to Vollerby that day? Found Tony on his own. Another argument breaks out. He loses it and kills him.'

'For that to work, Tony must have already dug his trench, found the something which excited him so much, and contacted Linda Vaux. Then Hansson utilises the hole to dump his boyfriend in.'

'It's possible.'

Anita scrutinised the second email again.

'So, we still come back to what on earth Tony found. It must have been more than just the body. If the skeleton itself is significant in some way, no archaeologist would be able to really tell until it was out of the ground. According to Eva, it hadn't really been disturbed – only enough to reveal the back of the skull.'

'Which is odd in itself. As Nour Haddad pointed out, the body was face down. So not your typical burial of an important Viking. So there may not have been any grave goods at all,' speculated Kevin.

'But we have to assume there was something in there... a weapon or something. Something for Yealand to get excited about. And, in your scenario, Hansson would have had to hide it, or get rid of it in some way because there was nothing in the grave.'

'He takes it with him.'

'He hasn't much time. He was straight off back to Stockholm, and then on to Peru.'

'Whatever was in there might not have been substantial. I mean size-wise. Trinkets... jewellery... He could have taken them with him. And as he hasn't been back from South America long, whatever Tony found could still be in Hansson's apartment in Stockholm. What about a search?'

'It's a thought. Though we'd probably have to jump through hoops to get a warrant.'

Anita laid down the paper in her hand.

'You don't look convinced.' Kevin knew Anita well enough to know when she hadn't taken an argument on board.

'No. I think it's an angle we've got to pursue. Though I have to admit' – she scrunched up her face – 'I still think Nordin is involved.'

'Is that because Hansson couldn't have had anything to do

with Linda's disappearance? I mean, you're right there: he was out of the country at the time.'

'Partly. I just think that maybe the answer to all this lies in Birka. That seems to be the common denominator.' She tapped the relevant email message. 'Tony himself mentions Birka.' She read aloud from the email: '*Of course, I should have known better. It all goes back to that bloody trouble in Birka.* Then he follows it up with *It was all so awful.*'

'So, a trip to Birka?'

'I think so. But I'll take Hakim.'

'Oh,' Kevin said, his bottom lip curling in disappointment.

'This may be to do with the death of a Swedish citizen. And I can hardly take you up there for a jolly. Isn't that the British expression?'

'It wouldn't be a jolly. Serious detective work.'

'At a famous historical site? Pull the other one. Remember, I know you only too well, Kevin Ash.'

CHAPTER 38

It wasn't until after the weekend that Anita and Hakim jumped onto the early Stockholm train at Malmö Central and began the journey that they both hoped might bring them closer to finding Tony Yealand's killer. The weather had turned and the window was streaked with rain as they pulled out of the station and started to build up speed through the suburbs. Living and working in the centre, Anita hadn't really noticed how Malmö was constantly growing. They passed through the satellite communities of Arlöv, where Hakim now lived, and Åkarp, once a sleepy village, now a desirable development of modern chalet-style bungalows; and on to the outskirts of Lund.

Hakim, on the other side of the table, was engrossed in his newspaper. It was refreshing to see someone of his age not flicking through his phone. She knew he would miss Linus while he was away, but, hopefully, they wouldn't have to spend too long in Stockholm. The young trainee, who had been foisted onto her by Erik Moberg all those years ago, had matured into a fine, perceptive detective; and had become a good friend. She realised how much she depended on him within the team, especially when things got tough. She could rely on Hakim one hundred per cent, and that was why she was so keen to have him accompany her on this trip north.

While they were away, she'd given Bea Erlandsson and Kevin two tasks. The first was to break the news of the discovery of Tony Yealand's body to Alice Asplund. Asplund had been the last person to see Yealand alive. Kevin had floated the possibility that she might even have killed him. On the surface, this seemed unlikely: she did, after all, stand up to Nordin on his behalf. In theory, she did have opportunity, but no obvious motive. However, Anita reckoned it would be interesting to gauge her reaction when she was told that Yealand had been murdered. The second task was to find out exactly what Ari Nordin had got up to when he made his trip to Malmö in the middle of his weekend in Denmark.

He slurped his ice cream. Strawberry. It had always been a favourite. Around him, there was the usual throng of summer visitors interspersed with a handful of locals. The ice cream booth was always a big attraction down by the harbour. There were kids everywhere, noisily rushing around in the sunshine. School holidays were always like this. It would be quieter when the kids went back in August. But they did bring their mothers with them, and they were one of the attractions of coming down here and grabbing a bench and an ice cream. To people watch – or mamma watch. The young women were a pleasant distraction, but Viktor Bjelk's mind kept leaping back to the visit of the two detectives.

Had he taken the right approach? When they'd caught him unawares with his planning scam, he'd been thrown. He'd had to think on his feet. He was good at that; it had been a useful skill in impromptu planning meetings when awkward questions had appeared from nowhere. He'd quickly recovered by appearing to be as frank as possible – a default setting which usually paid off. But had his outwardly casual attitude dispelled their suspicions or whetted their interest? He couldn't decide, and that was preying on his mind. He'd become so preoccupied that he felt ice-cream dribbling down his hand. He swiftly licked it off.

How had the police found out? In the same way that Brink had? They must have found what Brink had on him. He'd tried to be blasé about not having a problem paying. Initially, it had been a nagging inconvenience, but after various global financial fall-outs, his savings had been greatly depleted. The last time he had to pay, he'd tried to renegotiate the sum. Brink would have none of it. The woman had got exactly what she deserved. The world had been rid of an evil and manipulative bitch.

He took another couple of licks. The ice cream was fast losing its appeal. He'd always assumed that he was Brink's only victim until Anna-Marie had let slip that the police were onto Henning about something he'd done in the past. And he had been dragged off to the police station! That had set tongues wagging on the allotments. She wouldn't tell him what the indiscretion was; she was too frightened of her husband. What if Brink had been fleecing a number of people?

Any further thoughts were pushed aside when someone slipped onto the bench beside him. Talk of the devil... it was Henning Kristoffersson. Not one of Viktor's favourite plot holders, though they were virtually neighbours with only one cabin between them. He hoped Kristoffersson wouldn't mention his wife. More thinking on his feet might be required.

Henning dispensed with any casual greeting. 'I hear you had a visit from the cops.'

'How did you know?'

'Anna-Marie said they'd come when she was delivering those new potatoes.'

That wasn't all she was about to deliver when they'd been interrupted.

'Yeah.'

'What did they want?'

'Oh, general stuff. Had I heard anything the night Sigrid was attacked? As it happens, I hadn't. Of course, you weren't around, were you?' Viktor added.

'No. So they can't pin that on me.'

'I'm afraid Sigrid was being too nosey.' The comment was followed by another slurp of ice cream.

'Once a cop... She couldn't help herself from the moment that flaming dog was killed.'

'I think she was trying to solve Gerda's murder just to piss off that chief inspector,' said Bjelk. 'She was asking everybody questions as though she was still on the force. By the way, why did the police drag you in?'

'Misunderstanding.'

Bjelk started to gingerly crack his ice cream cone with his teeth.

'Did you have anything to do with Knut Fredriksson?' Kristoffersson asked.

Bjelk bit off a bigger piece of cone than he intended.

'No,' he said with his mouth half full. 'I lived in Ystad. My lawyer's over there.'

'Just wondered.'

Bjelk took that as confirmation that Kristoffersson was definitely one of Brink's cash cows. 'Why?' he asked innocently.

'Nothing really,' said Kristoffersson dismissively. 'It's just the police were trying to connect her death to Knut's old law firm.'

'Are they looking into all his old clients?'

'I don't know.'

Was Kristoffersson looking for someone in the same position as himself in the hope of using that information to deflect suspicion? Bjelk had no intention of helping him out.

'Gerda's no loss,' commented Bjelk as he finished off his wafer and licked his fingers.

Kristoffersson grunted in agreement. 'She blighted lives.'

'Did she blight yours?' Bjelk was intrigued to know what Brink had had on his neighbour.

'Just with allotment business.'

'Surely the police wouldn't want you to go to the station

just for that.' Bjelk couldn't help antagonising Kristoffersson, just pushing him that bit further.

'As I say, there was a misunderstanding,' he responded belligerently. He jumped up from the bench. 'Oh, and there was one other thing I wanted to say to you. Stay clear of Anna-Marie!'

This came as a shock. 'I don't know what you mean!'

'If I thought you were messing around with her, I'd kill you!'

'I don't think that's a word you should be bandying about right now.'

Kristoffersson hovered menacingly over Bjelk. His action had caught the attention of those sitting nearby. He leant down and spoke close to Bjelk's ear. 'Just a warning.'

'And if I ignore it?'

'I'll tell the police that I saw you on the path outside my cabin on the night Brink was murdered.'

Kevin was enjoying the ride. He hadn't come across Bea Erlandsson much and this was a chance to get to know her better. She turned out to be a thoughtful, interesting young woman. Anita had filled him in on Erlandsson's background in the force. She'd worked in the now-defunct Cold Case Group under a vindictive Alice Zetterberg and had escaped that by joining Erik Moberg's team, only to be landed with Zetterberg again. She was blossoming under Anita and was excited about the prospect of marrying her Brazilian girlfriend. As they sped along the E65 in the direction of Rydsgård, time passed quickly as they chatted happily. The Scanian countryside was bathed in midsummer sun. At this time of year, it reminded Kevin of the low, undulating landscape of Normandy with its wheat fields and apple orchards. He'd once had a holiday there and was telling an amused Erlandsson about how disastrous it had been. His elder daughter, Abigail, had started doing French at school, and he'd persuaded his wife, Leanne, that they should have a family holiday in France as a change from the usual trips to the beaches and bars of mainland Spain or the Balearic Islands. And camping would be fun, he'd said. He'd bought a large tent and all the equipment, and they'd driven down to Portsmouth. It had gone wrong from the moment the girls had both been sick in the car on the long journey south. The ferry crossing over the Channel had been rough and the weather during their stay had been poor. Leanne and canvas were not a good combination, especially when the tent flooded after a particularly heavy downpour. And the facilities didn't quite meet her expectations either: sharing the loos with large spiders and the wash room with other people's kids didn't appeal, nor did washing up in cold water and cooking on a spluttering gas ring at ground level. Abigail hadn't been much more enthusiastic, though Hazel, his youngest, still remembered the holiday with affection.

They turned off the E65 at Rydsgård and headed inland into more wooded countryside. Fifteen minutes later, they were driving up a rough track. At the end was an old stone farmhouse that had seen better days. The walls were sound but the corrugated iron roof needed attention, and the window frames were rotten in places. The garden was a wilderness and was surrounded by tall trees, which sucked out the light. This was Alice Asplund's summer home, and she was standing by the front door waiting for them; Erlandsson had rung ahead to warn her they were coming. Asplund was wearing an old pair of jeans and a green T-shirt that was blotched with white paint. There was paint on her hands, too. Outside the front porch was a rough wooden table with a flask of coffee and three mugs on it. Next to it was a bench and a camping chair.

'Sorry, I'm a bit of a mess,' she said in English when she noticed Kevin.

'Quite understand,' said Erlandsson. 'You've taken on

quite a project,' she added, casting an eye over the property.

'Yes. But it'll be worth it in the long run.' She waved for them to sit down and she poured out the coffees. 'I'm afraid I have no cookies.'

Kevin took his mug. He was too polite to ask if there was any milk.

'It's only a few days since we last spoke. Has anything happened?' Asplund asked as she perched on the camping chair.

'There's been a new development.'

'Concerning Linda?'

'No. Tony Yealand.'

'Has he turned up?'

'You could say that.'

'That's good. Where's he been hiding himself?'

'Vollerby. I'm sorry to have to tell you we've just dug him up.' Asplund appeared nonplussed. 'His body was in the field you were excavating.'

'Oh my God!' The colour drained from the archaeologist's face. 'How could he be...? It's impossible. I mean... I mean, are you sure?'

'We're sure. There's no doubt.'

Kevin was watching the woman's body language as the news was delivered. Her reaction was as expected: she was almost speechless; slightly incoherent. She'd been on his list of suspects simply because she was on the site the day Yealand was murdered. But without a motive, there wasn't much mileage in his hypothesis.

'Where? Where did you find him? On the main site?'

'No. He was where he'd wanted to dig but hadn't been allowed to by Professor Nordin.'

'I just can't believe it!'

'We have to ask you to take us through that day again,' said Erlandsson.

Asplund turned her coffee mug around in her hands, spilling some of the liquid on the table. She ignored the splash and seemed to concentrate on gathering her thoughts.

'Yes... yes, I see,' she said quietly. 'I was the last person to see him alive?'

'You're the last person who admits to seeing him alive.'

'OK.' She took a deep breath. 'So, I went down to Vollerby that morning. I oversaw the removal of the last of the equipment. Small earth digger, tents etcetera. The two guys who were transporting everything were there early. About eight. I got there at around the same time. Tony arrived a little bit later. Certainly before nine. The removal guys headed off sometime after nine. I went over to see Tony, who was pacing about and flattening odd bits of earth with a spade.' Both Kevin and Erlandsson had the same thought: that must have been the murder weapon; it wasn't on the site, so the murderer must have removed it. 'On the main site, you understand – he was nowhere near the anomaly. He said he wouldn't be long. The site looked fine to me as it was, and I suppose, looking back, it was surprising he didn't leave with me. Thinking about it now, perhaps he was waiting for me to go so he could start digging elsewhere.'

'That seems to have been the case,' Erlandsson agreed. 'So, you left the site about ten according to what you told us before.'

'Correct.'

'And after that?'

'I went back to the university department. Malmö, that is, not my department in Lund. I had a few things to sort out.'

'Can anyone corroborate that?'

'Yes. Yes they can. Ari Nordin.'

'Wasn't he meant to be in Denmark at the time?' Kevin asked.

'He was. He came over during the day. Around midday, I

seem to remember. He wanted to double check everything was tied up all right. We had a chat and then I didn't see him after that. I assume he went back to his family celebration.'

Erlandsson and Kevin exchanged glances.

'You didn't mention this before,' Erlandsson said accusingly.

'I can't remember you asking me.'

Twenty minutes later, they were back on the road. The lighthearted chit-chat of the journey over had been replaced by reflective thought. It was Kevin who broke the silence.

'I wonder why Nordin didn't mention he'd come over from Denmark on that Saturday.'

'Mmm. The impression he gave us was that he was in Roskilde the whole weekend. It's only when I spoke to his mother-in-law that we found out he'd come back to Malmö.'

'Odd isn't it? Meeting up with Alice Asplund to ask her about the site is innocent enough – and it gives him an alibi –'

'And her.'

'But what's strange is that he came all the way over from Roskilde to do so. Why didn't he just call her? And why didn't he mention his visit, if it was so innocent, to us?'

CHAPTER 39

On their arrival in Stockholm, Anita and Hakim made their way straight to the police headquarters in Kungsholmen. Hakim stared in awe at the impressive complex, which he hadn't visited before. Built in the imperial manner in the first decade of the 20th century, the older part, with its yellow stuccoed facade and central spire reaching high into the city skyline, is an imposing edifice, the style of which was replicated around the world as a symbol of law enforcement. But it was to the rear of this architectural gem that Anita steered Hakim – to a massive utilitarian block which could be found in a thousand cities. It was here that they had two appointments.

Their first was unsuccessful. Anita had hoped they could get a warrant to search Doctor Jan Hansson's apartment in an attempt to discover if he'd taken whatever Tony Yealand had found at the Vollerby site. She knew it was a long shot. The case for a warrant was very thin: a search for something unknown in the apartment of a man they couldn't prove was anywhere near the scene where another man, who may or may not have dug up the unknown something, was murdered. Even Anita wouldn't have issued herself a warrant on those grounds!

However, they had better luck when they talked to one of the officers who had been on the Hilma Moll investigation. Tindra Häggel had taken them through the details of the case again and agreed with the conclusion that Moll's death was just an accident. But when Anita filled Häggel in on their own investigations concerning Tony Yealand and Linda Vaux, an element of doubt began to creep into her mind.

'You're saying Ari Nordin had sex with two young women on the Vollerby dig?'

'Yes,' Anita confirmed. 'One's now missing. We suspect he has something to do with her disappearance. And now we have this murdered archaeologist who Nordin clearly disliked. But what's more pertinent is that Yealand was on the Birka dig but he wasn't formally interviewed.'

'No. I mean, everyone made statements but only Ari Nordin was officially interviewed. As far as we could gather, Hilma went off swimming by herself and got into difficulties. It was Nordin who found her. When it emerged that he was having an affair with her, it did raise doubts at the time, but the pathologist couldn't find any evidence of foul play. There wasn't any physical evidence that she'd been held under the water or anything like that. As for motive...'

'Trying to rid himself of an unwanted attachment?' Hakim suggested. 'He dumped the first of his students at Vollerby because she was too clingy.'

'And if Hilma was drunk, it might not take much to keep her head under the water,' Anita suggested.

Häggel pulled a face. 'My old boss won't be happy if you discover this wasn't an accident after all. He's a government adviser now.'

Can a cigarette take on a persona and express exasperation? When the tobacco burns red and brightly and the paper looks battered and bruised in the nicotine-stained fingers of Inspector Dan Olovsson, definitely. In fact, such was Olovsson's frustration with the allotments murder case that he lit a second cigarette from the embers of the first. He was loitering in the car park of Simrishamn police station. His protruding belly gave a rumble of hunger. According to his daughters, he should eat more and smoke less. It was a habit he felt disinclined to break; his fondness for nicotine had seen him through many a difficult situation. He persuaded himself that it kept him calm and sharpened his perspicacity. And he needed both these factors, as well as a dozen other attributes, to help him wade through this particular mire. He couldn't remember working on a case with so many possible suspects, all with good motives for murder. Yet the police hadn't got a shred of evidence to work with. Nor were they any nearer to finding Sigrid Clausson's attacker. It was all an incomprehensible mess.

His daughters were also always hinting that he should retire before the job killed him. But what would he do? Lie on a beach? He'd end up smoking even more out of boredom. He knew that their motives didn't entirely appertain to his health. With extra time on his hands, he could look after his grandchildren, perhaps do the school run. His mind flashed to the couple of schools he'd passed on his way over to Simrishamn that morning. He couldn't think of anything worse than standing at the gates making small talk with strangers. No, retirement wasn't for him. Besides, he enjoyed his job. He was the first to admit he hadn't set the world alight during his steady career, but now he felt he was making a meaningful contribution to Anita Sundström's team. She had confidence in him and always gave him and his ideas a fair hearing. He valued that.

Beyond the car park, the road was busy, as a train had just pulled into the station opposite. The doors swished open and a stream of travellers piled out onto the platform and, single-mindedly, headed for their cars or the expectant row of yellow Skånetrafiken buses parked in their bays. Some of the pedestrian passengers made a beeline for the town centre. A picturesque little town, Olovsson mused. But not for him. He couldn't wait to get back to Malmö and breathe in the heady mix of vehicle fumes and kebab aromas. And the quickest way back there was to solve this case.

He shoved the killing of Gerda Brink to the back of his

mind and began to focus on Sigrid Clausson, who was still lying in a coma in Ystad Hospital. He prayed that she would come round soon; an attack on a fellow police officer always gave him an uneasy feeling. Moreover, she might have information that could help them with the Brink investigation. His gut instinct told him the two cases were linked. He had gone over the attack in his head a hundred times, and now a niggle had wormed its way to the forefront of his mind. He would have to speak to Wallen.

That opportunity presented itself almost immediately. She came out of the police station as he was extinguishing his second cigarette. She raised an eyebrow in disapproval. He was surrounded by an ever-increasing pile of cigarette butts.

'I hope you're going to pick them up.'

'Yeah, yeah, 'course.'

Wallen was about to pass him and make her way into the town.

'Klara... there is something...'

'What?'

'About Sigrid Clausson's attack.'

Wallen sighed in desperation. 'If you've got anything new, *please* tell me.'

'It's the spade.' Olovsson's tummy gave another rumble. 'Sorry about that.'

'You said the spade?'

'Yes, the spade. It lived in the garden shed next to the decking. The shed hasn't got a lock.'

'Which is why it was easy for the assailant to find a weapon to hit Clausson with.'

'Yes, but she was found round the back of the cabin.'

Wallen sighed. 'That's why we think whoever it was was going to try and break in through the back window.'

'The thing is if Clausson disturbed the thief at the back of the cabin, how could he or she have got across the garden to the shed to grab the spade? Clausson would hardly have waited for whoever it was to get the weapon to clobber her with.'

'They had it with them already.'

'Yes. But it's not the sort of thing you'd use to break in through a window.'

'OK.' Wallen was now listening intently.

Olovsson hitched up his trousers. 'So there are two possibilities. Either this person had arranged to meet Clausson at the plot in the middle of the night and was waiting for her, armed with the spade. The other is that Clausson heard something going on at the back of the cabin and went to see what was up. Again, our mystery assailant had already got the spade from the shed...'

'And?'

'And was not trying to break in at all but was about to dig something up.'

After leaving police headquarters, Anita decided to stroll back to the hotel to take in the sights and sounds of the busy capital. It was early evening, and she got caught up in the crowds of commuters surging towards Central Station. Pushing her way through the throng, she headed up Kungsgatan and crossed pedestrianised Drottninggatan with its proliferation of smart cafés and bars, buzzing with energy and activity. There had been times when she'd missed all the sophisticated amenities that Stockholm had to offer – the theatres, concert venues, galleries and museums. She'd loved it when she was at the Police Academy, and later on when visiting her father. But now she found the place all a bit much. The character of the Stockholm she remembered was being nibbled away. Too many fast-food joints, too much traffic, too much noise. Malmö was more manageable, less manic, less pretentious. It didn't have to live up to an image, and was humbler as a result. And she could identify with the people; they seemed more real, not trying to be something they weren't. And if you wanted the big-city experience, you popped across the Bridge to Copenhagen.

She crossed the road on Sveavägen. She stopped for a moment and looked down. There, in front of her, was the metal plaque in the pavement marking the spot where Prime Minister Olaf Palme was assassinated in 1986 after leaving the cinema with his wife. Anita glanced towards the pedestrian tunnel through which the killer had escaped and disappeared into the realms of myth. There was still debate as to who had pulled the trigger on that fateful evening. Suddenly, Ewan Strachan came into her mind. She hadn't thought about him for some time. It was the Palme connection. Mick Roslin had been making a film of the events surrounding the Prime Minister's death. Roslin was another memory she'd tried to bury. She shook her head, clearing her mind of unwanted thoughts.

The hotel was tucked away on Luntmakargatan. Hakim was calling on a relative he hadn't seen for years. He described it as a 'duty call' to please his father. Anita checked in and went up to her room. She needed a shower. After freshening up, she went out and ordered a Hawaiian pizza the size of a swimming pool at the Italian restaurant round the corner.

As she drank the last dregs of her cold beer, she decided on an early bed. Tomorrow, she and Hakim were taking the boat out to Birka. They were to meet Professor Axel Råberg, who had run that fateful excavation six years ago. Maybe they would discover if the death of Hilda Moll was somehow linked to the events that had unfolded in Vollerby.

CHAPTER 40

Initially, the water had been choppy. Now, it was settling down and the day that had started wet was cheering up, which was just as well, as Hakim wasn't a good sailor. They had boarded the small tourist boat to Birka, on the island of Björkö, at the central Stockholm pier situated between the low-lying railway bridge which crossed Gamla Stan, and the iconic Town Hall, scene of the famous Nobel dinners, on the other side of the Klara Sjö canal. They could have used a police launch, though Anita would have had to justify the cost. And she was keen to trace the route that Tony Yealand had taken and discover how he had ended up joining the dig that year.

When the weather settled, she managed to get Hakim up onto the upper deck, where the view was uninterrupted. They sat among the other expectant passengers, who were marvelling at the sights of the city on either side of the fjord that was channelling them inland towards Lake Mälaren. On boarding, they had been greeted by a large Viking, named Ragnar (of course). This was the role that Tony Yealand had been playing six years ago when he caught the eye of the dig director, Professor Axel Råberg. Ragnar explained how the day would pan out and that he would keep the tourists informed about any points of interest they would pass on the way to the island. Once at Birka, he would conduct two tours – one in English, the second in Swedish. When the first group was on the tour, the other could have lunch in the restaurant. The young woman manning the bar/café counter on board the boat was also in Viking costume. It was a Viking away day.

During her time in the capital, Anita had seen many of its hundreds of islands which were strewn far out into the Baltic. Most of them were encrusted with the holiday homes of moneyed Stockholmers, though there were a few more modest dwellings which had been passed down through the generations. Every weekend during the summer months, their owners would head for the ferries or their own private boats and escape the city. The archipelago is the playground of Sweden's new super rich. The old socialist ideals which had been the Swedish mantra for generations had given way to capitalism on a grand scale: the country was now producing one of the world's highest proportions of dollar millionaires. But Anita had never before ventured inland to the Northern Archipelago. Here the story was no different. Many of the small islands they passed had several houses surrounded by trees and meadow, and even on the ones with more inaccessible terrain, a single dwelling clinging to a rock could be spied.

The boat made a few stops on the way, to pick up more passengers, including an enthusiastic walking group of spritely pensioners. Anita enjoyed the two-hour journey and by the time they moored on Björkö, even Hakim had perked up. Sitting in the middle of Lake Mälaren, Björkö is an unremarkable island that has a remarkable history: the settlement of Birka was one of the great Viking commercial centres of the 8th, 9th and 10th centuries – the hub of a vast trading network that spread its tentacles far and wide. But by the time of the Vollerby Vikings that Ari Nordin and his diggers had found, it had been abandoned. Now, all that was left of the town of Birka were some grassy hummocks peppered with a few trees. Rising above the complex of knolls, on a small rocky hill, was the island's most prominent feature – the Monument of Ansgar. This stone cross was built in the 1830s to commemorate the saint who, in the first half of the 9th century, had been foolhardy enough to accept the Pope's mission to convert the Swedes to Christianity. It was a tough gig, as the local population seemed quite happy with their paganism.

Axel Råberg was waiting for them on the small quayside. The professor was a compact bundle of energy, with uncontrollable grey hair that sprouted in all directions. He had a jolly, weatherbeaten face, and a chortling laugh, which made his eyes sparkle. He had extricated them from the general mass and taken them off in the direction of some rough-thatched, wooden buildings which were replicas of Viking dwellings at the time of Birka at its height. There was also an exhibition centre with models of the town, mannequins sporting contemporary dress and weaponry, and an impressive array of artefacts, both original and reproduction. Beyond the museum was a restaurant and tourist shop, both of which were filling up with the Swedish visitors. A booming Ragnar was busy corralling those who were taking the English-language tour, readying them for a route march around the landmarks.

The day was now hot, and Anita was glad she'd been liberal with the sunscreen that morning. She wasn't the only one enjoying the heat; as they neared the Viking houses, a thin, black snake slithered across the path in front of them. Thank goodness she hadn't brought Kevin with her – he'd have run a mile! She glanced at Hakim. He looked rather bored and disgruntled. She wasn't sure what he'd been expecting: perhaps something more from a UNESCO World Heritage Site. Råberg picked up on this.

'You've got to use your imagination. This place would have been buzzing. Merchants of every creed and colour from all over Europe and beyond made for this little island. Here, there was money to be made. Think of it: beads and ceramics from Eastern Europe, fabrics from Asia, Arab silver – all being traded for Swedish iron, skins and furs. Up to a thousand people would have been living here at any one time.'

Hakim took in the surroundings. 'There doesn't seem to be much to see now.'

'Underneath our feet is a different story. There are over three thousand burial mounds dotted around the island, including at least one of a female warrior,' he said, angling for Anita's approval. 'It's a veritable treasure trove for archaeologists like myself.'

They were standing next to one of the homesteads.

'This just gives you a flavour of what was once here,' Råberg said with a sweep of his arm towards other buildings that were in different stages of reconstruction.

'And it was six years ago that you first came across Tony Yealand?' He wouldn't know yet that Yealand had been murdered; that information still hadn't been released to the public.

'Yes. He was keen. Very keen.'

'We believe he was working on the boat we just came in on.'

'That's right. Dressed as a Viking,' he remembered with a laugh. 'Like that big fellow over there.' Ragnar was stomping ahead of his gaggle of tourists.

'And you took him on half way through the dig?'

'Yes. We had a place going spare, as one of my students had had to go home for family reasons. So why not? He had the requisite qualifications. When he left, he kept in touch for a while but, I must admit, I haven't heard from him for some time.'

'I'm afraid there's a good reason for that.' It was time for Anita to break the news. 'He's dead.'

'Dead?' Råberg was aghast.

'I'm sorry. That's one of the reasons we're here, Professor. He was murdered.'

Råberg looked shocked.

'We believe his death may have had a link with Birka. The

dig... the one that Tony joined –'

'I don't understand. I mean...'

'We can't give you any details other than that his death is connected with another dig.'

'Vollerby?'

'Yes.'

'I knew Tony was going to be there. He was going down with Jan. That's Doctor Jan Hansson. He's a colleague of mine at the university.'

'We know the doctor.'

'This is all too horrible!'

'As I say, we think the Birka dig may have a bearing on the case. I've read the police reports about the accidental death of Hilma Moll.'

'That was a tragedy. She was such a nice girl. Well... young woman. So much potential.'

'What can you remember about it?'

Råberg pointed towards the restaurant.

'We'd all got together over there. It was nearing the end of the dig and it was one of those impromptu gatherings. From nothing, it turned into a party. Mainly young people who'd been working hard letting off steam. I didn't know what had happened until Ari... that's Ari Nordin... came rushing back to tell us that he'd found Hilma's naked body. I made a statement at the time. We all did.'

'I appreciate that. What state was Nordin in?'

'Naturally very upset.'

'Did you know about his affair with Hilma?'

Now, he looked embarrassed. 'I got to hear of it shortly before Hilma's accident. I don't like that sort of fraternisation between senior staff and students. But I've been on enough digs to know these things happen.'

'Where was she found?'

'Over there,' Råberg said, pointing towards the lake.

They set off on the short walk to a small, narrow beach flanked by grass.

'She must have gone in here. This is where her clothes were found.'

'It's not that far from the restaurant,' Hakim observed, 'though the replica houses block the view. If she'd got into difficulties and called for help, would anyone have heard?'

'Pretty much everyone was in and around the restaurant. Music was playing... everything was quite noisy, so probably not.'

The lake water gently lapped against the shore; the aspect was calm and serene. On a day like this, it was hard to imagine someone getting into trouble out there.

'She was found just along from here,' Råberg said, indicating the strip of sand.

They trudged along the grass verge, trying to imagine Hilma's last moments.

'The police interviewed Ari Nordin a couple of times,' said Anita. 'Normal procedure after an accident of that type,' she qualified.

'Yes. They'd got wind of his affair with Hilma. That was awkward, to say the least.'

'Why awkward? Did they think he had anything to do with the incident?' 'Goodness, no! I say awkward because Ari's wife was coming to visit the site

a couple of days later.'

Anita and Hakim shot each other meaningful glances.

'How did he explain that one away?'

'Ari has his ways, as I've discovered over the years. I've seen him in action a few times – at conferences and the like. He plays away from home, as the English say.'

'So, he behaves himself on home turf?'

This produced one of Råberg's chortles. 'Have you met the formidable fru Nordin? She would have made a great shieldmaiden.' His eyes twinkled in amusement. 'I also believe she holds the purse strings. Or certainly, she comes from a wealthy family. A good reason for Ari not to rock the boat too much, wouldn't you say?'

They lapsed into silence. Hakim picked up a slim stone and tried to skim it. It managed two feeble skips before plopping out of sight.

Anita took up the thread again. 'Why did Ari Nordin so dislike Tony Yealand? We know there was some issue between them.'

Råberg tried to flatten his untamed hair. 'Right from the beginning, Ari wasn't keen on me letting Tony in on the dig. He didn't think he was a proper archaeologist. To Ari, Tony was just a glorified tour guide. Between you and me, he's a bit of a snob about such things. I knew Tony had an archaeology degree back in the UK, so I didn't see any problem. But it wasn't from what Ari regarded as a top British university. Bournemouth, I think it was.'

'No, I can't see what the problem was, either. But we know there was definitely something not right, apart from Hilma's death. We've seen an email Tony sent to a friend referring to his time here.'

'*It all goes back to that bloody trouble in Birka*,' Hakim quoted. 'But that sounds more like a specific event than just a general beef.'

'Well, yes. It may have had something to do with Hilma. She befriended Tony. Nothing sexual, you understand. Anyway, Tony wasn't that way inclined – you probably know he linked up with Jan later? I suppose Ari might have been jealous, though he had no reason to be. Tony and Hilma were just friends and liked to spend time together.' He shook his head slowly. 'I must admit, looking back, there was definite friction between them after Hilma's death. I wonder if they blamed each other for the tragedy.'

*

Anita was impatient to return to Stockholm. Having enjoyed the slow boat over to Birka, she now had to endure a chugging return to the city. As far as she was concerned, they'd done what they set out to do, and she wanted to get back to Malmö as soon as she could. She was even more determined to talk to Professor Ari Nordin.

While waiting to board the ferry, they grabbed a bite to eat at the restaurant, served by the same young Viking woman who'd been behind the counter on the boat on the way there. She and Ragnar would have had a long day by the time they finished.

They tucked into their tasty meat balls and lingonberry sauce and took in the view. They could see the lake from their outside table. It gleamed in the sunlight, and a light breeze rustled the trees at the water's edge. The same breeze gently rocked their ferry at its mooring. It was a perfect scene: nature joyfully embracing the summer. Sweden really was a beautiful country at this time of year. Anita was the first to admit that she rarely appreciated her surroundings; she took them too much for granted. Too involved with the seamier side of life. Which brought her thoughts back to Ari Nordin. Hakim read her mind.

'Do you think Nordin killed Hilma Moll?'

Anita put down her fork and took a drink from her bottle of beer.

'It's perfectly possible. He obviously disliked Yealand from the word go, but that dislike sounds to have been exacerbated after Hilma's death. Perhaps because Tony suspected him of drowning her?'

'The police report said Nordin was wet when he came here to the restaurant to announce he'd found the body.'

'Yes, but he said he had to get into the water to pull her onto the beach.'

'He's obviously a good liar, mind. He's managed to keep his numerous affairs secret from his wife.'

'Yes. And the accident, if accident it was, happened just before the wife was due to arrive. It was certainly convenient, avoiding a potentially awkward situation.'

Further speculation was interrupted by Anita's phone jumping into life.

'It's Klara.' She answered the call. 'Hi, Klara.'

Anita was silent as she listened to what Wallen had to say. Then she said, 'Yes. OK. Make sure you alert *Simrishamns Kommun* and the allotment committee before you start.'

'Some development?' asked Hakim, intrigued.

'The commissioner's going to love this. We're digging up somewhere else.'

CHAPTER 41

Kevin had the coffee brewing when Anita got out of bed at seven o'clock. The aroma had wafted through to the bedroom, and it was just the start she needed on what could prove to be a pivotal day. She and Hakim had managed to get on the last flight back to Malmö and they'd got a taxi from Sturup. It had dropped Hakim off first and by the time it reached Roskildevägen, Kevin was already asleep.

She slumped down at the kitchen table and he put a mug of strong, steaming coffee in front of her.

She grinned her thanks. 'By the way, I bought you this at the gift shop at Birka.' She handed over a small gold lapel badge fashioned in the image of a dragon prow of a Viking longship.

He was delighted and pinned it to his pyjama top.

She took a long sip of her coffee. At last, her British man was learning to make coffee the Swedish way. It revived her almost at once.

'Miss me?' she asked playfully.

'Not really. While you were having fun up north, I popped into Drumbar for a pint or two.'

'The Scots bar in Lilla Torg?'

'Yeah. Good atmosphere. I was in Taste of Britain, and Catherine and Karren recommended it.' Taste of Britain is a shop on Engelbrektsgatan that caters for expats and those who love everything British. When Kevin was feeling gastronomically nostalgic, he'd pop in for something from home. He'd got to know the owners pretty well.

'After your weird pickle, were you?' Anita pulled a face.

'Don't knock it. It perks up my sandwiches no end. Anyhow, how was Birka? Any use?'

'It was worthwhile. I'm satisfied we've got enough to pull Ari Nordin in for questioning. I think it's time we exerted a little bit of pressure on our professor.'

Klara Wallen had been surprised at how easily Anita had acceded to her request to dig up Gerda Brink's plot. She herself had been unsure as to whether it was worth doing, which explained why she thought Anita might veto the idea. The fact that the case seemed to have reached an impasse may have helped the decision.

She had sought permission from the council and the allotment committee. Both had grudgingly agreed. The optics weren't good, but everybody was keen for the police to solve the murder, and Clausson's attack, as soon as possible so that life could return to normal.

The briefing didn't take long. Olovsson was to oversee the operation and, though they'd co-opted a couple of uniformed officers to do most of the digging, Grahn and Brodd also volunteered to get their hands dirty. Wallen excused herself on account of not wanting to be there if nothing was found. She was, however, adamant in her instructions that the other plot holders were to be kept away from the area just in case they did find something. It was important that nothing slipped out into the public domain before Anita could be told and decisions made. She didn't want any undue speculation.

Ari Nordin had lawyered up. And judging by the cut of his jib, the guy was expensive. Bente Nordin had forked out for the best. And he was immediately on the attack when Anita and Hakim came into the interview room.

'I wish to make it clear that my client has been more than cooperative on several occasions, and bringing him in for questioning is decidedly crossing the line.'

Anita ignored him and spoke the time and date into the tape recorder. She listed those present and paused while the lawyer registered his name. Then she looked at him calmly and steadily.

'We are very grateful, herr Holmkvist, that your client has agreed to come in to answer more questions. When it comes to murder, we think that crossing the line is sometimes necessary.'

'It is unreasonable to believe that my client could be involved in such a crime,' Holmkvist protested.

'Professor Nordin is simply helping us with our enquiries at this stage. His name has come up in our investigations, both into the disappearance of the British student Linda Vaux and the murder of Tony Yealand.'

'I am here, by the way,' said Nordin in annoyance. 'I heard from Jan Hansson about you finding Tony's body down in Vollerby.'

Holmkvist tried to stop Nordin from saying any more. He ignored him. 'It's dreadful, of course, but I had nothing to do with it.'

'All right. Let's go back to when you first met Tony Yealand. It was on Birka?'

'Yes. He was a guide on the tourist boat from Stockholm. He showed interest in the dig, and Professor Råberg decided to take him on, as one of the students had dropped out.'

'And you weren't happy with that decision?'

'Not really. I didn't rate him. Simple as that.'

'We've heard from various sources, including Yealand himself, that there was at best antagonism between you – at worst, hatred.'

'Exaggerated.'

'How could you hear that from Yealand himself? He's

been dead for nearly a year!' butted in Holmkvist.

'From a couple of emails Tony sent to a friend shortly before he was killed.'

It was evident that this came as a shock to Nordin. A look of wary concern crossed his tanned features.

'He was friendly with Hilma Moll. Did that bug you?'

'Why should it? He was gay.'

'Were you having an affair with her at the time?'

'You don't have to answer that question,' Holmkvist interjected.

'Yes,' admitted Nordin. It was obvious the lawyer was beginning to get on his nerves. After all, his relationship with Moll had come out in the original investigation.

'Can we go back to the night that Hilma died?'

'The inquest said it was an accident. A tragic accident.'

'Our records state that the police interviewed you twice at the time. It seems they had their suspicions that it might not have been an accident when they discovered that you and Hilma had been having an affair.'

'And they also discovered their suspicions were unfounded.'

'But, Professor Nordin, the interesting thing is we've now discovered that your wife was due to visit you at Birka two days after Hilma's drowning. And the last thing you would want was to have Hilma around with your wife on the scene.'

'What are you suggesting?' This was Holmkvist.

'Hilma could have proved a huge embarrassment. And from what we hear, your wife is a force to be reckoned with. And, I believe, she is also a very wealthy woman.'

'That's a cheap jibe,' countered Nordin.

'Does your wife know about all your affairs?'

Nordin went quiet.

'I thought not. If she *had* found out about Hilma, what would have been the consequences, Professor? Divorce? Financial ruin?'

'My God, are you actually accusing me of killing Hilma?'

'This line of questioning is pure speculation,' interrupted Holmkvist before his client could go any further. Anita knew that was true.

'OK. Take us through the night that Hilma drowned.'

'What relevance has this to Yealand's death?' Holmkvist asked.

'You'll find out soon enough,' Anita said sharply.

Nordin took a drink of water before proceeding. 'There was a party at the restaurant. Everybody having a bit of fun. Too much drink, but not doing anyone any harm. I wasn't with Hilma.'

'But it was you who found her afterwards.'

'Yes.' His voice trembled. 'She was half washed-up on the beach. I had to pull her out of the sea.' He stopped to compose himself. 'We'd arranged to meet up later on. When she didn't show up, I went looking for her. That's when... well, you know the rest.'

'The party. No one seems to have seen her leave.'

'I certainly didn't.' Nordin paused reflectively. 'But I now know she left with someone.'

'Who?'

'Tony. Tony Yealand.'

'She left with Tony Yealand?' This was a surprise admission that didn't fit with the information Anita had gleaned from the police reports and statements. 'You didn't mention that at the time.'

'I didn't know at the time. Anyway, I had my own problems. I had enough trouble trying to keep my... my association with Hilma quiet. Unsuccessfully, as you know.'

'There's nothing in Tony Yealand's statement about leaving the party with Hilma.'

'He lied.'

'He lied? Why would he lie?'

'I would have thought that was obvious. It was his idea to go skinny dipping. It wasn't the first time he'd done it. He suggested it. But Hilma had had too much to drink. No wonder she got into trouble. He just left her out there. When she turned up dead, he wasn't going to admit it was his fault.'

'And how do you know this?'

Nordin grunted grimly. 'He told me.'

'Tony admitted it to you?' Anita remarked in astonishment. 'To Hilma's lover?'

'I don't think he even realised he'd told me. Late one night, about a week after Hilma's death, I found him down by the beach. He was very, very drunk. Almost incomprehensible. Sobbing his eyes out. It just all came spilling out... blaming himself. The guilt was eating the bastard up,' Nordin added with feeling.

Anita was beginning to understand where the hatred had stemmed from.

'Why didn't you mention this at the time?'

'By that time, the authorities had concluded it was an accidental drowning. If I'd brought it up then, it would only have meant renewed scrutiny of my relationship with Hilma.'

'And you couldn't have that with your wife around.'

'I can do without your sarcasm, Chief Inspector. When it came down to it, it would have been my word against his.'

Hakim took over.

'Let's move forward to Vollerby. We all know the background about Tony Yealand being at the site on Saturday the twelfth of August last year. We now know that was the day he was killed, and it was some time after he'd sent an SMS to Linda Vaux about his discovery. We are still unclear what that was all about. Now, you told us you were in Roskilde all that weekend, at your in-laws' fiftieth anniversary celebrations. But that wasn't entirely true: we found out that you came over to Malmö that day. Why?'

'I came to see Alice Asplund. Just to make sure everything had been cleared away properly.'

'You could have phoned her. That would have saved you a journey.'

'I could have, but I didn't.'

'Alice Asplund told us she met you when she returned from the site.'

'So, why are you asking?'

'Well, we've asked around the university and no one remembers seeing either of you.'

'There aren't many people around during the summer vacation, especially at weekends.'

'One of your own students was in all that day – in your department. It makes us wonder whether Alice Asplund was lying.'

Nordin turned to his lawyer with an exasperated expression. The lawyer nodded.

'OK, she was trying to protect me. I asked her, as a favour, to say we'd met up after I'd found out that my mother-in-law had told you that I'd gone to Malmö. I needed a reason that she and my wife would believe.'

'Why?'

'A colleague,' he muttered.

'A female colleague?'

'Yes.'

'It's amazing you have time to get any work done, Professor Nordin.' 'Inappropriate,' muttered Holmkvist, but Nordin took the remark on the chin.

'We'll need to check this colleague out,' Hakim said bluntly.

'Do you have to?'

'Of course we do.'

'She's married.'

'Married or not, she's your alibi.'

'I shouldn't need an alibi.'

'You most certainly do. You've already told us that you think Tony Yealand was responsible for Hilma Moll's drowning. You treated him badly on the dig, which is borne out in one of his emails and what other people have told us. You could have gone down to Vollerby after Alice Asplund had left that Saturday morning. You could have found Tony, who had made some sort of discovery. You coveted the object and, overwhelmed by your hatred of this man, you killed him and put him back in the hole that he had already dug.'

Nordin stared at Hakim in wide-eyed horror.

'That is simply not true! You must believe me!'

'Then there's Linda Vaux,' came in Anita as the professor was still reeling from Hakim's accusation. 'She came looking for Tony. She was intrigued to discover what he had unearthed. Of course, her reappearance would make people wonder what had happened to him. Where was he? Where had he been this last year? Of course, the murderer knew he was buried in that field. Linda had to be stopped.'

'Hang on there! I've already told *him*,' he said, pointing at Hakim, 'that I never heard from her.'

'We know she contacted Alice Asplund a month before she came over. But who was she most likely to go to first if not her lover from last summer? And if you'd already killed –'

The door opened behind Anita's back. She turned round angrily and saw Bea Erlandsson. 'What?' she demanded.

'So sorry, but you're needed on the phone.'

'Can't you see we're in the middle of an interview?'

'It's Dan. I think you'll want to speak to him.'

CHAPTER 42

Dan Olovsson was standing at the back of Gerda Brink's plot. There was very little of the garden area that had survived the digging process, just heaps of earth dotted everywhere as though the ground had been pounded by shellfire. The two uniformed officers were down to their shirt sleeves, and Grahn and Brodd had abandoned their jackets as the day got warmer. It was Brodd who had unearthed the two plastic bags at the back of the site, in the area behind the cabin adjacent to Thora Tarland's land.

The topmost bag contained twenty-one gold coins. On further scrutiny, they looked Arabic. The second bag was more remarkable. Olovsson carefully unpeeled the bubble wrap to reveal a small pile of gold panels about ten centimetres high and five centimetres wide. Most of the panels were dull and grimy, but a couple of them had had a cursory cleaning, revealing some beautifully worked cloisonné enamel depicting what looked like saintly or royal figures. On the edges of each panel were two tiny protrusions, mangled by age. Olovsson stared in wonder, instinct telling him that this was a thing of great antiquity. Carefully, reverentially, he placed the panels side by side. It was obvious that once, they would have been interlinked, forming some kind of chaplet or crown. It was an extraordinary collection to be found in the allotment of a known blackmailer. Had Brink extorted it from one of her victims? This was unlikely, as it didn't fit her *modus operandi* of extracting regular cash, as evidenced by her infamous notebook. And even if she had taken these items as a blackmail payment, why had she buried them?

Olovsson's brain was on fire. Now he brought the attack on Sigrid Clausson into the equation. It made complete sense that it was this... this treasure that the perpetrator was about to dig up when they were disturbed by the ex-detective. A far more plausible explanation than it being one of Brink's victims trying to break into her cabin.

The first thing Olovsson did was ring Klara Wallen, quickly followed by a call to Anita Sundström.

'This had better be good!' she snarled.

She was less snappy when Olovsson told her what they had found. When he'd finished, Anita said nothing. Had she gone?

'Right, Dan,' she said eventually. 'Take some photos on your phone. I need close-ups, especially of the coins. Send them to me as quickly as you can.'

Olovsson got Grahn and Brodd to take their discoveries into Brink's cabin and lay them out carefully on her table. Then he began to photograph them for Anita.

Anita returned to the interview room a few minutes after speaking to Olovsson.

'Sorry about that.'

'I think my client has answered enough questions for one day,' said Holmkvist officiously.

'We've nearly finished. To your knowledge, Professor, have there been any archaeological digs in or around Simrishamn in recent years?'

Hakim was taken by surprise at the question.

Nordin was puzzled, too. 'Not that I'm aware of.'

'Is this relevant?' Holmkvist asked.

'It could be.'

'Well, until you make your mind up, I assume my client can go.'

'Not just yet. I'd like to hang on to him a little bit longer,' Anita said, staring at her phone.

'This is ridiculous,' said Holmkvist, pushing his chair back and getting to his feet.

'You can go, herr Holmkvist, but I'd appreciate it if Professor Nordin remained for a few minutes. There's something I'd like him to see.'

Klara Wallen pushed her way under the police tape that Olovsson had set up to keep inquisitive plot holders at a distancc. By that time, most of the curious ones had left, though there was a journalist Wallen recognised who was still hanging about.

'Anything you can tell me about what's going on?' he asked.

'Nothing,' Wallen replied brusquely.

She found Grahn and Brodd inside Brink's cabin, and Olovsson busy snapping away with his phone. Spread out on the table was the treasure trove: twenty-one gold coins, and seven enamelled gold panels neatly placed in a row.

Wallen was mesmerised by the hoard. Even through the dirt, she could see that the panels were beautifully and intricately worked, each depicting a robed figure surrounded by birds and flowers. The figure on one of the two panels which had, to some extent been cleaned, wore a crown.

'So, what do you reckon to all this, Dan?'

Olovsson stopped clicking. 'Some kind of headpiece – a crown perhaps. You can see how all these sections must once have been linked. As for the coins, are they part of the same hoard, or something completely different?'

'And what was Brink doing with them?' Brodd mused.

'Another blackmail victim we don't know about?' suggested Wallen. 'Well, Dan, you were right. This is what Clausson's assailant must have been after. But who could that possibly be?'

'More to the point,' said Olovsson, 'where did all this lot

come from? Discover that and we'll have our attacker.'

'But does that bring us any closer to who killed Gerda Brink?'

There had been an awkward ten minutes before Anita's phone pinged. Holmkvist had chosen to remain with his client; it was more on the clock after all. Nordin sat there, silent and broody, and Hakim just looked perplexed, as Anita wasn't going to enlighten him in front of the other two. She flicked through the photos Olovsson had sent her.

'OK,' Anita said finally, straightening her back. 'Professor, could you look at these photographs, please? As you can see, they are of gold coins. Are they at all similar to the two coins that were brought to you by the antiques dealer, Thilde Meerwald?' She handed Nordin her phone.

He glanced at the first photo, then scrolled to a second.

'Can I enlarge it?'

'Be my guest.'

Nordin used his thumb and finger to widen the picture. He started to nod.

'This one looks like the two coins the antiques dealer brought to me.'

He moved on to the other photos that Olovsson had taken of the coins. He continued to nod his head. 'Definitely Arabic. Definitely similar.'

'That solves one mystery,' Anita said to Hakim. 'We now know who went to Meerwald's shop.'

With his eyes still firmly on the phone, Nordin asked, 'Where did you find these?'

'I can't say at the moment.'

Nordin absently scrolled to the next picture. He was about to hand the phone back to Anita when he stopped in mid action. His eyes bulged in amazement. His breathing became heavier and his mouth gaped. His hand shook and he nearly dropped the phone. He didn't speak but continued to flick through the photos. Then he stopped, enlarged one and gasped.

'Holy shit! It's not a myth!'

CHAPTER 43

After work on Friday, Anita and Kevin had decided to forego the pub, and they wandered into Pildammsparken instead. It was a pleasant evening, and the soft smell of summer made the walk more enticing. They weren't the only ones enjoying this quasi-rural haven in the heart of the city. The happy voices of children, the cackles of geese on the lake and the odd skateboarder whizzing past did nothing to inhibit the sense of peace and well-being they felt in each other's company. Pildammsparken was spread wide enough to persuade Anita that the bustling urban life was being lived in another place, and she knew she was lucky to have it on her doorstep.

They flopped down on a bench, and Kevin listened sympathetically as Anita, exhausted by the growing complexity of the cases she was overseeing, unburdened herself to him. He was a useful sounding board. She had spent much of the last couple of days with an increasingly agitated commissioner. The discovery in Gerda Brink's plot had thrown them all into a state of confusion.

She had described to Theo Falk – and later Kevin – the impact the photos from Simrishamn had made on Ari Nordin. His surprise and excitement at the images had superseded all other emotions – his anxiety, his anger, his frustration had vanished in a puff of smoke and derailed the entire interview. So much so that Anita had let him go – but under strict instructions that he was not to breathe a word about the discovery to anyone. If he did, he would need more than a fancy lawyer to keep him out of trouble.

He'd confirmed that the coins looked similar to the ones that Brink had shown to the antiques dealer, Thilde Meerwald. That was the main point of interest to Anita. She hadn't expected Nordin to flick on to the next images – those of the crown. But when he did, it was his reaction to what he saw that had changed everything.

'This is incredible!' Nordin could hardly hold the phone steady. Anita thought he was having a fit.

His wide-eyed expression passed from his lawyer to Anita and Hakim. 'Do you know what I think this is?'

'No.'

He shook his head in disbelief. 'This looks like the Basil Crown!'

Anita had heard Kevin mention it after his visit to Alice Asplund, but she hadn't been paying much attention.

Hakim was more aware of its importance. 'I thought that was meant to be a myth,' he said.

'So did I,' spluttered Nordin. He put the phone on the table for them all to see. He had blown up one of Olovsson's pictures: the stylised image of a white-bearded, haloed figure wearing a bejewelled golden crown with a sword at his side. It was difficult to make out the colours of the figure's clothing, but a gold haubergeon was easily discernible, and the tunic could have been purple: the colour of kings. Nordin was convinced. 'This is undoubtedly Basil the Second. The Byzantine Emperor.' He was almost pleading with them to understand the importance of the image.

'So, it's worth something?' Anita asked.

He gave her a horrified grimace. 'Worth something?' he expostulated. 'This is priceless! But it's not its monetary worth that's important. It's a stunning piece of history that most experts didn't even think existed.'

Where was Kevin when she needed him?

'Where in God's name did you find it?' Nordin demanded.

'I'm afraid I can't tell you that.'

Realisation dawned. 'Simrishamn! It is, isn't it? Is that why you asked about Simrishamn before?'

Anita said nothing; she couldn't exactly deny it.

'This has to be examined immediately. Authenticated... catalogued. And then exposed to the world!'

'Not yet, Professor. You're telling no one.' Then she had issued her stern warning about speaking to anyone else.

Later that day, the crown and the coins were brought over to Malmö, where they were sent off for forensic analysis. As they had been carefully wrapped in modern-day plastic, there might be clues as to who had handled them besides Gerda Brink. The consensus among the team was that Brink must have got the artefacts from someone else and then buried them in her plot. But who was that someone? And where had that someone found such a valuable hoard? There was also a strong conviction that the same person was responsible for the attack on Sigrid Clausson.

On her way home that evening, Anita ruminated about all the speculation. There were many imponderables, but the factor that sat the least comfortably with her was the connection between the priceless artefacts and Gerda Brink's blackmail operation. She needed to talk to Kevin.

'We're no further forward with Gerda Brink's murder, or Tony Yealand's, for that matter. As for Linda Vaux...'

Kevin knew that he would have to return to the UK next week unless something concrete on the Linda Vaux front turned up in the meantime. Superintendent Kellet had made it plain that he couldn't waste any more time over in Sweden: 'Leave it to the local plod.' Kevin would be returning empty-handed, which would be no consolation for Linda's grandparents.

They sat in silence for several minutes, each lost in their own thoughts.

Anita placed her hand over Kevin's.

'I've liked you being here.'

'I hope it's helped.'

'You've kept the apartment tidy, so yes.'

'It's nice to know I'm good for something.'

She patted the back of his hand.

'Come on, let's go back. I'm hungry.'

They made their way slowly towards the great grassy area surrounded by trees, known as The Plate. As they turned into the long avenue that funnelled them towards Roskildevägen, Anita's phone started buzzing. She took it out of her pocket.

'It's Eva Thulin.' Anita answered it. 'Hi, Eva. You're not still working on a Friday night?'

'You know me. Can't stop. Actually, I need the overtime. I'm having to pay for an extension. And before you jump to conclusions, it's a building, not my husband's.'

'I don't jump to conclusions. It's only your dirty mind at work. Have you anything for me?'

'I have, actually. Not sure how helpful it'll be.'

'Shoot.'

'We've examined the modern materials that the crown and coins were wrapped in – bubble wrap and plastic bags. Three sets of prints. One was Gerda Brink's – they were taken during her autopsy. The crown also had three sets and the coins four. Brink's prints were on everything. The others aren't on the database.'

'So, the only ones we know about are Brink's?'

'Hold your horses. Wait for this... we did manage to extract DNA off one of the sets of prints on the artefacts, and we found a match. They belong to that guy your lot dug up at Vollerby. Tony Yealand.'

CHAPTER 44

Kevin had suggested that Eva Thulin's news was a breakthrough... of sorts. Anita didn't quite see it that way. It only created more mystification and did nothing to further either of their murder investigations. But at least it did give credence to Yealand's last message to Linda Vaux. He certainly did find something, but how had it ended up in Gerda Brink's allotment?

One consequence of Thulin's findings was that the weekend was cancelled and the whole team was pulled in to the polishus. There were a few grumbles at first, but they dissipated when Anita told them about Thulin's discovery. They were all as intrigued as they were baffled.

First, Anita got Hakim to brief Klara Wallen's group on their investigation into the death of Tony Yealand and where they had got so far. Then Wallen reciprocated with her case. Now, through the DNA extracted from Yealand's teeth, they had a link between the two but could make neither head nor tail of the connection.

'So what we have,' Anita started in summary, 'is two separate murders, committed nearly a year apart, in different locations. Both victims were killed by blunt force trauma. That's the one thing they have in common. There's nothing else that, on the surface, ties Gerda Brink to Tony Yealand... other than the gold coins and what we now believe is the mythical Basil Crown. I think we can assume that the artefacts are the ones that Yealand found at Vollerby. His DNA is on the pieces of the crown and some of the coins. And the fact that his DNA is not on the plastic wrappings indicates that he didn't bag them himself. It's likely that the killer did that. Of course, whatever they were originally in would have rotted away by now. The finds would certainly explain his excited message to Linda Vaux. As for the coins, they seem to be the same as those taken to Thilde Meerwald's antiques shop; we can assume that Brink went to have them valued, as her fingerprints were on the other coins. Who the owners of the other two sets of prints are is a mystery, though one *must* belong to Yealand's murderer. Anyway, though Meerwald had the coins authenticated, Brink seems to have been frightened off doing anything more with them in case awkward questions were asked. So, how did she come by them? Why were they buried? We know that Tony Yealand couldn't have taken them to Simrishamn, as we believe he was killed the day he found them. There must be a connection between Vollerby and Simrishamn. Do any of our suspects in the Yealand case have a connection to Simrishamn? Conversely, do any of our Simrishamn suspects have a link to anybody on the Vollerby dig? That's what we've got to find out.'

'Does Linda Vaux fit into all this?' Kevin asked, as the missing woman was his priority.

'Again we don't know,' answered Anita. 'Whoever had the artefacts wouldn't want Linda coming over and stirring things up. Perhaps that's the reason she disappeared.'

'Which points to someone on the dig.'

'On the face of it, yes. Yet they ended up on Brink's property, which brings us back to Simrishamn.'

'It's now possible that Brink was killed because of the crown,' Olovsson pointed out. 'And it had nothing to do with her blackmailing operation.'

'That's a possibility.'

'And the killer came back after Brink's death to dig up the treasure and was interrupted by Sigrid Clausson,' Olovsson suggested.

'Again, that's a possibility.'

'And Ari Nordin?' asked Erlandsson.

'He was genuinely taken aback when he saw the photograph of the crown. And incredibly animated. Would you agree?' Anita asked, turning to Hakim for confirmation.

'That was my impression. Unless he's a fantastic actor. And if he *had* killed Yealand, he would have seen the crown on site. Then he would have had to hide it away somewhere. Why choose Brink's allotment?'

'Unless Yealand's killer passed the artefacts on to one of our Simrishamn suspects – or someone we haven't yet come across,' said Wallen. 'Who then used them to pay off Brink.'

'This is doing my head in,' moaned Brodd.

'You and me both, Pontus,' said Anita. 'As far as Nordin is concerned, I don't think he killed Yealand. His alibi checks out: he was bedding a married colleague. But I'm certainly not ruling him out of being involved in Linda's vanishing act.' She glanced around at the team. They had been working so hard, yet they had nothing to show for it. They had to find the missing link. 'Right, let's get on.'

By seven o'clock that evening, Anita had wound things up. They'd found one connection. It was Liv who discovered a detail they'd actually had in their possession all the time. Jan Hansson had been brought up in Simrishamn when his father had moved there for work.

'We'll speak to Hansson again next week. Look, take tomorrow off, and let's start again on Monday. I'll go over to Simrishamn in the morning. It's where the artefacts were found. Maybe we can uncover something else there.'

'What about at this end?' Hakim asked.

'I want you to double-check Hansson's movements in Malmö. Did he have time to go to Simrishamn after Yealand's murder took place? He admitted he went to Vollerby that weekend. No one saw him but he *was* in Skåne, so he could have passed the artefacts on to Brink. With this in mind, Bea, can you go and have a chat with Alice Asplund again and ask her if she saw any sign of Hansson that weekend? Both said they were at the site on the Sunday.

'Klara, you can look for a possible link over in Simrishamn. See if Hansson's father was a client of Knut Fredriksson's. Oh, and by the way, the commissioner wants to announce the finding of the crown on Monday afternoon. He hopes someone might come forward with information. Waste of time if you ask me. I suppose, Bea, while you're with Asplund, you can tell her that her precious crown has turned up.'

'Will do.'

They finished off by saying their goodbyes to Kevin, who was booked to fly back to the UK on Tuesday morning.

They all drifted away and Anita and Kevin had a last drink at The Pickwick on their way back to the apartment.

'It's all so frustrating,' Kevin said as his pint hovered close to his mouth. Then he took a deep draught of the beer.

'It's maddening,' said Anita. 'I feel we're so close, yet we seem to be nowhere nearer any solutions. The trouble is I can't make any sense of the latest development.'

'Try and forget it for a while. Let's have an idle day to ourselves tomorrow. Let's go down to the beach if it's nice.'

She gave a half nod of agreement. But Kevin knew she couldn't relax until she had some kind of result. These cases were all-consuming, and there was nothing he could do or say which would relieve her torment.

CHAPTER 45

Bea Erlandsson had followed Anita along the E65 as far as Rydsgård before turning off and heading inland. The murky drizzle that had descended as they left Malmö had gradually been replaced by an insipid sun breaking through. The forecast promised continued improvement. The last few weeks had been exasperating for all of them and Erlandsson could see the toll it was taking on her boss. She knew the pressure Anita was under trying to solve two murders simultaneously. The press and public weren't known for their patience. In the unremitting despondency within the team, her task today was being the bearer of some extraordinary tidings: news of the discovery of the Basil Crown. Asplund had been right all along. OK, she wouldn't have the satisfaction of finding it herself, but surely she would be delighted to prove all the doubters wrong. That in itself would boost her credibility and help her career. Erlandsson imagined that female academics, as in so many other professions, had to work twice as hard as their male equivalents just to hold their own. It was certainly the case in the police. That's why she always appreciated Anita's support. And Maria, too, had been a rock, tolerating with benign equanimity her unsocial hours and the emotional toll that such a demanding job inevitably took on her partner from time to time. Bea's thoughts strayed to the nice day they'd had together yesterday: a walk along the coast, followed by a lazy lunch. After a difficult few years, both professionally and personally, she was at last finding a level of contentment: she was happy in her job, and she'd found her soulmate.

She reached the turning off the main road and drove down the track to Asplund's house. The site was well shaded by trees, which only allowed disparate shafts of sunlight to break the gloom. Erlandsson didn't much like the location – she couldn't cope with being hemmed in like this. Asplund's car was parked at the side of the house, so she was around.

Erlandsson got out and made her way to the front door. She knocked and waited. There was no sound from inside. She tried again. Still no luck. She then tried to peer in through the grimy front window, but she couldn't make anything out. Stepping back onto the grass, she called out, 'Alice!' All was quiet. Maybe Asplund was round the back. Bea hadn't ventured round there on her previous visit with Kevin.

The house was definitely in need of modernisation. Asplund had taken on quite a project. At the back, there were some stone steps leading down to what was probably a basement. Erlandsson called again. Nothing. Had Asplund gone for a walk, or maybe a run? She was a fitness freak. In one corner of the garden was a medium-sized wooden barn. Most of the panels were badly weathered and some had wide cracks in the wood, and the roof was in disrepair. Another big job. Erlandsson stepped over to the barn. Could Asplund be inside? There was a padlock hasp and staple on the large double doors, but the lock itself was hanging loose. She put her weight against the door and gave a mighty heave. As it swung open, she was hit by a musty smell of age and neglect. It took a few moments for her eyes to adjust to the dimness inside.

And then her heart skipped a beat.

Anita entered the incident room in the Simrishamn police station to find that only Dan Olovsson was around.

He greeted her with a 'Morning.'

'Where are the others?'

'Klara and Pontus have gone down to the allotments. They're asking around about possible connections to Jan Hansson. At lot of the older plot holders might have known the family from back in the day. Joel is going though Knut Fredriksson's legal archives to see if there's any connection to the Hanssons and, by association, with Brink.'

'Good.'

'I'm here holding the fort. Coffee?'

'Go on.'

A few minutes later, they were sitting at the table with their drinks. Olovsson started his finger-drumming. Something was on his mind.

'Your thoughts, Dan?'

He stopped drumming. 'It's the timing that puzzles me. If it *was* Hansson, he wouldn't have had much time to decide what to do with the artefacts. They would have been as much of a surprise to him as they'd been to Yealand. He'd have had to react quickly, as he was due to go back to Stockholm and then straight off to Peru.'

'Your point?'

'Well, if it was him, he must have known Brink really well. Firstly, to approach her with the artefacts at such short notice, and then to trust her to look after them while he was away.'

'Except she wasn't trustworthy, was she? She was trying to get the coins valued. If Meerwald had offered her a price there and then, she might well have cashed them in.'

'That's almost by the by. Unless Hansson passed them on to someone else first, who just happened to be one of Brink's blackmail victims.' He coughed raspingly to clear his throat. 'But that would be too much of a bloody coincidence.'

'Normally, I would agree. But we're getting desperate.'

'Maybe the link is up there somewhere,' Olovsson said with a nod in the direction of the board.

Anita turned to look. There were far more photos on it

than the last time she'd been over.

'What are all those?' she asked, pushing back her chair.

'Joel's uncle took the shots at Knut Fredriksson's funeral for the local paper. A number of Brink's victims were in attendance.'

Anita stood up and went over to get a closer look. She gazed at the photos and picked out the Kristofferssons, Einar Wallter and Viktor Bjelk. Their heads had all helpfully been ringed in biro. Then she came to the one with Brink talking to the funereally dressed younger woman.

Olovsson saw that Anita was concentrating on the photograph. 'That's Fredriksson's niece. She gave the eulogy.'

'Oh my God!' she said slowly. 'That's our connection! That's Alice Asplund!'

Anita turned round as though in a trance. Suddenly, she snapped out of it. Everything was falling into place.

'Shit! I've sent Bea out to see her. Dan, we've got to move! Now!'

There was a tarpaulin over the roof of the Dormobile. It didn't hide the distinctive green-and-white bodywork. Erlandsson slowly advanced towards Linda Vaux's vehicle, her mind trying to process the information that the old Volkswagen was feeding her. Alice Asplund was the person the young student had come to – not Ari Nordin as she and Hakim had thought. *So why had Asplund still got the vehicle in her barn? And where was Linda?* The questions buzzing through her head distracted her long enough not to notice a figure suddenly appear behind her. Before she could react, she was knocked violently to the ground.

Anita had started the car by the time Olovsson wheezily climbed in beside her. She was about to drive off when she noticed that he wasn't armed.

'Where's your pistol?' she challenged.

'Inside.'

'Bloody get it!' She hadn't got her own firearm with her. It hadn't seemed necessary when she'd set out.

The delay made her even tetchier, and she impatiently gunned the engine while she waited. She glowered at a flustered Olovsson as he hurried back into the car.

They screeched out of the police station car park and broke the speed limit all the way to the boundary of the town.

Alice Asplund, in her running gear, forced Erlandsson down the stone steps leading to the cellar. Erlandsson's own pistol was pushed into the middle of her back. There was a key in the door, which she was forced to turn. Asplund shoved her into the room.

It smelt of damp and excrement. A thin strobe of light from the high, narrow window, which was at ground level, penetrated the gloom. As Erlandsson staggered across the floor, her head still pounding from Asplund's blow, she was aware of something or someone stirring. There, in the corner, was a figure sitting on a filthy mattress. As her eyes became accustomed to the dingy surroundings, she could see that it was a young woman with dank straggly hair, thin to the point of emaciation, dressed in dirty, soiled jeans and a T-shirt. She was barely recognisable as the happy, smiling girl in the photo they had of her next to her Dormobile in Denmark, but Erlandsson still knew who she was. Linda Vaux had been in here for over five weeks.

'It's OK, Linda,' Erlandsson said, trying to sound reassuring. Vaux instinctively shied away and said nothing.

'I'm afraid it's not OK,' said Asplund, her blue running singlet still sweaty from her run in the woods. 'You've given me another problem.'

Erlandsson could see that the hand holding her police

pistol was shaking slightly. It was obvious that Asplund wasn't used to wielding a gun. That made her even more dangerous – if she panicked, it might suddenly go off. She would have to try and calm the situation and talk her out of doing something drastic.

'Look, Alice, don't make this any worse for yourself. Why don't you give me the gun and we can talk about things?' Erlandsson held out a hand.

Asplund reacted badly to the suggestion. She raised the weapon so it was pointing at Erlandsson's head.

'It's too late.'

'No... no, it's not. Linda's still alive.'

'Tony's not.'

'What's that about Tony?' a weak voice said from the corner.

'She killed him,' Erlandsson said in English, realising that Linda can't have been following the conversation.

'Oh no, no!' the girl sobbed.

'I didn't want to do it, Linda,' Asplund said bitterly. 'It was in the moment. I... I had no alternative.'

'We've found the Basil Crown in Gerda Brink's allotment,' Erlandsson continued in English, perceiving that Linda might be a useful witness. 'You were proved right, Alice. It does exist.'

'Being *right* would have been no fucking use! Yealand would have got the credit for finding it. An incompetent fool like that solving one of history's greatest mysteries! It was *my* dream; it should have been *my* discovery.' Her voice rose; she was almost in tears.

'Did he call you?' Erlandsson asked.

'No,' she laughed dryly.

'Tell me what happened, Alice.'

'Why not?' She seemed to relax slightly, but the weapon was still aimed at Erlandsson's head. 'I decided to go back later that afternoon to make sure he'd done his job. And then I found he'd dug up this spot at the far side of the field. He was... he was so full of himself, so elated. He was sending a message to Linda when I reached the trench he'd dug. I didn't know why he was on such a high until he showed me what he'd found. There it was! *My* crown. It was real! I could touch it. It was like he'd stolen my life's work. I just snapped. I picked up his spade... and... and before I realised it, he was lying there. Dead.' Tears began to dribble down Asplund's cheeks. 'I'm not a murderer,' she said hoarsely.

'I know you're not. You couldn't help it. That's why you can't kill us. Keeping Linda alive proves that. If I'm unharmed, that will go in your favour, too.'

'What was that?' Asplund said suddenly.

Anita switched off the engine. The satnav had helped them reach the road end at breakneck speed then they took the track to the house at a more sedate pace. They could see two cars; she recognised the one from the pool Erlandsson had taken that morning.

Anita and Olovsson stepped gingerly out of the car, leaving the doors open.

'We'll take it easy,' Anita said in a hushed voice.

Olovsson pulled out his pistol.

'I'll go to the front. You go round the back. Don't make a bloody sound.'

Asplund stopped straining her ear and turned back to her captives.

'I don't want to harm either of you,' she said.

'There's no reason to.'

'Of course there is! You've left me no choice.'

'There's always a choice, Alice. How would you explain my disappearance? My colleagues know I'm here. My boss sent me. If I don't go back soon, you'll have half the police in Skåne on your doorstep.'

Erlandsson could see that Asplund was wavering.

'I'm so sorry, Linda,' said Asplund. 'I couldn't have you asking questions about Tony.'

Erlandsson took advantage of an increasingly distraught Asplund and took a step towards her.

'Don't move!' Asplund ordered as the pistol shook in her hand.

Erlandsson held up her hands in acceptance. 'Take it easy, Alice.' She was trying to remain calm but her insides were churning and her mouth was dry. 'This doesn't have to end badly.'

Asplund was sweating. She wiped her brow with her left palm. The tension and indecision were getting to her.

Erlandsson wasn't sure what to say next, her mind desperately sifting through options and topics to keep Asplund talking for as long as possible. She knew help wouldn't arrive. Her only hope was to persuade the woman to give herself up.

'Alice, one thing that can't be taken away from you is the fact that the Basil Crown exists. It wasn't a myth. You believed in it. You'll be recognised for that belief.'

'But I've ruined all that. Tony... what I did in Simrishamn...'

'You were a lone voice. No one believed you, but they've been proved wrong.' Was that a sound on the steps behind Asplund? Erlandsson kept talking. 'Your faith in the crown was never shaken. It's your legacy. No one can take that away from you.' Her lips felt cracked and her voice croaked. She forced herself to carry on. 'Don't throw it away. Please, Alice, hand over the gun. Let's finish it... now.'

Asplund was now openly crying. Little by little, she relaxed her grip on the pistol. Her hand came forward a fraction... slowly... slowly...

Suddenly, Olovsson burst into the room.

Asplund jumped in fright and the pistol went off. Almost simultaneously, Olovsson fired his own gun. Linda Vaux screamed.

CHAPTER 46

It was a week after Bea Erlandsson's death. The shock of it still hung in the air and wrapped itself like a blanket around the polishus. The whole force had been affected, but Anita's team had been nothing short of traumatised. This was the hardest time she had experienced since the murder of her mentor, Henrik Nordlund. Then, she had only had to deal with her own grief. Now, she had to handle a collective sorrow and be there for all her colleagues. It was an enormous burden to bear. Erlandsson had been well liked, and her death had touched everyone. Anita also had to cope with her distraught family, who had come down from Örebro, as well as Maria, whose life had been turned upside down in a moment. As for Dan Olovsson: he was taking compassionate leave. In all his years of service, he had never been required to shoot anyone before, and he blamed himself for Asplund firing the bullet which had killed Bea Erlandsson.

And who was supporting Anita? There was a nagging guilt she couldn't shift. It was she who had sent Erlandsson to Asplund's country house and, *ipso facto*, it was she who was partly responsible for her death. Kevin had repeatedly told her that she wasn't to blame. He'd wanted to stay and help her through the trauma, but he had to escort Linda Vaux back to Britain after her medical check-up and extensive debriefing. At least for one family there was a happy ending. But before he left, he persuaded a reluctant Anita to take her planned annual leave; he thought the break would help distance her from the tragic events.

Anita was supping her second cup of coffee in Commissioner Falk's office. The man across the desk was far less harassed and much more amenable now that the two murders had been cleared up. The solving of the crimes had given him a brief respite from his critics, and public sympathy, for once, was with the force after the killing of the young detective. He and Anita were taking part in a much-delayed debriefing.

'Please take me through the events, Anita. Fill in the gaps.'

It was a reasonable request. In the days that followed the death of Alice Asplund, Anita had been piecing together what they actually knew and what they had gathered from a distraught but clear-minded Linda Vaux. It all seemed to fit.

'I thought it all began in Birka, but I was wrong. Ari Nordin had nothing to do with anything... well, inadvertently. It actually all began with the geophysics results at the site at Vollerby. For some reason, Tony Yealand became obsessed with this anomaly. The dig team didn't have the time or resources to look beyond the main section of the site, which had already produced dramatic results. Yealand was tasked with clearing up the place ready to return it to agricultural use. Left to his own devices, he dug up the spot where the anomaly was. And he made this amazing discovery –'

'The Basil Crown.'

'Exactly. And the gold coins. It was this find that he referenced in his excited SMS to Linda Vaux. But it just happened that Alice Asplund had returned late in the afternoon on that Saturday to check up on Tony. She didn't trust him to do the job properly.'

That had been a real turn-up.

'Asplund must have been both ecstatic and horrified at what Tony had found. From what Linda told us from that final conversation in the cellar with Bea, Asplund had in her hands the culmination of all her dreams, and the means to establish her reputation forever. It would prove all the condescending sceptics wrong – the crown really *did* exist. The only problem was that Tony would steal her thunder. *He* had found it against all the odds. *He* would get the acclaim. This was someone that all the senior people on the dig regarded as a second-rate archaeologist. Stolen glory plus humiliation. It was too much for Asplund and it pushed her over the edge. She killed Yealand and pushed him back in the grave with the original Viking body, and then she covered her tracks. She was given an alibi by default, as Ari Nordin asked her to lie about them meeting up in Malmö that afternoon. That was to cover his own tracks: his liaison with someone else's wife. Asplund did go back on the Sunday as she said. That was for appearances' sake.'

'So, Tony disappears.'

'After his public break-up with Jan Hansson, no one was particularly interested in what happened to him. He wasn't missed until Linda Vaux decided to track him down. When she was unable to find him, she contacted Alice Asplund. This alerted the murderer and she arranged for Linda to come straight to her new country place, bought with a legacy left her by her uncle, the disreputable Knut Fredriksson. Linda drove straight into a trap. But Asplund couldn't bring herself to kill her in cold blood.'

'Thank God.'

'Indeed. In the meantime, after killing Tony, Asplund had to do something with the crown and the coins. She had nowhere to hide them. It was then that she rekindled her friendship with Gerda Brink who, as we know, worked for Knut Fredriksson. She'd know what sort of woman Brink was. We've seen Asplund's bank account – she took out a large sum of cash shortly after the end of the Vollerby dig. We can only presume that was payment to Brink for the favour of burying the crown and the coins on her allotment. I suspect that once she'd bought the country property beyond Rydsgård, she intended to transfer them there. Then they would stay hidden until she decided to make her discovery public.'

'How was she going to do that?'

'Plant them at some future dig and then miraculously discover them? I don't know. She wouldn't have got any satisfaction just sitting on them forever. She would need the academic world to know the crown really existed.'

'But things went wrong?'

'First, there was the death of the dog. It had been sniffing around Brink's plot. It must have worried Brink enough to kill the nosey creature. She didn't want it to dig up the crown and the coins. And then the greedy woman couldn't help herself and she took a couple of the coins to get them valued at Thilde Meerwald's antiques shop. She couldn't know that they would find their way back to Alice Asplund. It alerted Asplund – her treasure was out there and could easily be discovered. She took matters into her own hands and silenced Brink to protect the crown. But that left her with a problem – how to retrieve her treasure. She would have to move it, but she was unlucky that the night she chose, she was disturbed by Sigrid Clausson. She hit Clausson over the head with the spade she was going to use to do the digging.'

'So she left empty-handed.'

'Yeah. Probably frightened that she might have disturbed someone. Of course, then it became dangerous to go back. She probably hoped things would die down before the plot was taken over by someone else. But it must have been agony for her.'

'Academics,' Falk exhaled noisily. 'I'll never understand them. Some can get so obsessed. Anyway, Dan Olovsson has saved us the cost of a long-winded trial.'

'That's one way of looking at it.' Why did everything come down to budgets? 'That's no consolation for Dan.'

'No, no, of course not. By the way, any word on Sigrid Clausson?'

'Good news on that front. She's out of the coma and should make a good recovery. There appears to be no sign of lasting mental damage.'

'That's a relief. Well, Anita, there's been some excellent police work done on these cases. Or one case, as it turns out. Congratulations.'

'It's not the best of results,' she reminded him.

'Quite so. We can't forget how brave Bea Erlandsson was at the end. We must give her an appropriate send-off.'

'I think the family want it low-key. A humanist gathering.'

'Right, of course. Whatever they want.'

By the time Anita left the commissioner's office, all she wanted to do was go home and have the family round for a meal. She needed company and hugs. That would cheer her up.

But, despite what appeared to be a satisfactory conclusion to both cases, she couldn't get out of her head Kevin's parting remark: 'It's all a bit neat, isn't it?' She knew Kevin didn't like neat. Neither did she.

Anita was about to leave the office that evening when a phone call came through from Joel Grahn.

'I've just been to the hospital to see if Sigrid Clausson is all right.'

'That's very diligent of you.'

'Well, it was the right thing to do.'

Grahn's compassionate gesture only made Anita feel worse for not going over to Ystad herself to see the ex-detective. 'How is she?'

'Able to talk.'

'Did you tell her who attacked her?'

'Yes, I did. She was interested to hear about the case.' There was a pause at the other end. 'Erm... she wants to see you.'

'I'll try and get over as soon as possible. It's been full-on here.'

'I totally understand. It's just that she wants to speak to you, and only you. She says it could be important.'

Anita breathed deeply.

'Really? Everything's tied up. OK. I'll come across tomorrow.'

The next morning, she drove to Ystad. She was relieved that Clausson was recovering but still cursing her for getting involved in the first place. The team had gathered from other plot holders that she had been asking questions as though she was conducting the murder enquiry herself. Anita swore that there was no chance of *her* interfering with a police investigation once she was retired. She wouldn't want to see another cop, another witness or another criminal ever again when her time came. And she couldn't for the life of her understand what Clausson could possibly tell her that would have a bearing on things. Everything was done and dusted bar the paperwork – and of course the possible prosecutions of Einar Wallter, Viktor Bjelk and Henning Kristoffersson for the misdemeanours that Gerda Brink had threatened to expose. That was up to the prosecutor now, and any action taken would be through Ystad.

And, at first, what Clausson had to say seemed to be totally irrelevant.

'It's the dog.'

'The dog?' Anita spluttered uncomprehendingly.

'Yes, Oskar. It's to do with the dog.'

CHAPTER 47

As Anita was in Ystad, she called into the police station and sought out Joel Grahn.

'We need to have a word.'

Then she related what Clausson had told her about Oskar the dog. When she had finished, to her surprise, Grahn wasn't taken aback. In fact, the opposite.

'Something's been bugging me right from the start. That article about the boy who was killed in the hit and run. Anton.'

Anita couldn't recall it.

'The newspaper cutting I found when we searched Brink's cabin.'

'Yeah. I do remember now. It rather got forgotten when we found the cash.'

'The thing that got to me was that the more we discovered about Gerda Brink, the more that article intrigued me. Why had she cut it out? I got the impression that she didn't do anything without a reason. What was it about that event that she could exploit? The unfortunate family? I couldn't see how. Then I went back to my uncle and got him to blow up the photo that went with the article. Like the ones of the Fredriksson funeral, he had several different shots. And guess who I saw on it?'

Back in Malmö, Anita immediately got onto Liv. Could she run off two headshots for her?

The next morning, Anita headed into the city centre. The day was bright, though her mood was dark by the time she returned to the polishus. If only she had made sure this had been done earlier, the investigation could have gone in an entirely different direction, though she had to concede that at the time, there didn't seem to be any relevance. That oversight almost let somebody get away with murder. They might still get away with it, Prosecutor Blom gloomily predicted. Too much circumstantial evidence and not enough fact.

Anita called Joel Grahn and gave him instructions. They would meet in Brantevik, ten minutes outside Simrishamn, the following day. He was to bring a warrant with him.

The sunshine had brought out most of the plot holders, who were busy planting, pruning or painting. Anita, and Grahn clutching a folder had prepared their approach after their discovery in Brantevik.

Like many others, Thora Tarland was tending a vegetable bed: lettuce, onions and cabbages by the look of it. Her beloved apple trees were promising a harvest that her old orchard in Kivik had failed to produce. She looked up in surprise at seeing the return of the police. Anita stared at the woman's grey hair. Bloody grey hair!

'Could we speak to you?' Anita said.

'Is it about Sigrid? We're all so relieved she's going to pull through.'

'No, it's about you.'

This produced a scowl of irritation. 'What about me?'

'Can we talk inside?'

Anita noticed Tarland suddenly become nervous. That might make things easier.

They followed her into her cabin. It was laid out like so many of the others, though more spartan. Tarland had few possessions, but in pride of place there was an old photograph of herself delivering apples to the cider factory. It looked like a staged publicity shot. A reminder of more prosperous times.

They sat round the small table after refusing Tarland's offer of coffee.

'I hope this isn't serious,' she ventured.

'Murder is serious,' Anita replied unsmilingly.

'What murder? You've caught the murderer. It was that archaeology woman. The news is full of it.'

'Yes, you're right; we did think she'd killed Gerda Brink, but we were wrong.'

Tarland stood up, poured herself a glass of water from the tap and took a large gulp.

'I don't understand.'

'Let's go back to the beginning. Sometime late last summer, you must have seen Gerda and the "archaeology woman" digging at the back of Brink's plot. Only you could have seen them, as that particular piece of ground isn't overlooked by anyone else. I suspect it was late one night. You were intrigued. What were they doing? It looked like they were burying something. What could that be?'

Tarland didn't say anything. She stood very still, as though glued to the sink, staring back at her accuser.

Anita continued, 'The temptation was too much. You had to find out. You probably sneaked into Brink's plot when she was away and you did a bit of digging of your own. And you came up trumps! You found some ancient gold coins. Arabic dinars. A whole bagful. You only took two so it would be unlikely that they would be missed. Here you were, short of money, and just lying in a shallow hole right next to your plot, a possible fortune. Of course, you needed to find out what the coins were actually worth. So you took them into Malmö to Thilde Meerwald's antiques shop. I know this because I asked Thilde yesterday and I showed her this photo of you.' Anita gave Grahn a nod and he produced from his folder the headshot that Liv had found on Tarland's old orchard website. She was a bit younger then, but Meerwald had had no difficulty identifying her. The coins had become relevant to the enquiry when Asplund was exposed as Tony Yealand's killer, but they'd assumed the grey-haired woman Meerwald had described to Bea Erlandsson was Brink. Tarland's involvement would at least explain the fourth set of fingerprints.

'Despite the coins being authenticated by a couple of leading academics, it must have been frustrating for you that you couldn't get a proper valuation. You decided not to pursue it, as too many questions might be asked as to how you got hold of them in the first place.'

Again, Tarland remained stubbornly silent.

'Then there was the dog. Oskar. It's interesting that you accompanied Sigrid Clausson to see Inspector Grahn to put the blame firmly at Brink's door.'

'She killed it.'

'You were deflecting us from the real culprit. Oskar had taken to Brink's plot. She'd driven him away on a number of occasions. Did you see him scratching around the back where the coins were buried? You must have been worried that he'd inadvertently attract Brink's attention to the spot. And then she might check that everything was still there and discover the missing coins. So you killed the dog.'

'That's ridiculous.'

'You were seen the night the dog disappeared, carrying a large bundle wrapped in a blanket down to the shore. You returned only with the blanket.'

'Who said that?'

'We have a witness.'

'Who?'

This is what Sigrid Clausson had discovered in her own enquiries. She had wheedled it out of Anna-Marie Kristoffersson. Henning had been away on a trip and Anna-Marie had used the opportunity to pay a late-night visit to Viktor Bjelk. So as not to attract attention, she'd sneaked through the back gardens of the plots. It was while returning to her own cabin that she'd spied Thora Tarland. Then, through her darkened window, she'd watched Tarland come back.

'I can assure you, it is a reliable witness.'

Tarland sat back down at the table. 'Is that the murder you're accusing me of? A dog?'

'No. We're accusing you of the murder of Gerda Brink.'

Tarland tried to laugh. It sounded hollow. 'What rubbish! Why would I kill Gerda? I admit I couldn't stand the woman; not many people could. And as for all that stuff about gold coins! I don't know what you're talking about. The antiques woman you mentioned must be mistaken: she couldn't possibly have recognised me from that old photo.'

'No, I don't think you murdered her for the coins, though I'm sure she would have worked out eventually who'd taken them. No, we think Brink was doing what she did best – blackmail.'

Tarland took another drink of her water.

'What could she possibly blackmail me about?'

'Detective Grahn. Can you tell fru Tarland what you've found out?'

'Certainly.' Slowly and deliberately, Grahn pulled out from his folder the cutting they had found in Brink's cabin of the memorial ceremony for Anton Lagerberg, the boy who had died in the hit and run. It was sealed in plastic. Tarland winced. 'I see this means something to you.'

'It was very sad,' she said. 'The poor family.'

'Do you know where we found this cutting?' Grahn asked.

'I have no idea.' Her attempt at denial sounded unconvincing.

'We found it in Gerda Brink's cabin when we searched it after her death.'

A white-faced Tarland said nothing.

'Brink had scribbled a word on the back – *Garage*. Of

course, that meant nothing to us at the time. Neither did the cutting. Then we had the photo enlarged.' Grahn produced a blow-up of the people gathered behind the grieving family and the bench with its dedication to the child. 'That's you,' he said, pointing at the face on the very fringe of the photograph.

Tarland gazed at the image for few seconds before speaking. 'I don't deny being there. Why should I? My orchard was in Kivik. That's where the accident happened.'

'Yes. Your business. You suffered a couple of bad years. Poor crops.'

'It ruined me. I blame global warning.'

'Which is supposedly why you suddenly gave up driving.'

'It was. I realised the planet was going to pot.'

'And you manage without a car?'

'I don't need one. I can get the bus into Simrishamn. Or, if the weather's nice, I can bike.' She pointed out of the window. Her bicycle could be seen propped up by her potting shed.

'According to your neighbours, it was very sudden – you giving up driving, I mean.'

'It just hit me that I wasn't doing my bit to save the planet, however small that is.'

'Isn't it true that what really hit you was the realisation that you had killed a child?'

Tarland almost choked. For a moment she seemed unable to breathe. Grahn patiently waited. After a few seconds, she drank some more water then rubbed her mouth with the back of her hand.

'You must be mad!' Her voice cracked. 'You can't believe I had anything to do with that!'

'That's exactly what we do believe. And also what Gerda Brink believed.' 'There's no proof.'

'We have the proof. You and Brink both live in Brantevik. You have a garage next to your house. We believe Brink must have passed your garage one day when you had the door open

– and she saw something. Whatever, she found out somehow. That scribble on the back of the cutting – she was referring to *your* garage, wasn't she?'

Tarland's hand was trembling. She put the glass down on the table. She didn't speak.

'This newspaper report mentions a dark-blue Volvo that was seen at the time of the incident. The police reports say it was never found. Brink put two and two together and came to the conclusion that it was your car that was involved. It was still in your garage because you didn't know how to get rid of it. After the incident, you couldn't use it in case it was seen and identified. You couldn't take it to a repair shop or have it scrapped, because questions might have been asked, paperwork to fill in. So you left it where it was and decided to save the planet.'

Tarland was about to protest, then stopped herself.

'We know it was your car.'

'How –'

'Because we've been to your home in Brantevik. We found the car in your garage. A dark-blue Volvo. It has a smashed headlight and damage on the front. It's been taken away for forensic analysis. We're confident that will prove that your car was responsible for little Anton Lagerberg's death.'

A tear slowly began to trickle down Tarland's cheek.

'Brink worked it all out,' Anita continued. 'And, of course, she wouldn't let it lie if she could squeeze some money out of you. Is that what she did?'

Tarland was now openly weeping.

'She was blackmailing you, wasn't she? Or she was about to.'

'I couldn't afford what she asked.' Grahn and Anita had to lean forward to hear the words through the tears. 'I pleaded with her. She wouldn't listen.'

'Tell us about the night Anton died,' Anita prompted quietly.

'Oh, that poor, poor boy!' Tarland was now distraught. 'I... I was depressed because of the way the business was going. I... I'd drunk too much cider, and... and driving home...' She shut her eyes and rocked backwards and forwards. 'There isn't a day goes by that I don't relive that dreadful moment. I light candles for him at the church. God forgive me!'

Anita slowly stood up. Grahn followed suit.

'Detective Grahn, you can make the arrest now.'

EPILOGUE

Skania, summer AD 1017

Viggo Flatnose and Harald were as exhausted as their steeds. This was the third set of horses they had ridden almost day and night for the last eight days. They had been driven on by the fear that Yusuf's men had reached Vǫllrbý before them. The two Norsemen had rushed ahead, leaving their comrades to make their own way south. For the thousandth time, Viggo cursed himself for leaving Vǫllrbý. He had convinced himself that Bilal would never find him, or would give up and return to Miklagård or Antioch. Yet, in his heart, he had always known that the Arab would never abandon his quest. What the barbarian had taken was too precious.

They stopped in a woodland clearing, on the edge of a stream. Wearily, they dismounted and let the horses nibble at the grass while they drank thirstily from the cool water.

'We will reach Vǫllrbý before nightfall,' said Viggo as he splashed water over his face to keep him awake.

'What's that?' Harald said suddenly.

By the time Viggo had risen to his feet, three horsemen were staring down at them. There was no doubt as to the identity of two of them. No Norseman looked or dressed as these men did, though the other was of their kind.

'Is that Bilal?' Harald, who had not been on the voyage to Antioch, whispered.

'Yes, that's the evil-looking bastard.'

Bilal's face creased into a menacing grin. He said something in Arabic.

Viggo did not understand. 'What does he say?'

'He brings greetings from his master, Yusuf of Antioch,' Harald translated.

'What do you want?' Harald asked in the same tongue.

'Viggo Flatnose has something that does not belong to him. I have come to take it back.'

'If you lay a finger on Nadira, I will kill you.' Harald had always worshipped the Eastern beauty from afar. To his surprise, Bilal laughed out loud.

'You think we have come all this way to find that whore?' he said contemptuously. 'Though I'm sure my master would consider it a great favour if I brought him back her head. She brought him great shame.'

Harald was about to reply when the Norseman accompanying them spoke. 'You said nothing of killing the woman.'

'You will not have to do it. That will be my pleasure.' The Arab's honeyed tones were chilling in any language.

'No,' said Erik. 'That was not part of the bargain.' With that, he kicked his horse's flanks and rode off into the trees.

Though Viggo had not followed the conversation, other than the mention of Nadira's name, he calculated the odds were swinging back in their favour – two against two.

'You will harm the woman of Viggo Flatnose at your peril!' Harald said vehemently, fingering his sword.'

'Tell Viggo Flatnose that we will spare his woman if he gives us the imperial crown.'

'What crown?' Harald responded in shock.

Turning to Viggo, 'What crown? He is talking about an emperor's crown. I know nothing of this.'

'Has he not told you?' interrupted Bilal. 'It is the crown our master had made for the Emperor Basil. It is worth a thousand Nadiras.'

'It is of no consequence,' Viggo said baldly.

'That cannot be,' Harald said in angry confusion. 'These bastards have not come all this way for nothing.'

'I was sent to Antioch to guard it. When I took Nadira, I took the crown, too. It is worth a king's ransom. Or an emperor's.'

'And it has put Nadira's life at risk!'

'Hold your tongue! Keep him talking. Promise him anything.' Viggo was swiftly working out how to physically gain the upper hand.

Bilal was enjoying the Norsemen's altercation. 'Take us to the crown and we will leave you in peace,' he said. 'If not, you will both die here and I will force the whore to hand it over, before killing her.'

Harald spoke quickly with Viggo then turned to Bilal, stepping forward as he did so and obscuring his cousin. 'He agrees... he agrees to hand over the trinket.'

Bilal relaxed, and at that moment, an axe whistled past Harald's head and plunged into the chest of the second horseman. The man's cry died on his lips as he slumped to the ground. Quick as a viper's bite, taking advantage of the confusion caused, Harald leapt forward and with the small dagger he kept in his boot, lunged at Bilal's horse. The animal reared in fright and threw its rider to the ground. Though the Arab fell heavily, he was agile, and quickly gained his footing, scimitar at the ready. By this time, Viggo had unsheathed his rhomphaia and torn into Bilal, who managed to repel the attack with much skill, though he was forced back by Viggo's savagery. The combatants were equally matched as sparks flew from their clashing blades. Then Viggo overplayed his hand, and a mighty blow aimed at finishing Bilal's resistance missed its mark. The Arab deftly swayed away as Viggo lost his balance and fell on his face. Swiftly, Bilal raised his weapon. Viggo looked up and grasped his sword tightly, ready to enter Valhalla. But the gods were not ready for him yet. As he sprawled on the ground, he saw, to his amazement, Bilal's head fly through the air, struck from its shoulders by Harald's axe.

'Thank you, cousin,' Viggo said as he wiped the Arab's blood from his eyes.

He then went to retrieve his axe from Bilal's comrade. There was still breath in the dying man's body. Another blow silenced him forever.

'Now we are safe.'

'So is Nadira,' Harald said pointedly.

Viggo shrugged and wandered back to the stream. 'We will let the wild animals feast on these two.'

Harald stared at Viggo. Suddenly, he felt a burst of hatred for the man he had worshipped for years... the man whose faithful follower he had been through untold adventures, perilous journeys and bloody battles... the man he had whored with and roistered with in the alehouses and backstreets of the Byzantine Empire.

'Is Nadira just a trinket, too, like your precious crown?'

'No. I love them both,' Viggo said smugly. 'I will present the crown to the King of Denmark at Jelling. But for a mighty price,' he added with a throaty laugh.

Unaware of the rage boiling in the breast of his younger companion, he bent down to the stream to clean his blade.

It was the last thing Viggo Flatnose was ever to do.

Vǫllrbý, late summer, AD 1017

The stars lit up the sky for the gods to play. Summer was still clinging on but the nights were chill and the morning grass was soused with dew. Autumn often crept in early in Skania. The flame from the torch cast an eerie light on the hunched figure digging a hole in the turf. Harald stopped to wipe his brow. Why did Nadira want a hole so big and wide for such a small thing? But it was her decision, and he was happy to obey her instruction: 'Dig hard, dig deep'. It was over a month since he had returned to Vǫllrbý with the body of their jarl slumped over his horse and the tale of how they had been ambushed by Yusuf of Antioch's men. He had brought Bilal's head along as proof of his story. Viggo Flatnose had been given a fitting Norseman's funeral and much of his silver from the East was buried nearby in case he needed to pay the old gods, whom he had never forsaken. The tale that Harald had spun had Viggo meeting a brave death.

Harald had been surprised and disappointed at how grief-stricken Nadira had been. As their interpreter before she had learned her lover's strange tongue, Harald had believed that this was not a love match as far as Nadira was concerned. She was using Viggo to escape a life in which she was trapped. So it was with some optimism that, a few days earlier, he had plucked up the courage to declare his love for her and, as he was now the new jarl of Vǫllrbý, he wanted her to rule by his side. Her answer had been vague. First she said that they must put the past behind them. The Emperor's crown was to be buried. She said it had brought them ill luck and that it was cursed. This, Harald, as a Norseman, could readily accept, though he was sad to see such a precious object disappear into the earth.

Harald looked up; he stood knee-high in the hole. 'Is that deep enough?'

'A little more. It must be well buried to contain the evil.'

Harald continued to dig while Nadira planted the torch in the ground. She picked up a wooden cup which lay beside the bag containing the crown.

'You have done well, Harald, Jarl of Vǫllrbý. Here is your reward.'

Harald, still standing in the hole, reached up and took the cup.

'I have a deep thirst.'

As he raised the cup and drained it, a smile played upon

Nadira's lips.

'It has a strangely bitter taste. You have added one of your herbs or potions?' he joked.

'I have' was all she said.

He wiped his mouth.

'You have still not given me your answer, Nadira. We would make a fine couple. I am a man of importance now; I am strong and can protect you. I also have great wealth.' Harald patted a bag dangling at his side. 'In here are my gold coins from Miklagård. You will be the finest lady in all Skania. I can...'

Suddenly, his words died on his lips, his hand went to his throat and he began to choke. He stared at the woman looking down on him, with fear and wonder in his eyes. 'What have you done?' he croaked.

'It is Viggo's revenge.' Nadira's eyes gleamed and her voice shook with hatred. 'You take me for a fool, Jarl Harald. I tended to Viggo's body when you brought it back. His wound was not caused by any Eastern sword. His head was split from behind by a Norse axe – your axe.'

Harald sank to his knees as he desperately clutched his throat and tugged at the clothing around his neck.

'You will be dead soon. And you can take your gold coins with you to buy your way out of the snake hall of Náströnd.'

Harald slumped forward. He gasped and gurgled and rolled his eyes in fright. Nadira took up the torch and watched impassively the final grotesque twitches of Viggo's treacherous cousin.

Then she picked up the crown and tossed it into the hole.

NOTES

Vikings in the East

Being brought up and living in the UK, my Viking stereotype was the Norsemen, including my ancestors, who headed over from Norway and Denmark, and pillaged and then settled in Britain and Ireland; and others who colonised Iceland and eventually reached Greenland and America. Until I became familiar with Sweden, I hadn't paid much attention to the hordes of Vikings who ventured east into modern-day Ukraine and Russia and onwards to Constantinople (Istanbul) and the Middle East. Some even ended up in Baghdad and on the Caspian Sea.

These eastern-bound Vikings (Swedes, and Danes from what is now Skåne) were remarkable. They headed down the rivers and carried their longships over difficult terrain to move from one river to another or to avoid dangerous rapids. They helped create the city of Kiev and are believed to be responsible for the name 'Rus' (the word for 'rowers'), the people who were later to become Russians. The Kievan Rus were a mixture of Scandinavians and Slavs. Generally, these Vikings weren't so much conquerors, like their Western counterparts, but traders and seekers of wealth, though such peaceful quests didn't necessarily curb their violent nature.

Many joined the famed Varangian Guard. These brutal Vikings were initially recruited from Sweden by Vladimir the Great to help him regain his Kievan Rus kingdom. On achieving that aim, he was lumbered with 6,000 restless Norsemen. He managed to rid himself of them by sending them off to fight for the Byzantine Emperor, Basil II (976–1025). Their ferocity so impressed Basil that he turned them into his imperial guard, his own Greek guards having proved disloyal. Using Vikings was a deliberate choice – they lacked local political loyalties and could be trusted to quash revolts by Byzantine factions trying to destabilise the Empire. The Guard were handsomely rewarded for their fierce loyalty and unmatched fighting skills, bravery and viciousness. Many returned to their homeland as rich men. The story Viggo tells at the beginning of the book about the blinding of Samuel of Bulgaria's army is believed to be true. After the Battle of Kleidion on July 29th, 1014, Basil II is said to have captured 15,000 Bulgars and fully blinded 99 out of every 100, leaving a single one-eyed soldier to lead each cohort home. The shock is said to have caused Samuel's death.

Their Eastern explorations were of great economic benefit to the Swedes: trade flowed in both directions between Scandinavia and Constantinople (known to the Vikings as Miklagård) and the Middle East. Slaves, furs, skins, walrus-tusk ivory, honey and beeswax headed south – spices, silks, glass, silver, gold and slaves came north. This made the strategically located island of Gotland, in the middle of the Baltic, a rich trading centre. Another place to profit from the Eastern trade route was Birka, a town on a small island in Lake Mälaren, which is two hours by inland waterway from Stockholm. It was one of the Viking world's leading commercial centres, though it was abandoned by the time of Viggo Flatnose's story. Thousands of burial mounds on the island are testament to its importance. In its heyday, it was visited by Ansgar, a Benedictine monk who was sent to Sweden by Louis the Pious, the then Holy Roman Emperor, to bring Christianity to the Vikings. We have a personal connection to the saint, as our son Fraser played Ansgar in the Swedish historical documentary series, *Historien om Sverige*.

If you're interested in the Vikings, Birka is worth adding to your to-do list on a visit to Stockholm. Further reading could include Frans G Bengtsson's sweeping saga *The Long Ships*. Written in the 1950s, it's a wonderful story of a Viking's dramatic voyage through life. Rosemary Sutcliffe's novel *Blood Feud* follows Vikings to Constantinople, and I'd also recommend *Northmen: The Viking Saga AD 793–1241* by John Haywood.

Malmö University does not have an archaeology department.

Swedish allotments

Though the August Hagman Allotments is fictional, it is based on a system that has been part of Swedish life since the late 1800s. The purpose behind these allotment garden areas was to give the urban working class the opportunity to grow their own food and get away from the city for some much-needed fresh air. It was hoped that the working classes, who might otherwise be tempted to head for the pub in their free time, would get involved in more practical and worthwhile activities. Many of these low-paid factory workers had moved from the countryside, and the allotments allowed them not only to reconnect with their roots, but also to grow their own produce.

The concept originally came from Copenhagen, and the Swedish allotment garden movement was promoted by the Social Democrat politician, Anna Lindhagen (1870–1941), with the Association of Allotment Gardens being founded in Stockholm in 1906. Within ten years, thirty-seven Swedish cities had allotment areas. Today, there are 51,000 such allotments nationwide, with 66% having cabins (or cottages) on them.

The plot holders with cabins can stay in them overnight from April to September, but not during the winter: water and electricity are turned off at the end of the summer. But during the season, as well as the benefits of garden cultivation, the allotments often perform a social function and become a community hub for all ages.

Post-Brexit Sweden

The UK officially left the EU at midnight on January 31st, 2020. According to data published by the EU statistical office, 2,250 UK citizens were ordered to leave EU countries between 2020 and September 2022. Around half this number was from Sweden alone.

Half the problem appears to be that the Swedish authorities relied on informing Britons living in the country of the changes in post-Brexit residency through information published online. The result was that a number of Britons weren't aware of the deadlines. Stories have emerged of people who have lived for many years in Sweden, often with long-term partners and children, having applications rejected. Analysis prepared by the Migration Agency for the UK government and the European Commission found, by February 12th, 2024, that 2,286 Britons had had their applications for post-Brexit residency rejected. Unlike in Denmark, Brits who missed the deadline to apply for post-Brexit residency, will not be given a second chance. As a government spokesperson told the English-language digital newspaper, *The Local*, ignorance is not 'reasonable grounds' for missing the deadline.

Hundreds of British citizens have fallen foul of Sweden's strict application of the EU Withdrawal Agreement. In such a climate, it is understandable that certain people believed that Tony Yealand might well have had to return to the UK.

Cashless Sweden

Sweden is now regarded as one of the most cashless societies in the world. Though it's true that many outlets won't accept cash any more, banknotes are still used and accepted. All the main denominations of banknotes are still issued, though the older versions of some became invalid in 2017 (see *Mission in Malmö*), and most towns of any size will have ATMs. It is this cashless approach that so intrigues Anita Sundström and her team when they come across Gerda Brink's stash. Interestingly, this increasing tendency towards using contactless and mobile payments is worrying the Sveriges Riksbank (Sweden's central bank). They have called for the urgent strengthening of cash as a payment means in legislation. They have asked the government, or authority designated by the government, to review the position of cash and access to cash services by 2025 at the latest.

ABOUT THE AUTHOR

Torquil MacLeod was born in Edinburgh. After a brief career as a teacher and an even briefer one in insurance, in which he didn't manage to sell a single policy, he worked as an advertising copywriter in agencies in Birmingham, Glasgow and Newcastle before turning freelance. He lives in north-west England with his wife, Susan. The idea for a Scandinavian crime series came from his frequent trips to Malmö and southern Sweden to visit his elder son. He has four grandchildren, equally spread between Sweden and Essex.

Also by Torquil MacLeod:

The Malmö Mysteries
(in order)
Meet me in Malmö
Murder in Malmö
Missing in Malmö
Midnight in Malmö
A Malmö Midwinter (novella)
Menace in Malmö
Malice in Malmö
Mourning in Malmö
Mammon in Malmö
Mission in Malmö

ACKNOWLEDGEMENTS

Starting with the cover of *Myth*, I'd like to thank my good friend Nick Pugh for doing another superb job. I'm sure it's time I bought him another lunch. And thanks to The Knight Shop for allowing us to use one of their excellent Viking helmet images (www.theknightshop.com).

In Sweden, I am always hugely grateful to Fraser and Paula for their observations of day-to-day life in Skåne – and to Paula for her input on a tricky plot point. And no Anita adventure would be the same without the expertise of Karin Geistrand. Again, she can't be held responsible for my twisting of police procedure to fit my storylines. As an allotment plot holder, I was also able to tap into Karin's summer life, which, fortunately, isn't as eventful as the fictional ones in this story.

I'm also grateful to reader and friend Maria Fridefors from Malmö for her historical insights, and for generously gifting me the novel *The Long Ships* by Frans G Bengtsson. It helped fire my imagination.

As ever, I must mention Catherine and Karren, owners of the excellent Taste of Britain shop on Engelbrektsgatan in Malmö, for their unstinting efforts to sell my books, and for plugging them during various 'Eurovision' interviews.

Thanks also to Andy and Caroline at McNidder & Grace for their usual efficient service and helpful support.

Above all, I'd like to thank Susan for all the long hours of editing and polishing which ensure that what you read flows and makes sense.

I also really appreciate readers who have contacted me with interesting and supportive emails. They are great contacts with the outside world during what is often a solitary process.

Finally, this book is written in memory of Bern Haigh, a great friend and loyal Anita fan, who sadly passed away this year.

OTHER TITLES IN THE SERIES

Meet Me in Malmö ISBN 9780857161130

Murder in Malmö ISBN 9780857161147

Missing in Malmö ISBN 9780857161154

Midnight in Malmö ISBN 9780857161307

Menace in Malmö ISBN 9780857161734

Malice in Malmö ISBN 9780857161871

Mourning in Malmö ISBN 9780857162076

Mammon in Malmö ISBN 9780857162106

Mission in Malmö ISBN 9780857162380